WHEN THERE'S NO MORE ROOM IN HELL

LUKE DUFFY

1

A noise to his front snapped his head away from his binoculars and his hand instinctively reached for the weapon across his lap. Down the hill, about fifty metres away, a shadowy figure shambled, struggling to negotiate the steep and slippery grass bank. Steve remained seated and watched as the figure slipped, its feet falling away from under it and causing it to fall face first in to the grass and slide back down the hill before regaining its balance and trying again.

It looked like a man, though from this distance, Steve couldn't be certain. A quick glance left and right again and Steve was happy in his security. He reached into his pocket and pulled out a pack of cigarettes. He thumbed the top open and placed one between his lips. As he lit it, he could taste the smoke draw into his mouth, musty, and not as fresh as they used to be twelve years ago, but there were very few vices now, and as long as he could still find them Steve would continue to enjoy a smoke now and then.

He zoomed in with the binoculars again to get a better view of the figure below him. He adjusted the focus and saw that what he was looking at had once been a man.

It had seen him too, and was doing its damndest to climb the hill.

Steve continued puffing away on the cigarette as he studied the man.

Its skin was mottled grey and brown and stretched tight over its face, as thin as paper and dry as match wood. The corners of its jaw and cheek bones were visible, the skin having rotted and weathered away. What had been weeping, puss dripping sores were now dark holes in its face leaving the teeth and bone structure visible in places below the skin.

Eyes that had once read books, the Sunday papers, gazed at beautiful scenery and watched movies, now lay shrivelled and dry in their sockets. They could distinguish between light and dark, and movement and large shapes could be seen, but small details were now hard to focus on, and it was only a matter of time until the figure would be completely blind.

Wisps of dried, sun-bleached hair blew in the breeze, revealing much of the bare scalp underneath. To a large degree, it was nothing more than a skull with a thin layer of leathery skin covering the surface. Where there had once been a nose, now a dark hole in the middle of its face, almost like a cave in a grey mountainside

The figure emitted a low moan as it struggled to reach Steve, the vocal cords rasping in its dried out throat. The sound was more of longing, of needing than an attempt at communication. Its jaw flexed and gnashed out of instinct rather than hunger or frustration as it clawed at the grass with its bony rake-like hands.

Its tattered, ripped, and battered clothes that had once fit a living human frame, now hung in ruins from its emaciated shoulders and back. Years of exposure to the elements, dirt and grime had discoloured them to become the same colour as the figure itself. Where its jacket hung open, or was torn away, Steve couldn't tell; its ribs and sternum jutted out from its grey skin, a large cavity, where it had once had liver, stomach and intestines, now a black and empty cavern.

The figure never gave up, it never tired and it never lost interest, and never would, not as long as Steve stayed in plain sight. It would continue to try and climb the hill for the rest of eternity, so long as something kept its attention focused on reaching the summit.

Steve watched in wonder. After all these years, he still found that he couldn't help but study them. Their behaviour never seemed to change when they saw him. It was true that he had witnessed occasional differences in their behaviour, but he had found that it was always when they were unaware of him that they acted differently.

There had been times when he had witnessed them show interest, or even curiosity, in inanimate objects. A fleeting memory maybe pushing its way to the surface and for a moment reminding them of the things they had known before. A car or a book, even something as irrelevant as a cup, Steve had watched them clumsily try to manipulate items in their uncoordinated hands as though trying to cling to a former existence. Or maybe it was just a spark of the old human nature coming through, to study and to learn?

But in general, their existence was basic and single-minded. He knew that he couldn't reason with it, that no matter how much he tried, he would not be able to convince it to do anything other than come for him. He had been up close and personal with thousands of them over the years, and yet he still watched.

The same questions always formed in his head. Who was the man he was watching? What did he do for a living? Did he have a family, where are they now? Did he like simple things, movies, good food and pretty women?

Then other questions inevitably came to him; does he remember anything? Does he feel emotion of any sort? Is he aware of himself and what has happened to him? Questions that Steve could never answer, but nevertheless, questions he always pondered.

He could see a couple more figures staggering along the road. Slowly they made their way along the tarmac, occasionally bumping into vehicles, debris and sometimes, each other. Using his binoculars, he did a quick scan to check for any sign that they were likely to be coming his way. They weren't. He was either too far away for their bad eyesight, or they just hadn't yet noticed him.

He knew that on their own, they're easy to out-manoeuvre and deal with as long as you're careful, but in groups, then you're likely to have a lousy afternoon. However, for the moment, Steve was safe. He had the high ground, good range of visibility and mobility on his side. At the first sign of trouble, he could just walk away.

Without realising, a sigh escaped his lips with the last of his cigarette smoke. He looked down at his feet and then back up at the skyline of the city. Though he had never really been a people person, he sometimes missed the hustle and bustle of the past. It had been easy back then. If you needed something, you went shopping. If you were hungry, you went to the fridge, or even a restaurant. If you were bored, you did whatever it was that you found entertaining. Even the basics such as running a tap and having instant clean water, or flicking a switch and the room being lit from the light above was a thing he no longer took for granted.

But it wasn't just the amenities that he found himself sometimes longing for. He had hated all the Reality T.V., Chat Shows, and Soap Operas, as well as advertisements for crap he didn't need. The modern culture of everything being disposable, including people and marriage, everyone being too interested in what was happening with their favourite celebrity at the time, politicians screwing over the people they were supposed to be striving to make a better future for; it had boiled his blood.

But that was just it, it was all life. It was everyday, mundane, run of the mill, *life*.

"Actually, Mankind and civilisation was fucking shit!" Steve didn't realise he had said it aloud until the figure at the bottom of the hill stopped still and stared in his direction. A couple of seconds later it doubled its efforts to climb. The ones on the road hadn't heard him.

He looked down again and let out a silent laugh. "Aye, I always did prefer dolphins and gorillas to people."

2

"A career, what the fuck is that?" Steve scowled at his older brother Marcus. "To you, it's a chance at a future, to lay building-blocks to make your life and your future childrens' lives better, to contribute to the world, to make a difference to yourself and the people around you."

"To me, it's a life of subliminal slavery, working my whole life so that the taxman can squeeze my nutsack and then demand more. All the time, those fat wankers in the government offices get richer by the day. Shove it up your arse Marcus!"

Marcus shook his head in frustration, "Steve, you seriously need to grow up. Last month, you were stacking supermarket shelves. The month before that, you were laying bricks. Right now, well you're doing fuck all except being a 'rebel without a clue'. Where's that gonna get you?"

"Better off than you anyway. Don't tell me; since you joined the Army, all you've done is water ski and abseil for a laugh? Where were you this week? On a sandy beach somewhere, strolling along with Frank from the recruitment ads and a couple of pretty girls?"

"Actually no, I was on guard duty all week because Smudge didn't want to do his stint while he was off shagging some chick. He paid me for it though, so it's all good." Marcus tried to lighten the mood with a smile.

Steve didn't see the upside. He was still feeling like a captive audience while his brother, the hard man Paratrooper, gave him another lecture on how to run his life. Sitting against his bedroom wall, with his hands folded tight around his knees, he grumbled, "I can't be arsed with this Marcus, get off my back."

"Are you just gonna sit on your arse thinking the world owes you?"

Steve sneered, "Yeah, I just might actually."

"Like I said bro, grow up!" And with that, Marcus picked up his bag and walked out the door.

Steve loved his brother, though he could never show it, he just didn't know how. He had always looked up to Marcus and though he wouldn't admit it, Marcus was his hero.

Two years older than Steve, he had joined the army at the age of eighteen and had never looked back. Even as kids, Marcus had always been the tougher and more focused one. And Steve always felt as though he had been abandoned by him when he went off to join the army, though deep down he knew his feelings were unfounded. Marcus had hounded him for years to join him, to make him proud and at the same time, to give himself a goal in life. But Steve had always seen it differently. To him, joining the army was throwing himself as a pawn at the feet of the very government that he hated and despised.

Steve continued his life of rebellion. Working dead-end jobs until he was bored of them, or until he had enough money to see him through a couple of weeks of partying, then he would quit. Once the money had run out, he would be back to looking for work, or a way of making an easy earner.

At one point he found himself in a packing factory. For some reason, it got so hot in there, everyone just worked in their underpants. After a while, the fantasy of women joining the workforce became just that, a fantasy, and he soon moved on.

He was always known as a rogue, and he never professed to be an angel. If there was a way of making money that wasn't completely legitimate, or even downright against the law, he would take the chance if he thought he could get away with it.

Even going to the extremes of trying to be a cocaine dealer; risking being arrested and sent to prison, Steve had delusions of grandeur. Imagining himself driving around in a fancy car, wearing tailor-made suits and handmade shoes while living in a huge mansion-style house with a swimming pool. One week later, after tallying up his profits, he realised he had risked ten years behind bars for an extremely small return. Thus, his days of being a drugs baron were over and it was on to the next idea.

For years, he lived the life of a man who had no idea what to do with himself. That all changed when, at twenty one, he met Claire. For a while things were great and Steve began thinking of pinning down a steady job, so that they could live together. Then their relationship was blessed when Claire became pregnant. Steve was at a loss. All of a sudden, responsibility and maturity were hanging over him, and he felt cornered.

At first he found it hard to cope with, but then he began to realise that he owed this baby a future, to be a good father and give it a chance in life. When Sarah was born, he instantly fell in love with her. There and then she became his entire world, and he adored every minute he spent with her.

Soon, the relationship between Steve and Claire deteriorated and they went their separate ways, but that never deterred him. Though he was pretty much a weekend dad, he cherished his role as a father.

He never missed a school play, kept track of all the teeth grown and lost and never had to rearrange a weekend to have her. She always came first. And if it meant him missing out on an event with the guys or workmates, then he was always more than happy to do so.

When she stayed with him, at his rented flat on weekends, they would sometimes stay up late, watching kids' movies and joking with each other. Some days they would go on adventures in the countryside, or spend the day making cakes from a cookbook, then grimacing at their efforts afterwards while trying to eat them. When the time came that Sarah could no longer keep her eyes open, he would carry her to bed and sometimes just sit and watch her sleep for awhile.

Sarah had an amazingly sharp and sometimes dark sense of humour. Other times, it was completely off the wall and random. Steve once woke up and saw in the mirror, as he brushed his teeth, that his little angel had drawn a moustache on him in black marker pen while he slumbered in bed, too long for her liking. After scrubbing at it for an hour, while Sarah stood giggling, he resigned himself to the fact that he was to go through the next week with a faded grey moustache.

Conversations between Father and Daughter were always spoken in a language that was neither adult nor childlike. It was their way of communicating. Steve never spoke to her in a childish or patronising way and, in his eyes, which helped with her development and self confidence, and the fact that he was still a child himself at heart, it all came natural anyway.

"Dad, who do you think would win in a fight between Shrek and Spiderman?" Steve looked at his daughter, bewildered about where the question had suddenly sprung from as they both sat on the floor of the living room, building a house from Legos.

"I reckon Spiderman sweetheart, because he's faster and can tie Shrek up in his web. Plus, he's wearing tight Lycra and it would make him slicker than snot on a doorknob when Shrek tries to catch him."

Sarah considered this, "Ah, but what about Shrek being so strong though? Oh and he can kill fish with just a fart. So I think Shrek."

By the time that Sarah was ten, Steve began to feel redundant. She was more interested in spending time with friends, experimenting with makeup and playing on computers. He sometimes found himself having to bribe her with days out, just to spend time with her. Regardless, he would always be there for her.

Around that time, the world went to shit. After the terrorist attacks at the 2012 Olympics in London, which had killed thousands, war seemed to break out on every continent.

Steve could only look on as the world seemed to fall apart. He continued to go to work every day at the warehouse as he had done for the last five years. He was a foreman now, and on pretty good money. He had accepted his lot in life and felt content, but he was starting to grow concerned with the way the world was going, more for Sarah's sake than his own.

All the while, he kept an interested ear to the radio while at work, buying the day's paper on his way in, then watching the news once he was home again in the evening to catch up.

Very little information was coming out of Africa and South America; most of the news seemed to be centred round the numerous wars throughout the world, and particularly the events unfolding in the Middle and Far East. But still, it was strange that a virus that had the ability to kill hundreds of thousands was being kept on the sidelines. His old rebellious, anti-government feelings began to rise up inside him again. He knew all there was to know about the fighting in Iran, Iraq and the rest of the Middle East as well as Russia and Korea, so he started to scour the internet for more details on Africa.

No news websites were giving any more information than that which he already knew. A flu virus had broken out, spread by contact with infected people, similar to the Swine Flu pandemic of the year before when it re-emerged after the initial outbreak in 2009, but the African virus was even more aggressive. Whole villages and towns had died and many cities were becoming huge tombs.

But there was nothing about treatment, suspected origin or what the world was doing about it. *Was there any plan to contain it, other than blowing people out of the water as they fled? Who, if anyone, was studying it and breaking down its genetic code in order to find a cure?*

He spent a whole evening searching, but to no avail. It wasn't until the next day at work, during a break as he sat chatting to one of his shift bosses, he brought the subject up.

"Nah mate, you should look on the likes of 'youtube' instead. I've seen loads of mobile phone camera footage and personal blogs and reports from eye witnesses, and people are going apeshit over it."

Steve rubbed his head in sudden realisation of his stupidity, "Fuck's sake, why didn't I think of looking on them kind of sites?"

That evening, he could only look on in horror at the images and personal accounts of the people who had witnessed the effects of the virus firsthand. Piles of bodies could be seen as town authorities tried their best to control the situation. Men in white suits and masks setting fire to mass graves, before filling them in with bulldozers. Makeshift hospitals with the dead and the dying, crowds of infected people staggering around, wailing for help, coughing and vomiting while they lay waiting for the end as nurses and doctors wearing masks did what they could to ease their final hours.

Steve read on and learned that, according to the stories on the internet, 60% of the population were naturally immune, and of the remaining 40%, more than half of them developed nothing more than cold-like symptoms. Steve felt confused: *so why are there so many bodies? Why the mass graves being burned? Why the hospitals packed to the brim?*

It was obvious that there was, to a degree, a media blackout. Either no one was interested, or, more than likely as far as Steve was concerned, the powers that be had put injunctions on the different news stations to stop them reporting and showing too much. But no one could stop the internet upload. Even if the sites were closed down, others would always take their place.

According to what was being said by the majority, some of the infected would at first become sick, then after a couple of days turn violent and attack anyone they saw, except other infected people. This caused Steve to lean back for a moment and try to understand why people with flu would attack others. Something bothered him, more than just the fact that the world was at war and a virus was on the loose. He couldn't shake his sense of foreboding.

He stood up and walked to his kitchen. He had no particular need of anything; he just needed to get away from his computer to give his eyes a break. He flicked on the kettle with the intent of making himself a cup of coffee, and then decided he would get a cold beer out of the fridge instead and returned to his computer.

He read and sifted through more write-ups and personal accounts, until he came across what he presumed to be a kind of 'below the radar' freelance news blog that someone had decided to upload themselves, rather than it be taken and kept under wraps by the networks. What he read gripped him, horrified him and made him shake his head and dismiss it, all at the same time.

David Newcomb,

13/05/2015,

Sierra Leone, Freetown,

Two days ago the Sierra Leone government declared a country-wide curfew with the army patrolling the streets to enforce it. Anyone caught outside their homes, AT ANY TIME for ANY REASON will be dealt with as looters, rioters and rebels. From my hotel window, I have seen people being executed as patrols have caught them in the streets.

Regardless of what the reason, or need, for venturing outside, the curfew is final in the eyes of the totalitarian government. Whether you need food or if a family member is sick, or even to collect water, you are not to leave your homes.

I have seen a lot of bodies lying in the streets of so-called looters and rebels, summarily executed by the soldiers and left in the gutter before the clean up teams come along and collect them. People are sick, starving and the flu is breaking out more rapidly and becoming more widespread. Our hotel has no running water and we have to try to keep clean with bottled water. The toilets don't work, and we have to use buckets, which we then take into the hotel garden in the morning and dump the contents in a pit, which is then burned. Thankfully we still have electricity, but for how long we do not know. It's only a matter of time until everyone in the hotel becomes sick.

I dare not even think about trying to get to the airport or the embassy. Whether you are local or foreign to this country, the same rule applies and I fear I would be shot the minute I leave the hotel.

Trucks full of government soldiers patrol the streets night and day. This morning, I watched as a small group of people, who must have been sick, or so hungry that they could hardly lift their feet, staggering along the street towards the hotel. A patrol approached, and as the people moved towards the truck and raised their hands to beg for help, the soldiers gunned them down. Afterward, the troops dismounted from their vehicle and moved from body to body, shooting them in the head. Twenty minutes later, another patrol came and removed the bodies.

Before the curfew I was able to travel throughout the villages and report and collect stories on the epidemic and the effect it is having here. During that time I learned that many of the locals have begun to call the flu 'The Walking Death'. When I asked why they called it this, the answers made no sense. A tribal medicine man told me that death is now walking amongst us and that the age of man is at an end.

A mother with two young babies clinging to her told me that her husband had died two days earlier and that the doctors had taken him to the hospital. That night she was told by a friend that they had seen her husband chasing a dog in her village on the outskirts of Freetown.

A man told me that his sister died that morning, and in the evening when they were preparing her for burial, she opened her eyes and sat up, causing everyone in the room to panic and flee. He told me how he watched her, from a distance, as she emerged from their home and devoured a live chicken that she took from the pen at the side of their house.

Mothers attacking children, husbands attacking wives, friends attacking each other, whatever the reason, it seems that Freetown is about to go under.

Stories of curses and voodoo style rituals being performed on the sick and dying are rife. No one knows what is really going on, and no information or help is coming from the authorities.

15/05/2015,
Freetown has been abandoned by the government and the troops. Crowds of sick people are swarming the streets and many

of them have crowded around our hotel. The stench of the crowd is sickening; even with all the windows closed I can still smell them. Swarms of flies and other insects are surrounding them, and the sickly-sweet smell of putrefaction is everywhere.

It's almost as if they are rotting while still alive.

They are banging against the doors day and night, but there is nothing we can do to help them. All of the ground floor windows have been smashed in their attempt to gain entry and we have had to barricade ourselves inside. They are behaving extremely aggressively and even attacking each other to get closer to the doors in the hope of getting help first.

Everyone has taken to wearing surgical masks, to help with the smell and hopefully to stop us from catching the flu; more like Plague. We have decided to keep away from the windows due to the fact that the sight of us seems to excite them in the hope of receiving some kind of help from us.

At first we pleaded with them, told them that we had no supplies and that we couldn't do anything for them, but that just seemed to fuel their anger and they doubled their efforts to get inside.

I fear that it's only a matter of time until they break through the barricades and then we will become infected. Either that or, we starve to death.....

Steve rubbed his eyes. He was starting to get a headache, and filling his head full of silly stories from the internet wasn't helping him. He clicked to another site and continued to flick through stories, reports and blogs.

Speculation was rife. Theories were all over the internet on what was causing it and what was being done about it. All that Steve could understand was that there was no cure or vaccine for the virus.

One group believed that the virus came from a pesticide that had somehow caused the common flu virus to mutate. They claimed that the pesticide was genetically engineered by the Americans to aggressively hunt down and kill mosquitoes and their larvae. They had then released it in the tropical areas of South America and Africa and once it came into contact with the flu virus, it caused a mutation, creating the violent flu symptoms in some of the sick.

Another group took a similar stance, but with a cosmic twist. They believed that the common flu virus had been mutated by gamma radiation from a faraway supernova on the other side of the galaxy. When some scientists and enthusiasts challenged them on this, they were unable to produce any solid evidence of a supernova having recently been witnessed and the scientists discredited them outright. It occurred to Steve though, *It's a big arse sky and not all of it can be watched at the same time. Any theory is as good as another.*

On the 21st December 2013, not long after the invasion of Iran, a probe that had been kept secret until then, returned to Earth after having landed on and taken samples from Europa; one of Jupiter's many moons. Why they kept it secret until its return was anyone's guess, but some believed that it was because Europa is said to be the strongest chance of being a life sustaining planet in the Solar System other than our own. The probe had drilled its way through fifteen kilometres of ice to a liquid water ocean beneath its hard frozen surface. Then, on completion of its mission it had returned to Earth. People were now speculating that it had brought something back in the samples.

All manner of reasons were being thrown about, including, as to be expected, the religious versions. Some believed that the Four Horsemen of the Apocalypse had arrived; Pestilence, War, Famine, and that the final one – Death – was the Anti-Christ in the form of the new American President, who came appearing as a saviour and a man of righteousness.

Since the beginning of the millennium, the world seemed to have been steadily falling apart. Aside from all the wars, there were the natural disasters. There were droughts, famine, disease and earthquake after earthquake.

The tsunami of December 26th 2004 that originated from the Indian Ocean killed more than a quarter of a million people, and it was closely followed by Hurricane Katrina, which came up from the Gulf of Mexico and laid waste to much of Louisiana, particularly New Orleans. Each year was followed with more storms and earthquakes, Haiti, New Zealand and Japan. Japan was hit by an earthquake that measured 9.0 on the seismograph and was closely followed by a tsunami that devastated much of its eastern coast. After that, the Japanese Nuclear Reactors began to fail up and down the country as their cooling systems were ruptured and the reactors overheated. A huge ecological crisis broke out, with thousands of brave workers dying from radiation sickness as they laboured to bring the core temperatures down to a stable level.

Steve raised his eyebrows and exhaled loudly. They all seemed as good an explanation as the next in his eyes. Though he had never been religious, it did seem like the Apocalypse was at hand and the Day of Judgement was on its way. Disease was sweeping the globe, war was being fought all over the world, whole countries were slowly starving, devastating earthquakes had been a regular occurrence over the last decade, and he had always thought that the American President was a twat.

Two weeks later the news broke. The flu epidemic was set to become a pandemic. Cases had been diagnosed all over the northern hemisphere including Moscow, New York, Berlin, Paris, the Middle East and even London. A lid couldn't be kept on it any longer. But it was clear that the authorities wanted to minimise the damage, so they released only the information they thought necessary.

Details were sketchy. It was still claimed that the majority of the population would be naturally immune and that with advanced medicines and hospitals being what they were in the likes of America and Europe, the chances of surviving were much higher and that there would be fewer deaths. However, all precautions were being taken and anyone with symptoms was to go to the nearest hospital.

News reports began to acknowledge the flu problem in Africa and South America. Footage of deserted villages and towns were shown, with the reporters wearing protective suits and surrounded with armed protection. Clean-up teams were filmed using flamethrowers on mass graves and news reels of helicopters dropping supplies to Red Cross refugee camps, giving the impression that the rest of the world was starting to give a shit. The overall impression that the news channels gave was that, as bad as the flu was, it was nothing to worry about given the right attention and treatment.

Smiling faces of people recovering from the flu, and children sitting with their parents in the refugee camps eating in tents, were plastered over every report. It was said that the death toll was nowhere near as high as first suspected, and that most of the sick were making a recovery.

Even though Steve had read and seen numerous reports and photographs on the internet, he found himself feeling pretty calm about it. Africa and South America had always struggled with disease. The environment and lack of money didn't help, but here in the first world it could be dealt with and controlled much easier. Sarah had had her flu jabs, and he himself very rarely got ill, and even then it was nothing more than a runny nose. He put his initial concerns down to the shock created by the sudden rush of information, stories, speculation and rumours available once he found the right websites. Reading people's theories had only brought back his deep, and in his eyes, immature and naive suspicion that everything was a cover-up or conspiracy. He had to remind himself that he was a grown up now, that Area-51 didn't exist and that 9/11 was Al-Qaeda and not the C.I.A.

While having an after work drink in his local pub, he heard the strangest theory. The news on the TV in the corner of the room was covering a story on the spread of the flu virus in Europe and North America.

A clearly drunken man stood by the bar, one hand holding a stool to steady him. Slurring his words, he announced, "I'll tell you what folks." He raised his other hand as if to silence everyone in order to put the world to rights for all to hear. "I reckon that this disease shit is pretty bad."

Steve continued to slowly sip at his Jack and Coke. He caught the attention of the barmaid as she rolled her eyes. He grinned at her, knowing that she was thinking the same thing.

"John, give it a rest will you," she moaned, "We're sick of your theories on everything that happens in the world. Like when there was a documentary on JFK, you came in gobbing off about how he and Elvis were assassinated by the Norwegians."

"They were!" The expression in his face told everyone that he was completely convinced of it. Steve resisted the urge to ask him how he came to that conclusion for fear of scowls and hoots aimed in his direction from the rest of the people in the bar.

"Anyway," the drunk continued, "I reckon that a star blew up and made that probe thingy turn radioactive, then when it crashed back down, it mutated the mosquito killing thing, uh....pesticu...testicular....parsit...uh....."

"Pesticide?" The barmaid wanted to help him along to get it over with.

John's eyes lit up. He reached out and tried to click his fingers and failed completely, "Yeah, that's it. Anyway, I reckon that the pesticu...uh...fuck it, what she just said, mixed with the radiation and made the mosquitoes ride horses called War, Death, uh....Famish and uh....Dopey, I think...."

"John, you're shitfaced, again! Go home and sleep it off, will you? People are trying to have a quiet evening here." The landlord, a burly man, had stepped closer from his side of the bar.

"Aye, you're right. I'm gonna go and get a bag of chips I think." John staggered out the door, and a sigh of relief could be heard throughout the bar.

As people tried to carry on with their lives, the flu spread. Nearly every town and city, every country in the world, now had outbreaks of the virus. Businesses were closing due to the lack of staff. Shopping centres, normally packed with shoppers, were getting fewer and fewer customers by the day. Even at work, Steve found himself having to pitch in on the warehouse floor and help fill the gaps in the ranks, as people failed to turn up for work.

Blackouts were becoming common. At first only for a few minutes at a time, but as the days went by, more frequently and for longer periods. The news announced that the country was beginning to come to a standstill and that the Prime Minister urged the people to carry on as normal and that there was nothing to worry about.

A lot of people also decided that, even though they weren't sick, they would stay home and avoid crowded areas so that they wouldn't catch the flu. For a virus that the majority were said to be immune to, Steve noticed that a lot of streets were deserted and there was very little traffic on the roads.

That was until he went to the supermarket.

He had made plans to have Sarah that weekend and decided to stock up on all her favourite food and drinks. He arrived at the car park and saw masses of people, forcing their way in and out of the main doors. Shopping trolleys piled to the brim, people pushing and shoving to gain access or to leave with their goods before someone stole them. It seemed that people had become almost feral, and protected what they had as though anyone who even looked at them were a threat. He witnessed two young women rolling around on the floor, clawing and kicking at each other as their children looked on, screaming.

It was obvious that everyone was panic buying, maybe to stock themselves and their families up and sit and wait it out?

Steve found himself caught up in the moment and pushed his way in to the large building. His theory was; *if the whole town is panicked, how could I be the only one with nothing to worry about?*

He headed for the canned goods section. With a basket in hand, he grabbed as many tins of beans, meatballs, fruit and anything else he thought necessary, as he could. Next, he headed for the drinks area and snatched up two cases of bottled water. Finding himself short on arms, he took to kicking the basket along the floor in front of him with a crate of water under each arm as he searched the aisles for anything he thought he would need. Twenty minutes later, he had finished his sweep. Armed with two full baskets and two cases of water, he played the strangest game of football of his life as he kicked his goods to the checkout.

Once he was back at home, he took stock of what he had. He put away his shopping and placed the candles that he had bought in easy to reach places, making a mental note to make sure there was a lighter in every room. He didn't fancy the idea of Sarah panicking in a sudden blackout and running into a wall.

He sat down to gather his thoughts; *Fuck me, what's going on? It's only flu, and the news says there's nothing to worry about.*

His inner consciousness told him different; *If it's nothing to worry about, then why is the whole country in a panic? Why are people stocking up on food? Why are there blackouts?*

3

Marcus had left the army five years earlier, and had become a private military contractor in Iraq, getting paid to escort and protect VIP's as they travelled about. He didn't do it for the 'War on Terror', or so that he could make a difference; he was in it purely for the money and many of his old army buddies had done exactly the same.

Since the flu had hit the Middle East, the situation had steadily deteriorated. The extremists believed that it was a sign from God that they must continue the fight to rid themselves of the Infidel from the Holy Land, and began to increase their attacks.

With the hospitals being run down and neglected, the dead were piling up and every day, more and more funerals were being held. The number of riots, bombings, shootings, rocket attacks and kidnappings had gone through the roof.

Many of the Western organisations were, as far as Marcus could tell, slowly pulling out and hoping that no one would notice. All the bosses and company directors had made their excuses, and had fled for home. Now, the military was closing down and steadily retreating into the International Zone and a steady trickle of troops and material were loaded onto planes and flown out from Baghdad.

Many districts within the city had been closed off as 'Quarantine Zones' by the police and Iraqi army. Within those zones, the population was left to fend for themselves or die. Militants attacked the walls and the checkpoints from both sides, some of them being trapped inside. Their compatriots saw it as their duty to try and free them from the outside so they could continue the fight. The streets had become a battleground and casualties were mounting.

Very few people were arriving in country and more and more left each day. Engineers, diplomats, doctors, advisors, all of them headed for the airport and the airfields in the hope of getting a flight out of the Hot Zone. The backlog was ridiculous and people even fought with each other in the terminals in desperation of getting a seat on a plane, any plane.

Marcus' team snaked their way through the tight and congested dirty streets of Baghdad in their four, heavily armoured SUVs, with turret-mounted machine guns. Horns were blowing, people hollered, and in general, the Iraqi drivers did as they pleased without any consideration to the rules of the road, or other vehicles. It was like a game of dodgems.

They were on their way to drop their last two remaining clients at the airport. The rest had fled over the previous weeks, and the two nervous and wide-eyed men that sat, strapped to their seats, were keen to get out.

The convoy had to push through and stay mobile, avoiding becoming a static target in the narrow, confined streets. Every man in the team was poised, with their weapons ready for a possible attack.

They had all been in attacks, either from roadside bombs, rocket attacks and even small arms, with the insurgents actually wanting a stand-up fight with rifles and machine guns. It was new to none of them, and they were a hardened and experienced crew.

Gathered from a wide range of military backgrounds and nationalities, Marcus had nicknamed his team, 'The Foreign Legion'. He had two American ex-Special Forces, three South Africans, and even two Serbians who were thought to be wanted for war crimes. With a couple of Australians and New Zealanders thrown in to the mix, they were a highly multi-cultural bunch and no one could ever accuse them of not being tolerant of other nationalities.

To their right was a high curb with open waste ground beyond it and buildings in the distance with a densely built-up area to their immediate left. They came to a junction controlled by Iraqi Police and began to slow, keeping their distance from the traffic in front in order to maintain manoeuvrability. The police were holding the traffic and allowing the vehicles across from the left. They were making a poor job of it, and with the volume of traffic in all directions, the crossroads was almost at a standstill, even for the drivers who were supposed to be moving.

A series of loud cracks, like the snapping of a whip, rang out as incoming rounds flew overhead, causing the men to duck in their seats as they recognised the distinct snap of enemy fire.

"Contact right!" Someone screamed over the radio.

Marcus spun his head around to try and identify the threat. From his position in the commander's seat, in the second vehicle of the convoy, he heard the heavy 7.62mm machine guns begin to fire from the turrets on top of their vehicles. The distinct rapid thump as they unleashed their deadly, heavy rain of fire at their targets was almost comforting. Sini, the gunner in Marcus' own vehicle, was firing in three to five round bursts, never letting up the pressure on their attackers. His body was juddering as the recoil shook the weapon in his hands.

Green tracer rounds started to pass over the front of the vehicle a second later, after the shooter had adjusted his position, and were smashing into the side. Up and down the whole length of the SUV, Marcus could hear the thwack as the rounds pierced the outer shell of the vehicle and thumped into the hard armour plating beneath.

The driver, a burly guy from New Zealand named Eddie, began to try to push forward to get them out of the line of fire.

"All vehicles push through, push through!" Marcus commanded.

The turret gunners increased the rate of fire, and all the drivers accelerated to clear the immediate killing area. The fire coming in from the right had doubled and was now more concentrated and accurate as the insurgents became more determined not to allow the team to get away.

"Man down, Nick is down!" Marcus heard through his ear piece. He looked back over his shoulder to see that the machine gun in the third vehicle was no longer firing as Nick was pulled back inside. By now, all four vehicles were taking heavy fire and with nowhere else to go, the driver of the lead vehicle began trying to push his way through the static traffic ahead of them.

Civilian drivers had either raced off, or abandoned their cars to seek cover from the bullets whizzing through the air all around them. The Police had fled and the junction was now a mass of vehicles blocking all three lanes. It was impossible to push through and Marcus had to think fast.

"Reverse back. We're gonna have to try and push back the way we came." He gave over the radio. All four vehicles came to a sudden stop, and almost instantly began to back up, building up speed by the second.

Rounds continued to zip over them and into them. The gunners were screaming target indications to each other over the radios, trying to guide each other to the enemy positions, but for every enemy neutralized, another position took up the firing. The incoming fire never let up and soon the vehicles were beginning to smoke from heavy damage. Tyres and windows, even though armoured, were blown out. Everyone in the vehicles was being hit with shrapnel from the doors as they buckled under the continuous impacts, and also splinters of glass as the integrity of the armour was pushed to its limits.

The noise was beyond deafening, the continuous thunder of the machine guns above in the turrets, and the high-pitched cracks and snaps as the vehicles took round after round. The smell of cordite was thick in the air as the guns discharged their ammunition and the spent brass casings fell on to the floor of the vehicle. Marcus' eyes began to sting and water.

Marcus watched over his shoulder as his driver did his best to reverse at speed. The third vehicle was swaying as it tried to avoid debris in the road. A sudden ball of flame and a large puff of pale grey smoke erupted from the right hand side of the road between two buildings. It streaked across the open ground and smashed into the fourth vehicle with a heavy thud, quickly followed by a huge bang and flash of light. The SUV rocked from the impact and almost toppled onto its side. The vehicle was torn wide open, and debris flew in all directions. It exploded instantly and the three remaining vehicles slammed on their brakes.

For a short moment, Marcus watched in horror as a second rocket snaked in their direction. "RPG right," he screamed and instinctively crouched in his seat. The rocket was high, and passed over his vehicle. A third missile came at them, this time aimed at the front vehicle; the insurgents were trying to block them off by disabling the front and rear vehicles, causing them to be trapped in the killing area. It punched its way through the rear of the lead SUV, passing through without detonating but damaging the rear axle and drive capability in the process.

The crew of the lead vehicle began to bail out on the left hand side, using the SUV as cover from the enemy fire. All three of them began to hammer the numerous firing points with their rifles and machine gun.

The turret gunner, a tall skinny American named Jim, was naked from the waist down. The rocket, as it had passed through, had created a vacuum inside the vehicle, taking Jim's trousers with it as it punched through the other side. If it wasn't for the desperation of the situation, it would've been almost amusing to Marcus, watching him running about with his balls on show, firing a machine gun.

Marcus made a quick appraisal of the situation; moving forward was out of the question, and their retreat was blocked. The tyres were shot to pieces and they had no way of crossing over the central reservation. Civilian vehicles were left and right, with their drivers either dead or wounded, or having run for cover as soon as the shooting started. They were stuck in the killing area.

"Okay boys, abandon ship. We need to get out of this rocket magnet and get out on foot."

Eddie and Sini didn't need to be told twice. They grabbed their weapons and ammunition and bailed out to the left, taking up firing positions to the front and rear of the vehicle.

Marcus thumbed his radio. "Ian, we are gonna have to bug out on foot. How's Nicky? Have you got eyes on with the rear vehicle, any survivors?"

Ian's booming voice came back, "Nick is in shit state. He took one through the jaw, but he's still conscious and able to move. The rear vehicle is fucked mate. I haven't seen anyone crawl out and I think they're all dead, Marcus."

He couldn't afford to lose his head over it just yet. He needed to get what remained of the team out of the immediate area. "Roger that, Ian. You, Yan, and Nick, keep the clients close together and push to the far side of the road. The more vehicles we have between us and them, the better. All acknowledge."

A chorus of "roger" and double clicks came through his ear piece as everyone understood what needed to be done. Marcus remained crouched behind his damaged and smouldering vehicle as the crack of rounds continued to fill the air around them.

He pulled a smoke grenade from his tactical vest. "Stu, you got smoke?" he shouted to the lead vehicle. Stu didn't hear him due to the noise of the guns around him, including his own as he continued to suppress the enemy positions.

Marcus keyed his radio and asked again, "Stu, any of you lot got smoke?" He had to shout to be heard in his own head. By now, the whole team was throwing a hideous amount of fire power down on the insurgents, as they covered the retreat of the men from the third vehicle. The loud growl of the machine guns and the rhythmic crack of the rifles filled the air.

Stu looked in his direction and gave the thumbs up then, pulling a smoke grenade from his own belt kit, placed his finger into the ring attached to the pin. At the same time, Stu and Marcus stepped back and threw their smoke grenades over the vehicles as far as they could. A few seconds later, plumes of orange and purple were billowing in the waste ground, creating a smoke screen for them to retreat behind.

They had to act fast. Marcus knew that once they began to move and their suppressive fire stopped, the insurgents would release a hailstorm into the smoke, knowing that the team was covering their retreat.

"Move, move back to the others!"

A final long burst from the two machine guns and both Stu and Marcus' crews were sprinting across the road, running between vehicles and jumping high curbs as they headed to the rally point with Ian.

Rounds were zipping all over as the insurgents recovered and began firing into the smoke in the hope of hitting something. Some rounds smashed into vehicles as the men ran past them, others streaked and ricocheted off the road, while others flew overhead. The very air seemed alive with deadly flying pieces of metal.

Sini and Jim stopped ahead and, using a civilian car as cover, fired long shuddering bursts from their machine guns into the smoke, covering the rest of the team as they moved back. Marcus was bringing up the rear, screaming for his men to move faster, to get to cover. Once they were in position with Ian, Marcus and Stu returned fire in order to give Sini and Jim support as they moved to safety. Sini and Jim stopped firing as Marcus and Stu released a hail of rounds in the enemy direction and sprinted, bent double, towards the rest of the team.

They reached the area where Ian had mustered his crew and the two clients. Nick was sat leaning against the wall that separated the main road from the houses and flats beyond, holding a bloodied field dressing to his face and still carrying his weapon. Just from that split second of eye contact, Marcus knew that there was still plenty of fight left in him.

Everyone jumped down and quickly took stock of their weapons and ammunition, ejecting magazines and slapping in fresh ones, ensuring that they had the means to carry on the fight. Marcus eyed the two clients; they were crouched, huddled together with eyes like saucers.

"Other than Nick, anyone else hurt?"

All sounded off that they were okay and good to go. Marcus looked back toward the road at the burning hulk of what was left of the fourth SUV. He couldn't see any movement around it, and with a heavy heart, he had to assume that all were dead.

"Right, we can't stay here. We need to move into better cover before the ragheads grow some balls and do a follow-up." He looked further along the wall and saw what he needed, "There's a gap there. We can push through that and hole up in one of the buildings behind us until help arrives. Shit, did anyone hit their panic button? I forgot."

"I hit mine as soon as the rounds started coming in," Stu said.

Marcus felt a wave of relief, knowing that Stu had sent the distress signal through the vehicles transponder. It would then ping in the Operations Room back at HQ, informing the monitors that they have come into trouble and their exact location would show up on the map screen.

"Nice one. As soon as we go firm, I'll try and get mobile comms with the head shed and see what's being done. Me and Sini will take the lead and find a way through. Stu, you and your crew bring up the rear while Ian takes care of the clients in the middle. We'll have to sprint to the gap, you up for that Nicky?"

Not being able to talk, Nick just nodded, which caused him to wince with pain.

Stu and Jim stood up and poured more fire in the direction of the enemy. They couldn't see them, but they wanted to make sure that anyone following them up would stall as soon as the rounds snapped above them, giving the team the time they needed to cross the distance to the gap.

They ran. Past more static vehicles, through the gap and down a small embankment to a tightly packed housing estate situated twenty metres on the other side of the wall. They didn't stop running until they were in the cover of the buildings.

Marcus had already decided to himself that they would gain entry to a building that overlooked their vehicles on the road, for two reasons. Firstly, in the remote chance that there were any survivors from the destroyed SUV, and secondly, if the insurgents came up to check or loot the abandoned vehicles, they could hit them from their vantage point.

They forced their way to a block of dingy dark apartments and began climbing the central staircase to the upper floors. Stu left Jim, balls still on show, and his driver, Paul, to cover the entry point with a machine gun while the rest secured the top two apartments.

There was no room for manners and politeness, and they barged through the doors with weapons raised, treating everyone as a threat until they were sure otherwise. The two families were herded in to one room and Stu, with his pigeon Arabic, began explaining that they were safe and would not be hurt. The women were screaming and hollering at him, raising their arms and gesticulating to the heavens.

Ian brought in the clients and dumped them in the corner. Stu looked at him for help but Ian could only shrug his shoulders. "Don't look at me mate, you're the hearts and minds guy. I can only ask for cigarettes in Arabic."

Ian began tending to Nick and his wound while Eddie and Yan took up fire positions at the window. Ian cleaned it as best he could and applied a clean dressing that basically held his jaw to his head. He had lost a lot of blood and needed to be evacuated as quickly as possible. Ian set up an I.V and began to replace some of the fluids he had lost.

By now, the family was quiet and between the team, they maintained an overhead watch on the road and the entrances into the building while Marcus called for help.

After a short conversation, he passed on the information to the rest of the team: that an American patrol had been sent to help and should be there within the next ten minutes. No air support was available; something else that was in high demand, but short supply. Marcus pulled his marker panel from his vest, ready to signal to the Americans his position and that they were friendly. The last thing they needed was to get shot up by their trigger-happy rescuers.

"Hey guys." It was Jim hollering from the stairwell in his distinct Texan drawl. "Guys, can you ask the Jundies if they can spare me a pair of pants? My ass is freezing on these concrete steps."

A minute later Stu tossed him a black skirt.

"Sorry buddy, it's all I could find." Stu left Jim staring at the skirt in bewilderment.

Twenty minutes later the remains of the team were at the roadside as Marcus briefed the American commander on the situation. The rescue team, with APCs, pushed into the open area to the right of the road with the barrels of their armoured vehicles pointed toward where the attack had come from. They started to pound shells at likely enemy positions. Civilian safety and collateral damage wasn't taken into consideration anymore, especially after a heavy attack involving Western casualties. A recovery team then moved up to extract the dead from Marcus' team. Marcus insisted that he and his men help.

The charred and dismembered bodies of their fallen comrades were pulled from the wreckage. Marcus could feel his chest heaving and his eyes welling up as he dragged what was left of his friends into body bags laid out on the floor. Now and then he would recognise a piece of clothing or equipment, and he would realise which of his friends it was that he was carrying. They worked in silence, as the crescendo of the firing subsided from the APCs.

Once ready, the remaining vehicles had thermite charges placed inside them and were burned out in order to leave nothing for the enemy to use.

They returned to base as the damaged vehicles left behind burned and smouldered.

That night, Marcus hardly slept. As the commander, he saw it as his personal responsibility to secure and sanitise the equipment and personal effects of his three fallen comrades. Sasa, Joe, and Mike had all been good guys, good operators and good personal friends of his. With blurred vision through tears and cracked voices and choked throats, he and Stu went about doing what needed to be done.

The next day they had a chance to try and put themselves back together, to take a step back and decide what they were to do. The team was now four men short; with three dead and Nick severely wounded. They had no vehicles and had to wait until the company supplied them with new ones. And, inevitably, there would be at least one member of the team that would feel it was time to move on and leave Iraq. On that occasion, it was Marcus.

Over the years he had lost too many good friends. He believed it was only a matter of time until his luck run out, and he had a family to think of; his wife Jennifer and two young sons, Liam and David, who needed him. He needed them just as much.

He had been clever with his money and invested in property and saved. It wasn't as if he would go back home and find himself in a factory. His options were endless, but for now he just needed to get back to his family.

When he informed his boss that he was resigning and wanted the next available flight, he had been caught off guard with the reply.

"Marcus, everybody wants a flight. I'm sorry but there's a backlog the length of the Suez Canal and the likes of us 'mercenaries', as we are looked at, are at the very bottom of the priority list."

His boss, the Operations Manager named Mickey, leaned back in his chair and placed his hands behind his head revealing dark patches of sweat in the armpits of his shirt. "I'm sorry mate, but there's not a lot I can do. I want out too, but HQ has said it'll happen in due course and no one will be left behind. Iraq is gonna fold, Marcus, and everyone is expected to just sit tight for now."

Marcus felt his anger brewing, and checked himself before answering, "Roger that, Mickey. Let me know if anything gets said will you?" And, with that, he turned and left the office.

The last thing he needed to do was lose his temper now, to get arrested by the Americans for assaulting someone, and slung into an Iraqi jail cell, where he would no doubt be forgotten about and left to rot. Besides, Mickey wasn't a bad guy, and Marcus was sure that if he could, he would help him.

For the next three days all they could do was sit around and wait. During that time, Marcus decided to do his own checking up on the current situation. He learned that Iraq had pretty much been written off by the West. He'd even heard rumours that the troops in Iran were going to be pulled out.

Baghdad had an air of death about it, as if the population were just waiting to die. He saw reports about rioting and people attacking each other. New York, Washington DC, London and Berlin; the rest of America and Europe were having more than their fare share of unrest.

And he also learned that he wouldn't be leaving Iraq any time soon.

4

Steve heard his phone beep in his pocket. It was a text message from his brother, Marcus.

"Steve, things are getting bad here.
Looks like everything is going tits up,
How are things at your end?
I'll try and call you soon."

He hadn't heard from his brother in a while, and it was rare for him to call or text while he was away. Mostly, they stayed in touch through e-mail. If Marcus suddenly needed to speak to him then things couldn't be good.

Steve flicked on the TV and started up his computer. He wanted to do more research and find out how bad things really were. He hadn't paid much attention to the media for the past couple of days. It was the same stuff over and over; being told not to worry and that all would be okay. Only the scenery changed.

It was the same as he had just witnessed at the supermarket all across the country. Stocks were running out as everything was snatched up. Fuel was starting to run low at most stations and rioting had broken out all over. Special reports were shown of police in riot gear, forming lines of shields and being attacked by angry mobs, cameramen trying to continue filming with shaky hands as they watched the defensive lines being overrun and the police dragged to the floor.

London was under siege with mobs running loose in the streets. The government had declared a state of emergency in the capital, and many other major cities to the South of the country. The army was being called in to try to help with the over-burdened police.

Steve knew that this was the result of the flu. Though the media had done what it could to give accurate reports, not all the information had been passed onto them, to then pass onto the public, until it was too late.

Steve kicked himself for not keeping up on current events.

The Secretary of Health, along with the help of government scientists, had released a statement:

"The escalation of the flu virus has now reached a critical point,
with the spread now becoming harder to contain. Hospitals and

government health officials have informed me that the virus now seems to have mutated to a more virulent strain and can now be transmitted without coming into contact with another infected person.

"In essence, it's in the very air we breathe. Numerous new cases are being reported every day, and we advise that you avoid the already overwhelmed hospitals and remain at home if you suspect that you are infected.

"We still believe that the majority of people are immune and that the outbreak will eventually be under control. However, I've been informed that a small percentage of people have a violent reaction to the virus. These people are passing on a violent strain to people who are otherwise uninfected. Even if you already had the flu and recovered, contact, through attack, with the violent strain will cause you to have the same aggressive symptoms.

"We believe that in most cases, the aggressive strain is passed on through bodily fluids, mainly from bites.

"Health officials have advised that anyone suspected of being infected must be separated from the rest of their family. Avoid contact without face and hand protection, and anyone showing signs of the violent strain should be reported to the authorities immediately.

"I assure you that all is being done to bring this problem under control and you will be kept informed of any further information."

"Fuck me." Steve had his hand in front of his mouth holding his chin up from hitting the floor. "Why would people with the flu bite?"

He had read similar stories on the internet about Africa and South America, but had dismissed them as rumours. Plus, he never imagined he would be seeing it in his own country.

He decided to call Claire to check on the arrangements for Sarah that weekend. His theory was that as long as she was with him, he could protect her. Claire, even though a good mother who always wanted the best for Sarah, was a balloon without a string as far as Steve was concerned. She probably didn't feel the same sense of urgency and panic that Steve felt rising in his stomach.

He and Claire arranged that he would pick her up on Thursday; the next day, instead. The sooner he could get Sarah back to his flat, the sooner he would be able to think straight and consider the situation. He had no real intentions of taking her back on Sunday.

He had already decided, to himself, that school was out for the time being.

The next day, with both of them safe in his flat, he explained the situation to Sarah. Though she was only ten years old, he didn't want to brush over the state of affairs or paint it all in a prettier picture; he knew that Sarah was mature and intelligent enough to understand.

She took it well. "So does that mean I won't be going to school on Monday, Dad?"

"Sweetheart, I don't want you going anywhere, especially without me."

A smile spread across Sarah's face making her big green eyes sparkle more than usual. Steve wasn't sure whether it was due to not having to go to school, or because she knew her father was there to protect her no matter what. He suspected it was a bit of both.

"For now, we will just have to watch movies, play board games, and eat rubbish. Sounds like a perfect weekend to me, my little buddeo."

"Yup," Sarah replied, "me too, Daddeo."

That night, after Sarah had fallen asleep on the couch, Steve turned on the TV to check the news. Headlines were flitting across the bottom of the screen and flashing up behind the reporter as she sat at her desk. Steve struggled to focus at first through tired eyes, and strained to read the reports as they sailed along the bottom. He caught a glimpse of a word before it disappeared off screen: 'Cannibalism'. He felt the hairs on the back of his neck stiffen and stand erect.

He turned up the volume and listened as the reporter spoke:

"Civil unrest has escalated and continues throughout all major cities within the country, with the number of rioters rising. Police officers and soldiers that were trying to control the mass crowds have been attacked and a number have even been killed, with many more injured.

"Unconfirmed reports from the front lines say that many have been bitten and that there have even been reported cases of the attackers eating their victims.

"We take you live now, to the front line in Birmingham. Jessica Beal has more on the story."

The screen flicked to a pretty blonde girl standing in a dark street holding a microphone as police and army vehicles moved back and forth in the background and people in riot gear formed lines of defense.

She looked scared, and as she gave her report on the situation, Steve could hear screams, gun shots and something else in the background. It was like a throbbing, humming noise that could've been mistaken for a generator or even swarms of insects, only it got louder and louder.

The camera panned away from Jessica and zoomed in on the riot shield line of soldiers and police. They were standing their ground like Roman infantry behind their wall of shields, as police officers who had formed a line in front of them fell back and passed through them looking battered and bruised, many missing their helmets and other equipment. Many of them continued to run past the camera in panic, rather than stop to support their fellow officers and soldiers.

Shouts and commands could be heard as the newly formed line braced themselves. The crowd crashed into their shields, causing a ripple as the police and soldiers tried to steady the line. The humming had become louder and now sounded more like individual voices. But they weren't speaking, or shouting, or even screaming, it was more of a steady pleading, remorseful wail or moan. It was a chorus of despair and anguish, like the battle cry of some medieval ghost army.

The lines gave way, and some of the attackers ran. Others walked through the gaps, but they all fell onto the beleaguered men and women that were trying in vain to hold them at bay. Screams rang out from every corner as more and more of the mass of people poured forth, attacking everything in sight. In the dim light of the street, Steve could make out some of the attackers. Some looked like people you would expect to see in a riot, but others were wearing suits, some even police uniforms. Even young children seemed to be involved. Nearly all of them seemed to have some form of injury as well as bloody faces and torn clothing.

Jessica was screaming to her camera crew and soon the footage became jerky and distorted as the news people fled to safety. The screen went blank and returned to the news desk, focusing on a shaken reporter.

Steve sat in shock, not knowing exactly what he had just witnessed. The people attacking the police didn't seem to care about the law, or their own safety. They attacked in a wave, completely undeterred by the shields, the batons, and the riot guns.

He sat bolt upright, looked around the room and ran to his front door. He double-checked all the locks and bolts closed the windows and blinds in his kitchen then stood shaking as he leaned against the fridge.

"Shit, this is bad." His understatement didn't go unnoticed by himself and for the rest of the night he stood watch over the flat, regularly checking the news for further updates. It was more of the same throughout the country and it was clear that the army and police had no chance of stemming the tide of violence.

The next morning Sarah woke to see her anxious father carrying tools into the kitchen. She peered round the corner and saw that every cupboard had been emptied, with tins piled high on the table top. He was now dismantling the doors on the kitchen units and stacking them against each other at the side of the door. In the corner were crates of bottled water, with buckets and other bottles filled to the top.

"Dad, what are you doing?"

Steve spun to see her standing in the doorway, rubbing her eyes. Placing the screwdriver on the table, he approached her and crouched to look her in the eye. "Sarah, you know how I told you that things were getting bad outside, all over the country?"

Sarah scratched her head of long wavy brown hair, still looking half asleep, "Uh, yeah?"

"Well it's got a lot worse, darling. A lot worse than I thought and it looks like it won't get any better soon." Steve was doing his best to sound like he had things under control, but a glance around the kitchen told him that, once Sarah was fully awake and aware of what was going on, she would no doubt become frightened. "All you need to know is that I'm here and I won't let anything bad happen. Okay?"

"Righto, Dad." She turned and walked back to the living room.

It was still very early, and she fell back into a slumber on the couch. Steve wondered whether or not she had actually been fully awake and had understood anything he had said. No matter. As long as she was asleep, he could carry on with his preparations.

From what he could tell, they had enough food to last for weeks and the water he had put to one side would only be used in case the main water supply failed. He counted the doors and other pieces of wood he had collected and stacked by the door. *Plenty*, he thought.

"If I have to," he said aloud, "I can board up every window and door pretty well. Let's just hope I don't have to because IKEA might not be open for a while."

On the table, along with the food, he placed four boxes of candles, two maglite torches and every battery he could lay his hands on.

He then added a hammer, a baseball bat, and a scuba diving knife. He wasn't exactly over the moon with his arsenal but it was better than nothing. He was determined that no one would hurt his little girl.

Next, he went to his bedroom and returned with a small backpack that he used when he and Sarah went on their adventures in the country. Inside, he placed a sleeping bag, a thick jacket for him and one for Sarah too, a few tins of food and bottles of water along with one of the torches and spare batteries. He added an extra jumper and socks for Sarah and then placed the backpack to one side. Later, he added the baseball bat, sliding it through the straps on the side so that it sat vertical and easy to retrieve. He fastened it, and tightened the straps to ensure it was all secure and ready for a quick grab should things become worse and they needed to leave.

He laid out clothes for them both. He decided his walking boots were best for the situation and also donned his walking trousers and a T-shirt for the time being. He left his jacket with the backpack. He laid out similar, suitable clothes for Sarah, and he would insist that she put them on once she was awake, and only allowing her to take them off when she was washing.

Out of an old hard-wearing workman's belt he found at the back of a drawer; he added loops and fastenings from other straps and belts that he found, to act as his weapons belt. He strapped the diver's knife to his leg, and the belt would carry the hammer and second torch.

He was as prepared as he could be, and short of having a machine gun or a tank, he figured he hadn't done too badly at all.

He turned on the TV then, looking down at the remote, "ah, more batteries!" They also went into the backpack, and he happily resigned himself to having to turn the TV channels over manually instead.

During all his preparations, he couldn't shake the images of what was happening in the streets. All morning he had heard police sirens throughout the town, racing up and down the roads from one emergency to the next. Screams and shouts rang out from adjoining roads and streets, and it seemed to Steve that the chaos and violence had finally found his doorstep.

He sat watching more reports on riots, statements from army and police officials and more eyewitness accounts of what was happening. The words 'cannibalism' and 'devouring' were in nearly every report.

A blackout caused the TV to go blank. A few minutes later the screen came to life again. It was midway through some kind of announcement from the newsreader. She sat trembling, looking anxious with a piece of paper in her hand that had obviously just been passed to her to read with there being no time to set it up on the teleprompter.

She looked left and right nervously. Clearly uncomfortable with what she was about to read to the entire country. She glanced past the camera and, most probably, at her producer for confirmation that she was to continue with what she was saying.

"Uh...so far, no announcements have come from the government or their health officials confirming or denying these reports, but a number of independent scientists and laboratories, including Oxford and Cambridge, have agreed that these findings are, in fact, correct.

"As yet, we have received no theories on why or how this phenomenon has occurred but certain institutions are insisting that these changes have happened within the last five days, and that it is a global, and not a localised, problem..."

She trailed off and raised her hand to her ear. Steve found himself standing in front of the television, willing the information to pour forth again. He felt completely out of the loop. Something had just been announced and because of the power cut, he had missed it.

"Fucking power cuts," he said, automatically looking up toward the ceiling as though it was either God's will, or the power station that was actually situated on the other side of the light fitting.

He turned his attention back to the news desk:

34

"I have just received word that the Prime Minister is about to make an announcement. We now go live to hear the government's stand on this story." The reporter had somewhat composed herself again since her obvious discomfort at the announcement she had made, whatever it was.

The scenery changed from the pretty newsreader at the desk to the Prime Minister looking haggard, withdrawn and deeply stressed. This announcement wasn't going to take place in the usual settings. The background wasn't rows of old wooden and plush-cushioned seats with his party faithfully behind him to cheer him and heckle the opposition. It wasn't even his luxurious, spacious office with the antique desk and oil paintings on the walls behind. It looked more like a concrete-walled cell, with no furnishings and none of the usual trappings that he preferred to surround himself with.

He refrained from utilising the false smile and pleasantries that he usually used before telling the country he was going to hit them with more taxes, job cuts and slashes in government funding. He seemed more to the point, his expression grave and without the usual shit-eating grin as his hand reached down and yanked your balls off. In fact, the man didn't look like he was about to piss down the people's back and tell them it's raining at all. He looked more human, more like a real person with issues and problems on his mind. Big problems!

He took a deep breath and looked directly into the camera:

"Ladies and gentlemen, in the last hour I have received a number of reports on the situation as it stands at this very moment. Though shocking and hard to believe, I have had confirmation from a number of government sources that those who have died recently are returning to life."

He paused for a moment to allow the information to sink in. Steve felt his arse twitch and his arms become heavy.

"At the moment we have no solid evidence on the cause of this, but it is widely speculated that the flu virus, which has now swept the entire globe, has again mutated. I am informed that whether death is from the flu, natural causes, or even a bite from an infected person, anyone who passes away will reanimate and then attack the living.

"I have been in contact with the presidents of America, Russia, China, and France, as well as the German Chancellor, and many

other country leaders. They have all confirmed the same facts. Every country in the world is being stretched to its breaking point and resources have become minimal.

"I am in negotiations with the Chinese and North Korean governments to come to an agreement to end the hostilities and to focus on the more urgent matters on our home soils, and to work together to come up with a solution.

"At this moment I myself have no further information to give you and I'll now pass you over to Dr. Joseph Cox of the Department of Health."

Again, the screen changed to reveal a grey haired man in his late fifties, looking athletic and stronger than he should have actually been. But from the lines on his face, and his aged eyes, he was easily pushing sixty.

He wasted no time and fired straight into his findings:

"Over the past five days we have taken samples from numerous flu and attack victims. The findings were the same, but at different levels.

"While most of the flu victims, except for the aggressive strain, became lethargic and sick for up to a week with some making a full recovery, the bite victims became feverous and incapacitated within twenty four hours. So far, at the most, we have seen a bite victim continue to fight the virus for up to four days, before they succumbed and died before reanimating.

"On reanimating, they show no vital signs. Heart rate, blood pressure and core temperature are exactly what you would expect from any cadaver. They do not react to stimuli, or even recognise the people around them, and will attack on sight any living organism they encounter, including humans.

"The bite victims of the aggressive strain die, on average within seventy two hours, and then revive and attack the living within a few hours after death. The time period has been recorded from as little as two hours, to as long as eight.

"Now, we have found that all recently dead, reanimate. Whether they die from the flu, a bite or even a car crash, every dead body will rise and attack the living. The virus seems to have mutated once again and seems to be in the air around us, causing the recently deceased to revive. From what we know, the mutation does not mean that the living will be affected any further. It only causes the dead to reanimate.

WHEN THERE'S NO MORE ROOM IN HELL

"The bite victims develop a high fever, vomiting, headaches and eventually death. The results on revival vary. We have discovered that the fitter and more active the patient before death, the more mobile they are once they reanimate. Some of the cadavers on revival have been known to run, albeit at a slower and more uncoordinated pace than their living counterparts, and some can even problem solve with the likes of opening doors and using stairs.

"So far, only humans have been recorded as reviving after death, though the reanimated bodies will attack anything that is living including mammals, birds and reptiles. They do not recognise authority or even family members and will not react to emotional or sentimental encouragement. Their instincts are rudimentary and so far, we have discovered that they cannot be reasoned with, or bargained with. They recognise nothing of their old lives and all emotional attachment should be disconnected from family members who become infected.

"They do not feel pain in the sense that we do, and they can take injuries to all vital organs of their bodies, except the brain. We have discovered that the brain is the key to their revival and continued existence. Without the brain intact, the body cannot reanimate.

"I have been asked how this will affect the dead who have already been buried. For one, even a strong and healthy human being cannot force their way through six feet of soil covering them. Also, bodies that have undergone autopsies and embalming cannot reanimate. They have had their brains removed and without them, they are permanently dead.

"Though many will find that what I have to say as barbaric, it is nevertheless the inescapable truth; all dead bodies must have the brain made inactive, either by blunt trauma, as ruthless as it sounds, or by surgical removal. A heavy blow to the head or a gunshot will normally be sufficient enough to render the body inactive.

"We must remember that these are no longer our family and friends. Regardless of what we say or do, they will not react to their past lives, names, places, emotions or trinkets. They are nothing more than reanimated corpses that are, for some unknown reason, intent on killing and eating anything living that crosses their path.

"Any recently dead or suspected infected family member should be turned over to the authorities as soon as possible."

Steve felt dizzy. The room spun and his stomach did somersaults as he stood staring at the television. He turned to look at Sarah, who still lay sleeping on the couch. The feeling of panic and dread creeping up his throat was making him feel sick. He ran to the bathroom and hung his head over the toilet with one hand against the wall to support himself. The room was spinning and the walls seemed like they were closing in.

He didn't vomit; instead he leaned his back against the wall and slowly slid down it until he was in an upright foetal position, bracing his knees to his chest as he contemplated all that he had just seen and heard.

5

The police riot line had collapsed into pandemonium.

What was supposed to be a defensive line to contain the rioting crowd in that part of the city had crumbled almost instantly. It wasn't the fact that the men and women defending the line had just turned and fled in panic; initially they had stood their ground and been ready to repel the attackers.

But it was the way the attackers had assaulted the line that had caused it to disintegrate.

The police were trained and well equipped to withstand most civil unrest scenarios; armed with helmets, shields and protective clothing as well as riot guns and CS gas. Some of the men and women in uniform had even been in riots before and had experienced first-hand the effects of a full scale bombardment of bricks and petrol bombs hailing down on them. Even people assaulting their shields with clubs and heavy objects to try and intimidate them and break the line, was nothing new to some of them.

In most riots, the aggression slowly escalates, starting with chants and the rioters trying to provoke the security forces. Next would be the chunks of masonry and anything else that could be hurled over and at the shield wall. As the rioters would become braver and more daring, some would charge at the police and crash into and kick at the shields before retreating to cheers of the other rioters.

It was rare, even unheard of, that a full-on assault involving every member of the crowd would follow.

This time, the rioters hadn't used missiles to bombard the police. They carried no weapons or makeshift battering rams and they hadn't backed off when the first of the baton rounds and riot gas canisters had been fired into them as they approached.

They didn't even shout taunts or slogans. They had just assaulted the lines in one huge rush, without any noise, other than some kind of humming sound that they made in unison. At first it had been a steady, uninterrupted sound, but once they hit the shields, it had become clear that it was made up of thousands of voices creating the same low haunting gurgling moan. Just the noise in itself had unsettled a lot of the police units that were expected to stand fast.

They crashed against the shields like a tidal wave, their hands and faces pressed up hard and pulling against the clear reinforced plastic riot shields and visors that protected the police officers on the other side of them. With the weight of the crowd pushing forward, the lines began to buckle. Many tried their best to stand their ground and maintain the integrity of the shield wall, knowing full well that once one person broke or collapsed, the strength of the line would be lost; allowing the rioters to break through and exploit the gap.

It wasn't completely unlike ancient Greek and Roman warfare, relying on the men next to you in the Phalanx or Cohort to hold their position and maintain the integrity of the line against an assault.

More officers, who had been held as a reserve, came from the rear to help stabilise the line, pushing and propping themselves against the men and women already standing shoulder to shoulder and helping the already beleaguered defenders to stand fast.

Screams and shouts could be heard all along the wall of police as they encouraged each other, trying to steady themselves, or gave orders as the pressure against their shields increased.

The collapse had begun on the right flank, and the rioters had rolled up the line of defence like a plague of locusts. Within seconds the crowd swarmed through the gap.

More police were sent to plug the hole in the line but it was too late. The integrity of the shield wall was lost. The centre had begun to cave in shortly after the right flank had been forced back. With the rioters behind them and attacking the police that tried to retreat, the men and women in the front line, still fighting, had nowhere to pull back to. It became every man and woman for themselves as command and control were lost in the mayhem.

Everybody ran.

People were screaming all around, some from panic and others from pain. The rioters didn't just charge the police to break them up and send them running. They were actually intent on dragging them to the floor and swarming over them, tearing at them with their bare hands and gnashing teeth.

Tony could hear the screams, but nothing was going to drag him back. He ran like many others had and didn't stop. His only thought was to get as far away from the scene as possible and to safety.

He could hear his muffled footsteps through the fire retardant hood that protected his bare skin, as his booted feet pounded against the road.

The lenses in the respirator that he wore to protect himself from the riot gas was steamed and his vision was severely impaired. He had to angle his head as he ran so that he could see through the top of the eye pieces that were still free of the condensation. He could see the dimly lit street ahead of him and the light from the street lamps above. He ran directly down the middle of the road, the parked cars to his left and right helping as a channel to follow in his poor visibility.

His breathing was constricted due to the heavy riot gear that he wore, and the fact that he had to suck his air intake through a relatively small hole which was then restricted even further with filters inside the respirator. He could hear his own loud, short breaths within the confined and humid respirator that seemed to suck at his face like a squid.

His legs were burning and he pumped his arms to try and keep his speed up. But he began to slow, his chest heaving and his heart threatening to burst.

He turned a corner and found himself in an empty street on the outskirts of an industrial area. He slowed to a brisk walk and moved toward the shadows of a shuttered doorway. Leaning with one hand, propping himself up against the cold bricks, he tore at the respirator and lifted it from his face and over his head. The cool night air hit him and it felt good on his hot flushed skin.

He was dripping with sweat and sucking in the air as fast and deep as he could. His head began to spin and he felt the bile rising in his chest. From nerves, fear and exertion he couldn't control it and he spewed the contents of his stomach all over the wall in front of him.

He had no water and the taste of sick was soon replaced with a dry parched mouth that threatened to seize up on him, like a machine drained of oil. His lips were dry and his tongue felt swollen. Tony looked around, then walked to the curb and reached his hand into a small dirty puddle that had collected at the edge of the road. He scooped up a palm of water and slurped it up, swilling his mouth to gain moisture as well as rid himself of the taste of vomit. He spat it back out after a few seconds and then repeated the process.

Feeling more composed, he headed back to the corner of the street and looked down the road in the direction he had come from. He couldn't see anyone else heading his way. Had they all turned back? Was he the only one who ran?

Tony didn't care. After what he had seen, he had no intention of playing the hero and standing firm to help his fellow officers fight the crowd.

He looked down and shook his head. *Did I really see those things?* He fought with his inner self and tried to convince himself that he must be mistaken. But he knew he wasn't. He had seen it.

He turned and walked deeper into the industrial estate. He knew that he would hit the main road on the far side; he would turn right and that would lead him back to the station after a mile and a half. He didn't care about what would be said when he got there. Questions would be asked about what had happened and why he had run, but he wasn't concerned about that. *Maybe others who had fled had already made it there?* There was always a chance that the unit, or what was left of it, had been pulled back and regrouped at the station.

He struggled with his thoughts. He had seen the rioters' crash against the shields. Close up, he'd seen their faces, which were strange, sick, pale and gaunt. Their eyes had just stared at him, unblinking and vacant; some had eyes that were clouded over, looking like an opaque film covering the lens.

And the noise, that poignant noise they made. It was a lingering low groan that seemed to emit from every one of them. It made him shudder to think about it.

Some of them had horrible injuries too. He was sure he had seen people with eyes missing and even skin ripped away from their faces. He couldn't remember clearly, but he was certain that one of the people closest to him, attacking his shield like a berserker, had a hand missing. It was just a bloody stump, and his shield had turned red before being finally ripped from his grasp.

The screams of his colleagues still rang in his ears. He had heard the agonizing cries of his co-workers as they had been brought down and set upon by the mass of attackers. Before he ran, he had witnessed one officer being dragged to the floor and five or six people pile on top of him, clawing and biting at him. His high pitched screams had been cut off as one of the people had clamped their teeth around his windpipe and tore it away in a fountain of bright arterial blood that sprayed over their faces.

He continued to walk, constantly checking the shadows and over his shoulder. He was glad to be alive. He didn't feel much for the people he had left behind. He felt very little for anyone anyway, regardless of his current situation.

He had never allowed or wanted anyone to get close to him and he was happy in his own home, with his own company, without people prying. He knew he wasn't normal and his dark thoughts and desires sometimes surfaced when he was behind closed doors, but he did his best to counter that by being a good policeman.

Tony never gave people the benefit of the doubt or showed leniency, even for the pettiest of offences. He had been known to chase kids around the streets in his squad car after witnessing them riding their bikes in a 'no cycle zone'.

Once he had been suspended after being accused of hitting a young offender, but nothing came of it due to lack of evidence and the child having a record of anti-social behaviour. It was around that time that Tony had decided to take his frustrations out on the scum of the streets by making their lives difficult and stopping to question them at their every turn.

But in his private life, his behaviour had become more disturbing. He just couldn't help himself. At first he had fought with his morals and he knew that his urges and the movies he liked to download were wrong, but still, they satisfied his distorted needs. They excited him, and afterward he always felt calm and content.

Tony had never been well liked, even as a child. He had always been viewed as an outsider. Of average height and slight build, his appearance was unassuming, and with his balding hair and deeply lined but soft-featured face, he gave the impression of a hard-working friendly man, but he always harboured inner demons that he fought with from a young age, until finally giving in to them in later life.

He joined the police force and had found a new calling in life. He enjoyed being a police officer, even though many of his colleagues viewed him with suspicion and avoided working closely with him. He tended to rant to himself in a whispered tone and, more than once, fellow police officers had voiced their concerns about his mental status.

But Tony had accepted that he was different, and after finally admitting to himself about what made him tick, he had discovered a new peace within himself.

He heard footsteps behind him. The rapid hard pounding footsteps of someone sprinting along the street, and they were getting louder. Tony glanced to his left and right for somewhere to hide; he saw a low wall that was topped with a chain link fence. There was a gap where there would've normally been a heavy sliding gate, but it had been left open and he ducked behind it, out of sight from the street.

Crouching in his hiding place, he raised his head slightly and peered through the gaps in the chain link. Further down the street he could see a dark figure creeping along the wall of the warehouses across from him. He couldn't tell whether it was friend or foe, and remained still and concealed in the shadows.

The figure came closer and he could soon distinguish the uniform of a police officer in riot gear. Whoever it was, they were hurt and limping. The officer stopped and dropped into a squatting position against the wall of the warehouse. Tony strained his eyes to see if he recognised them. He couldn't, but he could hear sobs, and they sounded feminine.

He squinted at the end of the street, he saw no one else approaching and after a few deep breaths, he stood and walked out from behind the wall. The female officer hadn't noticed him and he was ten feet away before she finally looked up.

Startled, she pushed her feet out, thrusting her upper body up the wall and forcing her upright. The back of her uniform scraped and scuffed against the rough brick and she stepped to her right as if about to make a run for it.

"It's okay." Tony was holding his hands in front of him, palm first to show he meant her no harm. "I was down there with you when they attacked us. I'm police too." He swept his hands in front of him and downwards, as if presenting himself, so that she would recognise the uniform.

"Why are you up here? Did you follow me?" She looked scared and defensive.

Tony was doing his best to put her at ease. He relaxed his shoulders to reduce his height so they were closer to eye level and tried to soften his face and even offer a smile as he spoke. "I'll be honest with you, I ran when everyone else did. The line was broken and those people were attacking everyone in sight. I was scared, to tell you the truth. I think everyone was. I've never been in a riot before. I'm normally sat in a patrol car or at the desk."

She seemed to relax a little. "Yeah, I recognise you. You're Tony aren't you? I've seen you about at the station."

"That's where I'm planning on going now. There's no way I want to go back down there." He vacantly swept a hand in the direction they had both come from. "You may as well come with me. What's your name?"

"Elaine," she replied.

"Okay then, Elaine, we had better keep quiet and try not to attract any attention. From what I saw down there, I don't fancy that mob getting their hands on me."

Elaine looked at him, her face contorting as though remembering something terrible; the visions of the attackers clawing and tearing at her from behind the shields and then the images of her friends being attacked as they lay on the ground, hopelessly trying to defend themselves.

"They just didn't seem to care. No matter how much I hit them with my baton, they kept on coming at me. One of them even bit my leg." She looked down and rubbed her wounded calf muscle. "I don't think it's too bad, but it hurt like fuck."

Tony eyed her, weighing her up and wondering whether she was likely to be useful or a burden. "Yeah, I saw them biting people too. You think you can walk and run okay if need be?"

"I'll manage." She stood up straight and looked ahead. "We going that way then?" She pointed to the darkness at the end of the street.

"Yeah, hopefully we'll be able to get back to the station within the hour."

They began to walk. Elaine hobbled but she refused to allow herself to become a hindrance to Tony. She kept pace at his side; regardless of the pain she felt shooting through her leg with every step.

They covered the distance to the station in a relatively short space of time. It was late, close to midnight, and the streets and roads were deserted with no traffic or signs of life, otherwise they would've tried to flag a car down. Instead they had walked and now and then had been forced to hide in the shadows when they thought they heard people on the other side of bushes or walls that lined the side of the road. They took no chances; in the dark they couldn't tell who would be likely to help them or attack them.

As they approached the station they began to hear the sounds of trouble. The bangs of gunfire and the crashing of heavy objects and the smashing of windows echoed off the walls around them. They were still close to the main road, but they were entering an area comprising of shops and restaurants. There were more buildings there, and the continuous echo bouncing from the hard surfaces made it hard for Tony to make an estimate of where exactly the noise was coming from, or how many people were involved.

They had no choice but to carry on, creeping closer to the station. They were just a hundred metres away from where they knew the station would be. They stealthily moved along the wall of a designer clothes shop, keeping to the shadows, toward the junction that would turn left into the street of the police station.

Tony paused before turning the corner, taking a deep breath; he held his hand out behind him, signalling for Elaine to stay where she was.

Quickly he forced his head around the corner and took in the scene that lay before them. Just as quickly, he retracted and backed up to where Elaine was still standing. He continued to back up and collided with her.

"Tony, what is it? Are they here as well?" she hissed in a whispered voice.

Tony had gone pale with fright, his eyes had grown wide and he stared back toward the corner. He stuttered his words as he spoke. "They...they're...every...everywhere."

Elaine crept forward to the junction. She saw the roof of the station, and that was about all she could see of the building. Police cars and riot vehicles, some on their sides, lay abandoned in the car park in front. People crowded around the building, clambering and attacking the doors and windows.

Most of the glass had been smashed out from the windows and the attackers were climbing in through the open gaps. She could see silhouettes moving in the upper floor windows, some obviously her fellow officers, running from one room to another and battling to regain control of the police station, or just for their lives.

An officer stood on the roof of the building with, what Elaine assumed to be, a shotgun aimed over the edge, and pumped round after round into the crowd at street level. Even with people being killed around them, the rioters didn't seem to be fazed in the slightest and never let up their assault.

Elaine looked back to Tony, who still looked as though he were in shock. "What do we do? Should we try and help?"

Tony was just mumbling to himself, his eyes wide with fear, and slowly shaking his head, backing away all the time from the corner of the street.

She turned back just as two of the rioters rounded. She stepped back and gasped. They stopped for a second when they saw her, their bloodied mouths opening as if to speak, then suddenly snapping shut and grinding their teeth in anticipation as their hands reached out for her.

Their clothes were torn and covered in dark blood. Their hands, mouths and faces were also smeared with it and their eyes, even though they were fixed on Elaine and Tony as they backed away, were devoid of anything.

For a fleeting moment Elaine thought, *they actually look like the eyes of dead people.*

She backed up and this time, it was she that bumped into Tony. He was standing solid in his tracks and looking behind them. Others were approaching from the opposite direction. Tony, snapping out of his moment of inactivity, gripped Elaine by the shoulder, dragging her with him as he headed for the other side of the street, hoping to bypass the approaching rioters and flee to safety.

"C'mon, head for the other side of the street," he said, pushing her in that direction.

As they began to cross, more people turned the corner toward them from the direction of the police station. They shambled and hobbled, reaching out with their bloodstained hands and grasping at the air between them as they drew closer. There were now six of them in front and eight behind. The street was blocked by the approaching aggressors and so was their escape.

"Shit, what do we do?" Elaine was pushing back at Tony as he tried to guide her forward.

Tony glanced over his shoulder again, then back to the front. They were getting closer. Some moving much faster than the others as they staggered toward them on unsteady legs. He weighed up the odds and considered his options; he looked down at the back of Elaine's head and shoulders, then back to the corner of the street where he had planned to escape.

"I'm sorry, Elaine," he said.

She turned to speak but before she got a word out, she felt a heavy blow to the back of her head that knocked her off her feet and sprawled her on the ground. She wasn't unconscious, but she wasn't far from it. She could see the blurry silhouette of Tony above her then, felt the impact of his foot as he brought it down onto her left ankle. She felt and heard the bones break but the pain hadn't registered.

Tony raised his foot again and quickly brought it down, heel first, on her other ankle. The bone crunched under his heavy boot and there was a clear audible snap as it shattered. This time, she screamed. A loud gut-wrenching scream that didn't seem to end. The sound reverberated around the street.

All the time, the bloodthirsty rioters closed in around them.

Tony stepped back and looked to the corner. Only two were coming from that direction. He glanced down at Elaine who was trying to get to her feet. She rolled onto her stomach and began pushing herself up onto her hands and knees. She managed to get a foot under her, but as soon as her weight rested on the splintered jagged bones of her ankle the pain caused her to cry out again and collapse.

He began to back away from her, checking over his shoulder to make sure no more people had appeared in his line of escape. It was still just the two and Tony decided that he could deal with that many. He would just run through them.

Elaine was sobbing and pleading with him. "Don't leave me, please, don't leave me." She reached out for him, imploring him to help her up, her face twisted in an expression of agony and desperation.

Tony turned away; he looked straight ahead and sprinted for the next street. The two shambling figures ahead of him, a man in a police uniform and a blood-soaked fat woman wearing a torn flowery dress, raised their arms in his direction as if he might give himself to them. They looked almost grateful as he closed the distance, reaching out to him and moaning in harmony with each other.

He dropped his shoulder and hit the first one, the woman, sending her flying away from him, arms and legs flailing in the air as she crashed to the floor, landing on her back. He handed off the man by slapping his hands away from him, sending the police officer spinning with a stupid and surprised sounding moan.

By the time he reached the corner and turned into the next street, Elaine was screaming. It was a piercing shriek that rang out in to the night. The pitch raised and fell as her flesh was ripped from her body.

The searing pain of teeth as they punctured her skin and bit deep into her muscle caused her body to spasm. She fought them, but their numbers and weight, coupled with her already weakened state, was too much for her.

Her fingers were bitten off as she tried to fend off the snapping jaws; she could feel them being crushed in the teeth of her attackers, then scraped and snapped away from her by jagged and broken teeth.

Her screams began to lessen as she became weaker, but she remained conscious for a long time. Her limbs were pulled from their sockets and her stomach was split open as cold hands and bony fingers clutched at the skin of her midriff until it broke, popping and splitting open like a thick plastic bag that had been over-filled, revealing her warm internal organs, which were wrenched from her rib cage and spread across the tarmac.

Fingers dug into her eyes and tore them away; teeth sunk in and gnawed at the soft flesh around her face and neck.

Within a matter of minutes, Elaine was nothing more than a butchered and dismembered carcass, still steaming as the blood continued to cool in the night air.

Tony was at the far end of the next street and continued at a fast walk to save his energy. He was grateful when the screams finally stopped. They could've attracted every one of the things in the area and he would never have been able to get away.

Elaine hadn't been a burden after all, he thought.

6

Marcus and Stu sat watching the news broadcast. It was the American version and the President had released his own statement of the situation. But the story was the same.

"Those who have recently died are reanimating and attacking the living."

They looked at each other with wide eyes and slack jaws. Stu screwed up his face, "Is this some kind of wind up?"

"I don't think so, Stu. The U.S President doesn't strike me as the sort with a sense of humour."

Around them, the whole compound seemed to erupt in a hive of activity. People had obviously watched the same news bulletin and began running around asking each other questions in the hope that they had heard the story wrong.

Running to the Operations Room, Marcus burst through the door to find out what, if anything, was being done by the company. Everything was in turmoil; phones ringing, computers beeping and the watch keepers doing their best to gain communications with teams on the ground, shouting over radios to bring them in. Marcus could get no sense from Mickey, who was very shaken and pouring with sweat as he scurried from one desk to the next, to a phone and then to the fax machine.

The only information he did gain from Mickey was, "Marcus, the military have closed down the airport and all airfields for the time being. Military personnel and high ranking government officials are priority for flights. It looks like they had it all in place because they slammed the doors shut the moment it was announced. They're pulling out and not pretending otherwise now. In fact, it's a full blown retreat."

Marcus wasted no time and called his team together. Eight of them sat, stood, crouched and squeezed into the small room where Marcus lived. Some of them were big men, and with very little air getting into the room, the atmosphere became claustrophobic and hot. Some had an expression of bewilderment on their faces, having obviously missed the news broadcast, and wondered what all the activity was about. Others stood with grave faces, clearly in the know.

Yan had just a pair of underpants on and flip-flops on his feet, having been dragged out of bed by Stu.

Eddie was sweating and still in his gym clothes, looking confused.

"What's happening, Marcus?" Yan asked with his heavy Serb accent as he stood pulling his underpants out of his arse. His black hair was standing to attention on one side, making his usual 'male model-style' looks seem comical.

"Well," Marcus began, "some of you have seen the news, and a few haven't by the looks. I dunno how to say this, but from what we just heard from the President on the news, dead people have started to come back to life." He paused to let it sink in and noticed the faces of Yan, Eddie and Jim contort, then look about as if they were waiting for the punch line.

Yan motioned as if he were about to speak again, but Marcus cut him off, "On top of that, from what the reports from scientists are saying, the dead are now attacking the living as well and anyone they bite will die and come back as one of them. They think it's all related to the flu. So, it looks like things are about to get a lot worse around here."

"Jesus Christ, how the fuck could that happen?" gasped Jim. "I mean have you ever heard something as crazy as that? Are you sure about this, Marcus? I mean, you're a great Team Leader and all, but were you on the whisky last night, or any of that evil homemade shit that Yan drinks?"

Marcus was sat on the edge of his bed, hunched with his hands folded across his lap as if in prayer. "Fellas, I wish that were the case. But both me and Stu watched the announcement and saw the footage. Looks like Paul, Sini and Ian saw the same report." He looked to them to confirm it and that he wasn't just going mad.

Ian nodded slowly. "Aye, I saw it. As far as I can tell Jim, it's true." Sini and Paul nodded in agreement.

Eddie looked around. "Fuck me guys, so what is happening about it? Has anything been said about the situation in New Zealand?"

"I dunno, but I was told a few days ago, that I could be stuck here for months before they get me a flight. Now with this shit happening, even more people are gonna panic and head for the airport. Mickey told me just that the military have locked it down and the army have taken priority on flights, and that it's gonna take quite awhile until or, *if* anything becomes available for the likes of us. Short of hijacking a plane, we're pretty much fucked."

The room broke out in hushed individual conversations as people swapped what information they had with the men that had been out of the loop.

Ian looked over at Marcus. "So, what are we gonna do boss? We can't just stay here to rot. If this thing is as bad as it looks, and set to get worse, then we need to get home as soon as."

Marcus peered back up at his short but heavy-framed friend. Short curly blonde hair and far from an oil painting, Ian was as tough as he was ugly.

"Not sure buddy, like I said, we can't exactly steal a plane. The thought had crossed my mind, but with all the military around here we would be shot out of the sky as soon as we got airborne."

Ian folded his arms across his barrel chest and let out a long sigh that turned into a low whistle toward the end through his crooked teeth.

It was Paul who spoke up, silencing the chatter within the room. Paul came from Australia, and as big as he was, he came across as being reserved and quiet, and rarely spoke in a volume higher than a calm, conversational voice. Now he stood, pushing away from the corner by the door, so that everyone in the room could see him and he had their attention.

"It's obvious what you have to do, Marcus. You, Ian and Stu, and possibly Yan and Sini, need to make a break for it. It's the likes of me, Eddie and Jim that are fucked." He saw a couple of confused faces and continued. "As ridiculous as it sounds, your best option is to make your way home across land. There are four new vehicles for our team that arrived yesterday, and we have the keys too. Load up, get as much ammo and rations as you can squeeze in, and bug out."

Marcus looked at Paul, then at Ian and Stu, raising his eyebrows. "He's right you know. That's about the only option really." He looked back to Paul. "What about you? What are you gonna do?"

Paul shrugged. "Like I said, we're pretty much fucked. Eddie lives in New Zealand and Jim is from America. He could try getting out with the Yank army, but there's a lot of other American contractors about that will want to try the same. Me? I've got to find a way of swimming across to Australia I guess."

Jim glanced from Paul to Marcus. "Screw that! I'm coming with you Marcus, I've only got a dog back home and he's a pain in the arse. Besides, I've always wanted to travel Europe. Granted, this isn't what I had in mind, though."

Sini and Yan had both been talking quietly in their native Serbian. They nodded to each other having agreed on a matter, and Sini spoke. "Us too, Marcus. We're coming with you and we can make our own way home at some point."

Marcus eyed the Serb, Sini. Of average height, but with broad shoulders and a shaved head, and a scar along the length of his left cheek which he wore with pride as a trophy from the war in Kosovo, Marcus knew that Sini had every ability to make it home along with his friend Yan.

"So, what you're saying is that you want us to drop you off on our way home?"

Sini grinned. "Something like that."

The room became silent as every man contemplated what they were about to do. Paul and Eddie swapped nods with one another. They had decided to go their own way, and try a break out together. Neither of them held much hope for making it to their homes, but they had to try.

Stu looked at Eddie and Paul. "We'll help you with any prep you need to make, lads, and set you up as best we can. It might be an idea to find out if there are any others from your neck of the woods trying the same; best to try it as a group."

"I'd already thought that. I'm gonna go and see what the other Kiwis and Aussies are doing." They both turned and left the room and Marcus watched them with a feeling of helplessness for not being able to do more to get them home.

Marcus stood. "Okay boys, we may as well start prepping for our little adventure. Sort your kit out, and we will meet in the briefing room at 13:00, then we can start smashing out the details. Keep it on the quiet, though. I don't want Mickey and the head shed finding out what we're planning."

The room emptied as the men left for their own rooms to begin working out what they would need to take. Stu remained behind.

"You got any ideas of how we'll do this?"

Marcus shook his head. "Haven't a fucking clue, mate. Can't even think straight yet, and I'm still waiting to wake up from this mental dream."

WHEN THERE'S NO MORE ROOM IN HELL

"Well, it looks like we're having the same dream. Hey, maybe there's some kind of synaptic link between us."

"Yeah, and next you'll want to share a shower with me and play hide the sausage."

Stu laughed. It was good that they clung on to their sense of humour. "Don't flatter yourself, Marcus, I like pretty boys!"

That afternoon they began their preparations. Each man was given a list of jobs to do, from preparing vehicles to acquiring ammunition and rations.

Ian and Jim went to collect fuel and spare tyres. They stole as many jerry cans as possible to store extra fuel and every vehicle now had three spare wheels. They spent the whole afternoon trying to look like they were doing everyday maintenance as they began going over the four new SUVs, stripping out the extra seats and anything that was of no real use. They toiled in the hot sun, covered in sweat, oil and grime.

Sini had access to the armoury, and he and Yan had decided that they would steal a few spare machineguns and as much ammunition as they could without making it look as if they had ransacked the place. They made four trips to and from the armoury to their rooms, and by mid afternoon, they had enough ammunition and magazines to start their own invasion. Next, they turned their attention to gathering up all the rations they could.

Marcus and Stu spent the afternoon poring over maps and aerial photographs, studying routes and alternate routes. They knew that unforeseen problems on the road would inevitably force them to deviate, but as long as they planned as much as possible for eventualities, they would have a good idea of where they were going and how to get there.

They then scrolled through all the intelligence reports of the areas that they would pass through, gaining as much information as possible on the situation in those particular areas. It took a long time, and none of the information, since the announcement of that morning, could still be relied upon. Cities that were considered relatively friendly could've exploded into a hot zone in the past few hours, with anarchy and panic reigning.

On the other hand, areas that had been hostile could well be deserted of all enemy threats on account of them realising that there were more pressing matters to deal with other than blowing up or attacking convoys. The ground and the situation was fluid and it would be flexibility that would see them through.

They needed to go through their communications equipment. Anything they thought they would need, they would have to steal from Alan, the 'Comms Guy'. Alan was easy enough to handle; fat and lazy, he rarely ventured out of his office, and if someone needed something, he normally gave the key over, expecting people to get what they requested from the stores before returning the key to him.

But Marcus and Stu needed a little more than an earpiece or two. They needed spare satellite phones and batteries, vehicle mounted GPS systems, HF and VHF radios, and they weren't a hundred percent on how to install some of it. They decided on bribing him with a couple of bottles of whiskey in return for his help in setting the equipment up for them.

Whiskey was hard to come by, and they would lull Alan into thinking that they just wanted to be up and running with full communications for the team and their new vehicles. As long as it didn't affect him in a way that would mean him having to get up too early, or do anything strenuous, then Alan would turn a blind eye with disinterest at the situation and delight at his two bottles of whiskey.

Three days later, they had everything they needed. All that was left was the fine-tuning and details and the team to go through the overall plan together. It wasn't just down to the commander to plan; the whole team would have input. All being experienced ex-military from different armies and backgrounds, some would have suggestions that would work better for the task ahead, and Marcus would make any changes as necessary if they all agreed on a certain plan of action.

Paul and Eddie had teamed up with a bunch of other guys from another company. It was a sad farewell, and the team provided them with as much ammunition and extra weapons that they needed, including a vehicle.

Once they had everything planned, Marcus decided to give it another five days to see how things would pan out on the world scene. At that moment, everything was unpredictable and not enough overall information was known. In the meantime, they would go over and over the plan, their kit and weapons and ensure that nothing was missed.

Still, very little was coming from Mickey, and the general consensus was that they would be left to the last minute, if considered at all. The big wigs and powers that-be had taken care of themselves and their interests.

Marcus decided that it was time to call his brother. Sitting in his room, with the door locked to avoid interruptions, he dialled Steve's number. It began to ring and Marcus just hoped that the line wouldn't be unworkable and they could understand what each other was saying.

"Hello?" Steve sounded groggy.

"Steve it's me, Marcus. Is everything okay? Have you seen the news?"

"How could I not have? It's on every channel and people are flapping everywhere."

"Roger that, where are you? Are you safe? Do you have Sarah with you?"

"Yeah, we're safe and I have her here. I'm gonna keep her with me as well. I've boarded up the door and windows and we're okay for now. Sounds like the town has gone to shit, though. I've heard nothing but sirens for the last week. I think that the old couple who live next door have turned into them dead things, too. I heard crashing and banging yesterday and the old lady screaming, but now it's all quiet."

Marcus felt a rush of relief knowing that his brother had done everything he could to protect himself and his daughter. "Okay, Steve, listen; Iraq is going under. The military has seized control of the airports, leaving us stranded. We've decided not to wait about and make our own way out. Otherwise we could just be left here and...."

Steve butted in. "Hang on. Make your own way out? What do you mean?" His voice had a confused tone to it.

"I mean that some of the lads and me have decided that we will drive, and fight if we have to, all the way home. We've planned and prepped it as best we can and we decided that we'll make a push in five days. Everything here is in chaos, the city has gone apeshit and it is best that we allow a soak period."

"You're gonna drive all the way from Iraq, across the Middle East and Europe to get home? My geography isn't the best, Marcus, but how the fuck you gonna do that?"

Marcus sighed. "Doesn't matter how, Steve, but we're gonna give it a go. Beats sitting here waiting for things to get worse, which they will soon, I bet."

"Right, okay."

"What I need from you, Steve, before it gets any worse there, is I need you to get to a safe location. Staying in your flat is okay for the time being, but eventually you could find yourself trapped. I spoke to Jennifer when the news broke and also this morning and told her to sit tight, keep the boys with her and secure the doors. She's packed a couple of small bags for them, with food and clothes, and they're ready to move as soon as you get there...."

Steve butted in again, "As soon as I get there? I wasn't planning on going anywhere."

Marcus could feel a pang of anger but he forced himself to swallow it down. "Steve, I've just explained to you that you can't stay where you are. I've seen reports of this thing from America, and no doubt you have too. If their cities are falling, even though every other person has an arsenal of guns at home, what chance do you think you have with a hammer in your flat? You need to get to somewhere safer and more open and better defended. I dunno where, you'll have to work that out yourself, but I want you to get Jen and the boys for me and take them with you."

Steve was quiet for a moment, then, "Yeah, fair one. You have a point there, bro. I haven't a clue where to go though. I'm worried about taking Sarah out there, but as you said, here might not be safe for too long. Does Jen still have the four by four?"

"Yeah, she does." Marcus wondered where Steve was going with the question. "Why?"

"I was thinking that, we go to yours on foot to avoid the roads, and then we take the Range Rover. My car is a bag of shit anyway, and I couldn't rely on it."

"Sounds good to me, Steve, just don't scratch it." The quip was lost on Steve, and Marcus could tell that he was concerned, yet the cogs were turning in his head and he was willing to do what was necessary.

"Right then, that's what I'll do. It's too late in the day now though and I don't want to risk taking Sarah out in the dark. I'll check the area first thing in the morning, and if it looks good I'll grab Sarah and head for yours. It's only a few miles and I'll go through the nature reserve; shouldn't be too many people around at that time of the morning. I'll phone Jen for you and let her know the plan."

A smile spread across Marcus' face. His brother was doing him proud. Gone were the days of the rebellious boy who wouldn't do anything for anyone and shirked responsibility as though it were a heavy hand on his shoulder.

"It means a lot to me, Steve, and I owe you the world if you can do this."

"Like you said, mate, I've no real choice in the matter and Jen is my family too."

"Thanks Steve. I don't know how much longer we will have comms. If things are going downhill rapidly, the networks could crash too. So whatever plan you come up with, you need to let me know as soon as possible. I'll need to know where you are and what the situation is."

"Will do," Steve replied.

"Be careful tomorrow, Steve. Don't take any unnecessary risks and keep Sarah close. Give her a big kiss for me and tell her, Uncle Marcus is bringing her a tank."

"You too, Marcus. Phone me tomorrow."

They hung up.

Marcus felt calm and a sudden confidence in his brother that he had never experienced before. He had grown up and become a man. Amazing how kids change you.

7

Steve didn't sleep that night. Sarah lay dreaming and twitching on the couch dressed in the clothes that he had insisted she wear, while Steve stood by the kitchen window, listening to the sounds in the streets below and thinking about what he needed to do at first light.

On the horizon, through a gap in the barricaded window, he could see the distinct orange haze on the skyline of the town, telling him that a part of it, unsure which, was ablaze.

The sirens had stopped and it seemed now that everyone had been left to their own devices; the police and the authorities had either too much to deal with, or the infection had spread quicker than he had anticipated and they were all gone.

Over the last week, Steve and Sarah had sat and watched the TV, trying to gain as much information as possible. Sarah was scared. Steve was scared too, but he had to appear to his daughter that he had things under control and that she would come to no harm.

The reports had steadily gotten worse. Towns, cities and even small rural villages had been overrun by the virus. Army units in helicopters flew rescue missions to save people trapped on rooftops. Police cordoned off entire built up areas only to be overrun, and it shocked him at how fast the thing had spread.

Steve paused and thought. Though he didn't live in a particularly large city, there was still scope for a rapid spread. Hospitals, funeral homes and the riots themselves were all tinder for the fire. The flu had been going on for weeks, and the dead, according to the news, had begun to reanimate over a week ago.

He had seen numerous reports on the TV over the past week about the phenomenon that was sweeping the globe and bringing back the dead. Most of what he had seen was of figures shambling, tripping, and in general looking like they were shit faced. He couldn't see how it had spread. Though he did reason that he found the whole thing hard to believe, and in a larger scale, maybe that had something to do with it. As well as the general disbelief, he also saw the infected violent flu strain victims and the 'runners' as they had become known.

The violent flu strain, from what he could gather, was the final stage before the people of that particular strain died; taking anyone they could with them. Then there were the 'runners'. As the reports had said, some of the dead could run after reanimation, all depending on their condition before death. The likes of an Olympic Athlete could probably attack twenty people a day, Steve reasoned, on account of their physical fitness.

The more he thought about it, the more scared he became. But still, he hadn't seen hordes of the infected roaming the streets below yet, so as far as he was concerned, he still had the upper hand over the mounting enemy.

Early next morning the sun rose over the complex of flats that he lived in. Bird song filled the air, and when Steve closed his eyes he could almost convince himself that all was normal with the world. But he had to snap himself back to reality quickly before he became lost in his dream land. He needed to focus on his new situation.

He pulled out his phone and dialled for Marcus' wife.

"Jen it's me, Steve."

She sounded worried but in control and not on the verge of a breakdown. Steve explained the plan to her and told her to be ready to move when they got there.

He walked into the living room and gently shook Sarah.

"Oi, sleepy head, wake up lazy bones." He tried to make his voice as soothing as possible.

Sarah stirred. She groaned and curled into a ball.

"Sarah, you need to wake up sweetheart. Remember what I told you yesterday about our special job for Uncle Marcus? Well we're about to do it and I can't do it without you."

Sarah had always been hard to wake up. Every time she stayed with Steve, he had to keep on at her to get up for school in the morning. He never needed to shout or get angry; it just took gentle coaxing and nudging, then she would suddenly snap wide awake.

"I need you to listen to me. We have to look after ourselves. Things are bad outside and we can't trust anyone. Even people who we may have known for years or lived next door to. We have to be sure of everyone. Okay?"

"Are we leaving Dad?" she sat up and asked.

Steve smiled and stroked her hair. "Well, we can't go without breakfast, can we?"

"Good, cause my belly is touching my bum," she replied with a sleepy smile.

Steve warmed up two tins of beans and sausages and they ate the last of the fresh bread together, washing it down with mugs of hot tea.

"Oh I needed that, Dad. Are we off to see aunty Jen now?"

"Yup, we are, but I need you to wait here and guard the flat for five minutes while I check the area. Can you do that?"

Sarah still had a mouth full of bread covered in bean juice, and could only manage a nod and 'Mmm hmm' with puffed out cheeks and a thumbs up.

Steve slipped out, remembering to take a key with him. He ducked beneath the window of the old couple next door and crept to the stairwell and peered down. It was empty. Leaning over the balcony he saw that the courtyard and car park were clear too, the street beyond seemed quiet.

Retracing his steps, he stopped and held his ear to the door of his elderly neighbours. All was silent inside and he couldn't detect any movement. Creeping along, just below the line of view, he paused below the window ledge, his fingertips clutching at the wooden frame as he steeled himself. Curiosity had gotten the better of him and he couldn't resist the urge to see if anything of the couple could be seen. He breathed in sharply, as if he were about to submerge his head below water, and slowly raised himself, his heart beating like a bass drum in his ears.

Eyes; lifeless with pupils dilated to the point where the colour of the iris could no longer be seen, only the flat dull blackness of the centre that had expanded, stared back through the window, unfocussed and looking almost like faded black-and-white two-dimensional drawings due to the lack of blood pressure.

The old man's face was just inches from the pane of glass that separated him and Steve. His face had taken on a yellow hue with hollow cheeks and sunken eye sockets and his skin seemed to have taken on the same texture as waxy plasticine.

Steve gasped and fell back from the window, throwing his arms behind to catch him, ending up in a crab position. The eyes at the window watched him vacantly, unblinking. Steve felt the urge to run and hide but composed himself and, once again, slowly approached the window; though this time he kept his distance. He knew beyond any doubt that he was looking into the eyes of a corpse. Other than the small movements of its eyes as it followed him, the head was motionless, as if it had been removed and placed in the window.

Beyond the face of the old man, in the gloom of the living room, Steve saw movement as a figure walked through a door, distorting the light that shone from behind with its bulk. He squinted and moved closer, trying to see whether it was the old lady.

A pale yellowed hand slapped against the glass with a reverberating smack, making Steve jump back again. The old man had attempted to reach him; not realising there was an invisible barrier between them. The fingers, yellowed and shrivelled as if he had spent too long in a bath, clawed at the window in an attempt to grasp him.

The eyes fixed on Steve.

Steve saw that there was absolutely no emotion in the face peering back at him. No anger, no aggression, nothing. But the hands spoke its intentions. Where the eyes failed to even hint at what it desired, the clutching claw-like fingers spoke volumes.

His throat was dry and he found it hard to swallow. He gulped in air and did his best to control his pounding heart. He moved away from the window and headed back to the flat. When he got to the door, he found that the dead bolt was engaged. He pushed against the door again, thinking that it was stuck. The letterbox flapped open and he saw two bright green eyes scan him from the other side.

"Who is it?"

"Who do you think it is, bone head? Let me in."

"Sorry, Dad, but you told me to trust no one and always double check."

"You were half asleep when I said that, how can you remember?"

She released the dead bolts and let him in. Steve felt pride swell within him. Even though the situation was bad, his little angel had taken it in her stride and adapted to it. He stood in the hallway and peered down at his daughter. "You ready for an adventure?"

"Yup," she nodded, "I am."

Steve looked at her in seriousness. "Sarah, remember what I said about the bad people? Well there's a chance we might run into some. If we do, you might see me do some horrible stuff, but I want you to keep yourself close at all times, do you understand?"

Sarah sighed. "Dad, I watched the news, I know what they're saying and I know what's going on. I'm scared but I know that you will save me if anything bad happens. Oh, and my Mum too."

Fuck! Steve hadn't figured on Sarah being so aware of the situation. Over the days, Claire and Steve had spoken on the phone and he had reassured her that Sarah was safe but that he didn't think it wise to travel the streets; she should stay with him until things were under control. Though her mother was distraught and wanted her child home, she understood and agreed that Sarah should stay with him. There was no way that he was going to tell her of the latest plan until he was sure of what to do next.

He hadn't lied to Sarah, but to avoid her from freaking out at the contemplation of the dead returning to life, he had left that bit out and replaced it with 'bad people'. Now she brought her mother, Claire, into the equation.

"Okay, Sarah, once we get to aunty Jen's, we'll phone your mum. Okay?"

Sarah looked up and gave a big grin, with thumbs up again. "And Roy too."

Steve rolled his eyes. *Fuck sake, now I'm going to be rescuing her mother and her mother's boyfriend too. I'm gonna get fucking killed in this,* he thought.

Picking up the backpack and placing it by the front door, he adjusted his belt, removing the hammer; he figured that it was best to have a weapon in hand, ready.

"Remember what I said, Sarah. Stay close to me at all times."

They moved. He deliberately shielded her from the stares of the dead old man and his wife who had now joined him at the window. He felt a chill as they passed them and he avoided looking into their dead haunting eyes again. Sarah never moved more than a few inches away from his backside, keeping herself tucked in, safe behind her father's body.

They made it away from the flats and headed across the main road for the housing estate that backed the nature sanctuary. The estate was a mess. Houses looked abandoned; smashed windows and doors hanging from their hinges helped to complete the look.

Here and there he saw people hanging out of windows, warning them that the streets weren't safe and that they should get indoors and stay there. Steve just waved and kept moving. Even though he wanted to take them up on their advice, he had to carry on with his plan. It was no longer about what was best for just him and Sarah.

His palms were sweaty and he continuously adjusted the grip he had on his hammer as they walked. Whenever possible, they stuck to the middle of the road, allowing advanced warning of any threat from the houses to the left and right.

Sarah did as her father had instructed and stayed close.

Their eyes darted from side to side and with every few steps, Steve would glance back over his shoulder, making sure nothing and no one was following.

Deep in the housing estate they came to a junction. They needed to head straight across, but as was his new habit, Steve wanted to check the street to the left and right before exposing themselves as they crossed.

They both crouched and made their way toward the junction along a low wall, stopping every few steps to listen. Steve heard it first; crashing and banging was coming from the street to their left. The sound of something slapping and beating against wood mixed with another sound, the steady low hum of the infected. The sound sent shivers through Steve and he could feel panic grip him. He had heard it on TV, but in the flesh it was more haunting, yet almost sad.

Now and then the sound of a desperate mournful wail would come from within the sounds of the infected. Like the voice of a woman, exhausted and on the verge of giving up, but still searching for a child that she had lost.

Steve motioned for Sarah to stay where she was and he crept along the last couple of feet to the corner on his hands and knees. He glanced back at her, eyes bulging, and offered a smile of reassurance then peered around the corner.

In the street he saw a crowd of about fifty people. All their attention was focused on a large detached house, roughly seventy metres along the row. They all seemed to want to get to the front, pushing, shoving and pulling at each other. There was no visible aggression within the crowd, just a clear determination from every one of them to get to the house.

Their clothes hung from them as though they no longer fit, or had been worn for so long that they had become loose and shabby. Discoloured with dirt and blood and ripped and torn from a struggle.

Flies swarmed around the mass. Already, their colour had begun to change. Many of them pale and grey looking with dried, encrusted, almost black blood on visible wounds. Some were naked, or close to it, with hideous gouges in their flesh and swollen limbs. Where the blood had coagulated, their skin turned purple and made them look even more grotesque. Others looked fresh, and other than their wounds, looked almost normal. But it could never be doubted for what they were; their gait was unmistakable, shuffling and staggering without regard for the path or objects in front of them.

They were dead.

The entire group seemed to focus on the house. Their heads held up, their eyes fixed on their goal, steadily shuffling against the body in front, no doubt causing the ones at the head of the group to be squashed against the walls of the house from the weight behind. Now and then an individual infected would stop, raise its hands and let out a longing moan, flexing its fingers in an attempt to reach the house or something unseen to the others, doubling its efforts to reach the building while dragging and shoving at the bodies in front.

The banging, slapping and thumping continued. The wet slap as a bloodied palm or what was left of a mangled limb attempted to beat its way through the door. The thump as a body slammed against wood and the shuddering bang as hands smacked against windows.

Steve pulled his head back. His vision blurred and he felt the bile rising in his throat. He had seen a couple of bodies before, but they were of friends or relatives, embalmed and laid out in the funeral home dressed in their Sunday best, or gruesome images he had seen on the internet. But he had never seen so many in one place. Never had he seen the discolouration and grisly wounds with his naked eye. Never had he smelt the pungent odour of dried blood and the initial onset of decaying flesh. And never had he seen them walking about.

He looked at Sarah then quickly peeped around the corner again. Someone was in the house, he knew it. Maybe a family, maybe kids. His head swam. What was the right thing to do? He gripped his hammer and looked at it, hoping that the answer would come to him. Then he glanced back at Sarah and remembered, *'we have to look after ourselves'.* With a sinking feeling of shame, he moved back to Sarah.

"There's a load of bad people around the corner." He waited for a sign of panic from her, but she just watched him. "They don't seem to be interested in anything else except for a house further down, so when we move, move slowly and keep hold of my hand. Don't talk and don't make any sudden movements."

Sarah nodded, tight-lipped and eyes-wide. He gave her hand a reassuring squeeze.

As they were about to stand, an inhuman screech erupted from the right, followed by the sounds of feet running and slapping against the tarmac. Steve froze and held a hand on Sarah, forcing her down to the pavement.

Two infected, foaming at the mouth and arms raised out in front of them, were heading in their direction. Steve wanted to run, but in a moment of self control he quickly assessed the situation. Gripping the hammer, he prepared himself for the attack. Soon he realised that he wasn't the target and from the trajectory of the two screaming figures, he realised they were headed straight for the crowd.

They ran straight across the junction down the middle of the road, not more than five metres in front of Steve, and kept going, their momentum never slowing. He followed them with his eyes and watched in horror as they ploughed headlong into the mass of walking corpses. The two 'runners' didn't seem to pay any attention to the other infected, other than the fact that they were obstacles in their way, and began pulling and throwing bodies out of their path as they tried to reach the house.

But the dead paid attention to them. Dozens of the crowd surrounded the two and closed in until Steve could no longer see the two infected sprinters who had just passed him. The dead enveloped them and tore into them, biting and gouging at the flesh on their bodies. Even from where he was, Steve could hear the crunch of bone and the ripping of clothing and skin. Some of the crowd broke away and moved off carrying chunks of flesh or severed limbs, chewing frantically as though in fear of having their prize taken from them.

Less than a minute later and the crowd surged back at the house. Steve remained crouched, slack-jawed and wondering what he had just witnessed. He looked back at Sarah as if to ask what had happened. It dawned on him, what he had seen was two of the aggressive strain infected. Still living but oblivious to the dangers, they had been hell-bent on reaching the people in the house and the dead had seized and ate them.

They had to move.

Steve steeled himself and breathed deeply. His heart was pounding in his chest and his legs had begun to shake and feel weak. Sweat dripped from his forehead and into his eyes. It was a warm late spring morning, but it wasn't the heat that was affecting him. It was pure fear. He wanted to run away, bury his head under the duvet and imagine he was safe, but he had Sarah to look after and he needed to keep a tight grip on reality.

They stood together and steadily walked toward the corner. Slowly, they emerged into the junction and open view of the street to the left and right. They kept their faces toward the floor and with his eyes raised; Steve watched the opposite side of the road and the street ahead, painfully and slowly, come closer.

In the middle of their path was what looked like a slab of meat from a butcher's stall, red and glistening in the sun; the flies had already began to swarm over it. As they got closer, Steve noticed the yellowed skin still clinging to the meat and what looked like part of a tattoo. He couldn't tell which part of a body it was; only that it had belonged to a living person once. It made his stomach churn and he gripped Sarah's hand even tighter. He glanced from the corner of his eye, without moving his head, toward the crowd and was relieved to see that none were moving in their direction.

They stepped over the remains and continued to the other side. Once safely across, Steve pulled Sarah close and they crouched, hidden by the wall of a garden.

He whispered in her ear, "Okay Sarah, we're across."

He looked back around the corner and watched the crowd for a moment. He noticed a glimpse of movement in the upstairs window of the large house, and the infected seemed to notice it too. They became more excited, agitated, and surged toward the front wall of the house.

Steve once again felt like there was something he should do. But what? What could he actually do to help? There were too many of them and he wasn't ready to start risking Sarah's, as well as his own life, for the sake of strangers. He swallowed hard and moved on.

They continued through the housing estate. They saw bodies here and there with heads missing; others without limbs, pools of blood were everywhere and the buzz of flies and other insects feasting, was thick in the air. Burnt houses and cars littered the streets and they were forced, on a number of occasions, to detour around groups of infected. They saw uninfected people loading their cars and trucks, making a break for it. Others were dazed and confused and stood in their gardens, or walked along the street, watching others.

Cutting down an alleyway to avoid a street packed with more walking bodies, they were scared out of their skin by a dog that lunged at them from behind a fence where it was tied up in a garden. Steve considered setting it loose, but with the state of its mind unknown, they couldn't risk it attacking them. For all they knew, it would be completely insane with fear so they left it behind, moving quickly before the noise of its barking attracted the attention of the infected.

At the far end of the alley they came to an open area. A row of shops sat about fifty metres back from the far side of the road. The large windows were smashed and it looked like they had been looted. Steve didn't even consider taking a closer look on account of the scattered infected that he saw in the street.

To back track now would mean them heading into a possibly larger crowd of them. The only choice they had was to run across the open ground and, hopefully safety on the other side of the row of shops. He gripped Sarah in his left hand and wielded the hammer, ready to swing down on anything that stepped into their path.

Together, they ran. They didn't need to sprint; the area wasn't overly crowded but they needed to expose themselves as little as possible. As they broke cover, the shambling figures saw them and turned in their direction, moaning and wailing as they advanced. Steve tried to block out the sounds as he ran, knowing they would follow, and he focused on the far side, pulling Sarah who was whimpering now.

His heart was beating at his chest wall as if it wanted to jump free and run to safety by itself. In his ears, he could hear his blood pumping through their veins and his breathing was fast and heavy. The tingle in his spine forced him to keep going, as if a hand was just inches from grabbing his jacket and pulling him back.

They reached the row of shops and turned right, paralleling them, heading for the corner to the next street. A crash to the left and it was almost too late when Steve saw the figure emerge from the last doorway and lunge toward them.

Its pale, wrinkled, bloodless hands outstretched, its mouth agape, showing a black, swollen tongue and bloodstained teeth that snapped shut in anticipation. The dead, flat, fish-like eyes set on Sarah as it quickly closed the distance between them.

Steve turned his upper body to face the threat, pivoting on his leading leg and swinging Sarah quickly out of the way. At the same time he brought his right hand, raising the hammer, in a wide arc, aiming for the man's head. Still focused on Sarah, the creature didn't notice until the shock of the glancing blow from Steve sent him crumpling to the ground. Steve quickly stepped forward and brought the hammer down a second time and drove the head of the tool into the man's skull, the vibration shooting up his arm, jolting his elbow with the sudden halt in momentum.

He felt the bone give with a sickening crunch, and the body became limp. Its head hit the floor and Steve's arm went with it, still holding the hammer. It was firmly embedded and he had to angle the handle and push the hammer free, releasing a fetid odour and globs of clotted blood and brain matter.

Without a second thought, he turned and pulled Sarah along. She had become heavier, as if he was dragging her through treacle. Before any more infected could get closer, they had turned the corner and into a playing field that opened up before them. It was the start of the nature reserve.

They ran to the top of a small hill and stopped to catch their breath. Sarah was clearly shaken and in some shock. Steve stood panting with his hands on his knees. "Hey, remember what I said? You were bound to see something like that sooner or later."

Sarah blinked, and looked in her father's eyes, as though suddenly shaking off the trauma of what had just happened. "I know, Dad. Just didn't expect it."

She was strong, and Steve could see that she would recover after a quick rest, though he did worry about the long term affects on her young mind.

"Okay sweetheart, I understand that. Have some water then we'll get moving again. Hopefully there won't be too many surprises between here and aunty Jen's house."

For hours they played hide and seek with people and infected alike. Hiding in bushes away from the tracks, or taking detours, they trekked through the wilderness. The day had turned into a hot one and Steve had to force himself to keep his jacket on. As far as he was concerned, it was more protection from attack. If it were up to him, they would be wearing suits of armour.

Sitting in the shade of a small wooded area, they rested and ate some cold beans between them. Sarah didn't feel much like eating but he insisted, telling her she needed to keep her energy levels up.

"Sit here buddy and keep quiet. I'm just gonna move back to the track to check that the coast is clear. I'll only be a minute and you'll still be able to see me."

Sarah looked scared but she trusted him and did as she was told.

Steve pushed on to the dirt path and came out into a small clearing surrounded by trees, the path leading back in to the dark shade on the other side. He crouched in order to see the horizon of the path and to make sure that he saw no silhouettes moving along it in the gloom of the trees.

Satisfied that it was all clear, he began to head back to Sarah. As he moved off the path and back into the trees, he looked back over his shoulder once more along the track. Silently, a figure was sprinting toward him. For a split second he squinted to help focus, then he realised whether it was dead, infected or a perfectly normal living person, he didn't need to know. It was running straight for him and he needed to get away from it.

He ran through the trees, branches clawing at his face, twigs snapping underfoot and tripping over roots. But he never slowed his pace. Now the figure was in the woods with him and he could hear its heavy footsteps and moans as if it was pleading with him to stop.

Steve searched with his eyes as he ran. He was disoriented and couldn't find the spot where he had left Sarah. Panic gripped him. He couldn't see her and he assumed he was in the wrong place. He couldn't risk shouting for her to run in case she ran in the wrong direction and they became separated, or worse, she ran into the thing that was chasing him.

Reaching out for a thin tree, he swung himself round, never slowing, and used the tree as a slingshot. Gritting his teeth, he growled and raised the hammer. He could feel his aggression surge and the adrenaline pumping through his veins. For that moment he felt superhuman and he charged at the advancing 'thing' that wanted to hurt him and his daughter.

The gap closed and he threw a kick straight into the infected creature's midriff, sending it reeling backward into a tangled mass of undergrowth. Still growling he kicked at its head, stomping on it to stop it from moving. He brought the hammer down with his full force and, again and again, he smashed it into its skull. He felt no desire to stop; he felt only anger, a personal vendetta against the thing. Only after the head was no longer recognisable as once having been human did he stop.

Breathing heavy, with his chest heaving and his arms shaking, he stood with the bloodied hammer in his hand; flecks of the attacker's blood covered his clothes. He looked down at his bare hands, and wiped them on the back of his trousers.

Sarah was crouched not more than three metres away, huddled behind a fallen tree trunk, staring back at him. She stood up and looked at her father. He looked like a mad man, but she knew why. He was protecting her. She ran to him and flung her arms around his waist.

By late afternoon as the sun was starting to dip behind the tree tops, they made it to the quiet country lane where Marcus and his family lived. On one side was a high hedge with open farm land beyond. To the left was a short row of eight rustic looking quaint houses set back from the road and obscured by more high hedges, with the only gaps being filled with gates leading up the driveways and to the front doors. Behind the houses, a steady sloping hill and more farm land. It was pretty secluded and the chaos didn't seem to have touched the area yet out on the far outskirts of the urban area where it met the rural farmland and nature reserves.

Steve managed to breathe a sigh of relief when he saw Marcus' house and the large Range Rover still in the drive way. He looked down at Sarah, who throughout the journey had never let go of his hand when they were walking. He smiled; she looked like she had been dragged backwards through a bush, and no doubt he looked the same. They were covered in mud up to their knees; twigs and blades of stray grass clung to their hair. Their clothes were ripped in places and it occurred to him that some farmer could mistake them for infected and come after them with his shotgun.

They hastened along the road and walked up the drive to the house. Gently, he knocked at the door and peered through the letterbox, calling to them for reassurance. No doubt Jennifer and the boys would be scared out of their wits.

They could hear bolts and chains being released and the door cracked open a little. Jennifer peered through with tired frightened eyes. She squinted in the light then, her eyes lit up once she was sure it was him.

"Oh, thank God Steve! I was so worried for you both."

She opened the door wide for them to enter; she wasn't looking at Steve anymore, she was watching over his shoulder, her eyes darting left and right. She quickly closed the door behind them and replaced the dead bolts. Only then did she seem to relax and release a heavy sigh as though she had been holding her breath the whole time that the door was open. She probably had been.

She looked tired and far from her normal glamour, but Steve could still see the pretty woman that was his brother's wife. Jennifer had always taken great care of her appearance and her health but now, her mousy brown hair, normally flowing and shiny, was tied back in a tight and practical ponytail. Her jeans looked grimy and the walking boots, instead of her usual heels, made Steve realise that she was nowhere near as tall as she seemed. She wore no makeup and the varnish on her nails was flaking. Still, Steve had seen much worse from much younger women before the world went mad.

"How are you and the boys, Jen?" Steve tried his best to sound casual. "Have you spoken to Marcus?"

She smiled at him, then looked down at Sarah, stretching her arms out in the sign of wanting a hug. Sarah jumped to her and held her tightly. Jennifer looked back up at Steve. "We're fine, the boys are upstairs. All this is a bit hard for them to understand, even for me, come to think of it. I've never heard of anything like this."

"Yeah, me too. It's a lot to deal with and probably a lot worse for a kid." He ruffled Sarah's hair. "So, have you heard from Marcus today?"

Jennifer stood up straight again and Sarah walked into the living room. "Yeah, sorry, I spoke to him a couple of hours ago. He told me about their plan. How are they gonna make it half way across the world?"

"You know Marcus, Jen, he's hard as nails and if anyone can, he can."

She shrugged. "It's not some army manoeuvre, Steve, and even without all this going on it's virtually impossible."

"Ah but think about it, Jen," he interjected, "with all this going on, he has a better chance. With all the confusion, and governments, authorities and armies having the outbreak to deal with, he has more chance of getting through. They're gonna have their hands full with more important things than a bunch of blokes trying to get home."

Jennifer nodded slowly. "Yeah, I hope you're right, Steve."

"Don't worry, Jen. I'm here to look after you and the boys until he gets here. He said that comms could eventually be a problem with the networks failing, but I'll make sure he knows where to find us. I'll give him a ring in a bit once I've had a think of our next move and let him know we're all together."

They walked into the kitchen and made hot drinks for themselves and Sarah. Before long David and Liam made an appearance and they made no pretences about their excitement to see their uncle Steve. With one in each arm, Steve lifted them and hugged and kissed them. He hadn't seen them for a few months and he was surprised at how much they had grown.

"My God boys, you're gonna be big enough to beat your Dad up soon," he said as he squeezed them, causing them to squeal and giggle.

He watched them as they crowded Sarah, asking her a million questions at once and then leading her into another room to show her the latest toys and gadgets that they had received from Marcus the last time he had been home and spoiled them.

"They both have the exact same eyes as Marcus, don't they?" Jennifer spoke from behind him and he stared after them as they left.

He turned and gave her a faint smile. "Yeah, but luckily they take more after you."

"Oh you're such a sweet talker, Steve, but I know you're full of shit. Those two boys are their Dad through and through. They even have the same swagger when they walk and the reports I've had from their school, they're a pair of tyrants on the playground."

"Yeah," Steve nodded, "that's Marcus alright. He was the tough nut out of the pair of us and he was never shy of reminding me of it as we grew up. The bastard used to organise fights for me to toughen me up, and if I didn't win, then I got another kicking from him."

Jennifer was laughing. She hadn't laughed since forever, or so it seemed to her, and it felt good.

Steve decided that they should stay where they were for the night. With the light fading they didn't want to be caught out on the open road. Besides, they hadn't come up with a clear plan on what to do next.

"Steve you okay?" Marcus' voice on the other end of the phone was anxious.

"Yeah, fine bro. We're at your house now. Jen and the boys are okay and so is Sarah. The kids are playing upstairs while we try to work out what to do next."

Marcus sighed with relief. "Thank fuck for that, I was starting to flap. You going firm there for the night?"

"Yeah, it's dark now so we thought we would stay and work out a plan. I still haven't a clue where to go mate. It is nuts out there, Marcus. Me and Sarah were attacked a couple of times on the way here and I had to do them in with my hammer. I'm fine but I'm worried about how it will all affect Sarah."

Marcus was silent, then, "Yeah, I know what you mean mate, can't be easy for her. What about the farms around there?"

"Already thought about that one, Marcus, but the last thing we need is to stumble on a farm that's still occupied and some nervous farmer shooting at us."

"Fair one," Marcus replied.

"Besides, I want to get further away from the suburbs. If the towns and cities fall, then there could be thousands of them things wondering around here."

Both were quiet for awhile. Steve decided to pass the phone to Jen so that the two of them could talk while he paced the room and thought. With his hands in his pockets and shoulders hunched, as he always did when pondering something, he browsed about the living room; his gaze stopping at the framed pictures above the fire. One in particular caught his attention, and at first he didn't realise why.

He reached out for it to get a better look. Marcus, Jennifer, David and Liam, all wearing the same yellow t-shirts, stared back at him with huge smiles. Steve looked closer at the picture and read the logo on the t-shirt that his brother wore.

"Shit!" He exclaimed, causing Jennifer to pause mid-speech and look up alarmed. "I need to speak to Marcus for a minute Jen," he said reaching out for her to hand over the phone.

Holding it close to his ear he spoke in a fast excited voice, "I'm gonna take them to the Safari Park tomorrow."

Silence from Marcus then, "You what, what the fuck you on about Steve?"

"The Safari Park." Steve was getting louder and more excited. "I'll take them there tomorrow."

"Steve, you taking the piss, why take them for a day out? And the place is probably closed anyway with all this going on."

"Exactly." Steve actually enjoyed drip feeding the information and leaving his brother guessing where he was going with it. "Think about it, Marcus. The Safari Park is about seven miles from here, in the middle of nowhere, open spaces and it has its own walls and fences surrounding it."

The penny dropped on the other end of the phone. "Ah right, good thinking. But others have probably had the same idea..."

Steve cut him off, "I doubt it, maybe one or two, but the majority of people wouldn't think of the place. They wouldn't akin it to safety during a disaster would they? I only thought of it when I saw the picture above the fire, and you hadn't thought of it had you?"

"Yeah, that's true...."

Steve was getting more worked up about his idea and butted in again. "Anyway, even if others have thought of it, it's a big place and there's plenty of room for a lot of people. I wouldn't be surprised if a lot of the park staff headed there. They probably want to keep the animals safe, and at the same time, themselves. Because they know the area and being familiar with the place, that's probably what they would do. I even considered going to the warehouse where I work, because it's familiar."

"Fucking hell, Steve, you're turning into a master tactician. You should've been a General. Good thinking bro. You reckon you can get there okay?"

"I suppose so. We can take the back roads, the country lanes. The only main road is the one leading into the main gate and even that isn't that obvious unless you're reading the road signs. The actual main gate is set off from the road by a good one hundred metres isn't it?"

"Right, do that Steve, and let me know once you're there and how it all looks. If it all seems good, that's where I'll head for when we make the break out."

"Okay bro, I'll give you back to Jen while I work it all out." He handed the phone to a wide-eyed Jennifer and went looking for a road map.

8

In the weeks since the virus outbreak had hit the shores of Europe and America, and now with the plague mutating and reanimating the dead, civilisation steadily fell apart.

Before the information was released, that the bites from infected flu victims were infectious in themselves, many had become casualties through care. Nurses, doctors, family members and anyone who came into contact and was attacked by the violent strain, in turn, became violent and attacked others, eventually dying themselves and reanimating.

The infection spread quickly. Regardless of the situation and the attacks, many people still refused to believe that their friends and family would want to hurt them. The majority, feeling that the hospitals were overwhelmed, tried to treat their loved ones at home with blankets and soup. Entire households became infected and that lead to whole streets, districts and before long, towns and cities.

Areas were cordoned off and placed under quarantine. The infected within the closed off areas then attacked the people guarding them at the blockades. The virus jumped like a case of head lice in a room full of people standing shoulder to shoulder. It was almost like a small firework placed in a closed fist; with nowhere for the energy to be released, it exploded.

To begin with, the infected were still treated as being people with rights. So in the cases of people being attacked and in self-defence, killing the people attacking them, they were arrested and charged with murder or manslaughter. At the beginning, confusion reigned. A lot of people became casualties; rather than just smashing the heads of the infected, they would try to restrain them.

Then the news broke, and it was announced by the Prime Minister and the various world leaders, that the dead were returning to life and attacking the living. Also released was information on how to deactivate the walking cadavers. When the brain was destroyed, the body was then rendered unable to reanimate. But there was never any official word on what the public were to do when confronted with an infected person.

The governments, in their haste to explain the situation had forgotten to pass new emergency laws on how to treat and deal with the infected. The average person on the planet is a law abiding citizen with respect for human life, regardless of its form. So when confronted with a walking corpse or violent strain of flu, they feared prosecution should they hurt or even kill their attacker. This avenue of thinking helped to escalate the situation and the spread.

To add to the problem, many people had friends or family who became infected, or even died through natural causes at home. Once revived, they could not reason that the thing that had just sat up and now shambled toward them was anything other than their wife, husband, son daughter or even best friend. Emotion and sentimentality became one of the deciding factors for humanity losing the war against the dead plague.

People all over the world refused to believe that the dead could return to life. Even though the various religions prophesised it, many still buried their heads in the sand unable to contemplate the situation. No one had ever imagined that people could die, then come back and attack the living. So, a lot of people pretending to be ostriches had their arses bitten off in the opening stages of the spread.

Whole cities and towns were lost throughout the world, as the authorities tried to stem the spread and bring control and order back to the metropolis. What many didn't know until it was too late was that the dead and infected didn't feel pain on the same level as living people, or feel fear or consider consequences of their actions. Entire police and army units were sent in to secure this street or that square, only to be swallowed up and never seen again.

Human rights groups protested and spoke out on behalf of the infected, insisting that they still had rights and shouldn't be systematically destroyed, and that an alternative treatment should be used, though many had seen and witnessed that an infected person could infect two, three even up to five others before they were finally subdued and tied up.

The human rights movement lost all momentum when, in Paris during a march outside a quarantine zone to defend the rights of the walking dead, a group of roughly a thousand human rights activists were attacked by a swarm of the reanimated who had broken free and emerged from the cordoned area. At first, the protesters attempted to prove that treated with decency, and wanting to make a point for the cameras, the infected were just people and that approached in the right way, with respect to their rights, they could be integrated into society.

What followed was a bloodbath. At first, the protesters at the back stalled in confusion to the screams at the front. The people behind surged forward as the people ahead of them recoiled once they realised their mistake. The dead fell upon them all, biting, gouging and tearing their way through the crowd.

Some countries took a more extreme approach. Having lost cities and large areas to the infection, they tried reclaiming them by air strikes. No one pointed out that a reanimated body could continue to be a threat and move even without its legs or arms and one hundred percent burns covering its body.

Many of them were blown apart in the attacks. But the air strikes created more dead than they destroyed. Most cities were still heavily populated by the living; holed up and trying to survive. Once the bombing started, they were either killed in the blasts and the fires, or their defences were destroyed and left open to the dead. For all the reanimated they killed, the ranks of the dead were replenished by the collateral casualties of war.

Governments crumbled and were quickly and temporarily replaced by military commanders, religious zealots or weak politicians seizing their moment of power, who then sat and watched as the power they had grabbed crumbled to dust in their hands. The military in many countries were either destroyed or deserted, realising the battle was lost and fleeing to save themselves and their loved ones.

The religious groups who seized power never lasted long due to the fact that they insisted that it was a sign from God; they spent most of their time preaching and waiting for more signs, rather than dealing with the immediate problem and regaining control of their countries. Some even went to the extremes of making large scale sacrifices to the dead of their own people in the hope of appeasing their angry God.

The Third World countries were written off by the West and Europe. Africa and Asia were left to die, and America closed its borders and waterways along Mexico and the Gulf area. Whole army divisions were sent to those areas to shoot anyone attempting to cross onto U.S soil. In the meantime, the other states fell to pieces with the spread of the infection within their own borders.

For a short while, the U.S government tried, in vain, to remain in power and continue to exact a degree of authority and control over the people, but eventually, they too left their country to its fate.

Australia seemed to fare a little better. Having seen the effects of the outbreaks in the northern hemisphere, she closed her borders and placed her Navy and Air Force in a defensive ring around the continent, with orders to sink any and all unauthorised shipping approaching the exclusion zone; a threat that wasn't taken very seriously by a cruise liner that thought the rules didn't apply to them. Without hesitation, the ship was sunk and all hands went down with her.

Worldwide communications began to slowly deteriorate. Mobile networks became temperamental and even the internet showed signs of failure. With people dying or abandoning their posts, the daily maintenance that was vital to the upkeep of the smooth running global communications network wasn't being conducted, and the more delicate systems suffered.

Smaller news stations dropped from the air with only the big stations such as CNN and Sky News continuing to broadcast, though accurate updates from the ground became less and less frequent as the days went by, on account of the high number of casualties from reporters. Eventually, people were reluctant to go into the fray in order to get a story and most of the news came from other networks and the populations themselves.

City after city across the world fell silent, except for the moans and wails of the dead who shuffled aimlessly en masse through the streets. Any survivors were left to fend for themselves.

9

Sitting in his reclining armchair, Andy Moorcroft slept fitfully. His girlfriend, Susan, lay on the couch beside him. She had struggled to stay awake for days, scared to close her eyes in fear of what might happen while she slept, but eventually exhaustion had overcome her.

Andy's eyes shot open. Pulling the blanket away from him and letting it drop to the floor as he stood, he stared through the hallway and at the front door. The boards and cupboard still remained barricaded against the entrance, but he could hear the shuffling of the feet beyond the threshold with the occasional thump against the door.

He crept along the hallway and stood on his tiptoes until he could see through the frosted glass at the top of the door. Blurred but unmistakable, he recognised the tops of heads moving about outside. The sight never failed to make his heart skip a beat. He felt dizzy and returned to the living room.

The television was still on, but rather than the usual news reporters, all that could be seen now was the crazy static signal like thousands of ants scurrying across the screen. Andy shrugged. Either it was really all over and even the news stations had abandoned their posts, or they weren't receiving the signal for whatever reason. He tried flicking through more channels, but saw the same thing: nothing.

He looked down at Susan as she slumbered and decided that they needed to start thinking about the plan again. He shook her awake and they moved into the hall. Susan was nervous, her eyes were bloodshot and she looked ready to snap.

"Okay, you go first. I'll catch you if you fall."

The day before, Andy had smashed out the stairs with a sledgehammer, leaving a chasm below the top step, in case the barricade at the front door was ever breached. He was pretty sure that the infected couldn't climb rope ladders and it was impossible to reach a hand to the upper floor without the aid of a step ladder or something similar to stand on. He had left a few bed sheets, tied together and anchored to the upstairs floor, hanging down into the hallway as a way of getting up and down.

Susan climbed the rope, excruciatingly slow for Andy's liking, but she made it without falling. He followed and pulled up the makeshift rope, securing it against the banister. Without a word, Susan hugged him and began to cry in his arms. Her shoulders bounced with each outburst of tears and she sobbed uncontrollably.

"It's okay, Susan, we'll be alright."

He pushed her back, gripping her shoulders tightly, and looked in her eyes. No longer was she the stunning trophy girlfriend; she was a wreck and close to breaking point. They had not washed properly or changed clothes for days; her features seemed raw, but still beautiful without her makeup.

Andy had always been a bit of a playboy. With owning his own modelling agency and his film star good looks, almost black wavy hair and sparkling blue eyes, he could have any girl he wanted.

And he did.

Rarely had he kept any of his conquests on the scene for longer than a few months though. He would enjoy their company, show them a good time, then move on. He never liked the idea of settling down and having kids, sitting in the garden reading the papers or washing the family car on a Sunday. To him, life was all about enjoying the moment and keeping everything fresh and new.

Though the girls had been many, he had always strived to be a gentleman and treated them correctly with respect and chivalry. He always made it clear that he wasn't one to settle and he never filled them with false hope in the pretence that they could possibly tame him, but that never stopped them from queuing up to try.

Life had been good to Andy. Successful, handsome, charming, witty and a personality that glowed and lit up rooms by itself when he entered, the world was his oyster. That is, until the dead came back to life.

Now he stood looking at Susan who tried to control her emotions and strengthen herself, but with snot and tears running down her face Andy couldn't help but think how long it would be before she was out of the game.

She had been a stunning young model who had fancied her chances at taming the wild man that was Andy Moorcroft. With natural blonde hair, long slender legs, beautiful brown doe eyes and perfect olive complexion, he had been more than happy to let her try. Now, he feared that anything more than a pin drop would have her hanging from the rafters.

He led her into the nearest room and laid her on the bed. In the preceding days, they had moved anything of use upstairs. But Andy being Andy, they didn't have much to move, particularly in the way of food.

He had always been a minimalist when it came to furniture, opting for the contemporary look, and most of the time he ate out in restaurants or at client functions and friends' houses. So their measly few tins of soup and peas didn't last long, and he was scared of becoming too weak from hunger to not be able to do anything about the situation. So, he went over the plan in his head again.

He and Susan would climb out of a hole in the attic that Andy had made and carefully make their way along the roof to the gable end of the house. Using a makeshift rope again, and as quietly as possible, they would lower themselves to ground level. Once clear of the house, they would head for the shops and see what supplies they could find.

If they couldn't find any, they would check what houses in the area they could safely enter and make their way back to their stronghold. On the other hand, depending on how the situation looked once they were in the open, Andy had suggested that they might keep moving and look for somewhere more safe and secluded, or even head to the police station in the hope of finding help.

It wasn't exactly a solid plan, but he knew they had little choice. Either starve to death, wait for the door to come crashing in, or take the necessary risks in order to survive.

He walked to the window of the front upstairs room and exposed himself just enough to see the street below him. Hundreds of pale grey faces in a sea of swollen blackened limbs and festering bodies bobbed and jostled against each other. He had closed all the vents in the windows, but still the stench permeated into the house and he needed to keep a scarf wrapped around his face most of the time. Bloated flies crawled along the windowsill and over the glass panes. He could hear the buzz of the countless insects and the low steady moan of the dead outside his door.

He moved closer, careful not to be seen, and looked down the street to the junction. The day before, he had seen two infected people tearing down that same street and into the steadily growing crowd below, and witnessed as they had been torn limb from limb and consumed by the mass.

Shortly after, he had watched a man and a young girl walk slowly across the same junction. It had been obvious that they were alive and infection free and he had found himself willing them to safety on the other side of the street. At one point, when they were across, he swore that the man had looked straight at him. Even from that distance, the man seemed to see him in the shadows.

He smiled and thought to himself, *I hope you both made it buddy.*

He glanced down, back at the hideous sight below him. His top of the range sports car, once his pride and joy with its dull metallic grey paint and tinted windows, was now smeared in blood, bodily fluids and greasy dirt. Dents and scratches covered what surfaces he could see between the bodies, and his heart longed for the days when he used to drive it around with the top down and a pretty girl in the passenger seat. His shoulders felt heavy at the thought of moments like that being a thing of the past.

He turned away and placed the step ladder at the hatch to the attic. He woke Susan up again and gave her as much food and water as she could manage to hold down without baulking it back up.

"Susan, you need to get a grip on yourself. What we are about to do is dangerous enough without me having to worry about you losing the plot. I've already told you, you can stay here if you like, but I can't guarantee I'll come back. I might want to push on to somewhere else, and it would be too risky to come back for you and then drag you across the roof. Our escape could be cut off if any of them see me coming back."

She wiped her eyes and composed herself. "I'm okay, honest. Please, just don't leave me. Don't leave me Andy."

Andy looked hard in to her pleading eyes. "I won't, just do what I tell you and we'll be okay, but I need you to be strong."

She nodded her head and brushed her hair back with her fingers, trying even harder to control her fears. She looked up at him and they both exchanged a slight smile.

"Right then, let's do this. I'll go up first and you stay close behind me. Remember, shuffle along the roof slowly and quietly, and try not to let any of them see you."

They climbed out onto the roof and steadily made their way along to the gable end. The smell was overpowering, even through the makeshift masks that they wore tightly wrapped around their faces. It made Andy feel nauseous and he had to swallow hard to stop himself from vomiting into his scarf.

Once at the end of the house, he carefully lowered himself down the rope, pausing at the bottom and listening for any signs that they had been detected. Once he was satisfied that they hadn't, he waved for Susan to make her descent. It seemed to take an eternity and he became anxious as he waited and watched.

Safely on the ground, they made their way to the back of the property and down a short alley that led out to an adjacent street. It was clear, and they were soon travelling in a wide arc following the lay of the road toward the shops that they had agreed upon.

The streets were deserted and quiet with birds twittering, and gazing upward it seemed like a normal early morning. But looking back down to street level, the debris and scarred houses told otherwise. A car had smashed into a street light, toppling it onto the road and onto another car, crumpling its roof inward. People's belongings lay scattered around the doors and front lawns of houses. Smouldering ruins that had been homes to families, testified to the chaos of the previous week.

They reached the shops and Andy looked about the street and open area which surrounded it. Nothing stirred. He took Susan by the hand and walked toward a shop doorway.

"Wait here. I'll have a look inside and make sure it's clear."

He moved in, his feet stepping on broken glass from the door, the noise of it crunching underfoot, deafening in his own mind. He stopped and looked around at the interior of the shop; the shelves were all but bare. It had been ransacked and what little food was left was ground into the floor and unusable. He didn't want to venture into the dark bowels of the shop, in the hope of finding a store room, so he returned to Susan and they moved to the next one.

He pushed on the door, and a bell rang. He froze and winced trying to sink his head into his shoulders; nothing. Glancing back, Susan was staring at him, annoyed and frightened at the sudden noise he had made in the otherwise still air. He pushed the door fully open, the echo of the bell above the door still reverberating through the shop.

Again, the place was a mess and had little to offer, but Andy decided to take whatever he could find on the assumption that no matter where they tried, it would all be pretty much the same. He was halfway down the first aisle when he heard Susan scream. He spun on his heel and sprinted back for the door.

Outside, he came face to face with three infected that had Susan pinned to the wall at the side of the door. She had stopped screaming, her eyes had rolled to the back of her head and blood gushed from wounds on her arm and thigh. The three infected were oblivious to Andy until he reached for Susan.

One broke off from the others and lunged at him, arms outstretched with unblinking eyes fixed on him. As a reflex, Andy threw a straight punch to the creature's face. The impact shredded its lips as its teeth had come through the skin, crunching against Andy's bare fist. He punched again, and his attacker toppled backward in a heap on the floor, immediately trying to regain its footing.

Closest to him was a little girl, or what had been a little girl, of no more than eight years old. Her hair was matted in greasy locks to her scalp and her complexion pasty and pale, her eyes dead and hazed over. He knew what it was and he kicked at it from the side, catching it in the ribs and forcing it to lose grip on his girlfriend. At the same time, he grabbed Susan by the collar of her jacket. The two infected on the floor found themselves tripping over each other, and the third fought to get across them and to Andy as he dragged the unconscious Susan back to the doorway.

Andy pushed his back against the door to force it open, the dinner bell ringing loudly above again. He dropped Susan to the floor and slammed the door shut, wedging it with his foot. He didn't have time to deal with Susan right away; he needed to secure the door. Looking around at his immediate surroundings, he opted to drag the ice cream freezer that was just within reach and slammed it against the shuddering door as the creatures on the other side slammed their bodies and fists against it.

He reached down and dragged Susan across the shop towards the rear of the counter, holding her under the arms. He glanced out of the bay window and saw more and more infected approaching. He headed for the back of the shop and hoped to find a flight of stairs leading to the apartments above. He found them and had to carry Susan the whole way. She was unconscious and not responding. Her clothes were completely red with blood and a slick trail of the precious fluid snaked along behind them as he dragged her.

Reaching the door to one of the apartments, he had to kick his way in. With Susan still in his arms, he had to quickly swivel his head as a cursory check that they were alone. He slammed the door, placed Susan in the living room and dragged a chest of drawers from the nearest room to barricade them in. He began throwing everything he could move to the barricade, placing as much weight as he could behind the door knowing that with the narrow stairs leading up, they couldn't get much leverage to force the door open with their weight.

He turned to Susan and tried to stop the bleeding, placing anything he could find to act as a pressure bandage over the wounds, but it was too late. The femoral artery in her leg had been severed and she had bled to death. The heart had stopped and the blood had ceased pumping out from the damaged limb. She lay limp and lifeless.

Andy sat back against the wall with his face in his hands. He was covered in her blood and he suddenly felt an urge to wash it off. Running the tap, he cleaned himself as best as he could with the soap by the sink, scrubbing his hands and face.

He tore away his t-shirt and rinsed his hair in the flowing water, brushing it back with his fingers and studying himself in the mirror. He began to cry. His heart was close to exploding, his head was spinning and he felt sick. Most of all, he felt despair. His girlfriend lay dead in the next room, he was trapped in a strange apartment with no way out that he could see and there were lots of dead people chasing him, wanting to eat him.

He knew he had to secure Susan's body. He had seen the reports on the TV and knew that at some point, she would come back. He carried her already cooling body to a bedroom, tied her hands, legs and feet together with whatever cord and power cables he could find before tightly wrapping her up in the bed sheets and blankets, then closed the door.

He sat at the old dusty table in the living room. It looked like the place hadn't been decorated since the early 1980s; with colourful and strangely shaped patterned wall paper and thread bare carpets.

He found a flight style jacket hanging in the hallway and put it on. The pounding at the door had subsided; *maybe they had given up, lost interest?* He sat in silence and gathered his thoughts. His adrenaline had abated and now he felt exhausted. His hand throbbed. He looked at it and the knuckles were cut and swollen.

He assumed that he must have done it when he broke into the flat, the heat of the moment temporarily numbing the pain.

Now it hurt and felt like it was on fire.

It was almost dark when he woke. A splitting headache erupted between his ears and his body was coated in a light sweat, yet he felt cold. He leaned forward on the old flowery-patterned couch and held his head. He felt sick and weak and his limbs ached and throbbed.

Something had awoken him and it took awhile until his senses adjusted and he was able to recognise the occasional thud of something heavy, hitting something hard. *Were they at the door again, trying to find a way in*? It wasn't the door; it was coming from the next room and Andy realised what he was hearing.

He stood, steadying himself with an outstretched arm against the door frame. He was dizzy and his legs threatened to give from underneath him at any moment. He staggered toward the bedroom that he had left Susan's body in and listened at the door. The thud came again. It didn't sound close to the doorway, so he quietly and slowly twisted the knob in his aching hand and peered inside the room.

He couldn't see anything in the failing light of the day, so he opened the door wider and stepped inside. In the gloom, he could make out the cocooned shape of his once girlfriend, wrapped in the sheets, struggling against her bonds on the floor next to the bed.

He moved closer, careful not to alert her to his presence, and crouched by the writhing form. Her hands and legs were still firmly tied from what Andy could tell, and the muffled grunts and moans told him that the bedding was still wrapped tightly around her and didn't seem to be coming loose.

He stood to leave and, for a moment, lost his balance, forcing him to throw a leg back to steady himself, creating a thud of his own. The body stopped, a louder, more desperate moan emitted from the wrapped figure and it began to struggle all the more against its restraints. Andy watched, expecting it to suddenly burst out of the sheets and attack him, but it didn't. It made no more headway than it had before it had heard him.

He reached out and carefully pulled back the sheets that were wrapped around the head. First he saw the blonde hair, tangled and dull, come into view, followed by the pale forehead, and then the dead eyes that turned and stared at him. He recognised Susan, but he knew it was no longer her. All that she was had died and the thing in front of him was something foul and spewed up from hell.

The eyes frightened him; they didn't seem evil or malicious in any way. They just stared blankly. No recognition of him, all warmth and affection was gone. Not even anger or hate. Anything would've been better than the flat, black lifeless eyes.

He replaced the cover over her face as she opened her mouth, letting out a long, loud wailing moan. Her teeth snapped shut as his hand reached closer.

He closed the door and returned to the living room, the sounds of struggle and the moans in the next room becoming unbearable. He slept again, not through want or need, but his body just succumbed to it. Through the next day he lay shivering, head spinning and slowly getting worse. He passed in and out of consciousness, rarely awake fully enough for his mind to gain control of the situation and produce a clear thought.

Eventually he woke and it was dark again. In spite of his condition, he decided that he needed to get back to his house.

He checked the rear window that looked out over an alleyway that ran the length of the shops at the back. He would make his way along that and hopefully home, to safety.

His hand had gone from being a dull ache that he was able to ignore, to a searing burning pain that ran the length of his arm, like thousands of tiny hot pins embedded below his skin. He lifted the sleeve of his jacket. The hand was swollen to nearly twice its normal size. The cuts on his knuckles were red and purple and looked like mini volcanoes, obviously infected. The veins in his arm stood out from the skin, thick and red, they led all the way up to his shoulder and he could feel a sore swollen lump beneath the skin of his armpit where his body fought to keep the infection at bay.

"Shit!" he exclaimed to himself. Something must've been on the door or the frame, a rusty nail or hinge, and he had caught an infection from it. He looked again at his knuckles, clearly the starting point of the infection.

It dawned on him; he had punched the infected in the face and must have been cut by its teeth.

"Shit! Oh shit." He began to panic.

Searching below the sink, he found a bottle of bleach and began pouring it over the wound. The pain caused him to grit his teeth and screw his eyes shut. He forced his head hard against the wall and poured again. It hurt just as much as the first time. He didn't stop pouring until the bottle was empty. He found White Spirit, also under the sink, and did the same again. By now, his flesh was almost dissolving from his hand, or so it felt that way. He was causing himself chemical burns, but as far as he was concerned anything was better than the infection from the dead.

Next, he ran it under the flowing tap, hoping to flush the wound clean. He scrubbed at it with brushes and scouring pads, opening the cuts and causing the blood to run into the sink, all the time stifling the urge to scream from the pain.

He found an old first-aid box made from a biscuit tin and discovered a couple of bandages and surgical tape inside. He looked for antiseptic cream, but couldn't find any. He began wrapping his hand tightly in the bandage and he secured it by winding the tape around it. It would have to do and hopefully, he had cleaned it out sufficiently. Once he was home, he would clean it again and apply fresh dressings. He had creams and antibiotics at his house, and he hoped that they would be enough.

He struggled through the window and climbed down the steel steps that led to the rear of the shop and into a small yard. He opened the old wooden gate to the alley and made his way, quietly and carefully, along the narrow passage, hugging the wall.

By now it was pitch black. No street lights cast their glow into the shadows; lights didn't shine in the windows, aiding him to see where he was going. He looked up, the night was a cloudy blackness above him and without even ambient light he was virtually blind.

He reached the mouth of the alley and looked out onto the open street. He could see dark figures moving about in the gloom. Now and then a moan or sigh told him that the streets weren't empty, or safe. When he thought the coast was clear, he made his way in the open. Travelling back to the street he and Susan had come along, he headed for home.

The houses on either side of the street appeared as dark bulking walls closing in on him. The static cars were more like black mounds that would suddenly appear as he was about to walk into them. His head was spinning from fever and his legs shook and trembled even as he walked. Fear twisted his stomach into knots and he constantly felt the ice cold tingle of fingers lightly running the length of his spine.

It wasn't until he was almost on top of them that he saw them. He stopped dead in his tracks. A crowd stood in front of him. His senses detected them only after he knew they were there, and he slowly began to back away. He had been too focused on getting home and relied too much on his sight in the near pitch black, instead of his hearing and sense of smell. He could hear the scrape and scuff of feet dragging along the pavement and road as they shuffled about, the sound of their moans and grunts.

And he could smell them too. The sickly-sweet smell of decaying flesh was thick in the air. He had smelled dead animals in his life, just as most people had, but nothing smelled like the dead bodies of human beings. Whether it was due to people's diet or just their genetic makeup, Andy didn't know and he didn't care. All he knew was what dead people smelled like and there was a large crowd of them in front of him.

Quickly, he backtracked the way he had come. He knew he wasn't far from his house, but he didn't want to risk detouring in the dark. Why the dead were in that particular street, he didn't know. Maybe someone had been there, or still was? Either way, they were blocking his path and he had to find somewhere to hide until first light.

Fifty metres up, he moved in close to a house. It looked undamaged from what Andy could tell and he decided to try and find a way in. When he reached the door, he found it open. Not damaged in any way, just left open. In the pitch black he tried to scan the interior. Standing perfectly still and working hard to control his breathing and the beating of his heart in his ears, he listened for signs of movement in the house. Nothing stirred.

Gently, he closed the door and released the catch. He walked through the house, with his hands held before him to fend off any surprise attacks, and once he was sure there was no one home he barricaded himself in the front bedroom and wrapped himself up in the quilted bedding.

His mouth was dry and his throat hurt, his whole body hurt. It felt like he had been in a fight with someone twice his size. He squinted in the first rays of sunlight and held a hand up to shade his sore, stinging eyes. He felt worse than he had the night before. He trembled uncontrollably and every part of his body seemed to scream out to him in pain. Worse still, he had lost control of his bodily functions. His jeans were soaked through and he could tell just from the smell that he had shit his pants. His stomach churned and he leaned over the bed and vomited the contents of his gut onto the floor by the bedside table.

He was worse, a lot worse and he knew it. He could hardly think a clear thought and he found it painful just to sit up. His hand had turned black and his forearm was the same colour. He couldn't see veins anymore, and movement in his fingers was none existent.

With his good hand, he reached for the windowsill and pulled himself up to see out into the street. He looked up and down the road and saw no movement and decided that he had to move there and then. The urge to make it home, to his familiar surroundings, was overpowering and he was determined to do it.

He staggered into the street clutching his injured arm close to his chest. Every step sent jolts of pain up through his legs and into his spine. He struggled to walk in a straight line and stumbled from one obstacle or wall to another, using them to balance himself.

In his state, it took him a long time to make it back to the gable end of his house. The knotted bed sheets still hung from the roof and he felt a wave of relief at having made it. He could still hear the shuffling and moaning of the crowd around the corner in front of his house, but it no longer seemed to bother him. He had made it home.

He gripped the rope with his good hand and tried to pull himself up. Immediately, what little strength he had left failed him and he tumbled back, losing his grip and landing hard against the concrete. He raised himself to his knees. With hands on his thighs he breathed deeply, gathered his strength, and assaulted the wall and rope once more, using his damaged hand too. The hand failed to grip and once again he fell.

Determined not to give up, he tried and tried in vain to climb the rope, all the time becoming weaker with each assault. Eventually he became too weak to even climb back to his feet to try again and he dragged himself to the wall. He leaned against it and quietly sobbed, knowing he was doomed.

His legs had lost the strength to move and his arms were useless. His vision blurred and he opted to just close his eyes and wait. The fever seemed to subside and his head stopped aching. A feeling, almost of euphoria, swept over him as he accepted his fate. He rested his head back against the wall and drifted in and out of a delirious state for the rest of the day. His body was numb; he felt no more pain and in the brief moments of clear thought he found himself remembering happier times.

Images of his childhood and his younger days, on holiday for the first time without his parents, flitted into his mind. His friends' weddings, birthday parties and Christmas and New Year celebrations, the women he had known, and for a moment, he wondered where they were and if any of them were okay.

During the middle of the night he had a moment of clarity. He felt nothing and it seemed as though it was just his mind that was still alive. His eyes watched the starry night sky, blinking in the cool air that brushed against them, savouring the feeling of the breeze on his face. He could feel his life-force ebbing away; there was nothing he could do about it. His body was dead, and he knew that the rest of him would soon follow.

As he stared into the night air, his final breath escaped his lungs with a long sigh. His eyes closed and his head slumped, still and lifeless.

Andy Moorcroft was dead.

10

The hospital had been closed off and a defensive perimeter was placed around it. Anyone who found themselves inside when the gates were closed soon realised that they were a permanent resident, for the time being at least.

The soldiers and police were to protect the people and patients inside and, regardless of the injury or emergency, no one was allowed in or out of the perimeter. The hospital was in lockdown mode. The idea was that as soon as adequate transport and manpower, as well as a secure location became available, the hospital would be evacuated. But in the confusion, it seemed to have been forgotten.

For a whole week, the gates remained closed and a steadily increasing crowd of infected pushed and tried to force their way through the gates and barricades. Gunfire became a part of everyday life; the soldiers having to constantly fend off attacks, or to try and thin out the crowd and the weight against the perimeter walls.

People had stopped approaching the hospital in the hope of treatment and protection ever since the incident on the second day of the lockdown when the soldiers, becoming nervous and seeing a particularly rowdy crowd of people as a threat to the integrity of the safety barrier, had opened fire, killing three of them in the process. Now all they could see was the slowly decaying mass of flesh that relentlessly pressed itself against the barricades.

The grounds were large and, having also been a teaching hospital, there were more buildings than usually found in hospital complexes. Even though there were plenty of rooms and accommodation, with the number of soldiers and police, patients, doctors and nurses and the many people who had sought sanctuary there before the gates were closed, overcrowding had become a problem.

People fit themselves in wherever they could, and with the initial influx of people and lack of a cohesive chain-of-command and method of control and quarantine, it was inevitable that infected would slip through. Also, people dying from natural causes, with the main bulk of the police and army busy guarding the perimeter and wards, it was hard to police each individual group of people.

Outbreaks of the infected would spring up suddenly and soldiers would rush in to bring control back to that particular area. It was widely suspected that the troops took no chances, and any building that had an outbreak was liquidated.

Still, the doctors and nurses of the hospital controlled the wards of patients and they maintained their oaths and cared for the sick and the dying. Even though they had seen time and time again what happened to a bite wound or anyone who died, they insisted that everybody deserved the utmost in care and treatment while they still lived.

Terry was a poor excuse of a man in society's eyes; he always had an excuse and never failed to find time to sneak off from his ward duties to snooze or have a sly cigarette.

Being a porter wasn't really a career choice, but more of a job he'd landed in. He had no interest in doing the best he could and was always looking forward to getting paid and getting to his local bar. He found it ironic that he was actually in a job that was all about caring when all he cared about was his next drink, which was something he never tried to hide.

The way the doctors and nurses treated him, and looked at him, as he crossed paths with them in the halls and corridors of the hospital, was proof enough to him what type of person they all thought he was, and he bitterly accepted it and believed it himself.

He had never been married and had very few friends. After he left home at the age of sixteen, he had pretty much cut himself off from what family he had and set about trudging through an existence that he neither asked for nor wanted. Life to him was a burden, and it seemed to take forever.

Leaning against the wall by the fire exit, Terry was having a smoke break when the commotion in the hospital started. He ran his nicotine-stained fingers through his greasy brown hair. His physical being showed the signs of a dishevelled, heavy drinking and chain smoking man who had long since given up on himself. The oversized porter uniform that hung from his skinny, narrow shoulders and reeked of stale smoke, the lines on his dry, haggard face, all showed an age far past his actual thirty eight years.

More from curiosity than concern, he flicked away the strained cigarette butt and pushed through the fire exit. He followed the noise and commotion to its source. Screams, shouts and the sounds of crashing and banging had become the norm within the hospital.

The brightly lit corridors were packed with hysterical people; doctors, nurses and patients alike. He found himself pushing his scrawny frame through the bedlam. Screams seemed to fill the corridors and Terry soon realised that he was the only one heading in the direction of the commotion. People bumped into him, spinning him like a coin, yet he still headed in the direction from which they came.

He spotted a doctor rushing toward him.

"Doc, what's going on?" He tried to grab him by the arm, but the man didn't seem to have any intention of stopping and pulled away. Terry saw that he was terrified, and watched as he fled towards the exit, his lab coat flowing behind him as he burst through the door and into the sunlight.

Not actually thinking why he was going against the rest of the crowd, or why his fight or flight instincts weren't doing their normal flight behaviour in accordance to Terry's nature, he found himself at the epicentre of the carnage.

A ward had been kept to one side for the infected and the dying, with the doctors hoping to be able to deal with the corpses before reanimation, but someone had dropped the ball. The doors had been battered down and corpses had rushed into the rest of the hospital, tearing through patients and staff alike.

He stood in an open area that had corridors leading to it, which further along, was the 'Doomed Ward' as they had begun to call it. The infected filled the corridor from one wall to the other and stalked their way along it toward Terry. He could see commotion further within the crowd as one or two faster moving corpses pushed and shoved, trying to reach the front of the column to get to the living first.

On realization of his situation, Terry turned to follow the panicking nurses and doctors only to find blood-covered infected patients and hospital staff blocking his route back to safety as they poured up through a stairwell from a lower floor. He was cut off. Everything seemed to slow down for a split second and he found himself taking in what he was seeing and still not believing it was happening, or that it was possible.

The eyes of the infected where not that of wild people but of people in some kind of shock, and if not for the blood and flesh hanging from their mouths and wounds, or splatter on their clothes, they wouldn't have looked so threatening.

Terry came back to his senses as one of the bloodied figures lunged at him. Side-stepping the fat half-naked, gore-covered female patient, he rushed for a set of double doors and burst through, hoping to be able to make it to the exit only to find more carnage and atrocities going on over the floors of the corridor. He ran past scenes of brutality that he would never have thought possible. Blood smeared the walls and floors, the screams of the infirm that had been left to their fate clawed at his ears.

He reached a T-junction, glimpsed behind and saw that a large group was closing in on him. He turned to look if the corridors to the left and right were clear, when a sign to the right caught his eye.

Instantly, a sinking gut-feeling hit him hard and he realized he had a choice to make. The sign said 'Maternity Ward', and he knew that just past the next doors and to the right, a room housed the incubators full of newborn babies, defenseless against the barbaric atrocities that he had seen throughout the hospital.

His body was aching to just turn and run for the exit that was only fifty meters in the opposite direction and clear of any threat, but he knew he had to act, and there was no one else to take the brunt of what needed to be done.

Tears formed in the corners of his eyes as he contemplated his fate and the fate of the babies.

Terry mumbled in a nervous low shaking voice, "I can't leave `em, God, I can't leave them."

He turned to the bloodthirsty mob and screamed, "Fuck you, I'm not leaving them. You've got to fight me first."

With tears streaming down his face, he did not run but marched with purpose through the double doors; the ward was deserted of hospital staff. They had fled in blind panic and left the young babies to die. Terry felt disgust rise inside of him. They had spent years looking down on him and judging him as an arsehole, and now it was them who proved themselves to be the moral cowards.

He rushed along the corridor to where he knew the incubators would be. He turned and forced his way through a glass door to the right leading into a room full of peacefully sleeping infants, totally oblivious to their own agonising fate.

He stopped for a moment, and the sounds of the little babies gurgling, whimpering and snoring almost dropped him to his knees.

In contrast to what he had just witnessed, the room was like an oasis of tranquillity in a sea of madness.

Pushing over a large set of metal shelves in front of the door, he knew it wouldn't keep them out for long but he needed to stall them. He searched desperately with his eyes, pleading for an option of escape for him and the babies. Even if there was a route out, there must have been more than twenty full incubators in the room. There was no way he could save them all.

The now sweating and distraught porter started to push the incubator trolleys to the other side of the room as the first hands of the pale-blooded, vile-looking figures started to bang on the glass of the large viewing window and the door, pressing their faces against the panes and gnashing their teeth, which clanked on the glass, making the hairs on Terry's neck stand on end.

Terry stood his ground in the vain hope that the soldiers stationed at the hospital perimeter would come to his rescue. He could hear gunshots in the distance but they sounded like they were outside the main building. From the sound of things, the chaos had spread throughout the entire hospital complex.

Within a few minutes the glass door and the windows that spanned the length of the room were covered with the horrific faces of the infected. The thumping of fists on glass, of grinding teeth, was unbearable to him and the babies who began to cry hysterically. Terry looked around; the babies somehow knew that there was danger.

"You fucking bastards," Terry yelled with tears flowing down his cheeks. With all the children pushed into the corner he stood in front of them like a frantic goalkeeper ready to take on whatever came his way.

He turned to try and comfort the little soft-skinned babies, speaking in a quiet soothing voice. "Okay, Terry will look after you, ssssssshhhhhh. Terry won't let them take you."

At that moment, the once unreliable porter heard the cracking of the glass and the scraping of metal on tiles as the shelving slid across the floor. The door was forced open due to the sheer weight of the mass behind it.

He turned toward the crowd as they pushed their way inside, staggering into the room and heading for Terry and the babies. Wiping his face dry on the back of his hand, Terry whispered, "Come on then you bastards," so as not to alarm the children or let them hear him swear. He almost laughed. *So he wasn't a complete arsehole after all.*

The first bloodied body staggered towards him and he hit it with full force in the mouth, knocking it to the floor. He grabbed a metal tray that sat on a table by the wall and pelted at the head of the next to reach him, knocking it to the floor and swinging for the next.

A yellowed wrinkled hand grabbed his arm and he pulled away just as the gaping black maw of what had once been a young woman bit into his hand, severing the skin on his fingers and almost stripping them to the bone. He screamed, feeling the teeth clamp over the fingers and shear the skin from them as he pulled away. The pain was sharp at first, and then became a burning sensation as hot blood gushed from the wound and trickled down to his fingertips.

A couple more creatures tumbled forward over the first that fell. He swung and thrashed with a ferocity that a wild tiger would be wary of, but the things just didn't care and kept on the same steady pace and momentum. He spat and gasped as his tar laden lungs fought for air, while his limbs used up every bit of oxygen he had until they began to burn with the build up of lactic acid. Kicking and punching, he tried to keep them at bay and away from the defenseless babies that wailed behind him.

His head spun and his mouth was dry; every part of his wiry frame burned and felt heavy with exhaustion, but he kept on going. Not even able to open his mouth, he knew his body was failing as the things kept biting and pulling at him. One of them alone didn't seem much, but every time he knocked one down, another took its place, sinking its teeth into his flesh.

The burning, crushing pain of their blunt teeth clamping down and breaking his skin was immense and unbearable. He felt broken and ready to lose his fight, and so he turned and scooped up two of the nearest babies, forcing his way into the corner between the wall and the edge of a fixed wall unit. The gap was just big enough for him to wedge his shoulder into and he pushed with all his remaining strength to make sure that he couldn't be pulled free.

He felt his left shoulder dislocate. Even the pop and the agonising pain, like a mini lightning bolt that shot through him, wasn't enough to deter him and force him to lose his grip on the baby in that arm. He was losing blood from the numerous bite wounds and he was weak and lightheaded, but he pushed harder, burying himself deeper in to the gap.

Face down and crying with panic and despair, and guilt for being unable to save the defenseless newborn children that wailed higher and harder as the first of the abominations set on them, devouring their soft fleshy torsos and limbs, he stared down at the two he had rescued. They stared back at him in silence, their faces just inches from his own. Then he felt the hands tugging at his legs.

More teeth clamped down into his flesh. He screamed into the faces of the babies as chunks of skin and muscle were ripped from his lower limbs. He felt the fingers digging into his soft tissue and snapping the tendons and ligaments, tearing away at him. His body juddered and convulsed as he was torn apart. He screamed uncontrollably and his eyes and ears threatened to burst. The pain made him nauseous and he had to angle his head so as not to vomit over the babies in his arms.

He was close to passing out, and by now, as he lost more and more blood, the pain became a distant sensation like the echo of thunder hundreds of miles away. The sounds of the infected and screaming babies now seemed to be in another room as his senses began to fade. He couldn't even scream anymore, and the pain he seemed to accept, just as he had accepted his fate.

All the determination he had left was to hold onto the two little, once bundles of joy.

Terry's vision started to fail and he couldn't lift his head. All his limbs were numb and feeling too heavy to even move slightly as the fluids he needed to live flowed out of his exhausted, bloodied body. He slumped as the last of his life left him and his small frame, and all of what weight it had fell onto the two babies who were now alone and only had the body of their hero to protect them.

That seemed to be enough to save them, as the infected lost interest once there was nothing left to hold their attention or for them to eat. They thinned out from the room in an unemotional search for more victims to tear apart and devour.

The babies had fallen silent in Terry's dead arms. One had suffocated and died but had still escaped the terrible slaughter that the other babies had to endure. The other lay silent, falling in and out of sleep and staring up into Terry's lifeless face.

Broken limbs and small bodies lay all over the floor in a tangled bloody mess, gnarled to the bone and unrecognisable as human forms. Gore, blood and shreds of internal organs mixed together in the mess, and had been trodden and dragged about the room underfoot leaving a grisly version of a modern art painting behind.

Terry's body still lay wedged into the corner between the unit and the wall like a cork in a bottle. He had suffered numerous bites and gouges to his upper body, but for the most part that area was still intact. His legs and pelvic area that had still been exposed were nothing but bloodied bone, his left leg completely gone below the knee, carried away from the scene and gnawed upon away from the hungry group.

His intestines and other internal organs had been dragged through the cavern created after his genitals and backside had been ripped away, with hands reaching in past his pelvic bone as far as possible, to tear out the still warm and blood-filled organs from within.

A few hours later, Terry's torn and bloodied shoulders twitched, his head moved slightly in a slow, awkward circular motion like he was coming to after being clobbered unconscious, then his eyes flicked open.

With a vacant gaze he looked at the babies in his arms for a few moments as if trying to work out what he was going to do with them or even what they were. The conscious baby boy, tightly wrapped in his blankets, stared at Terry in silence as if he knew that he was his saviour.

A deep, unreasoning, uncompromising instinct registered in Terry. Realizing what he had in his hands, Terry dropped the dead baby, his face showing no expression but his mouth gaping open, baring his nicotine-stained, yellowed and broken teeth.

He lowered his head and paused. The baby continued to look into his dead eyes. Terry let out a grunt, and then he sank his teeth in.

11

She ran and ran through the corridors; the echoes of her pounding feet reverberating from the narrow walls of the hospital. Her heart was pounding, about to explode from her chest, tears streamed down her face, but still she ran.

Pausing at a junction, she leaned in close to a wall and risked a quick look to the walkway left and right. There was no one in sight, but she could hear the occasional crashing and banging further in the distance to her left. That was where she had to go.

Her stomach churned, the fear gripping her throat and forcing her to hesitate. She leaned with her back against the wall, staring up at the ceiling and sobbing with the knowledge that she was going to die soon, and a terrible death it would be at the hands of the hideous creatures that had spread throughout the hospital.

But she had to do it. She couldn't bring herself to run away as the others had done.

For five years, Helen had been a maternity nurse in the hospital. She had wanted to be a nurse since a very young age, and as she had matured her maternal instincts had grown with her. So, when she left school, that's what she set out to be and she had loved her job. She had loved the babies; each and every one of them. She cared for them as though they were her own, and when babies died, or were born sick, she felt the pain too. It never got any easier for Helen, but she felt that it was her calling in life.

Now, everyone in the hospital was either dead, walking dead, or had fled to safety. As she had heard the commotion and gunfire erupt, she had forced her way against the fleeing tide of people from the far end of the hospital and headed directly for the maternity ward. Along the way, she had stopped people, doctors and nurses included, and asked what was being done to help the helpless newly born. No one could give her an answer; they were set on saving themselves. Blind panic made them forget about their duties and obligations, but instead focus on saving themselves.

Helen found herself as the only one still heading into the bowels of the hospital.

Of only a slender build and delicate features, she was what most would call beautiful, but now, in her time of need, these traits would do nothing to help her. She needed to gather from her inner strength, as she had always done in life when faced with something too physically challenging for her slight frame. Her determination in everything she applied herself to was what helped her to not just overcome, but excel, in almost everything she did in life. Including kicking the shit out of an ex-boyfriend who had tried to grab her by the throat one time.

Helen slowly turned the corner, tightly gripping a fire axe in both hands. She advanced along the corridor. Her knuckles had turned white as she clung onto the handle, and she was ready to swing it down onto the head of anyone she saw as a threat, alive or dead.

She stopped at a set of double swinging doors and, standing on her toes, peered through the small square windows set two thirds of the way up. The corridor ahead was empty, but she could see that the infected had been there. Doors and windows were smashed, tables lay overturned and medical equipment and paperwork lay scattered throughout the wing. Amongst the damage and detritus, Helen could see blood stains and smears along the walls and the floors.

Further along and to the left, past the nurse's station, were the doors that led to the maternity ward. She took in a deep breath, glanced back along the corridor in the direction she had come, then quietly pushed her way through.

The sickly tang of blood was thick in the air, forcing Helen to breathe through her mouth instead. Careful not to create any noise, she picked her way through the mess and broken glass of the ward, choosing each step with deliberation.

She turned the corner and pushed open the door to the maternity unit. The smell of blood was stronger there and her heart began to skip beats. She moved faster along the short corridor, no longer bothering to tread carefully. The windows to the postnatal ward were gone, having been smashed in, and what shards of glass remained were bloodied. Even from a distance as she approached, she could see that the incubator room had been attacked.

Her knees were trembling, her heart racing and aching in her chest cavity, and her mind praying beyond hope that her worst fears hadn't come true. As she came to the gaping empty window frames and smashed door, she lost all hope and a whimper of despair escaped her throat. She reached for the door frame to steady herself before she collapsed and viewed the scene in front of her.

Tiny, smashed and dismembered bodies lay scattered across the floor. Bloody handprints and smears were covering every surface. She wanted to drop to her knees, to bury her head in her hands and cry her heart out. But instead she dropped the axe as a mixture of nausea and nerves got the better of her. She threw her head forward and vomited all over her uniform and shoes. It was uncontrollable, and before long she had completely emptied her stomach and was dry-heaving and convulsing as her gag reflex tried to bring up more.

Composing herself, she wiped her mouth and nose on the back of her sleeve, picked up the axe and forced herself forward into the room. A noise in the corner grabbed her attention, the dull thud of something banging against the steel unit at the far end of the incubator room. For a moment she felt a pang of hope rise inside her in the chance that some of the babies had survived, but as she drew closer she caught sight of the stripped-to-the-bone legs and shredded lower torso of a man face down in the corner.

She walked up behind him and saw that what was left of him was trying to free itself from the small gap. Then she saw what he had in his hands. She staggered back; her hand reaching to her mouth and letting out a sob of heartfelt pain and disgust. The axe clattered against an incubator stand and the man began to try harder to pull out of his trap.

In a moment of fury, and feeling the hate and revenge course through her, she moved forward, raising the axe in both hands and smashing it down into the man's head, shearing off a portion of the left side of the skull and ear. She brought up the axe and struck him again and again. It was only after the final blow, which left nothing but a pulp of bone and blood, did she realise that she was screaming.

She was breathing hard and trembling uncontrollably, the axe shaking in her hands. A moan behind her spun her round and she saw the corpse of a doctor entering through the doorway. He stumbled on uneasy legs, like a drunk trying to walk in a straight line as he bumped into the frame of the door. His face was almost completely missing with just one vacant and milky coloured eye remaining. The bare blood-covered bone of his cheeks and jaw glistened in the light. His doctors' overall was covered in gore and ripped and shredded in places. His trousers were missing and a large portion of his right thigh was gone, leaving an oozing deep red indentation with tatters of muscle and flesh hanging from it. His genitals had been ripped from his groin and lengths of skin and sinew hung between his legs like a grotesque tail, dripping blood that trailed behind him. He shuffled forward clumsily, raising his one remaining arm and clutching with his fingers at her.

Helen lifted the axe again and stepped to her left and forward, raising the weapon like a baseball bat. She swung directly into the face of the doctor, smashing through the teeth and almost severing the upper part of the skull from the lower jaw.

She felt the impact travel up her arm and into her shoulder and she had to force her right leg out in time to stop her from colliding with him from the momentum of her swing. The eye was still fixed on her as the legs gave and he crashed to the floor, with the axe firmly embedded in his face.

She put her foot on his chest and heaved the handle free and headed for the door. She didn't want to look back, for fear of not being able to move from the sight of such an atrocity against such defenceless and innocent babies. So she ran, and kept on running until she was free from the hospital, past the broken perimeter and in the open street where she found herself alone.

12

It had only been ten days since the worldwide acknowledgement and announcement that the dead were returning to life, but the plague and its results had been raging for months. Starting in remote areas of Africa and South America, then spreading to the Middle East and Asia, before eventually leaping and taking hold of the northern hemisphere and, after a while, mutating once again to become an invisible blanket across the world, causing all the dead to rise.

The virus had spread like wildfire through the heavily populated cities and within weeks, the literal death grip of the virus was firmly wrapped around the neck of civilisation and the future of the human race.

The dead from the flu and bites had been returning for some time and the eventual confirmation and acknowledgement of the catastrophic effects of the virus were too late to stop the spread or change the outcome. Even before the time of the latest mutation and the subsequent announcement, the virus was in full swing. Leaping from person to person, some would suffer the usual effects of flu symptoms while others turned aggressive and attacked the people around them, causing them to eventually die and then come back to prey on the living.

By the time of the final mutation, thousands upon thousands of corpses that had not been autopsied or embalmed lay in morgues, funeral homes and in their beds, began to reanimate virtually overnight and add to the already increasing spread of attacks from the aggressive strain and unacknowledged, already reanimated.

Within weeks of the flu virus spreading to Europe and North America, the world had become a giant tomb and the lid slowly closed over seven billion people.

Now, Andy Moorcroft's body lay still. It sat slumped, shoulders against the wall of the house with legs spread in front and its chin against its chest. The body's skin was pale and yellowed slightly, and its hands had turned a deep pink as the blood had settled there.

The crowd of dead still clambered at the front of the house, though the group had thinned out a little with nothing to hold their interest anymore.

Large grey clouds gathered in the night sky blocking out the moon and stars and blanketing the landscape in complete darkness. The usual lights of the cities and towns were slowly failing. The horizon no longer had the glowing haze of the nocturnal lighting that automatically came on at a specified time.

Many of the once brightly lit motorways and roads that ran through the country like a network of tarmac arteries and veins were now dark. The road signs no longer lit and the electronic boards offering cautions and traffic announcements of the road ahead were dark blank windows that hung above the once busy lanes below that, in many places, had become a stalled mass of cars, buses, caravans and trucks.

Some areas were without power, with no one to maintain the power grids and continue to supply the houses and streets with electricity. Many streets became eerie dark corridors of brick and cement with houses and buildings standing as black monoliths against the charcoal sky.

Heavy drops of rain began to fall, splashing hard on the surfaces of the roads and rooftops, causing a crescendo of noise. No longer was there the noise of people to dull the sound of the rain. There was no chatter in the homes. TVs and stereos had stopped blaring out their entertaining noises and the sound of car engines and horns had ceased to add to the ambient sounds of the night. Even the animals had taken to hiding during the night time and sat in the safety of the shadows, watching quietly from a distance.

The rain confused some of the infected that roamed the streets, causing some to search in the direction of the sounds of the droplets bouncing off car roofs with metallic thuds, then stalking in different directions with confusion as they heard the rain bounce from other objects nearby.

Others stopped and stood, gazing directly above them as the rain cascaded down their slowly rotting faces and blistering skin and into their shabby clothes, waterlogging them and creating an even more pathetic and bedraggled appearance as their clothing hung from their bodies with the weight of the water.

Andy's once immaculately styled and cleaned hair became plastered to the forehead, looking greasy and unkempt. After nearly six hours of complete stillness, the left hand twitched, very slightly at first, but then with more deliberate movements. It was soon joined by both legs bending at the knees as the rest of the body tried to sit up. There was no breath escaping from the deflated lungs and no fresh intake.

Andy was still very much dead.

The head raised and the eyes opened, staring into the sky. It had been the last thing Andy had looked at in life and the first thing Andy saw in death. The vibrant twinkling eyes of a man in his prime with everything to look forward to had been replaced by the lifeless, flat, misted eyes of a corpse. The good looking features were unrecognisable as the blood pressure had ceased, causing the nose to seem more like a crooked beak and the lips to become thin colourless lines around the mouth.

It had stopped raining and the stars shone again. As Andy stared into the night sky, something stirred inside. It wasn't a conscious thought but more of an instinct and it was forcing the body to stand up. Clumsily, like a newly born gazelle taking its first steps, the body of Andy Moorcroft struggled to its feet. It stood for a moment staring at the wall of the house, then gazing at the floor and eventually, its hands as it raised them slightly. Reaching out with both arms, it tried to grasp the wall. As the fingers touched the brick, something registered in the misfiring brain and pulled the hands back and studied them before reaching for the wall once more and following it to the back of the house.

Unless there was something to grasp their attention and force them in a certain direction, the dead rarely took shortcuts and instead, followed the linear paths and roads that acted like a guide to their badly functioning brains, unable to reason that there were quicker and easier ways of getting about.

Andy's body bounced from the wall a few times as it lost its balance and scraped the hands and face against the rough brick, creating raw scuff marks on the skin. The pale pink flesh underneath became exposed but with no blood flow, as would be expected from the living. The body continued to the rear of the house and along the garden path toward the gate leading into the alleyway. It was still open and Andy's reanimated corpse was soon shuffling clumsily along the dark empty street.

No thoughts occurred in its brain, not even memories or desires. The powers of deliberation weren't there and there was no real reason to walk in that particular direction. Andy's body just walked and followed the path in front of its shuffling uncoordinated feet.

The eyes took in what objects they could see in the gloom but nothing in the brain registered what they were. Cars and houses held no meaning anymore; it was just instinct that recognised them as obstacles that needed to be negotiated.

The legs kept moving automatically in the same direction that the street curved without even seeming aware that the sky was brightening and the night was coming to an end.

Only when the sun cast the first long morning shadows of the buildings and the first birdsong erupted did Andy's corpse look up. It stopped and stared into the pinks and purples of the morning sky and watched as the night faded into the horizon. Shadows of trees cast in the road moved gently in the breeze and Andy's dead eyes watched them. Somehow it knew that the moving shadows were not something that it could touch, and although at first the clumsy figure had reached out as though to grasp for them, it paused and followed the length of the shadow to the source.

The tree swayed gently, its leaves rustling. Andy stood below it and looked up into the branches. Reaching for the tree, the fingers touched the bark then pulled back; the dark eyes studied the wrinkled digits on the hand and the green smudge that the bark had left on the fingertips.

For a long time, the body of Andy Moorcroft stood staring up into the tall tree. Watching the branches sway and in a hypnotic state, Andy's body too was swaying rhythmically with them. The birds had fallen silent, as all the animals had learned to do when the dead were close, but it was the tree itself that held Andy's interest.

For hours the body stood there. Nothing other than the tree attracted any attention. There were other bodies moving in the street, slowly shuffling in different directions and occasionally bumping into objects, but nothing registered in Andy's less than perfect mind other than the tree and its hypnotic movements.

A sound, different to the tree, forced Andy to stagger back into the road. It wasn't the sounds already heard like the wind or the rustling leaves. It was different, and Andy's badly functioning mind knew that it needed to follow. No reasoning told Andy why the sound needed to be followed, no memories of the sound came forward, no emotions or thoughts about why it was important to move toward the source, just a driving force that surged through what was left of the brain urged the body along.

It staggered along the street, the sound becoming louder, rumbling in the ears as it drew near. It was another object that caught Andy's attention. Another moving object, but it moved much quicker than the tree and the other figures shambling about in the street as it ran down the garden path and to the car that was creating the noise. Andy's pace quickened and became an uncoordinated staggering and jerky run as some deep primeval need caused it to move toward the moving figure. Raising both arms in front and grasping at the vision, even though it was still a distance away, Andy wanted it. Nothing explained why, but it was an urge that would force the once successful young businessman forward, regardless. Every part of Andy's dead body felt drawn to the moving figure.

Something deep inside was travelling through Andy's body and it soon erupted from the throat; a gurgling sound that turned into a long needy groan. A feeling, a strong unmistakable feeling, surged through Andy.

More than anything, he wanted, needed, to get closer. He didn't know why, but he had to get closer no matter what.

The man spun and turned in his direction and stared for a moment, then disappeared into the car and sped away.

Andy followed at a brisk but clumsy pace until the car had gone from sight and he couldn't hear it anymore. His legs slowed and he watched into the distance in the direction that the car had gone and let out a deep sorrowful groan.

Then, as though he had forgotten all about it, Andy continued to walk.

13

Jennifer was pacing the living room, wringing her hands and now and then opening the blinds in the window just enough with her fingers to look outside. She was nervous and didn't like the idea of venturing out into the open. She had seen the reports on the TV and listened to the radio. The night before, Steve had given her a rough account of what he and Sarah had experienced on their journey to her house. And none of it inspired confidence in the plan to her.

As far as she was concerned, they were safer where they were.

Steve had argued, "Jen, if it continues the way it's going, then eventually, they'll be running up and down the road just outside. And if they find out you're in here, then you'll be trapped."

"But," Jennifer had argued back, "what if we get there and those things are there too? I think we should wait here for Marcus."

"Jen, you know as well as I do that it could be months before he makes it through. In the meantime, we need to get ourselves safe and organised for him." He let out a sigh and raised himself from the couch where he had slept the night before. "I know you're scared, Jen. Fuck me, I am too. But we can't stay here. I know the best route to get there and, I promise if it looks like it's too much of a risk, then we will turn back. Okay?"

Jennifer crossed her arms and wiped a tear from her eye as she nodded. "Okay, Steve. You're right."

Steve placed his arms around her and gave her a reassuring rub across her back. He promised to look after them and that was exactly what he would do, as if they were his own.

"Right then, do we have everything we need?"

He walked into the hallway and looked down at the bags and boxes he and Jennifer had packed the night before. They had taken all the food that could be used as well as cooking pots and other utensils. They had filled large plastic water containers and grabbed whatever spare clothing and camping equipment that they thought would come in use. A couple of sleeping bags that they had found amongst Marcus' old army gear had been a great addition.

On top of the pile, they had added what they could use as weapons, mainly tools from the garage including a small hand axe that Steve had added to his growing collection on his belt. He looked back at Jennifer who was holding a small lump hammer in her hands and staring down at it.

"Jen, if anything happens, just get out of the way. Marcus will skin me alive if anything happened to you." He grinned slightly as he said it, doing his best to calm her nerves. She returned the smile.

He pulled out his phone and began calling Claire, Sarah's mother. The line was dead. He had tried the night before and had the same then. He had text and told her of the plan in the hope that she was still safe and that she should stay where she was until he came for her. He received no reply and he avoided telling Sarah. Instead, he just said that he was waiting till they got somewhere safe, then he would go for her.

They loaded the boxes and bags into the back of the Range Rover and Steve began checking over the vehicle. The tank was three quarters full, all fluids were good and the tyres looked like new. It was spacious and comfortable inside and he couldn't help but let out a little chuckle to himself as he sat behind the wheel listening to the engine. It was Marcus' pride and joy, and no matter how many times Steve had asked for a drive the closest he ever got was riding shot gun.

He left the engine running and went back inside to check on the rest of them.

"Okay, listen up. I've already explained where and why we're going and all I need from you kiddies, is that you do exactly as us grownups say." He looked down at Sarah and winked, she beamed back at him. "Whatever happens, you stay in the car unless we say otherwise. Okay?"

Liam and David actually seemed quite excited by it all and answered up with an enthusiastic, "Yup."

Steve could see that Sarah looked a little less like she was on an adventure than the other two and he moved over to her, dropping to one knee and speaking quietly, "You okay buddy?"

She looked back at him. "Yeah, do you think there'll be many of them out there, Dad?" She nodded towards the door as she spoke.

"If there is, then it shouldn't be a problem as long as we're careful. We've got uncle Marcus' big car remember, and that can get us through anything. What I need from you though is to look after David and Liam. You're the oldest, so you're the boss of the kids, and on top of that, you're a veteran and they're not."

Sarah looked confused for a moment, screwing her eyebrows together and eyeing her father as though he has lost the plot slightly. "A veteran, isn't that an animal doctor?"

He smiled and looked down, before looking back up into her innocent curious eyes. "No darling, that's a veterinarian. A veteran is someone who has been there and done it, like you did yesterday on the way here. Like soldiers who have been to war."

"Ah." She understood and seemed to inflate slightly with pride.

Once in the car, Steve inched out the heavy, but surprisingly easy to handle, vehicle into the road, he and Jennifer constantly glancing left and right. At one time, they would have done that looking out for other vehicles approaching; now they did it looking out for infected. The road was clear and Steve spun the wheel, forcing the vehicle to turn left.

They passed down the quiet country lanes; Steve driving and Jennifer navigating, and through small scenic villages. The streets were deserted with most people having either fled, or staying indoors. The government had urged people to keep off the streets and to avoid heavily populated areas. It seemed that most of the country still tried to do as they were told. As far as Steve felt, it was a bonus and meant that they were less likely to run into trouble; broken down traffic or otherwise.

The children remained calm and quiet in the back, with Liam falling asleep, resting his head on his brother's shoulder. Sarah watched out of the window at the fields and scattered farms as they headed deeper in to the countryside. Even Jennifer seemed to relax and became less nervous.

Three miles into their journey, the road narrowed and Steve had to slam on the breaks to avoid crashing head on into the rear of a broken down small white van.

As the Range Rover came to a screeching halt, Steve swore into the steering wheel, "I fucking knew things were going too smoothly." Jennifer began to look nervous again. "It's okay, Jen. I'll just have to see if we can get around it, and if not, then we'll look for a different route on the map."

Just one look at the narrow gap between the side of the van and the high hedgerow told him they would have to backtrack the way they had come. He was about to curse again when he saw movement from in front of the van. He had already put the van in gear and was about to back away. The figure moved into the open and then raised a hand. It wasn't the clumsy hand of one of the infected, or the lunging movements of a walking corpse.

"Wait, please wait," the woman shouted. She began to work her way around the side of the broken down vehicle and in their direction. Steve lifted the clutch as though he was about to reverse, when Jennifer put her hand on his forearm.

"Steve, wait. She wants our help. We can't leave her."

Steve flushed, feeling annoyed. "I told you, Jen, the same as I told Sarah yesterday. We have to look after ourselves. We don't know who she is, or if she's infected."

"She doesn't look infected, Steve. They don't talk, do they?"

"Not that I know of," he replied.

He was looking back at the woman as she came closer. She didn't sprint and she didn't hobble. Instead, she trotted toward them, in all, looking pretty normal and unthreatening. He squinted, trying to focus better in the low morning sun, and noticed that she wore a nurse's uniform. He pressed a button and the window came down with a mechanical whine.

"Stay where you are. Don't come any closer."

The nurse stopped dead in her tracks. "Okay, but please don't leave me. Take me with you. I'm alright. I've not been infected or injured." She pleaded with him.

"We have to help her, Steve. If you don't, I will." Jennifer was adamant.

He rolled his eyes, knowing that if he tried to reverse back Jennifer was likely to either hit him or even jump out of the vehicle to help the woman.

"Right, okay. But I want to check her out first. Shuffle over and get behind the wheel once I get out. At the first sign of trouble, reverse down the road a couple of hundred metres. If I don't show up after a while, then leave."

Jennifer nodded and slid across; Steve stepped out onto the road, pulling the hammer free of his belt and lowering it to his side.

"Stay where you are," he gestured to the woman as he spoke, "and if you come any closer, I'll not hesitate to use this." He raised the hammer slightly and saw in the woman's face that she understood as she nodded.

He slowly inched his way toward her, scanning all around to the sides and rear, wary of a possible attack. When he was close enough, he stopped. With just five metres between them Steve could see that the nurse, although looking tired and smeared in blood and dirt, was extremely attractive; small, but perfectly proportioned with jet black hair. In another time and place, he would have wasted no time in trying to chat her up.

But he eyed her with suspicion now. "You need to move your van. We can't get past otherwise."

She glanced back over her shoulder at the broken down vehicle and then back to Steve. "It won't move. I don't know what's up with it. Can I come with you?"

"Just move the fucking van will you? I can't risk letting you come with us." He was using the hammer as a pointer, alternating it from the nurse to the van.

She looked at him pleadingly, tears streaming down her face. "I told you, I'm okay. I'm not infected. This isn't my blood." She looked down at herself as she said it, sweeping her arms in a gesture to the stains on her clothing, then back up at Steve. "Please?"

He looked back at Jennifer, unable to read her expression through the window because of the reflection of the low sun. He turned back to the nurse, his heartstrings were tugging at his chest. He had always been a sucker for a pretty face, and even now, in the middle of nowhere and at the end of the world, he still felt the need to be the protecting alpha male for the damsel in distress.

Feeling awkward and unsure of how to place his words, he swallowed hard and looked down at his shoes. "Right, okay. If you want to come with us, I need to make sure you're safe, okay?"

The nurse nodded without saying a word. The desperation in her face told Steve that she would comply with anything he said as long as it meant safety.

"Uh...okay then. Now, listen..." he shuffled his feet like a school kid who knew he was in trouble and trying to think of a story to get him out of it. "I'm no pervert, so don't take this the wrong way, but I need you to take your clothes off."

A look of shock and a defensive instinct seemed to spread across the woman's face, but before she could say anything Steve cut her off, raising his hand. "Look, for all I know, you could have bites and shit underneath your clothes that you're hiding. I have my daughter and my brother's family in the car, and I'm not letting you anywhere near them, or me, before I know you're not infected."

The nurse seemed to understand and nodded slowly. Looking about, she began to undo the buttons to her tunic and removed it, letting it fall to the floor revealing a black lace bra underneath. Then she started to loosen her trousers. Steve wanted to look anywhere but directly at her, especially in her eyes. Regardless of his best intentions, he still felt like a pervert.

Her trousers were slid to the floor, and surprisingly, the first fleeting thought that ran through Steve's head was, *and she's actually wearing matching underwear. Women never do that!* He instantly shook the thought away.

"Raise your arms out to the side and slowly turn around."

The nurse complied and though she had a perfectly flawless and toned body, he concentrated on looking for bites. He made a conscious effort not to lick his lips, even though it wouldn't have been through lust; they actually were dry in the crisp morning air, but he didn't want her to see him as a leering predator.

She had done a full circle and now stood facing him. Steve looked down at his boots and then back at the car where Jennifer was. He still couldn't see her through the window and wondered what was going through her mind.

He turned back to the nurse. "Okay, you look fine to me, uh...I mean okay," he stumbled, "you can put your clothes back on now."

She pulled up her trousers and picked up her tunic, all the time watching the man in front of her and seeing how clearly uncomfortable he looked.

She smiled slightly and spoke. "Okay then, I've shown you mine, now you show me yours."

Steve looked up, shocked, and only when he saw the expression on the woman's face did he return the smile with a shake of his head. "I'm sorry, but like I said, I had to be sure."

"It's okay, I understand. I'm Helen by the way." And she walked toward him with her hand outstretched.

"I'm Steve," he said shaking her hand.

He walked back to the Range Rover and introduced her to Jennifer and the children. Her eyes lit up when she saw them and she made a conscious effort of putting them all at ease as she introduced herself with her perfect tried and tested bedside manner.

She looked back at Steve. "I don't think the van will budge, Steve, and I don't know where you were heading, but you won't get there along this road."

After a cursory look at the broken down van, Steve confirmed that he wouldn't be able to move it. Sarah was now in the front seat as Jennifer and Helen sat in one of the many back seats and chatted. Jennifer looked completely relaxed, finally having someone on her level to talk to and to vent with. She searched through the bags and handed some clean clothes to Helen to change into.

"They might be a little long for you, but they're clean at least."

Helen was happy to change and her hospital scrubs were thrown out of the window.

Liam and David were just as interested in the new arrival and kept on butting in on their conversation as the two women spoke about what was happening, what they knew, what they were doing and what they had experienced.

Helen only briefly spoke of the hospital. Glazing over the details and giving them a rough idea of what the situation was there. The memories of the maternity ward were too painful and fresh in her mind; she couldn't risk becoming a blubbering wreck over it just yet.

Steve looked across at Sarah. "Righty dokey kiddo, I guess you're the new navigator. It's alright though; I pretty much know where I'm going from here."

He reversed the vehicle back down the long narrow road and drove an alternative route.

An hour later and they turned onto the main carriageway that led toward the Safari Park. Both sides of the road were deserted and Steve couldn't even see any traffic in the far off distance. As they approached the slip road that would filter them into the park, he noticed a figure up ahead beneath the trees before the entrance to the main gate.

Everyone in the Range Rover was silent, having seen the figure rise to its feet and step into the road, watching them approach. When they were no more than fifty metres away, the figure turned and ran toward the gate, scaling the fence and jumping into the park, disappearing into the shadows on the other side.

Steve braked. "That's that idea out the window then. They're in the Safari Park too."

He began to put the car into reverse when Helen put her hand on his shoulder. He looked down at her fingers gently clasping him, and followed her forearm up to her neck and the curve of her chin until he was looking her straight in the eyes. She glanced from the road and straight at him, making him blink with sudden discomfort.

"You may not be a pervert, Steve, but you've definitely got a one track mind. Or do you not get out much?" She grinned at him and, to save him any further torture, she pointed with her finger at the gate. "Look, from what I've seen, the dead can't climb a fence like that, and I don't think the aggressive strain infected can either. Plus, they would've run at us, not away from us. So they must be alright," she concluded.

Jennifer had noticed the look in Steve's eye since he had introduced Helen to them. "Not just a pretty face is she Steve?"

He could feel his male pride and masculinity ebbing as these two women teased him. "So, what do we do then? The gates are closed, and if they're infection free, they might not want to risk letting us in. And we don't know their strength, so we can't barge our way in."

Jennifer leaned forward. "We can just try talking to them instead. Show them that we're not a threat and that we have children with us. Maybe the fact we have a nurse might convince them too?"

Steve cautiously drove the car toward the gate. Stopping short twenty metres so that whoever was watching could get a clear look at him as he approached on foot. He deliberately kept his weapons out of sight and tried to look as harmless as possible.

Large trees stretched far off to the left and right of the gate into the distance, obscuring the high wall that the main gate was built into. The foliage hung over the road and met high above in the middle, casting the entrance into shadow and making it difficult for Steve to make out anything beyond the railings.

Over to his right, he could hear the buzzing of flies and insects, and as his eyes adjusted he could see something in the long grass. There were a number of bodies lying just off to the side of the road. Steve couldn't tell how many; ten, maybe twelve, all piled together unceremoniously. A draft of wind brought the sickly smell of the dead to his nostrils, the pungent, almost warm smell, like a mixture of raw sewage and sun baked garbage, of rotting flesh assaulting him and causing him to turn his head in disgust.

Putting it from his mind, he walked to the gate, his arms out from his sides to show he had no weapons and intended no harm.

"Hello?" he called. He paused and after a few seconds called again. "Hello, is there anyone here?" Still, there was no answer. "Look, we don't want trouble. We saw you as we drove up, so I know there's someone there. I have two women and three kids in the car. We just want somewhere safe to stay."

After a minute's silence, as Steve tried to peer into the gloom, he heard a voice.

"Are any of you bitten? Is there anyone else with you?"

"No and no," Steve replied. "We are all well and it's just us. One of the women is a nurse too so maybe she could be of help?" He was doing his best to sound harmless and even convince them that they could be of use.

A man approached the gate, middle aged with grey swept back hair and overweight but with sure and steady steps. He carried himself as though he knew how to handle his self and the intended effect wasn't lost on Steve.

"I'm Steve," he smiled and reached a hand through the bars of the gate with his best friendly smile face.

The man watched him warily and kept his distance. He nodded over Steve's shoulder, toward the Range Rover. "Tell them to get out of the car and come to the gate."

Steve complied, and soon the whole group were stood in front of the fence as the man gave them the once over.

He eyed the kids last, then smiled at Sarah, who smiled back. He looked back at Steve. "I'm Gary, Park Ranger here." He took Steve's hand and shook it. "I'll open the gate and let you in, but promise me this. You'll follow me all the way to the main building and once there, you'll undergo a quick check over just to be sure." He gave a slight squeeze to Steve's hand as he said it.

"No problem, Gary, we understand and we'll be happy with whatever sets you at ease."

Helen looked across at Steve. "Seems like everyone wants to see me in my knickers today doesn't it?"

Gary smiled and moved to the control box by the side of the gate. It slid open, and soon Steve was following Gary in his old Park Ranger Land Rover, zebra stripes and all.

They stopped at the main administration building in the centre of the park. It was an old mansion-style building with red and orange brickwork and high reaching chimney-tops and large windows. It occupied the highest part of the grounds, nestled within a clump of ancient trees on one side and wide open stretches of grassy fields to the other, a winding road leading up to it from within the wood.

From the main entrance all the way up to the admin buildings, it was mainly forested area with breaks here and there for gift shops, restaurants and picnic and play areas with a small lake. Further past the main building, from what Steve could remember from his childhood, was a high chain link fence that led into the Safari Park proper.

Gary escorted them inside from the gravelled parking area, immediately to the front of the building. More people were in the lobby and looked surprised to see the new arrivals. It was only then that Steve realised that most of them were wearing the same clothes; green t-shirts with black combat style trousers, Park Staff. He had suspected that he would find some here, and judging by the number, he guessed that there were maybe ten of them that he could see at a glance.

"This is Steve and his gang," Gary said introducing them, "they've agreed to let us check them over, and Helen here is a nurse too."

A few of the people from the park eyed them with suspicion, but the rest smiled and even approached the new group. They were led into separate rooms to the side of the main door. Steve was checked over by Gary himself, while the children and women were dealt with by two other female staff members. Ten minutes later they were back in the lobby and hot drinks were brought out for the adults and juice and chocolate for the children.

Everybody began to relax and they were given a quick layout of the grounds and the measures that had been taken to ensure their safety.

Gary began, "We keep pretty much to the main building here and we can monitor the main gate on the CCTV. Jake is in the security room now, it's his shift. It was him who told me over the radio that a vehicle was approaching when I saw you. I go down there now and then and clear the gate area of any stragglers that turn up. That's what I was doing when you interrupted me." He smiled at the group and feigned mock annoyance. "No one else here likes going down there, so as the Senior Park Ranger I see it as my duty to do it, as well as check the walls and fences with the others."

"Does the wall go all the way around then?" Jennifer asked, taking a sip from her tea.

"Yeah, pretty much," a young red haired man said from the couch with a chess board on a coffee table in front of him. "There's only one area that isn't stone wall, but that's a high fence with a steep drop below it on the other side," he looked over at Gary, "we gonna finish this game then old man or what?"

Gary looked back at the group. "Sorry, you'll have to excuse Kevin here. He fancies himself as an up and coming chess champion. Only thing is, I only taught him how to play a month ago."

"Yeah, and I give you a regular kicking at it too," Kevin interjected, smiling at the group.

Gary sat down in front of the chess board and continued to speak to Steve, Jennifer and Helen. "So, the walls aren't an issue. We have food but it won't last forever. We cleared out the restaurants in the park the other day and closed them down to save power. We have running water from the wells and there is enough room to make everyone comfortable."

"What about power?" Helen asked.

Kevin didn't look up from the board as he studied his next move, but answered, "Generators. They're in the basement and we have our own independent fuel supply here too. We've closed down all unnecessary buildings, utilities and attractions in the park to save power, but as Gary said, that won't last forever either but we have plenty for now."

"What about the animals?" Helen asked.

Gary answered, "They're still here, and we've continued and intend to continue to look after them for as long as we can. All the fences to the paddocks are safe and secure and we have plenty of food and medicine for them, though eventually, for the likes of the lions and tigers, fresh meat could be a problem."

Steve raised his eyebrows, wondering what would happen when the likes of the lions and tigers run out of meat, but said nothing. "Sounds like you've got it pretty well set here and you're in for the long haul. You don't think that things could get back to normal?"

Gary looked at Steve, a serious expression on his face. "The army can't control it, and the police can't. The Prime Minister has disappeared into a bunker somewhere and the rest of the world, including the so called superpowers, are on their knees. So no, I don't think things could get back to normal. Do you?"

Steve felt a little stupid. "Fair one," was all he could say.

Gary looked ashamed. "Sorry, I didn't mean to bite your head off. I just get a bit worked up sometimes when I think about the scale of this thing. I haven't heard from my son for over a week and I'm worried. He was down South somewhere, on business, when it all started to go bad. He was trying to get home, but I don't know where he is now."

"I take it your phones aren't working?"

"Sometimes, sometimes not, I think it won't be much longer before they stop working altogether. We do have a radio here that we used to use, before the days of the internet, to speak with other parks and even countries that our animals were indigenous to, when we had problems or needed advice. It was cheaper than using the phone and quicker than writing letters. Not used it in years though, but I was thinking about setting it up again and seeing if we can get anything from it."

That reminded Steve, he needed to call Marcus and try Claire again. "Yeah, maybe it would be a good thing to have. Do you remember how to use it?"

"Not sure. Been years since I last even looked at it but if we get it working, I'm sure it'll all come back to me, and Jake is a whiz at the technical stuff. If in doubt, I'll read the manual."

Steve nodded with a smile. "Always the case with us men isn't it, read the instructions as a last resort. I'm gonna see if I can use my phone. I'll be outside, Jen, and I'll let you know if I manage to speak to Marcus."

Gary looked at Kevin. "Sorry young man, but the game will have to wait. I'm gonna give the newcomers the guided tour and introduce them to everyone. I'm sure the other children will be happy to have a few new play mates to join them on their endless games of hide and seek about this old building."

"Other children? So we're not the only ones here?" Liam asked

"Not at all," Gary replied with enthusiasm, "there are five others here, three girls and two boys." He looked at Jennifer and Helen. "Some of the staff managed to bring their families in with them. There are eighteen of us altogether, including my wife, Karen, and she's on cooking duty tonight so you're in for a treat." He walked ahead of them, humming as he went, with Sarah, Liam and David close behind.

"Will we get to see the animals?" Sarah asked him.

"I don't see why not. I think it would be good for them to see kids still showing them an interest. Animals aren't much different from us you know. They still need to know that they're wanted, now and then, and that someone cares."

Sarah turned to the rest and grinned from ear to ear. She loved animals and the thought of having an entire safari park at her fingertips filled her with excitement.

Steve couldn't get an answer from Marcus. He got the usual overseas dial tone, but there was no answer. He hung up and typed out a lengthy text message, giving him the rough details of where they were and how things looked.

Next, he tried Claire again.

14

Roy was starting to get on her nerves. Claire watched him as he paced about in their bedroom where they had taken to spending most of their time to keep out of sight from the street below.

He had steadily become more and more anxious and by now he was more or less in a constant state of panic. Since the news had broken, he had refused to believe what was happening. He had stood and argued with the TV and radio, demanding to know how the dead could come back to life and start eating people and what the government was doing about it.

He had always lived his life through a set routine. He went to bed at the same time every night, went to work on the dot every morning. Even his rare nights out with friends were organized and arranged to the letter. Claire always suspected that he had Obsessive Compulsive Disorder. Even his wardrobe and sock drawer was neatly arranged accordingly and now, with the world turned on its head, his carefully packaged life had been pulled apart and he was unable to deal with it.

"For fuck sake, Roy, will you just sit down and relax? I'm the one that should be in a panic. My daughter is out there somewhere and I can't get in touch with her. I don't know if she is safe or not, but I'm managing to hold it together."

"She's with Steve. They said they would be heading for a safe place." He stopped and turned to her. "I just feel like we're trapped here, Claire, and that eventually those things are gonna come crashing through the door."

Claire rolled her eyes. Sometimes she had to wonder what she saw in him. There had never been any real adventure or excitement between them. At least with Steve she had never known what was going to happen next. But with Roy, it had been the stability that she had gone for. With someone who was so regimented and set in their ways, there wasn't much chance of a spanner being thrown into the works.

He was never late and she doubted that many other women would find him at all interesting. Though, without doubt, he was an attractive man. He was, nevertheless, a dull bore. She didn't even get excited sexually by him. Their bedroom activities consisted of a once a week twenty minute session that left her feeling unfulfilled and wondering why she even bothered.

Now, with the chips on the table, she also discovered that he was the sort to crumble at the first sign of trouble.

"Your van is parked up against the front door, Roy. There's no way they can get past that and I haven't seen any of them driving cars. Besides, there's only a few of them right now and if need be, we can always get out. Steve may have had a plan to get somewhere safe, but how do I know he got there? He told me not to try and phone him and that he would call when he gets there. That was last night and I haven't heard anything since."

She knew that with her determination and fitness, the things outside wouldn't be able to get her. There was only a few of them staggering about in the street at that moment and nothing had stirred in the area for the past few days. Not since the crazy man had driven his scooter along the road screaming something about being a 'Mobile Restaurant', then set fire to himself before disappearing out of sight.

Claire was a keen runner. She had been since her school days and although she knew full well that she wasn't the most academic of people, she made up for it with her physical abilities. She had always kept herself in top shape and four years earlier, as well as her running groups she had discovered an all women's Karate Club in her area. She had never missed a session since, and won competition after competition; something she suspected that Roy resented. She did her best to stroke his ego but there was always the invisible wall that went up whenever she spoke about her achievements to him. Instead of being proud and full of encouragement for her, he either dismissed her interests as a waste of time or changed the subject just as quickly as she had brought it up.

Now she was passed caring about his feelings. In the time of crisis, she was proving to be the Alpha, while Roy became a frantic bag of nerves. She would have to drag his arse through this if he was to survive.

"Right, they said they were headed for the Safari Park, so why don't we head there too?" She looked up, hoping that the suggestion of a course of action would bring Roy into a calmer state with his mind more focussed.

Roy sat down and sighed, "Because we don't know if they actually got there, and if they did, if the place is safe or not. We could be heading into a thousand of those things."

"Yeah, true. He did say to sit tight for now and he will let us know. God I hope Sarah is okay." She leaned forward from the bed and placed her face into her hands, rubbing at her tired eyes with the palms.

Roy placed his arm around her. "I'm sure she is, Claire. Steve wouldn't take any unnecessary risks. He's a good Dad regardless of his many faults."

They sat and watched out of the window for a while, neither of them speaking. For the last week or so they had cried, argued, talked and none of it had gotten them anywhere. Claire had become resigned to the fact that the planet had gone to rat shit and her only concern now, was Sarah.

Her phone began to vibrate in her pocket, then the theme tune to The Simpsons began to emit from her jeans. They both stared at each other for a second, apprehensively, before she reached into her pocket and pulled out her shocking pink mobile phone and flipped it open. It said 'Dick Head' on the screen, her contact name for Steve.

Claire fought back a feeling of dread and pressed the green button.

"Steve? Thank God, where are you, is Sarah okay?"

She heard his voice at the other end; it sounded distant but the line was clear. "Yeah, she's fine. We all are...."

She stood up and began to pace the room as he spoke, holding one hand cupped over her unused ear and the phone to the other.

Roy was sitting on the bed and following her with his eyes, trying to work out what was being said, the feeling of angst building inside him the more he was left in the dark.

Claire looked at him and recognised the familiar look of apprehension in his face. She pulled the phone away from her ear and spoke. "It's Steve. They made it to the Safari Park and they're all safe. There are other people there too." She placed the phone back to her ear and continued to pace about, nodding, humming and throwing in the occasional 'yes' and 'no'.

Roy assumed that Steve was giving her instructions and explaining what the next plan was and what she needed to do.

"Steve? Steve, are you there, can you hear me?" She looked at the phone then tried to call him back. The line was dead again.

"What's happening then? What did he say?" Roy was eager to hear what he had told her.

"Well, before the line went dead, he was saying that they have a secure wall all around the park and they are living in a mansion with other people. He said that he is gonna come for us within the next few days and once he has it all organised, he will let us know and that we are not to move from here until then."

Claire was clearly relieved. Sarah was safe and that was all that mattered. She didn't savour the idea of dying herself, but as long as her daughter was alive then she could deal with anything.

She sat down heavily on the bed, and before she knew it the tears were flowing uncontrollably. Everything caught up with her, and now that she knew Sarah was out of harm's way, she could afford to let her guard down for a moment and all the tension and strain was released in a deluge the moment the wall came down.

Two hours later, she awoke on the bed. Roy had tucked her in and left her to sleep. She must've cried herself out and the exhaustion must've been following close behind the tears because she couldn't remember stopping crying.

She threw off the bed sheets and walked to the bathroom. She could hear Roy moving about in the room next-door and it sounded like he was looking for something as he rummaged through cupboards.

"What are you doing, Roy?"

He was leaning over a large black canvas bag and looked up, surprised to see her. She stood watching him, her eyes squinting in the light that shone through the window from the rear of the house.

"I'm packing some stuff love." He sounded almost cheery. "If we're gonna be leaving soon, then we need to have some things don't we? I'm just grabbing what I think we need."

Claire scratched her head where her hair was standing on end. "Ah right. Well, I'm gonna see about getting cleaned up. I need to wash, I feel like the floor of a public toilet, so I'll have a look at how much water we have in the tank now; may as well use it because whether Steve gets here or not, we'll be leaving soon anyway."

"How do you mean?" He looked concerned now and Claire could see the panic returning to his face.

"And you're the one with the degree? Think about it, what are we gonna do? Spend the rest of our lives locked in here? Plus, my daughter is safe and sound and I want to be with her whether Steve makes it here or not, and I'm not going stinking like the arse end of a tramp."

She and Roy spent the rest of the day and night searching through the house, looking for things they would need. It was more to keep themselves occupied than anything else and now that they had a focus, they both felt better about the situation. Even Roy seemed more masculine and less like an empty wetsuit.

They each packed a bag with clothes and food and a bag for Sarah too. Claire had insisted that she would probably need clean clothes and a few of her personal belongings, such as her diary and photo album as well as her favourite teddy. Now all they had to do was to wait for Steve to call.

15

It was still early morning in Baghdad and the sun wouldn't be up for another couple of hours, but with much of the city ablaze, it seemed more like late evening as the sun was beginning to set. Visibility was good and Marcus decided that the time had come to leave.

During the previous days, reports of other teams from other companies making a break for it had come in. Some had been successful but others had found themselves trapped within the city and in need of help. But help would never arrive.

Marcus and Stu had opted for a route that would take them through the less built-up outskirts of the city. Though the journey would be longer, there was less chance of running into difficulties and finding themselves trapped like the others, unable to escape.

A city-wide curfew had been announced, but with the American forces too busy pulling out, there was no one to enforce it. It had been left to the Iraqi security forces and the city had soon crumbled into mayhem as a result.

Orders had been passed down to the teams that no one was to attempt a break out from the city and that all vehicle keys and weapons were to be handed over to the management staff at each location, so that they could be centralised and redistributed.

Management were in panic. They had finally realised that the teams had the upper hand. They had the vehicles, the weapons and the experience to get out for themselves. After years of the men on the ground being shit on from great heights by the people who sat behind desks and computers, telling them to 'put up and shut up' and to 'just make it work', the tables had turned and management soon realised that they would more than likely be left behind and not even considered as the teams bugged out.

The teams themselves scoffed at these orders to hand over their assets and dismissed them out of hand. Few members of management had the nerve to approach the teams and demand the keys and weapons. Rumours of people being shot in other companies by people holding grudges were already doing the rounds. With panic and confusion reigning and other priorities, no one was likely to care about some desk jockey getting his comeuppance.

"You think Mickey will come for the keys?" Ian asked Stu.

Stu huffed, "He's a fucking dick if he tries and thinks we're just gonna hand them to him. No one else has and I think Mickey knows that Marcus would just tell him to shit and fall in it."

They were standing in the parking area, keeping watch over their vehicles. Over the past week it had occurred to them that if everyone else thinks of escaping, then weapons, ammunition, kit, equipment and even vehicles would be a priority as it had been to Marcus' team. When it comes to survival and every man for his self, it was prudent to post guards.

Soon, Marcus and the rest of the team arrived and began the final checks and preparations to leave. The tension was thick in the air. They all knew of other teams trying for the same thing and being swallowed up within the city. He had received the text the day before from Steve informing him that they were at the Safari Park and what the situation was, and now it was their turn to take their chances.

None of them had been out into the city since the contact that had left three of their men dead, but they had seen and heard enough. Reports flooded the operations room of the virus spread and the hordes of infected that roamed the streets. Any civilian that was able and had the means, had tried to flee the city, but the majority had never gotten far. With the road blocks, unorganized roadways, burning streets and civil unrest, they had been easy prey for the masses of dead and infected in the confusion of a city brought to its knees.

News footage and reports showed the dead and infected staggering through streets around the world and attacking people, but it was still hard to believe; the dead had actually returned to life and now fed on the living.

Gunfire and explosions could still be heard from within the city as the survivors fought off the dead as well as each other. Militias had taken control of individual districts and as well as fighting the common enemy, the infected and the dead, they also fought each other and the security forces. It was hard to believe that even with all that was going on, loyalty to certain Imams and religious and political views were still strong enough to make them wage war on one another.

Marcus had decided to take three vehicles with two men in each. The gun turrets would be left unmanned until needed. Marcus had reasoned that most of their trouble would be from stalled traffic and blocked roads rather than armed attack. Ian and Jim would take the lead with Marcus and Sini in the second vehicle, leaving Stu and Yan to bring up the rear.

They loaded up and began the final checks of their personal kit and weapons, making sure that it was all easily accessible and ready to use. Marcus checked that his M4 rifle was ready to fire and that the magazine was firmly attached. Next he checked the pistol on his hip and his spare magazines in his assault vest and in the grab bag at his feet. Every man in the team was doing the same thing.

"All call signs this is Marcus, radio check."

"That's good to me mate," Stu answered.

"Strength five to me," Ian said.

Marcus clicked the send button again. "Roger, that's Lima Charlie all round. Lead off when you're ready, Ian."

"Roger that mate. That's us mobile."

They left the car park just as the first rays of sun touched the tops of the buildings. Marcus looked over toward the operations room as they passed and Mickey was stood there watching them. Marcus expected him to be ranting and raving and trying to stop them, but Mickey just waved and over the radio they heard, "Good luck boys".

There was nothing to say in reply so Marcus just gave him the thumbs up.

It was obvious that Mickey had been aware of their preparations but he had done nothing to stop them. Marcus doubted that it was due to fear and more to do with him being a decent man. He probably knew that the end was coming and that eventually the International Zone would be overrun and that it would be too late by then to escape. He hadn't asked any of the teams to hand over their weapons or vehicles and probably had his own plan of escape. Marcus hoped that he would make it as he watched him walk back to his office.

They headed south through the International Zone and toward the 14th July bridge that crossed the river Tigris from the safe area and into the southern part of Baghdad. The plan was that once across, they would head east through the outer edges of the suburbs and pick up the road North toward Ba-qubah and from there, they would continue North along the length of Iraq and toward the Turkish border.

Everyone knew all too well that it would be easier said than done. They had studied every map and aerial photo they could find, checking routes and scrutinising streets and towns. Any information and intelligence about the cities and towns along their intended journey was gathered and a number of alternatives had been discussed and planned should the primary plan go wrong.

One of the alternatives was to head for Syria. But that would mean travelling through places like Fallujah and Ramadi; cities that were trouble even at the best of times. Now with the world falling apart and the militias in those towns seizing control with no one to stop them, it would be a tough job to get through untouched. On top of that, those places were densely populated and if they didn't receive trouble from the militia, then it was a guarantee that they would from the infected.

The primary choice was the best that they could come up with. After Ba-qubah the only large cities on their route were Kirkuk and Mosul, both easily bypassed as long as the roads were still accessible.

The decision had been made to try and make the entire journey to the border in one day and be in a laying up position close to the crossing point by last light. That would leave time to have a look at the actual border crossing and any obstacles or problems, and to take the necessary action from there.

"There's always a chance that the border could be heavily manned," Stu had said during the planning. "With all the shit going on, the Turks may have brought extra troops and armour into the area to stop the flood of refugees and the likes of us too."

Marcus had agreed. "That's just a bridge that we will have to burn as we cross it. By the time we get there, it'll be too late to turn back I reckon and we'll be committed to whatever course of action the enemy and ground dictate."

Jim looked up, his eyebrows knitted together. "Enemy? We at war with the Turks now?"

"We are at war with everyone my friend. It is survival of the fittest," Sini laughed and slapped him on the back then looked to the rest of the group for approval in his statement.

"Sini is right lads," Marcus nodded to him, "anyone who gets in our way, we have to treat them as a threat. Every person out there is

WHEN THERE'S NO MORE ROOM IN HELL

gonna want our food, weapons and vehicles and they're not gonna ask nicely if they think they can just take it from us. Plus, I promised my missus I'll be home for Christmas."

The group let out a bout of nervous laughter.

As they reached the bridge they began to slow down. The checkpoint was still manned by the American Army, as they knew it would be, and it would take some smooth talking to explain what they were doing and get through. The cover story that the team had agreed upon was that they were tasked with rescuing a bunch of western reporters from the Sheraton Hotel.

If it was any other checkpoint manned by the Iraqi Army, they would have just barged through, but the Americans had an M1 Abram's Tank pointed straight at them.

As the lead vehicle approached, an officer stepped from the other side of the tank and waved them forward. He gestured something to one of his men and the road was made clear for them to continue. The two APC's that completely blocked the road were manoeuvred just enough to let the team through.

Sini raised an eyebrow at Marcus and as they passed the American guards; the officer waved and shouted to them, "Stay safe guys and God speed." Everybody waved in return. The first hurdle was crossed.

"That's the call sign complete." Stu spoke over the radio informing Marcus that the whole team was through the checkpoint.

They continued across the bridge toward the first junction. The ground was littered with countless corpses that had been picked off by the snipers that flanked the checkpoint. The soldiers had probably taken no chances and had more than likely shot infected and non-infected alike as they had approached the bridge.

Bodies lay sprawled in the morning sun, some on the hard tarmac and others entangled in the chicanes and barbed wire; all had shots to the head.

"Roger that, Stu, okay Ian, hang a left at the second junction."

They turned east and headed through the suburbs. A low drifting smog from the numerous fires clung to the ground. Buildings smouldered and crashed cars and dead bodies were everywhere. Some bodies were nothing more than skeletons, others were burned or dismembered, lying in pools of festering and bloated entrails and clotted blood. Debris was all over the road and the drivers had to pick their way through as the commanders in the seat next to them kept an eye open for the infected or any other threat.

Apart from the bodies and trashed vehicles and buildings, the streets seemed deserted. Packs of dogs scurried between houses and along alleyways feeding off the corpses', and birds swooped in to pick up the bits left behind when the dogs dropped their guard. Swarms of flies were thick in the air and, even from inside the vehicle, Marcus and Sini screwed their faces in disgust at the pungent smell of the bodies that littered the streets.

Marcus watched as they passed a broken down car. Across the hood lay the body of a man sprawled on his back, his arms and head hanging down to the wheel arch. His rib cage looked like it had been torn open, with dried blood splattered all around him and his rib bones pointing up into the sky. His skin had turned black and green as it lay baking in the hot Spring sun. His hands were gone from the wrists down and a large dog had its snout buried into the wide open skull, smearing its face with blood and gore. A cloud of black bloated flies took to the air as the vehicles passed the corpse, and the dog turned and growled at the men in the trucks as they passed, as though protecting its meal from them.

After crossing another junction, Ian's vehicle came to a shuddering halt and began to reverse. The rest of the team followed suit and Ian's voice came through the radio, "Back up, there's a huge crowd in front of us about fifty metres up."

The team continued to reverse.

"Man the guns but hold fire for now." Marcus was climbing into the turret as he spoke. "Do they look like infected, Ian?"

"They look it to me, Marcus, and they're heading for us too. Fuck, there's shit loads of them coming from the side streets too."

Without time to think, Marcus had to make a decision. Turn back or try and push through? He didn't like the idea of heading back because there was nowhere really for them to go other than back to the I.Z or into the city and neither option was appealing.

"Fuck it. Put your foot down, Ian, we have to try and push through. Use your guns to try and clear us a path. We'll be right behind you doing the same."

Ian's vehicle lurched forward and began to gather speed as he blazed away with the gun in the turret. He fired directly ahead and into the crowd and Marcus and Stu fired left and right, trying to keep the mass of infected at bay.

Over the roar of the guns they could hear the crowd. The loud constant hum of the moans with individual wails and cries from the dead. They all surged toward the moving SUVs with no consideration for the damage that the vehicles and guns were doing as they tore through the crowd. They were completely focused on reaching the vehicles.

Many did reach them, only to be slammed out of the way as the bumpers smashed into them, or they were dragged underneath and chewed up by the heavy armoured wheels. Some sprinted at the sides of the trucks and bounced off, rebounding back into the crowd or to the ground.

Marcus looked down as he fired into them. They were just a seething mass of blackened, foul-smelling, growling figures and couldn't be recogniscd as being in anyway human. He saw no features in their faces, just the gaping mouths and swollen blistered skin. They attacked relentlessly and some literally exploded on impact with the vehicles as the bumpers pierced the skin and caused the gasses and entrails to escape from their rotten, bloated bodies.

The heavy armour of the vehicles was impenetrable and there was no way that the crowd could get through it. But Marcus feared that enough of them could get in front and underneath to cause the team to lose momentum and traction on the road surface.

"Keep going. Don't let them slow us down," he yelled. "We get stuck here and we're fucked!"

The last of the rounds on the belt of ammunition fed through his gun and then stopped. Quickly and without thought, through years of practice, he lifted the top cover, cleared the feed tray and placed in a fresh belt of two hundred from the ammunition tray. He slammed the top cover back down, gave it a tap with his fist and pulled the cocking leaver back to feed the first of the link and belted rounds into the machinegun. In all, it took just a few seconds and he was soon staring down through the sight again firing at the attacking mass of diseased faces.

With ringing ears, and the fast rhythmic crackling of the gun as it shuddered against his shoulder and vibrated through his body, he watched as body after body fell. Sweat was dripping into his eyes making them sting and blurring his vision, but he couldn't afford to wipe them clear. He had to keep up the rate of fire.

He could hear the other guns firing, and in his peripheral vision he could see Stu's vehicle as it swayed and rocked over the piles of bodies that it crushed beneath its wheels. His own SUV was doing the same. Marcus was being jolted and tussled around in the gun turret and, on a few occasions, his rounds flew in to the air as he clung to the gun for balance and the barrel was forced upward.

The SUVs struggled, pushing hard against the weight of the crowd. Ian was ploughing ahead and leaving a trail of smashed and twisted bodies in his wake. Though for every walking corpse they lay to rest, another soon took its place and filled the gaps as they clambered to reach the men in the trucks. They pulled and pushed and tore at each other in their determination to reach their prize, only to be cut down or crushed under the wheels once they reached it.

The air was thick with the stink of the dead and the cordite and smoke of the hundreds of rounds fired into them. Bodies collapsed all around as hot 7.62 mm sized pieces of metal spat from the machineguns and punched through them. Limbs and entrails covered the ground like a thick repulsive swamp, with the broken bodies of the dead mixed in as the feet of the others stepped on them and trampled them beneath.

Sini had his foot pressed down hard on the accelerator but the vehicle was slowing. They were losing momentum. The wheels were losing traction even though they were in four wheel drive. The sheer mass and weight of the crowd that filled the wake of Ian's vehicle was straining the engine to its limit. Bodies and limbs were clogging up the wheels and the drive shaft and they were reduced to a crawl. All the time, more and more of the relentless shambling creatures attacked the convoy.

Marcus noticed the loss in momentum and screamed down through the turret, "Sini, put your fucking foot down, get us outta here."

"This is as good as it gets, Marcus. There's just too many of them under the wheels."

Sini was steering the vehicle left and right, trying to shift the piles of corpses from underneath and gain just a moment of traction on the road in the hope that they could then gain power. It was no use; the ground was too soft and fluid.

Marcus never let up his rate of fire. He felt panic rising within him. The thought of being slowed to a halt and stranded in a sea of rotting walking corpses that wanted to do nothing other than tear him apart and eat him, filled him with terror. It occurred to him that many other teams could have succumbed to the same kind of onslaught and were either overwhelmed or even trapped and surrounded, unable to move from their vehicles.

He stole a glance to the left and saw that Ian was almost clear with his truck and swerving through the thinner edges of the crowd. Between Marcus and Ian though, was a swarm of grotesque heads and faces and arms, crammed shoulder to shoulder, surging toward them. They were coming from every direction, spilling out from buildings and the streets and alleys that ran between them.

He heard Ian's voice through his earpiece. "Stu, Marcus is pretty much dead in the water. I'll do what I can from here to clear the path for you, but you're gonna need to close up and ram him forward."

"Roger that, Ian. We're struggling ourselves. The ground is thick with the fuckers," Stu replied.

Marcus looked to his right, and through the crowd he saw the upper part of Stu's SUV rocking as though on a choppy sea. To Marcus, it looked like there were thousands of the infected between their vehicles, but Stu was approaching at a steady speed. Yan was aiming his bumper straight for the rear of Sini and Marcus' vehicle.

Ian was laying down a tremendous weight of fire into Marcus and Stu's path. The butt of the machinegun pounded into his shoulder as the belted ammunition rattled through the feed tray and into the chamber. Below his feet, the pile of link and used cases grew rapidly, creating a slag heap of brass and steel. His fire never let up and his barrel was beginning to smoulder and glow red with the heat of thousands of rounds thundering through it.

Stu gripped the edge of the turret as the vehicle made contact with the rear of Marcus' SUV, causing them to jolt hard and bounce about in their positions. Without letting up on the pedal, Yan pushed the SUV to its limit. The engine screamed with the effort and threatened to burst, but the vehicle kept on going, the wheels spinning and gripping in turn and they began to make headway.

Rounds began to whizz down the sides of Marcus and Stu's SUVs as Ian concentrated his fire to the left and right of the line of advance. Red tracer rounds whipped through the air with their loud cracks and dozens of bodies continued to drop on both sides of the road.

The progress was slow and the ammunition stored in the turrets was dwindling fast, but all three vehicles were making progress with Ian's pushing forward and Marcus and Stu almost clear of the tightly packed crowd.

Finally in the clear, the wheels gripped the hard dry tarmac and the engines roared as the gears changed. The filth-coated SUVs raced away from the scene as the dead vainly staggered after them.

A few kilometres further along, Marcus, heart still pounding in his chest, called a halt on an open stretch of road that was flanked by open wasteland and provided them with good all around visibility. Marcus, Stu and Ian dismounted while the drivers stayed behind their wheels in case of the need for a quick bug out.

The first thing needed to be done was to restock and reload the machineguns in the turrets with ammunition. Thousands of rounds had been fired and the depleted supplies stored within the ammunition bins, directly below and inside the turrets, were replenished from the crates in the rear of the vehicles amongst the other supplies and stores.

The SUVs looked like they had been driven through an abattoir. Smears of what looked to Marcus like grease and rotten chicken skin, covered the side of the vehicle in long streaks as the dead had attacked and been brushed aside by the heavy trucks. Thick dark smears of congealed and coagulated blood were splattered over the windows and doors. Around what was left of the cracked mirrors and door hinges, chunks of flesh and cloth were caught as they had been torn from their owners by the momentum.

At the front, around the grill and engine bay and in the wheel arches was a tangled mess of hands and feet. Even a mangled head was caught between the wheel and the steering arm. Slivers of green, brown, and deep red putrefying meat covered the bumper and already the flies were starting to swarm.

The stench hit Marcus, and without warning he projectile vomited all over the hood of his SUV, adding to the already stomach churning mix. He couldn't control it; it came from his mouth and his nose and the more he tried to hold it in, the more violently it forced its way out. The whole content of his stomach was sprayed over the noxious soup of body parts and gore as his driver, Sini, sat watching from behind the wheel, cringing and grimacing with every new addition of gory artwork added to the surface of the hood.

"Thank you, Marcus, and once you're finished, could you do a shit on the windshield for me please?" Sini was grinning, waving at him from inside. "It's not quite disgusting enough for me yet."

Marcus couldn't speak. He tried to look up as he staggered to the edge of the road with watering eyes and raised a thumb to Sini as another bout of dry-heaving shot through him making him convulse. It took him a couple of minutes to regain control of himself. Once composed, wiping strings of bile and snot from his face, he set about checking along the opposite side for damage. With no damage found, and an empty stomach, he climbed back into the passenger seat.

Sini offered him a bar of chocolate.

They were moving again and approaching another built-up area within a few minutes. A car screeched to a halt as it shot out from a side street and stopped just in time to avoid being hit side-on by Ian's vehicle. The driver looked up in horror, expecting the machineguns to rattle and turn his car in to a perforated tea bag. If the turrets had been manned, no doubt Ian would have done so. As it was, the Iraqi behind the wheel of the civilian car thanked his lucky stars and reversed back allowing the rest of the call sign to pass.

Stu watched in his rear view mirror as the car then followed in their wake, keeping its distance.

"That vehicle is following us up, Marcus."

"No worries, Stu," Marcus replied. "Just keep an eye on him and let me know if he looks like he's closing up."

The streets in that area seemed untouched by the chaos of the rest of the city. None of the buildings appeared to be damaged by fires and there was a lack of infected, or anyone else for that matter.

Further along they ran into a makeshift barrier spanning the width of the road made from cars and concrete blocks that were known as T-Walls. In the narrow gap in between, Ian could see that rolls of barbed wire that blocked their route. Jim slowed to a halt and Ian began to speak into the radio but was cut short by the appearance of two men emerging from a building to the right.

Ian's eyes grew wide as he saw the Rocket Propelled Grenade Launchers that they carried, "RPG right!" he screamed into the handset and Jim slammed the SUV into reverse. The rest of the team followed suit, but Stu's vehicle then halted.

"RPG rear," was heard over the radio.

The civilian car that Ian had nearly T-boned had followed, stopped fifty metres back, and the driver had stepped into the street carrying a launcher of his own. There was nowhere for Marcus and his men to manoeuvre to and there was a split second pause as they expected the rockets to punch into them. Nothing happened.

All three Iraqis were in perfect firing positions, yet they held their fire. They had caught the team off guard. The turrets were unmanned and everyone knew that if there was any movement to use the machineguns, the Iraqis could fire their armour piercing rockets into the three SUVs before they got their first rounds off.

One stepped forward and lowered his launcher. He waved a hand to the other two, who then relaxed their grip, but kept them pointed in the direction of Marcus and his team.

"We do not wish to fight you." The accent was strong Arabic, but the English was near perfect. "But please, do not try to use your machineguns or we will have to fire. I want to speak with you."

Marcus spoke into his radio, "Lads, don't make any move toward the turrets, but be ready to debus at the first sign of trouble. Ian, Jim and Sini take the two on the right. Stu, you and Yan take out the bloke to the rear. I'm gonna get out and see what this cunt wants."

Standing in the street, Marcus and the insurgent eyed each other with suspicion, like two gunslingers meeting for a quick draw to settle an argument. Marcus carried his M4 at his side with his finger along the trigger guard. The safety was off and it was ready to fire, but he kept it pointed to the ground to give a less aggressive appearance. He didn't want a re-enactment of the O.K Corral for the sake of a misinterpreted gesture.

The Iraqi, a slim man who looked no older than twenty five, lowered his RPG and approached him. "I am Hussein, what is your name?"

"I'm Marcus. If you're not intending on blowing us up, what is it you're after?" He was straight to the point and wasn't in the mood for pleasantries.

Hussein smiled and cocked his head. "This used to be our area and we fought you Americans for many years to defend it. But now, it will soon belong to the demons like the rest of the city. They are the enemy now."

"I'm not American, I'm British and if you think that we will give you our vehicles, then I promise you, you'll be dead before the first rocket is fired and your boys will soon follow you to Paradise."

Hussein seemed cocky and smiled as though untroubled by the threat. "My friend, I told you, we do not wish to fight you, and we do not want your vehicles. We want to come with you. We have lost many men over the last weeks and we are all that's left. Those with families returned to their homes but many who stayed were killed on these streets. Anyone who was still alive fled two days ago. All the people who lived here have gone and there is no need for us to be here now."

Marcus began to laugh; part in relief and part astonishment. "Are you serious, why should we take you, and more to the point, how could we trust you? You and your lot have no doubt planted hundreds of IEDs aimed for the likes of me. For all I know, you could be responsible for the deaths of some of my friends."

"And you could be responsible for the deaths of some of my friends, Mr Marcus. This war has caused much suffering. But there is a new enemy now." Hussein pointed down the street at two infected that had turned the corner and was heading in their direction. "Them!"

Marcus turned just as the Iraqi to the rear of the call sign swapped his RPG for a rifle that he un-slung from his shoulder and fired a shot into the head of each approaching figure. They fell to the ground and didn't move.

Marcus looked back to Hussein. "He's a good shot. You rag-heads normally can't hit a barn door."

"I told you, Mr Marcus, we have been doing this for many years."

"Yeah, and no doubt looking forward to your seventy two virgins when you finally get slotted in the process?"

"I'm not here to become a martyr and I didn't do this for religion; I did it for the money. For every attack we did, we were paid. The bigger and more successful the attack, the more we got. We are not much different from you, Mr Marcus. I am sure that you and your men are not here for the 'War on Terror' or because you want to make a difference."

Marcus couldn't stop the smile from appearing on his face. "You know us pretty well, and where did you learn English?"

"I studied it at school, and learnt from movies too. The best movies are American, so I needed to understand the language."

Marcus nodded. He had met many Iraqis who spoke near perfect English just from movies and books. In many, even the American accent had rubbed off.

He looked back at his team who sat in their vehicles watching him intently. Marcus knew that every one of them had their weapons in their hands just below the line of the windows and would spring from the vehicles in the blink of an eye, firing into the insurgents before they had time to react. He had manoeuvred himself into a position that gave him a side-on shot at the closest insurgent carrying an RPG, and with Hussein no more than a step away now, he could easily deal with him, leaving just the man to the rear. He didn't worry about him though. He knew that Stu and Yan would drop him in the blink of an eye.

Marcus saw Hussein's eyes shift to his left to check his disposition and, to Marcus' amazement, Hussein placed his hands in his pockets and positioned himself to make it even easier for Marcus to deal with him and his men.

"I'm no fool, Mr Marcus, and I am serious about wanting to come with you. You can trust us and you can even take our RPGs. I only ask that you allow us to keep our Kalashnikovs."

Stu spoke over the net. "We're starting to draw a crowd here lads."

They looked back down the street from where they had come. Scattered figures shuffled toward them. Some were running and the Iraqi to the rear of the call sign began firing accurately aimed shots into the heads of the lead infected as they approached to within fifty metres.

Reaching for his radio, Marcus spoke, "These blokes are coming with us. They could be useful."

A torrent of curses and abuse flowed into his earpiece. He had expected it.

"Everyone shut up. They're coming with us, no discussions. They're not fanatics and we can use the extra firepower and local knowledge." He turned to Hussein. "You will travel one in each vehicle and tell your boys to hand over their launchers. You'll sit up front in the passenger seats and there'll be someone behind you all the way with a gun, ready to blow your face through the windshield if we think for a moment that this is a stick-up."

Hussein smiled. "I understand, Mr Marcus. I promise you, my men just want to get away from here, as you do. We will help you in anything you need."

The barrier was moved from the road and the three Iraqis were split between the vehicles. They were searched for extra weapons and anything concealed before they were allowed in. Hussein sat in Marcus' vehicle. Sini eyed him with a look of disdain. He sighed and shook his head then put the vehicle into gear.

"I hope you're right about these fuckers, Marcus." He turned to look at his commander.

Hussein spoke, "He is right my friend. Our war is over now and the new one needs us to fight together."

Marcus looked from Hussein to Sini and nodded. "There you have it, Sini, and we're all best mates now. But I'll drop him like a bad habit if he tries anything." He fixed Hussein with a stare and the look was returned.

Hussein relaxed and nodded in understanding and agreement.

Ian's voice came through the radio. "That's us mobile."

The team rolled forward again.

16

"Ssssssshhhhhh," Amy turned to look at her younger brother with her index finger pressed to her lips. "You've got to be quiet, Robert, they're still out there and they'll hear you."

He was shifting from one foot to the other. "I'm bursting for a wee though," he whispered through clenched teeth, wincing at the thought of having to hold it in for much longer.

His brown wavy hair was standing on end from grime and grease. Neither of them had washed or changed clothes since the morning that they had left for school nearly two weeks prior.

She looked at him and pulled away from the window. She crawled on her hands and knees and took his hand in hers. "Okay, follow me and don't make any noise." They crawled to the door of the classroom and into the corridor.

Class photos and artwork covered the walls of the interior walkways of the school. Some very basic drawings in child friendly paint, of spiders and butterflies from the younger classes and others, more detailed, showing off the growing talent and ability of the older children in the school. Amy had more than one piece of her own work on the walls and her teachers considered her to be among the brightest and most talented of her year.

They walked down the corridor, their footsteps echoing through the hallways and into the high ceilings that helped to carry the sound throughout the school. Even though the school was empty, there were no teachers or pupils and it was doubtful there ever would be again, Robert and Amy still insisted on using the childrens' toilets.

"Right, hurry up, Rob. I'll wait here for you."

Amy leaned against the wall with her arms folded and glancing left and right along the corridor as she pushed herself forward from the wall with her foot and allowed her body weight to bring her back against it, bumping her shoulders against the hard painted plaster and then repeating the process by pushing off with her foot again.

Robert had gone into the boys' toilets and Amy would always continue to use the girls'. Even with no one to tell them what to do, they still followed the rules. A minute later, Robert came out wiping his hands on the back of his shorts.

"I think there's only a bit of water left, Amy, and most of the toilets won't flush anymore."

"I know. But it's probably better that way really, because they would probably hear outside. Remember when you sneezed at the window? They nearly got in. The less noise we make the better."

Amy was ten years old and had always walked to school with her brother, who was two years younger than her. She took her older sister duties seriously and made sure that Robert never fell afoul of bullies or trouble. On a few occasions, she had even stepped in and found herself in a fight against another boy. Though only a skinny little girl, she was tough and knew exactly how to fight with her wits as well as fight dirty. She was fully aware that Robert was a typical boy and she felt that she needed to always be in the background to steer him right. Amy loved her brother, but he was always an 'ungrateful pain in the neck' as far as she was concerned.

They had set out together as usual, having given 'Mum' a kiss goodbye at the door and began the fifteen minute walk to the school gates. They had been kept at home by their parents for the whole of the previous week. Mum and Dad had been scared of them catching the flu and as the reports of unrest and violence mounted, they had been kept close and safe at home.

Over the weekend 'Dad' had become ill. Their Mother suspected the flu and spent the days caring for him while he lay in bed with fever. She had decided that it would be best to have the children out of the way and that they had missed enough school and their education was suffering needlessly.

Amy was glad to be going back, and along the way she and Robert had talked as though it were just another normal school day. They arrived at the main doors and, even though they were open, no one was around. They made their way to their respective classrooms and sat and waited for the other pupils and teachers to arrive, but after a while, Amy realised that something was wrong and that no one was coming.

She fetched Robert and decided that they should head home. On arriving at the end of their street, they were greeted with a scene of chaos. People were running in panic to and from their cars loading cases, boxes and family members and fleeing with screeching tyres down the road.

Screaming could be heard from some houses and sirens blurred from the next street.

She gripped Robert's arm and they hurried home. The door was open and the front window was smashed. She called for her Mother and checked the whole house. Even Dad was gone.

A pool of blood in the living room by the broken glass of the bay window filled her with a feeling of dread. She choked back the tears she felt welling up as she composed herself enough to stop the fear from spreading to Robert, and set about writing a note to her parents, informing them where to find them.

Without anywhere else to go, Amy decided that they should go back to the school and wait for either their parents, or the teachers to arrive. All she knew was that they should get away from their street.

Back at the school she noticed that the reception doors weren't just open, as she had thought earlier, but they were actually smashed off the hinges. Something reddish brown was smeared along the walls of the reception area, and what was left of one of the doors had a dark, dried stain that took up a large part of the carpet in the centre of the room.

They walked through the inner doors that led into the main part of the school, and Amy grabbed a chair from a nearby classroom and used it to step on and reach the bolt locks at the top.

Robert asked, "Where is everyone? Where's Mum and Dad? Our street didn't look like that this morning when we came to school. Do you think the nasty people that Dad told us about have been there and went to our house?"

Amy was beginning to cry. She had held it back for the whole time, but now the thoughts of being stranded and away from her parents made her feel vulnerable and alone.

"I don't know, Rob. Dad was ill, so he should've still been in bed, like he was when we left, but he wasn't and I don't know where Mum could be. Maybe they ran away?"

"Would they run away without us? Do you think they'll come to pick us up when the bell goes?"

"I don't think the bell will ring today, Rob. No one else is here, and I think that was blood on the walls and floor at reception."

Robert glanced back down the corridor toward the doors, then back to Amy with a look of concern on his face. "Can we go to the canteen then, Amy? I don't want to be here, near the doors. They scare me."

"Me too, c'mon, we'll go to the canteen then."

It had been thirteen days since they had last seen their parents or home and they had been living and sleeping in the school ever since. On the second day, a car pulled into the car park but pulled away before they could get to a window to shout for help. When they did call for help, strange people turned up. Some ran and some seemed to walk in funny ways, slow and staggering. Amy assumed that they were the nasty people who had messed up her house. They banged at the doors and windows, making strange noises, and Amy and Robert had decided to keep out of sight from then on.

They tried to occupy themselves by watching the recorded movies and programmes on the TV in Amy's classroom. The normal TV channels had stopped showing their favourite programmes; they had become a collection of doctors, policemen, soldiers and people in suits talking and arguing, and pictures and videos of people fighting all around the world. But since the power went out, they had begun to spend more time in the school library reading books to each other and playing board games.

Amy decided that they needed to help themselves to the food in the store rooms and freezers of the canteen. She felt guilty and feared that she would be called a thief, so she insisted on leaving a list of everything they had taken and a note saying that their parents would buy it all back when they came for them.

She knew deep down that they wouldn't be coming. In the past two weeks she had grown up fast, and just from watching the horizon from the classroom windows she had seen that things were bad and unlikely to get better in the near future.

The streets had become deserted. She didn't see cars and buses travelling along the roads anymore like usual. In fact, she couldn't remember the last time she saw a plane in the sky. The only thing she did see was more and more of the nasty people on the street. She could tell it was them by the way they walked. They didn't seem to be going anywhere in particular and wandered aimlessly.

Amy spotted a dog at the main gate before the car park as she stood in the shadows of a classroom one day. It had been sniffing the air and began barking at the small crowd gathered by the school doors. Immediately, four of the group broke away and sprinted toward it. Luckily, the dog had time to react and ran away yelping. Amy hoped that the dog had got away safely and she regretted not being able to have found a way of letting it into the school. It would've made a nice pet and they could've looked after it while they waited.

Now, sitting in a dark classroom with her legs hanging limply over the edge of a desk, she watched the glow on the horizon fade into darkness, spelling the start of another black and cold night filled with the sounds of moans, shuffling feet, thuds and bangs from the people outside the main door, and the occasional cries of panic and pain in the distance. They had taken to sleeping in the staff room on the large leather couches with blankets they had found around the school.

Robert sat on the floor, playing with a toy car he found in one of the classrooms and Amy sat watching him, staring and with a blank mind.

"I miss Mum," Robert said as he continued to drive his small car around at his feet.

"Me too," she replied.

"And I miss Dad,"

"Me too again," she knew it was going to turn into a game now.

"I miss McDonalds,"

"I miss Pizza Hut,"

"I miss SpongeBob." He began to giggle.

"I miss iCarly,"

"Well I miss my..."

Robert suddenly stopped what he was doing and looked up. Amy hadn't heard it, but when her eyes met her younger brother's, her ears tuned in and she could distinctly hear the sound of an engine approaching.

She jumped down from the table and ran to the window. She saw the beam from the lights as it approached the bend in the road beyond the school grounds. It was still on the blind side and out of sight but it was getting closer, fast. She could hear its engine racing.

"Quick, pass me the light." She held out her hand for the large heavy torch they had found in the caretaker's room and raised it against the window, just as the car came into view in the gloom.

It took the bend at speed and Amy frantically flashed the light on and off in the hope that the driver would see them. It continued on without slowing, and was soon speeding away out of sight. Amy felt herself deflate.

"Did they see us?" Robert asked.

"No, I don't think they did."

She was about to turn away and head out of the room when she heard the engine again. The car was coming back. Both of them stood on chairs at the window, Amy flashing the light and Robert waving his arms, but neither of them making any noise for fear of attracting the attention of the group outside, below the window.

The car was reversing back the way it had come. It reached the area in front of the gate, and then it came to a halt and it flashed its own lights in reply to Amy's torch.

A gasp of relief escaped her causing her breath to steam on the window. She continued to flash and wave the light but to her horror, the car slowly began to pull away. She waved faster, as though the more she waved, the more likely the car was to approach them; as if it was one of her interactive console games that she had at home where she would jump about to control the movements and speed of the characters.

She looked down and noticed that the crowd was moving away from the school and heading toward the car. When they were about twenty metres away from it, the car pulled away. Amy realised that whoever was in the car was luring them away.

She was sure they would be back.

"They're gonna come back, Robert. They just need to make sure there's none of the nasties here before they come in is all."

Robert reached out and held her hand as he stared out the window. "I know sis. They'll be coming back."

Within a couple of minutes, they saw the headlights of the car approaching again and before long they had pulled into the car park. Only when the lights had been switched off did Amy recognise the car. It was a police car.

A man stepped out from behind the wheel and headed for the main doors. Amy grabbed her brother by the hand and dragged him from the room.

"C'mon, Rob, we have to let him in."

Robert was trotting along behind her as she led him to the reception doors, which they had avoided for the past two weeks.

"How do we know he's not like the others?"

"He's a policeman, and he has a car. I don't think the nasty ones can drive, Rob."

They reached the door and saw the beam from a torch light moving across the reception area on the other side. A man stood there in the gloom of the doorway that led outside, scanning the room before entering. He saw the children reaching up to open the bolt locks at the top of the door and moved toward them.

Amy opened the door and the man shone the light down the corridor behind them and then over their dirty, dishevelled faces before pointing it to the floor.

He crouched down as he came close and smiled warmly at the two children. "Don't be afraid, it's okay. I'm a policeman. You're safe now, and I'll take care of you. My name is Tony."

17

They had thrust their way north from Baghdad, through the mayhem and hordes of infected, headed for the Turkish border.

The journey had been far from uneventful and they considered themselves to be lucky to have made it through at all.

After breaking out from the capital, with Hussein and his two remaining fighters joining the team in their bid to escape the meat grinder that was Iraq, they had passed through numerous villages and towns as they fled along the main roads and tracks that crisscrossed the country. They tried to keep clear of the populated areas as much as possible, but sometimes it was unavoidable.

In places the roads were packed with static vehicles, most of them abandoned. Many of them with their dead occupants entombed inside. Some of the stalled cars, trucks and buses were peppered with bullet holes, showing the tell-tale signs of ambush and attack. Others had burned, and whole sections of road became impassable with the charred, still smouldering skeletons of wrecked and destroyed cars.

Marcus had pushed his men hard. Angry survivors had fired at them with machineguns and rifles and even rockets on one occasion as they passed through villages and small towns. Their reaction had always been the same, to pour heavy, thunderous firepower at the firing point in reply from the machinegun turrets on the tops of the vehicles, suppressing the enemy until the team was clear of the field of fire.

Further on, American Apache gunships had buzzed them and lined up ahead, hovering low above the road as though about to attack. Ian had thought quickly and pulled the American flag from his glove box and frantically waved it at them through the armoured glass of the windscreen.

Whether the pilots believed that they were on a legitimate mission or not, Marcus was unsure, but they moved off nevertheless and allowed them to continue. They could still see them in the distance to the West, paralleling them. As they travelled along the road they watched as the same two helicopters attacked a column of Iraqi tanks that were travelling at a right angle toward the team and may have been headed to cut them off.

Marcus silently thanked the pilots and watched them turn back South and disappear across a ridge line, leaving the column of destroyed and burning tanks in their wake.

As the team approached a town called Tuz, just south of Kirkuk in the northern section of the country, they had halted on a deserted stretch of road to observe the route leading up to the outskirts. They knew the town, and to sum up the general feeling, Stu, while planning a previous mission in to the area, had commented, "The hostility that the locals feel toward Western security forces is matched only by their hatred of soap."

Marcus climbed out from his vehicle and walked to the front of their small convoy where Ian was already observing the road with his binoculars.

"How are we looking, Ian?" he asked.

Ian lowered the field glasses and handed them to Marcus without taking his eyes away from the town. "Looks deserted. I can see a few infected moving about in the main street, but other than that, nothing that looks like real trouble."

Marcus raised the binoculars and scanned the buildings and rooftops. He hummed as he did so, acknowledging Ian's observations. "Can't see any signs of an ambush, but you fucking never know with this place."

He keyed his mouthpiece and spoke to the rest of his men. "Pardon the pun guys, but the place looks dead. We'll push on. Keep the speed up and be ready on the guns."

Ian and Marcus moved back to their respective vehicles and up into the turrets. Stu was already manning his gun at the rear of the call sign.

"That's us mobile," Ian sent over the air.

Within a few hundred metres, the three trucks were travelling at speed, racing toward the town and aiming for the far side.

Tuz consisted of a cluster of buildings and residential areas that straddled the main road running South to North through the centre. Most of the buildings were dilapidated single-story breeze block and wooden shacks.

Ditches lined the road and collected all the waste and trash that ran from the homes and businesses and flowed into the oily, stinking water that filtered into the outskirts, acting as a medieval-style open sewer system. Plastic bags and bottles clogged every ditch and dead animals, left to rot at the sides of the road, would be in abundance while people stepped over them and ignored the stink as they continued with their daily routines.

Before the plague, the roadsides would have been packed with trucks and cars being repaired and refuelled at the countless small mechanics garages that ran the length of the main street, with hundreds of people milling about and staring with hatred and contempt at the team as they passed through.

The checkpoint at the Southern end of the town was unmanned, another indication that the place had fallen to the dead. The stretch of road that cut through the built-up area was no more than a couple of kilometres long, and Marcus hoped to be clear to the other side of the town and back on the open highway within just a few minutes.

Midway through, Ian saw a gaggle of infected that crouched over what must have been a body in the centre of the road as they tore at the scraps of flesh, still clinging to its bones. A couple of them heard the approaching vehicles and rose to their feet. They began to stagger toward the convoy and then broke into a sprint, headed directly at the lead vehicle.

"Straight at them, Jim, don't try to swerve at this speed, you'll roll the vehicle." Ian turned the turret and began to fire into their path.

Zaid, the insurgent that had been assigned to Ian's vehicle, sat in the passenger seat. He braced himself in his seat as they closed the distance to the first of the infected.

Jim stomped his foot down on the pedal, hoping to squeeze a little more power from the engine. "C'mon you ugly fucker!" he snarled through gritted teeth as he aimed the front of his vehicle directly at the lead sprinter.

The grill of the SUV slammed into the midriff of the first body. It folded immediately with its lower limbs being dragged under the wheels and its head smashing down hard on the steel hood of the vehicle. It burst like an overripe watermelon and its brains and thick sticky blood was splattered all across the windshield.

Ian felt a slight bump as he continued to fire when the body was crushed beneath the wheels.

The second approaching infected was slightly off centre from the line of approach and it was hit with a glancing blow that sent it hurling through the air in a tangle of smashed and broken limbs. It landed ten metres away with a wet smack, sounding like a large, fresh slab of meat being dropped onto a tiled floor.

The remainder of the infected, still feasting on the carcass in the middle of the road, were completely unaware of the heavy steel monster approaching them. Only one looked up at the very last instant, as the bumper smashed into its pale, gaunt face. Ian felt more of a jolt as the vehicle ploughed over the organic speed bump.

The dead began to materialise from the houses and streets after hearing the roar of the engines and machinegun. They reached out longingly for the speeding black vehicles, as though they expected the team to stop to satisfy their ravaging needs. The loud chorus of moans as more and more of the walking corpses gathered could be heard over the engines.

Some sprinted for the roadside, but by the time they reached it the team had already passed them, and their clumsy efforts to give chase were no match for the momentum at which the SUVs charged away from them.

Marcus, Stu and Ian didn't bother to waste the ammunition from the machineguns by hosing them down. They were no real threat. Unless a crowd appeared ahead of them, speed and the heavily armoured SUVs themselves were their best weapons at that moment.

The last of the vehicles passed through the final checkpoint on the far side of the town. Like the first one, it was unmanned, except for a dead Iraqi policeman who stepped into the path of Stu's truck and was obliterated by the heavy wheels.

"That's us complete." Stu informed Marcus that the entire call sign had made it through.

Marcus was about to reply when Ian's frantic voice sounded in his ears. "IED right," he hollered.

All three vehicles swerved to the left and over to the opposite side of the carriageway in an attempt to put as much distance as possible between the expected explosion and themselves. The people sitting in the passenger positions to the right of the drivers made themselves as small as possible in their seats. The men in the turrets ducked down and braced for the shockwave and flying shrapnel.

The team was travelling too fast to be able to stop in time. If they braked at that moment, they would have come to a halt in the centre of the killing area. Instead they had to try and push through.

A deafening roar, followed by a wave of heat and a temporary vacuum, caused every ear to pop within the team, followed by a loud ringing. Vision was distorted as the shockwave jerked the eyes in their sockets and caused the brain to rattle inside the skull, which had an effect similar to being unexpectedly punched in the jaw.

The pressure wave forced the lead truck to tilt momentarily onto its two left wheels before it rocked back over to the right, forcing it to swerve across the road as Jim fought for control.

Bangs and thuds echoed throughout the vehicles as shrapnel and debris slammed and embedded itself in the outer steel casing of the vehicles.

The three drivers, hardly able to see through the dust storm created by the blast, unable to hear due to the ringing and popping of their ears, and incapable of any other thought through the concussion of the explosion, accelerated away from the danger area and concentrated on keeping their vehicles on an even keel.

Stu, regaining a moment of self control after being tossed about in the turret, gripped his gun and began to scan for any sign of a follow-up with small arms fire or vehicles from the surrounding area. Nothing stirred, except for a large grey and brown cloud behind them.

"Fuck me. The bastards hit us with a fucking daisy chain," he called over the net.

Whoever had planted the row of improvised explosive devices had used a method known as a 'daisy chain', made up from a number of devices strung together and lining a length of road and set to go off as one, and intended to ensure maximum damage to a convoy.

The daisy chain intended for Marcus' team had been spotted by Ian as he scanned the road to the left and right from his vantage point in the turret behind the machinegun. It had been planted too close to the roadside and they had avoided it before it caught them in the kill zone as they had roared at full speed out from the town of Tuz.

They had had time to cross to the opposite carriageway, and as a result the only damage done was that they were peppered with a few chinks of shrapnel, cracked outer layers of armoured glass, and Stu had a damaged rear wheel. The vehicles were fitted with run flat tyres and they continued for ten kilometres before they decided to stop and check over their trucks while they replaced the wheel.

They needed a break, and Marcus decided that they would pull off from the main road and travel along a dirt track to lie up in a piece of dead ground for one hour to give them the chance to get some food and recover their senses after the shock of the attack.

"So then," Ian turned to Zaid as they both sat tucking into their rations. "How does it feel being on the business end of one of your IEDs then?"

Zaid looked at him blankly, understanding nothing that had just been said to him.

Hussein, chewing a large chunk of tuna, spoke for him. "He doesn't speak much English, Mr Ian."

"Okay then," Ian turned on Hussein with venom in his voice. "Well, what did you think of it? You've probably planted plenty of the fuckers but never been on the receiving end. It's a shame none of you were killed, so you would know how it feels to lose a friend in one."

Hussein had stopped chewing, his eyes glanced down at his feet and for a moment Ian thought he would not reply.

Then he spoke. "Mr Ian, we have lost many friends too. My brother was killed in an attack from American helicopters who took him and his friends for terrorists planting a bomb by a road; they were actually repairing a water pipe. The helicopters fired rockets and machinegun bullets into them and there was very little for us to bury after that.

"I have lost other friends too, Mr Ian. Friends that had nothing to do with what I did, and some have been killed by private contractors such as you."

"Ian," Yan was standing with a cup in his hand and staring at him. "Leave it mate. We've all had a belly full of this war and suffered our own losses. The world has changed dramatically in recent weeks, and these lads are willing to work with us instead of against us. They did okay today and we've a long way to go, so we may as well let the past be."

"Yan is right, Ian," Sini looked over from the back of his vehicle as he continued to unload boxes of ammunition. "They may be cunts, but they're our cunts."

Everybody burst into laughter, including Marcus and Jim who had been standing off to the side sharing a coffee and studying a map. Even Zaid laughed, though it was doubtful that he understood much of what was said.

Marcus steered them towards a town named Zakho to the west of Dihok, just a few kilometres east of the border. They bypassed Kirkuk and took the lesser roads that led them North between the two large northern cities of Erbil, and Mosul.

All three were major cities and densely populated. Everybody in the team knew that they would be nothing more than a seething mass of the dead and infected by now. With the tightly packed streets and narrow roads, the populations would've been quickly overcome with the virus and the dead would've multiplied at an incredible rate.

Most of the route was flanked with hilly scrubland and open desert with very little in the way of populated areas. The largest urban districts were nothing more than hamlets and farm complexes made from mud bricks and corrugated iron.

The call sign had no reason to stop. They spotted people watching them from around corners of buildings and walls, usually children, frightened and hoping that Marcus and his men were not going to be stopping to rape and loot, as no doubt others had done in some areas.

Marcus' main concern was to reach the border area before nightfall and find a lie up position where they could rest and, at the same time, get visual confirmation on the crossing point and plan their next move from there.

On a secluded stretch of desert road that would normally have seen no more than ten vehicles per day, the convoy came upon the rear of a mass of people headed north; live people. They were refugees, no doubt having walked from Mosul or Erbil and now headed for the border as well.

They saw the approaching convoy, they turned and pleaded with Marcus and his team to take them, to give them food and water. The wretched mob looked starved and close to collapse, but Marcus and his men couldn't do anything for them. If they helped one, they would have to help them all and their supplies were limited.

Instead, the drivers had to gently push their way through the crowd, using their bumpers to nudge them aside, blowing their horns and waving the refugees out of the way.

The noise of the mass pleading and hammering at the windows and against the sides of the vehicles began to unnerve the men inside. With a concerted effort, it could've been possible for the crowd to have climbed up onto the vehicles and maybe overpower the team.

Marcus ordered the turrets to be mounted. "Use your pistols if anyone climbs up, fire warning shots first." He added the last part after he caught Hussein's eye.

There had been hundreds of the refugees and it took a lot of pushing and shoving with the vehicles before they made it through, leaving them behind to survive or die on the road.

It was getting late and the team was approaching the foothills that led up to the ridge line overlooking the border crossing point, west of Zakho, situated roughly four kilometres to the North. They had made the journey in one day as planned, regardless of the problems along the way. They had done well and the strain was starting to show.

Sini, Jim and Yan were starting to struggle with the vehicles as fatigue overcame them. The last thing they needed was to be killed in a road traffic accident due to someone falling asleep at the wheel.

They found a piece of dead ground a few hundred metres along a narrow dirt track that led away from the main road and into the foothills. They had cover from view and it was easily defendable from attack. Marcus doubted that there would be many people travelling that area anyway, especially at night. It was off the beaten track and secluded enough to allow them the chance to relax and recuperate.

Marcus and Stu both wanted to get a look at the border before it was too dark. The rest of the team would stay in the dead ground and refuel the vehicles from the jerry cans and clean and oil the weapons and replenish the ammunition, while Marcus and Stu would head out and try to find a track that would lead them up to the top of the ridge.

"Mr Marcus, let me come with you," Hussein said as he stepped forward.

Stu huffed, "Why would you want to come with us?"

"If we are going to be working together, then we need to see how you do things. I don't want us to be just passengers, Mr Stu. We will do all we can to earn our place with you."

Marcus nudged Stu. "He's got a point, Stu, let him come along." He nodded to Hussein and moved back to his vehicle to collect his weapons and assault vest.

An hour later and Marcus, Stu and Hussein were walking along the ridge line toward a point that would give them the best view of the border. What they saw disheartened them. The border itself followed the line of the river Nahr Al Khabur that formed a natural barrier between the two countries, with bridges and control points in key areas.

The main crossing point consisted of a large terminal complex that spanned a wide area on the Iraqi side of the border, with buildings and warehouses and open spaces for large trucks and cargo to be stored or unloaded and checked before being allowed to cross.

Two bridges spanned the river leading into Turkey. They were now blocked off with huge concrete barriers and upturned cars to block anyone or anything from crossing. At the Southern point of the bridges was a large chain link fence, topped with rolls of barbed wire.

On the Turkish side, they could see a large number of tanks and men occupying defensive positions that covered the bridge; anyone who approached would be obliterated before even reaching the fence.

Beyond the defensive line, about ten kilometres to the North, as he peered through his binoculars, Marcus could see helicopters taking off and landing. Obviously a reaction force of gunships, no doubt in case anything more of a threat than the refugees and infected turned up that the ground units couldn't handle without air support; the Iraqi Army still had a lot of units in the field and many had probably gone rogue by now and would be looking to save themselves.

Blackened cars and trucks littered the roads approaching the bridge and gate area. Thousands of bodies, many of which had probably been living healthy people before they were mowed down, covered every inch of tarmac and asphalt.

As they peered through their binoculars, they saw the swarms of infected that travelled West along the road coming from the direction of Zakho. A large black throng of bodies were steadily making their way toward the crossing point. Marcus thought it would be interesting to see how the Turks reacted to the crowd, but they couldn't wait around to satisfy their morbid curiosity. Judging by the amount of armour and the helicopter gunships, it would more than likely be a one sided fight anyway.

"Well, that's a no go," Stu sighed. "What we gonna do now buddy?" He turned to look at Marcus, hoping he had other ideas and options in mind.

"Fucked if I know, Stu. I hadn't really thought past this part. And I didn't expect the border crossing to be so strongly defended, but we should've frigging known it would be. I think we were just trying to be optimistic mate." He smiled at Stu.

To Stu, it looked more like the resigned smile of a man who had done what he could and could do no more.

"There must be another way."

"Maybe there is," Hussein said. "What about moving further West along the river?"

Stu scoffed, "And where to, Syria?"

"No, I mean just a little further along than where we are. Iraq has thousands of unofficial border crossing points. It is a country that is pretty much landlocked except for Basrah in the South. How do you think we got most of our weapons that we used against you?"

"Yes, AK47s were easy to get here, but what about the Russian made shaped charge explosives, and the Stinger missiles and French anti-tank weapons? They were all brought across the borders with Iran, Turkey, Jordan, Saudi and Syria. Smuggled in goods vehicles or ferried through un-surveyed crossing points, or even brought in under the noses of the Turkish and Iraqi Army guards that manned the smaller crossing points all along the country."

"Where did you find this bloke, Marcus?"

"I'm not sure mate, but he's proving useful." He turned to Hussein. "Do you know of any crossing points up here in the North?"

"Sorry, I do not. But there will be many. They're normally close to small villages and towns that face each other on both sides of the border."

"Ah, that makes sense," Stu added. "We may as well go firm for the night and push out, paralleling the river at first light. What do you think?"

The three of them returned to the rest of the group and informed them of what they had seen at the border and the plan for the next day.

The weapons had been cleaned and Sini and Yan had started a small fire in the centre of the vehicles. For a while, they all sat and discussed the options in front of them, studying maps and aerial photographs, looking for villages close by the river that they thought would hold a crossing point.

They saw one that looked feasible. It was roughly fourteen kilometres West of the main crossing point at Zakho. The village on the Iraq side didn't even seem to have a name, but the one directly opposite, in Turkey, was called Ovakoy.

It was nothing more than a cluster of farm houses, close to an area where the river was relatively narrow. They saw no bridge on the maps or the photos, but they did notice what looked like tracks that led down to the water's edge and continued on the other side.

"Man that has to be a crossing, maybe a ford. But you can bet your arse that it'll be guarded. Whether the Turkish government knew of it before or not, they probably do now and they aint gonna leave it open for them dead fucks to just waltz across." Jim, with a smouldering cigarette between his lips, was leaning over Ian's shoulder staring at the aerial photograph he was studying.

"Yeah, thanks for that, Jim. Do you mind pulling your cigarette outta my fucking ear now?"

Hussein, Zaid and Ahmed, the third of the insurgent group, sat talking, sharing a mug of tea in the evening air. Their weapons were close by and ready to use; an indication, as far as Marcus and Stu were concerned, that either they were worried of being attacked by the team during the night, or anything else that approached. Or, it showed that they were experienced and disciplined and they took care of their weapons and they kept them within reaching distance.

"What do you think the score is with them then? Do you think they're genuine?"

"I dunno, Stu. To be honest, there's something about Hussein that I like. He speaks openly and says what he thinks. He doesn't seem to mince his words, and in my book, that's always a good trait. Don't get me wrong though, the minute I suspect he will fuck us over, I'll rip his throat out. I suppose we'll see, won't we?"

The next morning, just as the sky began to brighten in the East and before the sun had risen above the horizon, everybody was in their positions and ready to move. Marcus decided to put the Iraqis in the driving seats, partly to free up people to man the guns and also to begin to test them out as members of the team. All the time, the vehicle commanders would be watching and keeping an eye on them.

They headed West along dirt tracks that were barely visible except for the tyre prints of trucks that had travelled them in the past. There were no villages or farms between them and the possible crossing point and they expected to see no one along the route.

Marcus was studying his GPS and guiding the lead vehicle along the tracks and paths. By mid morning they were approaching the village on the Iraqi side of the river. The village was a kilometre ahead of them with the ground rising slightly to their right, obscuring their view of the river that lay just five hundred metres to the North.

He knew that just South of the village would be a crossroads where they would need to turn right to pass through the hamlet and onto the bank of the river facing Ovakoy. They were completely in the dark about what the river would be like. They didn't even have any information about the village and Ian had recommended that they stop short and send out a reconnaissance patrol to have a look at the crossroads and village before they moved any closer.

The team went static and everyone gathered around Marcus for a quick set of orders on what needed to be done.

"Stu, Ian and Yan, you three will push forward and conduct the recon. Take Ahmed with you in case you need an interpreter. His English isn't the best, but he does seem to understand most of what's being said."

Ahmed smiled, "Thank you." He actually seemed genuinely pleased to be counted as a member of the team.

Marcus nodded to him in acknowledgement and continued speaking to the rest. "Don't push into the village. Just get eyes on. The main thing I want to know is if it's occupied or not, and if it is, by who? Also, don't get carried away and decide to approach the river. We'll do that once we have a decent position that we can lie up in and defend if need be."

Everybody understood what needed to be done and after a quick chat between Stu, Ian, Yan and Ahmed, they were ready to move and pushed West toward the junction.

Two hours later they returned, informing them that the village was deserted – devoid of both the living and infected. They had crossed the junction and pushed a kilometre further to the West to ensure that there were no other buildings in the area or roaming infected. They reported that they had seen neither.

Happy with their findings, Marcus decided that they would move up to the junction and form a defensive position just to the East of it, with the vehicle-mounted machineguns covering the approach routes and continuing to use the upward sloping ground to their right as cover from the river and anyone who may be watching from the other side.

Once in position, they began preparing for the next reconnaissance patrol. The task was to get an idea of what the river and crossing point consisted of directly North of the village. Marcus wanted to lead the patrol himself, not that he didn't trust the others to do the job properly, but because he wanted a clear picture in his mind of what they were up against to help him form a plan.

Marcus and Ian crept through the village, contouring the slope as closely as possible so that they didn't expose themselves in the open. Hussein and Stu followed at the rear. The four of them pushed up to a position where they had an over watch on the river and opposite bank. They lay along a raised irrigation ditch and observed the scene.

In front of them, just a couple of hundred metres away, were motionless bodies all along the road. Civilians and soldiers lay mangled and twisted together where they had been mowed down by machineguns as they approached the river.

Some had lain dead for as long as a week from what Marcus could tell. Their bodies had blackened in places, and as the gases inside them expanded in the heat of the sun, the bodies had bloated, forming grotesque inflated lumps of rotting flesh with limbs sticking out erect from their bodies.

There were a number of vehicles, filled with bullet holes, with shattered glass, burst tyres and dead occupants, littering the sides of the track.

Even a burnt out tank lay close to the river, its gun pointing to the ground like a dying monster. The presence of a destroyed tank indicated that there were more than just armed guards on the far side.

"Fuck, there must be an anti-tank unit over there at least, maybe even another tank," Ian didn't sound too pleased about the prospect of having to go up against armour.

"There," Stu pointed to an area two hundred metres beyond the river and slightly to the right of the track, "looks like a T-72, and it's dug in."

The barrel was pointed straight at the spot where the track disappeared into the river. It had moved into a 'hull-down' position that left just its turret visible above an embankment of dirt that surrounded it, acting as a layer of protection.

A hundred metres further back from the tank, just below the brow of a small hill and to the left they saw a heavy machinegun position. The weapon was a Dushka 12.7 mm heavy machinegun. Even though their vehicles were armoured, just the Dushka on its own could chew them up without much effort, even without the tank.

"Shit, this doesn't look good at all does it? We could always cross on foot further downstream, but we need the vehicles if we want to stand a chance of getting anywhere." Marcus was thinking out loud.

"I'm not going anywhere without the vehicles mate," Ian stated.

There looked to be roughly twenty men manning different positions beyond the river. Whoever had sighted the positions, though, lacked experience. They were placed in a linear formation with all their fields of view concentrated on the East and the crossing point. From what could be seen, they had paid no attention to their flanks whatsoever.

The defences had no depth other than the tank and the machinegun position. If attacked, the men in the front line defences had no fall back positions and no one to support them as they moved. Normally, there would be at least a second line of defences to the rear of the main line, creating depth.

The heavy machinegun on the hill, though in a good position to cover the track and support the defensive positions in front of them, didn't look to be manned with any discipline. Neither Marcus nor any of the others could see anyone manning the gun and observing their arcs of fire.

It was more than likely that they conducted a passive sentry duty, and instead of being proactive and watching the approaches, pushing out clearance patrols now and then, they just reacted when and if they were warned by the troops closer to the river of people approaching. Maybe they had become complacent from boredom?

Marcus also noted that the Dushka would have to be mounted on a tripod because of its size, weight and recoil when fired, meaning that from its position, it could cover the river, but nothing directly below it on the slope of the hill due to the lack of depression in the tripod it rested on.

For hours, the four of them sat and watched the routine of the Turks on the opposite bank. Now and then, they would see troops walking in and around the buildings scattered along the Northern side of the track that led up from the river.

They identified what appeared to be the command centre. A single storey mud hut to the right and slightly to the rear of the defensive positions had an array of antennas and wires outside and on top of the roof. People seemed to be coming and going constantly from the building.

There were two guards who patrolled the riverbank. They walked from East to West for a hundred metres, then turned and headed back. Normally they would then sit by a low stone wall and smoke cigarettes and chat. They both seemed to be more interested in their conversations and smoking than actually being alert and a forward warning to their comrades.

As they watched, they saw a man and a woman approaching along a track that ran close to the river on the Iraq side. They walked slowly and apprehensively, picking their way through the bodies and vehicles that surrounded them as they moved closer to the crossing point. They were not infected from what Marcus could tell, and there was a young girl of no more than four years old with them, who he presumed was their daughter.

The soldiers that were sitting by the wall saw them approach and stood. They hollered something to the rear and a few more soldiers appeared, swaggering confidently as they eyed the approaching family.

They waved for the family to cross and come closer. As the man and woman reached the far side with the child in tow, the soldiers began to crowd around them, laughing and jostling one another, clearly drunk.

They started to push and shove the man and before long, someone hit him, knocking him to the ground. The others began to kick and beat him with the butts of their rifles. They laughed whenever one of their comrades failed to connect with a good enough hit for their liking and encouraged each other along, giving tips on how to give the perfect butt stroke. The man, at first, repeatedly tried to stand under the blows, but eventually he was left in a heap and lay bleeding from numerous cuts to his head and face.

The little girl was crying and clinging to her mother's leg for protection. One of the soldiers, having lost interest in using the man as a human football, grabbed the little girl from her mother and dragged her away. He forced her to sit on the ground and then dragged the man over, who was almost unconscious, and threw him down beside her.

The men closed in around the woman. At first they shoved her from one to the other and laughed as they tugged at her clothing. She was terrified and she cried and pleaded as they battered her to the ground.

They crowded in on her and ripped the remaining clothes away from her exposing her pale, soft skin. She tried in vain to cover herself by holding her hands across her breasts and between her legs.

The men grabbed her arms and legs and splayed her across the ground and began to take it in turns raping her, all the time, her husband and daughter forced to watch at gunpoint. Her screams echoed around the hills, and eventually she had become limp and silent as they continued to beat and ravish her.

Marcus, Stu, Ian and Hussein watched in horror. Their faces tense, and Stu pulled away and sagged down the embankment, refusing to watch anymore.

When the soldiers had had their fill, they stood and walked back to the husband and young girl, laughing and joking, slapping each other's backs and congratulating each other on their masculinity while the woman lay whimpering and curled up in the foetal position, bleeding profusely from between her legs.

They dragged the woman and her husband and child to the river where they were dumped together, side by side and face down. A soldier, who seemed to do most of the talking and appeared to be the highest rank of the group, pulled a pistol from his belt and shot each one in turn through the back of the head without so much as a blink, then waved to a couple of his men and gestured to the bodies. The men nodded and dragged the family to the riverside and dumped them into the water, allowing the current to wash them away downstream.

"Fucking bastards." Ian's face was clenched and Marcus saw small traces of tears well in his eyes.

"That's settled then," Marcus announced. "We hit the fuckers."

Marcus and Ian split from Stu and Hussein, leaving them in position to continue observing while they decided to move to the West along the river, in an attempt to find a secluded crossing point that could be forded on foot and would give them cover from view.

They wanted a narrow point of the river that was not too deep or fast flowing that would cause them to be swept away when they tried to cross. Three hours later and they approached Stu and Hussein from the rear.

"Stu," Marcus whispered from ten metres away trying to get his attention. "Stu, you deaf shit."

This time Stu turned around.

Marcus held up a thumb to him, asking if all was okay. Stu returned the gesture and Marcus signalled for him and Hussein to move back to him and Ian.

Once they were all together, they made their way back through the village and to the rest of the group where they collated all the information they had gathered.

Sini began to heat up some water for them to make coffee and tea and prepared some food from the rations.

"What we got then guys?" Jim was keen to know what they had seen.

Marcus sat down on a box and everyone gathered around with chocolate bars and mugs of tea while he explained the situation, using the map to point to positions they had plotted.

"We've got a defensive position on the far bank, with one tank that we can see and a heavy mounted machinegun, and roughly twenty infantry in defensive positions."

He then went on to give details of their layout, weapons, communications, discipline and routine. At the end he told them about what they had done to the family who had crossed the river.

Curses and mutterings went around the team as they pondered what they had just heard.

"We are gonna take them on aren't we, Marcus?" Yan wanted to know.

Marcus looked up and eyed each team member in turn. "Well, what you all think? We have to cross somewhere. We won't get far on foot so, what do you think?"

"Fuck it, I'm up for it," Stu said.

Jim was just as keen. "Hell yeah. Let's nail 'em."

The team were in unison. They all wanted to attack the position. All they had to do now was work out how to do it.

Marcus already had a basic plan in his head and Stu suspected that he knew what he had in mind.

18

It had been two days since Steve and his small band of refugees had arrived at the Safari Park. They had settled in amongst the many rooms available and he had made a point of making sure that Jennifer and Helen's rooms were close by.

He felt accountable for them and he had to stop and check himself now and then. It had taken the world falling apart for him to see himself as a responsible leader, but he was far from uncomfortable with it. In fact, it gave him a higher sense of purpose.

Maybe I should've joined the army after all? he thought.

On the first night, most of the people in the mansion had gathered to hear what news, if any, could be gained from the steadily faltering networks that still remained on air. A large TV screen had been placed in the main foyer, and although it was on for the majority of the day anyway, it had become a sort of ritual for everyone to congregate around it at the same time every evening.

Everybody watched intently as the images flashed across the screen and the trembling voices of reporters in the thick of the action gave running commentaries on what they were witnessing.

Entire armies across the world had been literally swallowed up as they fought to stem the tide of the rapidly increasing hordes of infected that spread across every continent. Nearly every major city in the world had fallen or was about to fall. Much of the fighting had spilled into the villages and small towns scattered throughout the countrysides of the world.

The bulk of the Western armies were still either fighting their way out of the Middle East, or already en route in troop carrier ships and cruise liners that had been commandeered to facilitate the huge amount of men and equipment as they raced back to their respective countries to help with the wars on the home fronts.

Large evacuations of mainland America and Britain were in progress, and thousands of refugees flocked to the many islands that lay scattered off shore. Around Scotland and the South of England, the numerous islets that sat just a short boat ride away from the mainland and giving a degree of security, were flooded with people who sought to escape the tidal wave of dead and infected that ravaged all in their path, leaving only more dead in their wake.

The Channel Islands had been declared as 'off limits' to anyone fleeing the mainland and it was soon suspected that it had been made into a 'safe haven' for the rich and powerful, including politicians and royalty.

There were reports that rogue military units from the Royal Army, Royal Navy and Royal Air Force had seized control of the Channel Islands and claimed them for themselves, causing a war within a war as rebel units and others still loyal to the government engaged one another to gain control. The last reports to come from Jersey were that all efforts of a counter attack had been repelled, leaving the government troops badly mauled and in retreat. There was no news of what had become of the rich and powerful who had escaped to the safe zones, and rumours soon broke out of revolutionary-style retribution being carried out against them by the breakaway military groups that had gained control of the islands.

The people gathered in the lobby, watched in silence and shock as the video footage showed throngs of panicking people rushing at the ferries and boats at the docks in the hope of getting passage to the safe areas. In some ports, infected overran the security cordons and ploughed into the crowds and tore through them and onto the boats as they consumed the thousands of refugees. Some of the boats and ferries were able to get away in time, but others floundered and became easy prey as the mass of infected charged aboard and wreaked havoc throughout the decks.

There was no good news and people began to turn away as they had had enough of the carnage that seemed to infest every corner of the globe. Eventually, everyone retreated into their own areas and while some carried on with what they were doing beforehand, others remained silent and withdrawn as they slowly lost hope for the future.

Steve and his small band of survivors had met everyone there by the end of the first night. Some people were cheery and polite. Others were distant and clearly struggling to come to terms with events. Some had lost people close to them and one or two just sat in a daze, staring into open space and silent. Others cried continuously and openly, sitting and rocking themselves as they relived the horrible events that had happened to them and remembered the people they had lost.

Steve felt that he could easily get along with the whole group. All, except one. A large fat mouthy woman named Stephanie who had been one of the management staff at the park beforehand and still believed that she was; walking around and speaking loudly and dictating to the younger members of her staff. She was a bully as far as Steve could tell and always spouted negative drivel to anyone who was in earshot.

Steve knew he was going to have a problem with her at some point, and it almost happened on the first night. She sat eating a huge plate of food with her husband, Jason, sitting beside her. She spoke loudly about how she believed that eventually, society would collapse and it would be up to the strong leader sort, like her, to lead humanity out from the dark.

Sophie, an attractive young blonde haired girl no older than eighteen who had also worked at the park commented, "But you were only promoted last October after being here for sixteen years. How come it took so long for your leadership skills to surface?" She was goading her and Steve had to stifle a smirk at Sophie's comment.

It was obvious that the two hated each other with a passion. Stephanie glowered at her nemesis from across the table and snarled, "When the time comes you skinny bint," she pointed her fork at the young woman, "I'll see to it that you get what's coming to you."

Sophie sat grinning at her with her arms folded. She was confident and knew she could probably kick ten bells of shit out of Stephanie before she even knew what had hit her.

All the time, Jason sat nodding at her every word. *Clearly henpecked*, Steve thought. He was a scrawny weedy looking man, and it was obvious who the dominant one was in the relationship. Helen commented later that she suspected Jason of being a 'feeder', supplying his wife with all the junk she could eat because he was turned on by obese women.

"Eh, people actually go for that?" Jennifer was shocked by the concept.

Helen replied, "Yes, and actually, it's more common among men. I've seen a lot of it, especially at the hospital; huge fat women being brought in for one reason or another, and their skinny little husbands following closely, no doubt smuggling in a big bag of cakes for them." She burst into laughter at her own comment, probably remembering a particular experience of it.

"Nah, not for me I'm afraid. Give me a size ten any day, with great legs," Steve announced, shaking his head.

"Good to hear it," Helen nudged him and gave an over animated wink for all to see, "but you've already see me in my underwear haven't you, pervy Steve."

Jennifer started to laugh at his discomfort. Steve flushed red and smiled sheepishly.

Karen and Gary were the life and soul of the group. Despite the situation and the fact that they worried about their son, they always seemed upbeat and positive with easy smiles and a quick wit.

Karen had been an instant hit with the children. They warmed to her like a Grandmother they had only just met, and the fact that she spent most of her day singing and baking probably had something to do with it.

She constantly told stories to the children and adults alike, and Steve couldn't work out whether or not they were true at times, but even so, he too enjoyed the soothing sound of her voice and listened to her tales intently, almost hypnotised by her soft tones.

He had promised Sarah that he would go for her mother, and now he was getting ready to uphold that promise. He had told Claire he would be on the way, but he was still wondering how he was going to do it.

"So you're planning on going back out there then, Steve?" Gary was standing watching him as he unloaded all the kits they had stored in his brother's Range Rover.

Steve sighed as he turned to face his new friend. "I have to, Gary, my daughter's mother is out there and I owe it to Sarah to bring her back, or at least try."

"I understand, Steve, I really do. That's why I'm gonna be coming with you." He smiled. "You can't do it on your own mate, and you'll need all the help you can get. Kevin has volunteered too."

Steve brushed his hands together as he dumped the last of the bags on the gravel at his feet. "I can't ask you to do that, Gary, I really..."

He was cut off as Gary spoke, raising his hand in front of him to silence him. "You've asked for nothing, we offered and it's settled. Though, my wife isn't too impressed with the idea."

Steve nodded. "You're a good man, Gary."

"That's what my wife says too." He was grinning. "Anyway, let's get a brew and work out what we need to do."

Steve, Gary and Kevin sat in the lobby on the large leather sofas discussing their plan.

"Best thing is to get in and out as quickly as possible. I'll phone or text Claire when we are on our way and give her a rough estimate of when we'll be there. We should take the route I took getting here actually, mainly country roads and that."

Gary and Kevin nodded in agreement. "Yeah sounds good," Kevin said.

Later, they found themselves sitting together again. A kinship of sorts had formed between them. As three people who were about to go and face a terrible danger together, they were drawn together from sharing in the knowledge that they could very well soon be dead.

"I'm still struggling to get my head around all of this you know," Steve spoke and nodded towards the doors, indicating the outside and the situation beyond.

"What's there to get our heads around, Steve? It was inevitable that humanity wasn't going to last. We are like a star that burned brighter than others, but faded sooner." Gary sat back in his seat, one hand stroking his short white beard as he spoke.

Kevin looked at him. "Gary, you been at the whisky again? I haven't a clue what you just said."

"Are you looking for theories on what is happening, or why?"

"Both," Steve replied.

"Well," Gary began, "what is happening is quite obvious. For some reason, a plague has swept the globe and caused the dead to rise and attack the living. From what I can gather, it began on the Southern hemisphere and spread North. Originally, it was flu, and it mutated again and again and now it's become like some kind of spore, drifting through the air and reanimating corpses. People are still becoming sick with the flu strain, and some become aggressive and attack others before they succumb to the illness and die, then come back as the walking dead.

"I've seen lots of reports from the so called experts and none of them can give solid answers. But one thing I have gained from the reports is; they have no need of nourishment, there's no real reason why they feed on the living. All their internal organs are dead and inactive and slowly rotting away at the same rate as the rest of their bodies. Apparently, it's a deep instinct that has been triggered by the portion of the brain that reanimates, and they seek only warm living flesh. Not all of the brain comes back. Only the central core still shows any sign of activity. And that is where the method of destroying them comes in; they can only be killed by a gunshot or heavy blow to the head."

Steve nodded. "That'll explain a lot. From what I've seen, there's no reasoning power amongst them, no speech or any higher level of intelligence. I believe that they're dead, but I still can't get my head around it. I've never heard anything like it, except in the Bible, and that doesn't say anything about the dead eating the living when they rise up on Judgement Day. You think it could be biologically engineered?"

"You can listen to all the religious nut jobs spouting off about the 'End of Days' on the internet, or watch the nerdy man wearing a lab coat with a comb over trying to baffle us with formulas and such when they have no idea what is actually causing it. Maybe we aren't supposed to know why this is happening.

"Think about it. Look at the dinosaurs. For over one hundred and sixty million years they ruled the planet. Granted, they never learned how to make fire and never landed on the moon. But their reign was a long one, and they thrived from species to species. They never damaged the planet or waged war on each other. There was a healthy balance in the ecosystem and although fierce and brutal as it must've been at times, they stayed in line with nature."

Steve nodded, understanding where Gary was taking his train of thought, "Yeah, but still, they became extinct and then we come along."

"Yeah we did. But we didn't show up the day after all the dinosaurs had died did we? There was a gap of about sixty million years before anything resembling us started to walk the earth."

"And your point is?" Kevin asked.

"My point, young fellow, is that maybe Mother Nature became bored of the dinosaurs and killed them off, then took some time off before deciding on her next big thing. Maybe she wanted something completely different? Something that could adapt to her changes in nature, to be able to think and create new things and ideas? Maybe," he paused and leaned forward, a stern look at Steve, "Maybe she wanted to create a species that had the potential to rival her in its beauty and creativity?"

"You're just being poetic Gary," Kevin huffed.

Gary turned on him, waving his finger. "Don't play the dumbass, Kevin. I know you're smarter than that. You no longer have to sit there writing in silly ways in text messages anymore and deliberately mispronouncing words. Those days are gone and it's the people who can think for themselves and adapt that will survive this."

Kevin looked at Gary feeling ashamed for his ignorance. It wasn't the first time he had been reprimanded by him. Gary and Kevin had become close, long before the dead began to rise, and now, Gary looked on the young man as a son.

Steve watched the two with interest and saw the close father and son style bond just from their body language. "So, what you're saying is, is that Mother Nature screwed up?"

"Well, yeah, sort of. Or maybe we were just an experiment that she's gotten fed up with."

Kevin had put his grown up head on. "And now she's getting rid of us? Surely there's easier ways to do that?"

"Yes, there is, but you know me, I'm not religious at all, but the Bible bashers always say that God works in mysterious ways. Well, I say the same for old Mother Nature. You ever heard of Necrotizing Fasciitis?"

Steve and Kevin shook their heads.

Gary continued, "It's a flesh-eating virus. Maybe our dead are now just a new version of it? What if Mother Nature has watched and thought 'Okay, you want to act like a virus? Well I'll show you' and this is a result? I believe that she has tried to warn us throughout history, but in our arrogance, we ignored the signs.

"The most recent being the tsunamis and earthquakes that have killed millions over the last decade, and that strain of swine flu that broke out in 2012, it was stronger and deadlier than the strain of 2009, but still, we carried on, out of control and with our heads buried deep in the sand and as a result, this sneaked up and now we're getting our arses bitten off."

Steve was enjoying the conversation and wanted to hear more of what Gary wanted to say. "So, we pissed her off?"

"Absolutely," Gary exclaimed, "we pissed her off good I think. Consider this," he glanced from Kevin and Steve in turn, then down to his fingers, pushing them back as though counting off his points of view, "we humans, that is, anatomically modern-appearing humans, originated in Africa about two hundred thousand years ago. It took from then until the late eighteen hundreds for the human population to reach two billion.

"If you look at the life of the Earth as a clock face, imagine it had started at twelve o'clock with its birth, and it was back at twelve o'clock now having done a full rotation, then humans only arrived in the last fifteen seconds."

He paused so that Steve and Kevin could take in what he was saying and judge the time scale for themselves.

"Now then, in just over one hundred years, the population has more than tripled from two billion, to seven billion. That's against nature in my eyes."

"How do you mean, against nature?" Kevin asked.

Gary ticked off another finger. "Because, of the rate of expansion. Only up until recently have we been able to vaccinate, cure and eradicate certain diseases. Smallpox for instance, killed thousands. Now, it doesn't exist, apart from a small amount in a test tube in a lab somewhere.

"Left to nature, many of the natural illnesses and defects that plague man would kill us. Look at families, they used to be huge and it was common that some of the children born to a man and woman wouldn't make it to adulthood for one reason or another. Death during childbirth was a common occurrence once and people born handicapped or disabled rarely survived. Don't get me wrong, I'm not saying that was a good thing, I'm just saying that the chances of survival through life had risen for everyone during the twentieth century."

"Right," Kevin butted in, "before you tell me off for 'dumbing down' again and send me to bed without supper, you really have lost me, Gary."

Gary smiled at him and nodded. "What I'm getting at, Kev, is that the mortality rate has dropped amongst humans, and as a result, the rest of the planet has suffered."

Another finger was ticked off. "It's my opinion, and this is just an opinion mind you, that Mother Nature never intended for us to take the path that we did. I believe that she wanted someone that could interact and live alongside nature, as well as advance and think for themselves. But maybe she got our programming wrong when she created us?

"Instead of a species that lived in harmony with its surroundings, we developed into something more like a virus. We spread and multiplied and ravaged the planet, destroying everything she had created for us. We, Homo-Sapiens, annihilated Neanderthal Man as well as thousands of other species of animals and brought many more close to extinction. We polluted her beautiful atmosphere, waged war on one another.

"Eventually we became what we are now. And that is my next point." He was in full flow and he pushed back yet another finger. "What are we now? Well, what were we before the dead started to walk? We were consumers. The word consumer and its usage to describe us, causes my piss to boil, but it's become a byword for the human race. It's perfectly acceptable now and seven billion people consented to the label that the governments, banks and big corporations labeled us with. But the label is pretty accurate. Like I mentioned before, we became like a virus. We went forth and multiplied and along the way, consumed everything in our path."

He paused, no one else spoke and he continued. "In the twentieth century man became the scourge of the earth. The industrial age was in full swing and all matter of crap was being pumped into the atmosphere. Oil became one of our main sources of power and at that point, man found his true greedy self. No one bothered about the damage that we did to the planet. The air was filled with the by-products and nobody cared. Land was destroyed and carved up to make way for the oil derricks and pipelines. Look at the wars over the stuff. During the Second World War, many of the main objectives of all the armies involved were to seize, or destroy and cut off the enemy oil supplies. The Falklands War, there's oil beneath those islands and I don't believe what was said about it being a matter of national pride, it was a war waged for oil. The two Gulf Wars were for black gold. And I don't care how much any government spouts off with their token gestures for the environment by raising fuel tax and toll booths. Even when there isn't open fighting, the oil war wages. People are killed, whole towns subdued, countries trodden down. It all boils down to money. And it's the politicians and oil barons that sit back and reap the spoils.

"Then came the nuclear age, followed by the digital age; the nuclear age had its own side effects and everyone has seen enough video footage of nuclear test sites and Hiroshima and Nagasaki to know the destruction we could cause the planet. Even when it is so called used for good causes, such as energy, look at Japan a couple of years ago after the earthquake. Remember the damage?

"And, most recently, something that I believe was the most destructive age of all; the digital age. Not in a physical sense, but in a moral one. The whole planet was plugged into the 'world wide web'. Information was accessible to anyone who wanted it.

"The human race has been turned into mindless drones that sit in front of TVs or computers and soak up the rubbish pumped out in the name of entertainment. Celebrities; it has become perfectly acceptable to take someone from the street with no talent whatsoever, an IQ well below average and turn them into multi millionaires with books being written about them and perfumes made with their names on for no apparent reason other than they were so called entertaining on some stupid reality TV show through being so ignorant and stupid.

"People have become addicted to drivel that is readily available through a wire that is plugged into your home and into your computer or TV. The next step would've been just to plug it into the back of our heads and no one would then need to live their lives, they could *virtually* live them and the corporations would control the masses like in that movie about the robots taking over.

"Look at pornography. It was once a taboo and not easily come by unless you knew where to get it, or a friend had a secret stash that he bought from Amsterdam. Now, all you have to do is click on the internet and anything you want is there in front of you. Simple, straight forward sex isn't enough anymore, it has to be extreme and shocking. Children being exposed to it, children being manipulated and abused by it.

"Look at us, our technological advance in the last century has been at an extraordinary rate. When man landed on the moon, the power they had in their computers back then was no more than what we have in the average calculator or digital watch now. But they did it and reached beyond the boundaries of human limitations. Now, with the knowledge and equipment available, we should've been colonising Mars and looking to travel beyond our Solar System. Instead, the technology was wasted. In my opinion, Mother Nature is not just angry, but she is ashamed of us."

Steve whistled through his teeth, a long low-sounding whistle. "Jesus, when you put it like that, Gary, I feel quite shit about us."

"Well that's the conundrum, Steve. In small groups, closely knit communities and families, maybe like what we have here now," he swept his arm across the room, "we do well. Throw us into a giant city with millions of people crammed so close together that we have to build huge concrete structures to inhabit like rats, and then we become viral. We fight and we squabble and we consume and kill. Greed has overcome us fellas and Mother Nature has finally said 'enough is enough'"

They sat and talked until late in the night. Helen and Jennifer had sat and joined in with the conversation and offered their own thoughts and feelings on the situation.

Soon, it had turned into an open debate, with glasses of whisky and more people joining in. Jake, the man who had been in charge of all of the parks electronic systems and communications, was very animated in his descriptions and his theories. It was apparent from the start that he was gay but the more glasses he drank, the more camp he became.

Steve found him hilarious and Helen and Jennifer had taken a shine to him also. "See, I've even got my own fag-hags at the end of the world," he declared.

Finally, Gary announced, "Well, it's been interesting, but some of us are up early aren't we, Steve? We need our ugly sleep." He made a short bow to the congregation and walked away, headed for the stairs.

Helen seized the chance to catch Steve alone. She pulled him to one side in the hallway when he came back through from the kitchen as he headed for the stairs.

"Steve, do you really have to be going out there tomorrow? I mean, it seems like a big risk to me and after all, you have your daughter to think about."

"That's why I'm not taking her, she's staying here," Steve replied.

"Don't be coy, Steve, you know what I mean." Her eyebrows knitted together as she spoke and her tone was deadly serious.

"Look," he sighed, "she's the mother of my daughter. It's not that I feel some sense of loyalty or duty to her, but it's for Sarah that I have to do this. I explained the same thing to Gary."

She nodded, "Okay, I don't have kids myself, so maybe it's harder for me to get my head around, but be careful out there, Steve."

"I will."

"I haven't thanked you properly for helping me."

He went to butt in but she spoke over him. "If you hadn't taken me with you, I'd be dead by now." She reached up on her tiptoes and kissed his cheek and whispered, "Be careful, Steve, please?"

She turned away and walked up the stairs to her own room, leaving Steve standing at the bottom rubbing the patch on his cheek where he had felt her warm lips kiss him. He looked around to see if anyone had witnessed the exchange and then climbed the stairs, whistling cheerily to himself.

That night he lay in bed, thoughts running through his mind.

To start with, about the day ahead of him and what could happen and how they were to do it. Scenarios of the possible obstacles raced through his mind and before he could think through a solution to one foreseen mishap, another scenario would crop up. In the end he resigned himself to the fact that he was just going to have to deal with it as it came and react fast on his feet.

Still, it didn't help him to sleep.

Then, his mind started to drift to something else, and he fell asleep thinking about Helen, the lovely Nurse Helen.

19

"Okay lads, this is the plan." Marcus stood in front of his assembled team with a notepad in his hand containing timings and specific orders for individuals.

Ian and Stu had built a scaled sand model of the area. It showed their current location, the village on the Iraq side and the river. Also it showed the opposite hamlet and the far side with the high ground and enemy positions, including the tank, machinegun position and suspected command post and surrounding buildings. Jim had insisted on donating a cigarette packet to denote the tank.

The model was layered and showed the relief and lay of the land in 3D. If there was a hill on the opposite bank of the river, then there would also be a scaled down version of it on the model. It needed to be as accurate to the ground as possible so that everyone could get a clear view in their mind's eye of what lay in the target area and immediately around them.

It was also orientated to the ground with a North pointer and an indication of the scale and distances between features. Marcus pointed to various positions for people to sit in relation to the ground and their tasks, so that they could get an idea of what the landscape would look like ahead of them during the actual mission.

It reminded Jim of a battlefield that he had built as a child in his garden for his toy soldiers that he had then stood over, pretending to be a general high up in a helicopter observing his men as they advanced.

The team worked from a system that they had learned in the army. While Marcus planned the operation to the last detail, the rest of the team conducted what was known as 'concurrent activity'.

Stu and Ian built the model and the rest of the men checked, cleaned and oiled the weapons. Ammunition and magazines were checked and redistributed. Then they went through and reorganised their personal kit, making sure it was sufficient for the task.

Any unnecessary weight would be left behind in a cache area, so that the team could move fast and carry more ammunition during the assault. Everyone stripped their kit to 'fighting order', ditching everything except ammunition. Anything that wasn't to be used in the assault was left in the vehicles.

With everyone seated around the model, Marcus began.

He had a radio antenna in his hand that he used as a pointer for the model to indicate positions as he explained the mission. The rest of the men settled in to listen to the plan as they sipped their coffee and smoked cigarettes.

Marcus began by explaining the model in detail, pointing out the various features that related to the map and the description of the model. The tank, machinegun position, buildings and even the river had all been added to the model using a range of different materials such as ammunition boxes and the blue towel that Ian had ripped up and shaped and added to act as the river.

Next he gave them their individual missions and tasks. He looked to Stu first of all who sat directly across from him on the Southern side of the model. Stu, being the team's second in command, would be in charge of the 'Fire Support Group'.

"Stu, you and Jim will be the FSG with the vehicles, along with the three Iraqis." He nodded to Hussein, Ahmed and Zaid. "They will drive the vehicles and Jim and your self will be the gunners."

He then turned to the remaining three members who sat on the Western side of the model facing East.

"Ian, Yan, Sini and I will be the assault group." The three men nodded in acknowledgement. "Yan, I want you as the gunner for the assault. Dismount one of the machineguns from the turrets and grab as much linked ammo as you can carry without being hindered. The rest of us," he pointed to himself, Sini and Ian, "will be carrying spare boxes of ammo for the gun too. You'll suppress the enemy positions while I, Ian and Sini assault them."

With everyone now aware of their specific tasks, he moved on. "The situation is, we have a defensive position on the far bank with one heavy machinegun," he pointed to its location on the small hill on the model with his radio antenna, "a tank and a line of shell scrapes directly in front of the river. We believe that there are more men billeted in the village that begins fifty metres to the rear of the forward line. We haven't identified any rear protection positions and it seems they've concentrated all their attention directly to their front. Altogether, we estimate between twenty and thirty infantry."

He swept his antenna again over the area of small cardboard ammunition boxes that had been used to simulate the buildings.

"This here," he pointed out a box that had been painted red and had a twig in the shape of an antenna sticking out from the top, "is what looks like their command centre. If they have any idea what they are doing, they more than likely have a mobile reserve to the rear in the city of Silopi, located about ten kilometres North, between this position here, and the border crossing at Zakho. From what we saw last night from the ridge line, it looks like they have air support too."

With the situation on the enemy complete, he went on. "The situation of friendly forces, lads, you know as well as I do, there fucking is none. So there's nothing to tell on that matter."

A low titter resounded amongst the group.

Marcus continued, "Okay, the mission. Our mission is; to destroy all enemy forces in the defensive position within the objective area and withdraw to the North into Turkey." He looked over the group. "It's as simple as that." He then repeated the mission statement. "To destroy all enemy in the defensive position within the objective area and withdraw to the North into Turkey."

"That's pretty fucking straight forward. I like it," Sini commented with nods and grunts of approval from the others.

"Okay then, this is where it gets complicated. Execution and concept of operations," Marcus said as he then went into the details of how they were to do it.

Stu and Jim would provide covering fire from the turret mounted machineguns from two of the vehicles, with the third vehicle remaining just to their rear to act as a backup. They would push forward through the village with their lights off and engines cut to avoid detection, allowing the gentle slope of the track as it dipped toward the river to carry them into position. Stu and Jim would park their vehicles on the South side of the raised irrigation ditch that would provide them with a degree of hard cover from the tank and heavy machinegun on the hill.

They were to hold fire until the signal came from Marcus to engage their primary targets. Stu would be on the left hand side of the track with the best view of the suspected command centre hut.

"Obviously, Stu," Marcus looked up from the model, "we don't have night vision, but hopefully, there'll be enough light at that time of the morning for you to identify the building."

On the signal, Stu would then begin to fire into the command centre in the hope of killing the people inside and disabling the radios. With the building being made of mud brick, the rounds would pass through the walls as if they were not even there and before long, the hut would probably collapse in on itself as the bricks disintegrated, and in the process, cut communications with any reinforcements that they have to the rear.

At the same time, Jim would engage the heavy machinegun position further up on the hill with his turret gun. He would continue to fire burst after burst into it until he was sure that it was neutralised.

"Jim, unless you nail the machinegun crew, then we in the assault team are wide open from our left flank. Most of our attention will be focussed on dealing with the tank and the dismounted infantry in the trenches and buildings, so be sure you destroy them before you switch fire to any secondary targets." Marcus raised his eyebrows and Jim nodded that he understood.

Once the two primary targets; the command centre and Dushka, were out of action, the fire support group would then switch fire to suppress any troops coming from the buildings in the village. The assault group would be advancing across their front from left to right and it would be up to Stu and Jim to keep their line of advance free from enemy reinforcements.

Marcus looked at Stu and Jim. "Remember though, we don't have an unlimited supply of ammo, so get plenty of fire down, but don't waste it if you don't need to."

They both returned with nods and thumbs up gestures.

He turned to Ian, Yan and Sini. "We will push to the West, about a kilometre, and cross the river at the point that Ian and I had a look at earlier. We will then move along the river bank and form up on the start line to the West of the position. Sini and Ian, you will be on the right. I will be in the middle and Yan will be on the left with the machinegun.

"Once we get to the start line, Yan will take up position where he can support the assault with a clear view of the trenches and the village. We will leave the spare machinegun ammo with him and he will act as our immediate fire support as we," he pointed to himself, Ian and Sini in turn, "assault the position."

Yan spoke, "I'll probably be just a hundred metres away from the enemy machinegun position so, please, Jim, kill them with the first burst will you?" He gave Jim a broad smile.

"Will do buddy."

"Have you two finished flirting? If so, can I continue?" Marcus eyed the two in mock annoyance. "The attack will be initiated by me firing an RPG into the tank. You two will carry one each as well." He nodded and pointed to Sini and Ian. "The moment you see the flash from the rocket leaving the tube, Stu, Jim and Yan, plaster your targets. It all needs to go off at the same time, and we can't give them a moment to recover.

"Yan, you will fire on the trenches ahead of the assaulting team, switching fire to the next one along as we go. Be careful of your arcs and keep one eye on us at all times. The last thing we need is a blue on blue and being killed by our own fire support.

"Once we have rolled up the trench positions, Yan, switch fire to the nearest buildings ahead of us. Stu, at that point, you and the rest of the FSG will ford the river and push up behind us looking for further targets in depth.

"That's when Ian, Sini and I will begin the final assault through the huts. Hopefully by then, Stu's group will have pretty much destroyed the place and it should be just a case of sweeping it clear."

Everyone was clear on how it was to be done. "We haven't had the chance to see what their night routine is like, but if their daytime routine is anything to go by, then their security is probably pretty lax. We don't know if they will conduct a 'stand to' or not at first light, but it doesn't matter, 'cause we'll be hitting them just before first light anyway.

"Once the position is clear, we will do a quick check to ensure all enemy are dead and deal with any of our own casualties, then sort our ammunition out and take anything that may be of use. Within a few minutes of the final assault, I want to be heading North like a herd of startled gazelles."

He then went on to detail the 'actions on'. It was a list of 'what if?' scenarios and how they would deal with them. What if they were spotted before the attack was due to start? What if there was a breakdown in communications, if they got lost on the way or walked into an ambush? All these questions needed to be pre-empted and they had to have a clear idea of how they would react to each problem as a team.

"Timings; we will move from here at 03:30 to be in our positions by no later than 04:45. Once there, go firm and wait out. H-hour will be at 05:30, just before first light."

They then synchronised watches to ensure that they all had the exact, to the second, same time as each other.

"The time will be 18:37 in six, five, four, three, two and one." A series of different beeps went off as every member of the team pressed the buttons on their watches to set the time to the exact second.

"Shit, missed it."

The beeps went off together, except one. For as long as Marcus could remember, from his time in the army, to the present day, someone always hit their button just that little bit too early or too late and would then have to run around to find someone to re-sync with after the briefing was over. It was Ian's turn to miss it.

"Fuck sake, it would be me wouldn't it."

Next, he went into the service and support phase of the briefing. "Get a good scoff in you tonight and try and get a kip. The weapons and ammo are squared away. Yan, let me know how much link for the gun you're carrying once you're sorted. All other kits will be left in the SUVs.

"Now then, prisoners." He drew in a deep breath. "We take none. You all know what they do to anyone from this side, and on top of that, we can't carry them and we can't leave them behind in case they make comms with their mates in the reserve."

A grumble of agreement resounded from the throats of all assembled. After what they had witnessed and heard, none of the team felt like taking prisoners anyway.

"Radios will be on channel two. We will do a comms check before we leave here, then radio silence until one minute before H-hour to confirm everyone is in position. Once we go noisy, then I want regular updates from Yan and the FSG on what you're doing. Okay, any questions?"

He paused for a moment to allow for any suggestions. None came. "To summarise, Stu and Jim, hit your primary targets as hard and as quickly as you can. We can't afford a moment for the machinegun or radios to get used.

"Hussein, Zaid and Ahmed," they nodded in anticipation, "stay focused, and do exactly as Jim and Stu tell you. Don't get scared or panic, and remain behind the steering wheel of your vehicles.

"It's surprise, speed and aggression that will get us through this one. The harder and faster we hit them, the less chance they'll have to recover. Keep up the rate of fire and momentum and make sure you're all communicating with each other as you move.

"Once the position is taken, we will quickly reorganise ourselves and check for survivors and anything of use. Once complete, we'll push north as fast as we can to the main crossroads and then turn West."

They conducted a set of rehearsals, with everybody standing in positions that related to where they would be during the attack and what they would be doing. It was known as a 'walk through talk through'. It was just a rough set of rehearsals that put everyone in the complete picture; so that they knew where they would be in respect to everyone else once the shooting started.

The orders briefing was over and everyone moved off to finish their preparation or just to sit with their own thoughts. Everyone was scared, despite the brave faces and wisecracks. Anyone who says they're not afraid before an attack is either insane or lying.

It's the most unnatural thing in the world to do.

Every instinct says not to do it, not to move forward into the hail of enemy fire, the explosions and shrapnel, the man with the gun pointed at you, but it's the years of training and experience that carries professional soldiers forward, when most people would turn and run in the opposite direction.

There is also the sense of duty. Not duty to the crown or government, but the duty to the friends fighting alongside. A soldier doesn't fight for a cause or an idea; he fights for the man at the side of him and the men of his unit.

Stu and Ian sat together as they ate. "Bit outnumbered aren't we?" Ian spoke the same words that Stu had been thinking.

Stu passed his mug of tea to Ian who began slurping away at it. "Yeah, but like Marcus said, we hit them hard enough, we should come out on top. Plus, you saw them yourself; they're not exactly switched on are they?"

"Aye, that's true. Anyway, you've no brew left so I'm off to have a nap." Stu watched as his friend stood and walked away toward his vehicle.

Marcus sat alone thumbing the buttons on his phone as he typed out a text to Jennifer. Before he pressed send he deleted the message. She knew that he loved her, he didn't need to worry her by texting her before an attack and leaving her wondering if he was okay. He would try and call them after it was all over.

It was time to move. The night sky was pitch black and with only a scattering of stars. There was no moon and the landscape was a dull, dark grey around them. Their bodies cast dark silhouettes and it was a while before their eyes began to adjust to the darkness.

They felt grateful for the lack of moonlight, it gave them the extra cover they needed. All it would've taken was for a glint of moonlight to reflect from one of the windows of the vehicles and their plan could be compromised.

There was a slight breeze drifting from the open flat plain of the Iraqi landscape to the South. A chill in the air made the men shiver as they stood close together, anxious to get moving and get the job out of the way.

They gathered around the vehicles and listened in as Marcus gave a set of confirmatory orders, roughly outlining the task ahead. Nothing had changed in the plan and everything was set to go.

Both groups then separated, Marcus and his assault group headed across the junction and toward the West in a wide arc, avoiding getting too close to the river, while Stu and the remainder of the FSG began to push and shove their vehicles across the crossroads and turned right toward the tip of the village.

Even with the ground at a slight slope, it was still difficult to push the heavy armoured monsters through the junction. They had disabled the brake lights and any interior lighting to avoid being detected. Once they had completed the right turn, the wheels turned easier as the SUVs gathered momentum and slowly rolled toward their positions.

The assault group walked one behind the other, with Marcus leading the way. They passed through a field of dying crops and turned North toward the river. They couldn't see it but they could hear it and it grew louder in their ears as they approached. It was perfect cover for them, but Marcus knew it was a double-edged sword. Though it stopped the enemy from hearing them as they drew closer, it also prevented Marcus and his men from hearing anything beyond the river. A battalion of tanks could've parked up in the enemy position and he would never have known.

As they advanced, he heard a sudden commotion behind him; the sound of a weapon being dropped and a body hitting the floor, followed by a grunt and a groan. Had Ian fallen as he walked at the rear of the group?

He heard more grunts and sounds of a struggle, then, he heard the lament of one of the dead.

Marcus sprinted back to the rear of his team. In a heap on the floor he saw three forms as they struggled against each other. Sini was underneath and Yan was crouched over the top, pulling at the body that struggled in between them, trying to pull it away from his friend on the bottom of the pile.

Ian appeared on the other side of them as he ran up from the rear. He stopped short when he saw the body of the infected, thrashing at Sini as he held it away from him, his hands thrust under its chin, holding it at bay.

It grabbed at his head and neck, trying to pull Sini's face closer to its mouth as its teeth gnashed together, over and over. Yan tugged at the clothing of the creature and began to drag it away. He swung both arms to the right and the body tumbled to the ground and away from Sini.

Sini was fast; he drew the knife he had attached to his assault vest and rolled to his left and up into a crouch, the weapon raised and the weight of his body carrying him forward toward the corpse as it struggled to gain its footing for another attack.

Sini closed the gap fast and slammed the blade deep into the top of its skull, burying it to the hilt, feeling the point puncture through the hard bone and into the soft brain inside. He caught his balance before he collapsed with it. The knees of the creature collapsed from underneath and the knife came free in Sini's hand.

He looked down in disgust and wiped the blade on the back of the now permanently dead man sprawled in the grass. The smell of the body assaulted their senses. It had the stink of a corpse that had been left in the sun and that's exactly what it was. It just didn't lie in the sun, it walked in it.

Marcus eyed him and gave him the thumbs up. It wasn't a 'congratulations on a job well done' or in appreciation of his skill; it was a question asking if he was okay and unscathed. Sini patted his body and checked his neck for any damage before he returned the gesture and nodded.

He crouched and picked up his weapon and Yan patted him on the shoulder, nodding, then walked on ahead, close on Marcus' heels.

The river was just fifty metres away and Marcus signalled for his group to stop. Alone, he pushed forward to check the opposite bank as he crouched in the reeds by the waterside. It was clear, and he returned to lead the others across.

Stepping into cold water, during the middle of the night, is never a pleasant experience. It reminded Marcus of his army days. In fact, the whole thing did. He thought that he had left the crawling about in the dark, and conducting recce patrols and river crossings, far behind him when he became a private security contractor.

Marcus had seen plenty of action in his days as a paratrooper. He was involved in operations in Northern Ireland, Africa, the Middle East and the Balkans. Now, he was about to go into battle again, but this time, he invaded a country for his own reasons and with just eight other men. *Better than doing it for weapons of mass destruction that can't be found. Or the war on terror, which was really the rape for oil,* he considered to himself. The thought amused him.

Leading from the front, Marcus pushed to the bank and slid into the water, keeping his weapon above the surface. The cold hit him immediately and he inhaled deeply as the water level reached his groin area, stabbing at him like a thousand needles.

He knew that Ian, being much shorter, would be up to his chest and he didn't envy him. He walked ahead, being careful to place his feet so that he wasn't knocked off balance by the current and swept downstream.

He heard the faint splash of water as Yan slipped in behind him and they ploughed the twenty metre width of the river to the other side. The water pushed at their right hand side, trying hard to sweep them along as it flowed to the West.

When all four men were standing on the far bank, they paused and checked to see that they were still undiscovered. After the soak period, and happy that nothing was stirring, they continued to move to their objective, hugging the river for a few hundred metres then turning north to their forming up position and start line.

His stomach felt hollow and his mind was asking a thousand 'what ifs?'. Stu knew that everyone, including the Iraqis who sat behind the wheels would be asking themselves the same questions.

Every man knew his job, but no amount of training and preparation or experience of battle could block out the apprehension. On the other hand, they all knew that once the first shot was fired, all nerves and doubts would be dropped and the fight carried through on pure adrenalin and aggression.

The clock ticked slowly by and far to the East, on the horizon, the faintest glimmer of pink began to show on the otherwise deep purple, sky.

Marcus lay watching the open ground to his front. The wind caught the wispy strands of grass in front of his face and caused them to brush against his chin as he lay on his stomach with his rifle pointing toward the enemy position.

To his left, he could just make out the faint silhouette of Yan and the machinegun, propped on its bipod legs in front of him. Beyond him, Marcus could barely see the shape of the hill as it touched the horizon. Somewhere, just below the crest, he knew was the Dushka heavy machinegun position, but he couldn't see it in the darkness. The thought of that monster being there. and having the perfect angle on him and his men as they advanced across its front, made him shiver.

He glanced to his right and squinted, trying to focus. He remembered that, to be able to see objects in the dark, he had to scan with his eyes in a sort of figure of eight pattern and once he located it, he should look to the side of it rather than straight at it.

He saw the outline of Ian and he knew that Sini would be just a few metres to the other side of him. All were ready, their weapons were in their shoulders and the safety catches were off with their right index fingers along the outside of the trigger guard.

Marcus looked down at the RPG. It had no night sight capability and he sincerely hoped that there would be enough light for him to be able to identify the tank once H-hour came. The rocket was primed and ready, just the safety catch needed to be clicked to fire and, hopefully, the tank would be neutralised.

He cupped his hand tightly around his watch and brought his eye down to squint as he pressed the button on the side to illuminate it; it read 05:18.

It was close now. He looked at the far Eastern horizon and saw the first glimmers of the pink dawn slowly forcing the inky blackness of the night back toward the west. He looked toward the enemy positions and was now able to distinguish the shapes of the trenches as the dark churned soil contrasted with the lighter coloured grass and scrub of the riverside.

The knot in the pit of his stomach clamped tighter. The cold bony fingers that he felt gently grazing down the length of his spine, and forcing shivers through his body, increased. He felt slightly nauseous and trembled with nerves. Even with everyone else around him, he felt alone.

He slowly, without making sudden movements, raised the RPG into position across his forearms in front of him, ready to be brought up onto the shoulder at the last minute, and fired. He checked his watched again. It was just under two minutes before the attack was to be initiated by him.

The light was almost perfect for a dawn attack. He could see the machinegun to his left, the trenches ahead of him and the tank, about two hundred metres away and in a perfect position for him to get a side on hit.

Marcus brought his mouth down close to his radio and spoke in a low voice, "All call signs, comms check."

"Stu, good to me."

"Jim, strength five."

"Sini, loud and clear."

"Ian, good to me mate."

"Yan, you're good to me."

All the team had acknowledged and Marcus replied, "That's good to me all around. Thirty seconds, stand by, stand by." He released his finger from the transmit switch and cradled the launcher. He looked back up to his left at the machinegun position.

"Shit," he whispered under his breath. It was in clear sight, and if he could see them, then as soon as he knelt up to fire the RPG, they would be able to see him He could now see movement from around the position of the gun as men began to move about in the first light of dawn.

They were now committed and it was too late to move back. "Fuck it," he whispered. "Jim had better nail `em from the off."

Yan had the butt of the machinegun in his shoulder and his finger lightly touching the trigger, waiting for Marcus to fire.

Marcus had a grasp on the pistol grip and trigger of the launcher with his right hand and his other hand on the forward grip. He looked at the tank, then in one swift movement raised himself to his knees and threw the launcher onto his shoulder, praying that the men in the machinegun pit wouldn't notice him before he could fire.

He pressed his eye to the rubber around the eyepiece of the sight. A second later, and he could see the ground in front of him, magnified and with the black vertical and horizontal lines and aiming points within the sight.

He raised the launcher slightly and the tank came into his sights. He steadied his aim, let out half a breath and then held it as his finger took up the slack on the trigger pressure. The RPG was steady, and the aiming mark was right in the centre of the broad side of the tank.

With a whoosh and a loud bang that sucked at his lungs as the air pressure changed and enveloped him in a cloud of white/grey smoke, he felt the launcher jerk against his shoulder as the missile left the barrel and raced toward the target. He had lost sight of the tank in the shroud of smoke that engulfed him but there was nothing he could do about it now. The RPG would either hit or miss; either way he wouldn't see it due to the cloud.

Immediately, he dropped the launcher and raised his rifle to his shoulder.

He heard the fast crackling of rounds being fired from his left. Yan was already firing into his targets, stitching all along the edges of the trenches in short controlled bursts; the used brass cases already piling up beneath the ejection opening of his gun as he kept up the rate of fire.

All around him, Marcus heard the clatter of weapons being fired as the entire team poured their deadly fire into the enemy. He heard the automatic fire from Yan to his left and the single rapid shots from Ian and Sini to his right as they suppressed the closest enemy trench. Streaks of red light flew forward from their barrels as the tracer ignited and marked the line of trajectory of their rounds through the air.

Directly above him, more tracer rounds zipped overhead, looking like laser beams accompanied by the ear-splitting crack of the air displacement as the rounds from Jim's machinegun hammered at the Dushka position.

Jim had been poised and ready. The butt was firmly jammed against his shoulder and he peered down the sights at the dark shape of the enemy machinegun position on the hillside. To his ten o'clock position, he saw the puff of smoke as Marcus fired the RPG and before the rocket had hit its target, as it streaked across his front, Jim had depressed the trigger of his gun and his rounds began to thump into the enemy position.

He could see them striking against the sandbags, bursting them open and the contents spilling over the edges of the gun pit as they collapsed. His rounds churned up the dirt all around the Dushka. As the weapon jerked and battered back against his shoulder and the ammunition fed through and into the chamber, he saw bodies trying to get to their feet behind the machinegun, only to be chopped down as his relentless fire smashed into them. They jerked and fell, bleeding and dying before they had even had a chance to man their weapons.

He fired another long burst to be sure, then swung his gun around to the right to begin suppressing anyone attempting to return fire or mount a counter attack from the buildings. Indiscriminately, he pounded at the mud huts, one after the other, obliterating whole sections of their walls.

Ian saw the strike of the rocket as it hit the target. The tank rocked on its tracks with the impact and a shower of sparks erupted for the entry point as the warhead of the RPG had smashed through the hull.

He and Sini fired their rifles together. They had no visible targets from the trench area yet, but they fired nevertheless. Anyone in the shell scrape contemplating even sticking their head up to join the fight would soon be convinced not to, as the rounds smacked against the tops of their trenches, sending splashes of dirt showering over them as they huddled at the bottom for cover.

It was shock and awe, the faster and harder you hit them, the less chance they have to recover before you've closed the gap between you.

They could hear Marcus to their left. "Move, move," he was hollering over the din of the battle.

Yan stepped up the rate of fire and they could see his tracer rounds as they poured into the second position. They heard confused shouts from the enemy and their screams of pain and panic.

Marcus and Yan provided cover fire as Sini and Ian advanced forward.

Sini jumped up. "Moving," he screamed and he ran forward five metres then dropped to one knee and began firing at the enemy trench to his front. "Move," he shouted over his shoulder to Ian.

Sini had now begun to fire and it was Ian's turn to move forward. "Moving," Ian shouted in reply as he sprinted forward. He got down to Sini's left and continued to fire as Sini bounded forward again. They continued covering each other with fire and manoeuvre as they closed the gap to the first position.

Marcus and Yan began to smash away at the next trench with their fire support as Sini and Ian approached their line of fire from the right. Marcus saw the final bound as Ian jumped up and charged, screaming, into the enemy position, closely followed by Sini.

Marcus tapped Yan hard on the shoulder and shouted that he was moving to follow and support Ian and Sini. Yan remained where he was and kept up his rate of fire to cover the assault team.

They had no bayonets but Ian jumped into the trench and thrust the muzzle of his weapon into the face of the terrified soldier who had been cowering at the bottom. Ian was still roaring with aggression as the barrel smashed through the soft tissue of the man's cheek and deep into his skull.

Ian felt the bone give and collapse inward as he put his weight behind the thrust and the man screamed a gurgling, wet howl. Ian withdrew the barrel and thrust again and again until there was a hole the size of his hand in the man's face and the soldier had gone limp and silent. His barrel had chunks of pink skin and red meat seared to it as the flesh had instantly cooked and stuck to it.

Sini dropped in beside him and changed his magazine and Ian did the same, ready for the next position. Marcus had followed them to the first position once it had been taken and left Yan to keep the fire support going.

They were all now in a blood lust and all three began to fire and manoeuvre again to the next position, leapfrogging one another as they closed in on the horrified Turkish troops. They roared and screamed as they approached, firing and moving alternately, and crashed in on the men who threw their hands up in surrender, but it was too late; the momentum and aggression had taken over and they fired into the two enemy soldiers as they landed on top of them, pumping round after round into their chests and faces and seeing their features crumble in a pool of blood and smashed bone.

Marcus charged the next position with Ian and Sini giving him cover fire. Their rounds zipping close to him as he ran. As he closed in on the trench, he saw an arm raised, holding an object that was about to be thrown.

"Grenade!" Marcus screamed and fired, as he charged, into the face and neck of the man holding the explosive. His throat erupted in a fountain of bright red blood as a round smashed through his neck, and he dropped from sight and to the bottom of the trench with the grenade still clutched between his fingers.

Marcus dropped to his stomach as it exploded. The low but deafening thud of the concussion as the deadly weapon detonated within the confined space of the defensive position made Marcus' ears ring as he crawled toward the lip of the trench.

A plume of black smoke rose from the hole in the ground and Marcus raised himself and bounded the last couple of steps, firing into the position on full automatic, screaming as he charged.

The grenade had done its damage. There was little left for Marcus to shoot at. The charred and torn open torso of a man was all that was left in the bottom of the trench.

"Position clear," Marcus called back to Sini and Ian, who then joined him in the trench and readied themselves to assault the final dugout.

Stu had taken out the comms centre just as quickly as Jim had destroyed the machinegun. He could hear the fire fight and screaming as Marcus and his group closed in on the trenches. He turned his fire to begin suppressing the troops in the buildings with Jim.

Men ran everywhere, some half naked, and they were mowed down before they could even see where the fire was coming from.

Three men tried to escape a hut that was untouched by their fire at that moment. As they piled out of the door, weapons in hand with the intention of either fleeing or joining the fight, Stu fired a long burst into them and they fell into a tangled mass at the foot of the entrance.

Hussein sat behind the wheel of the SUV that Stu was firing from with a panoramic view of the battlefield in front of him. His jaw hung open and his eyes were wide like saucers as he watched the attack unfold in front of him with awe.

He could see the red tracer rounds flying all over from every angle, the sounds of the multitude of weapons as the team unleashed their own version of hell onto the Turkish positions. He could hear screams and watched as men collapsed under hails of bullets. He couldn't help but admire the ability and speed of Marcus and his men.

He thanked the angels that watched over him that he hadn't fired the RPG on the day he first met Marcus. Judging by what he was seeing, he doubted he would've lived for long afterward.

Yan could see Marcus, Sini and Ian advancing from trench to trench. They were closing in on the last position and it was time for him to switch fire onto the buildings housing the infantry.

He was scanning for movement around the huts when he caught a glimpse of the tank; its main gun was moving. He had to double check and, sure enough, the gun was slowly rotating and it was aiming for Marcus, Sini and Ian.

"Marcus," Yan screamed into his radio. "Marcus, the tank. There's someone still alive in it." He saw Marcus raise his hand to his ear from the last trench then look up toward the smouldering tank.

Yan saw a flurry of arms and gestures as Marcus realised what was happening, and then Sini was pulling the RPG from his shoulder, struggling to get it into the aim.

Whoever was in the tank had managed to survive the initial blast from the rocket and was now manually turning the turret with the hand wheels in order to fire it at the assault team.

Yan was praying for Sini to get the launcher fired before the tank could.

A loud boom and the tank rocked on its tracks as the gun emitted a puff of smoke and a flash from its main gun. A fountain of earth and shredded sandbags erupted from the trench that Marcus, Sini and Ian had been in. Yan felt his heart skip a beat but he couldn't stop firing, he had to keep up the pressure on the enemy. He had to continue with the task; the village wasn't yet clear and he poured a heavy weight of fire into every hut he saw still standing.

Marcus was blown off his feet and back down into the bottom of the trench. He felt Ian and Sini land on top of him and crush him down into the dirt. He pushed up with all his strength and managed to crawl out from underneath. Sini and Ian were still alive, dazed and rattled, but still alive.

Ian was staring at him, unblinking and smeared in mud. "What the fuck just happened Marcus? Did the tank just fire, and how the fuck are we alive?"

Marcus was scrambling from the trench. "Because it was a fucking anti-tank round, move before he reloads with high explosive," he shouted.

The gunner in the tank had forgotten, in his haste and probably wounded state, to change the ammunition type and a solid shot of depleted uranium, designed to take out other tanks and not effective against infantry, had ploughed through the top of the trench and deep into the ground behind Marcus and his assault team.

The velocity of the round is what makes it so deadly against other armoured vehicles, and it had been the shockwave and air displacement as the round travelled between them that had thrown Marcus, Ian and Sini to the floor of the trench.

Sini climbed out and began to manhandle Ian out of the trench. He grabbed the RPG and placed it on his shoulder, took aim and fired it into the tank. It hit directly below the turret and the steel monster shuddered in a blinding flash; black smoke began to pour from it.

"Stu, do you see any depth positions?" Marcus was panting over the net.

"No mate, I think they're pretty much done."

"Roger that, move the FSG up to my position. Watch for any other positions that we have missed and cover us as me and the assault group do our sweep."

Stu acknowledged, "Roger that, Marcus, that's us moving now."

Marcus looked to Ian and Sini. They were pouring with sweat and panting for breath. They had a damp layer of dirt that covered them from head to toe and steam was rising from them as they knelt and changed magazines, ensuring they had fresh full ones on before they started their clearance of what was left of the buildings.

"Yan, you okay up there?"

"Yes, Marcus, all good here. Can't see any movement at all."

"Roger that, Yan, come down to our position and make sure there's no one still alive in the trenches behind us. Me, Sini and Ian are gonna do a quick sweep. From the looks of it though, Stu and Jim did a good job at levelling the place."

"No worries, Marcus," Yan replied, in an almost jolly tone. "On my way,"

He got to his feet and picked up his weapon and ammunition and began making his way to the first of the trenches with his pistol in hand. He walked from one to the next and fired a single shot into the head of each body he found, ensuring they were dead for good.

He glanced behind him and considered moving up the hill and taking care of the dead around the heavy machinegun position.

"Fuck `em," he said to himself, "if they get up and walk about after death, they deserve it."

He continued to move along the line of trenches, taking whatever he thought would be of use, including a few high explosive grenades he found amongst the bodies of the dead.

A few shots rang out as Marcus and his assault team finished off the remaining wounded still writhing among the ruins as they swept through the rubble of the village. Twisted, mutilated and bloody bodies lay scattered all around the piles of mud brick and straw roofing that now lay in smashed piles. Wounded lay mixed in with the dead, moaning and clutching at horrible wounds as they squirmed or tried to crawl to safety. Marcus, Sini and Ian moved amongst them, coldly dispatching anyone still alive with shots to the head.

Within a few minutes, Marcus and Ian returned from the ruins of the hamlet with an unwounded Turkish officer.

Sini followed a minute later and spoke to Marcus. "He's the only one left alive. They're all dead, Marcus."

Marcus nodded and turned to Ian and then to the officer. "Oi, you speak English?"

The officer nodded vigorously, hoping to earn brownie points. "Yes, yes I speak it very good." He even cracked a smile.

Ian stepped forward and grabbed him from behind, placing his mouth close to his ear and growling, "Good, because now you're gonna fucking die, cunt."

Ian kicked him forward and the officer let out a yelp and landed on his knees.

He looked from Marcus to Sini to Ian, panic in his eyes as he kneeled in the mud. "Please."

Ian raised his pistol and pointed it at the man's head. The image of the woman being raped over and over burned in his memory, the sobs and tears of the little girl as she cried for her mother and father and for the soldiers to stop hurting them, the sight of the three of them being thrown face down into the mud and then shot like sick cattle, flashed behind his eyes.

The officer raised his hand. "Please, I am..."

The loud echo of the shot cut him off; his face crumpled in the middle, just below his nose and a spray of red and grey brains exploded from the back of his head. His hand dropped and his body slumped to the side and landed in a heap on the dirt track, the thick syrup-like blood spilling from his head and collecting in a puddle around him as he lay in the mud where he would remain.

Marcus looked up from the body to Ian, then spoke into his radio. "All call signs, cease fire. Close into my location and start the reorg."

Within five minutes, they had collected anything of use, including four RPG rounds to restock the launchers and some mapping showing the Turkish dispositions throughout the whole of the East of Turkey. That would make it easier for the team to bypass the troop concentrations and pass through undetected.

"Stu, did you check to see if the radio was working? It would be useful to know if they managed to get any messages off before they were killed," Marcus asked as he folded the maps and stuffed them into his pocket.

"I highly doubt it. I think they were dead within the first couple of seconds, Marcus, and the radio is shot to pieces, so I don't think any signals got out at all."

Marcus nodded his approval. "Well, I guess we will soon find out, won't we? Just be ready for drama on the off chance that they managed to call for help."

The team rolled out from the scene of carnage and sped away to the north, leaving the smouldering, bloodied field and broken bodies of men in their wake.

20

"What do we do?" Kevin was sat in the back seat of the Range Rover.

Steve and Gary looked at each other then back at the gate that led out onto the main road from the Safari Park. A group of a dozen infected had gathered around the entrance over the previous couple of days and they clambered at the railings when they saw the vehicle approach.

Steve had seen them on the CCTV when Jake called him into the security room that morning. The infected just milled about without paying too much attention to the steel gate. For some reason they had remained close, as though they knew there was something or somebody inside.

Now, they rattled and pulled at the railings and each other as they moaned and reached for the black vehicle on the other side containing the three living people. The gate would hold; there was no question of that. It would take thousands of bodies pushing against it to force the thick steel hinges, set into the concrete base attached to the walls, to buckle and collapse.

But the problem that Steve, Gary and Kevin now faced was how to get past them. They had known they were there and Steve hoped that a solution would have presented itself on the short drive from the mansion to the gate, but nothing popped into his head that resembled a solid plan.

He shrugged. "I haven't a clue to be honest. We can't just open the gate and drive out; they would get into the park before Jake could close it again from the control room."

He looked to Gary for input with questioning eyes.

"Maybe that's exactly what we have to do, Steve?" He replied.

"Eh, you mean let them in?"

Kevin gripped the headrest of each of the front seats and pulled himself forward to speak. "Hang on old fella, we open them gates and those walking bags of puss are gonna come piling into the park."

"Not necessarily. If we get a few people down here, armed of course, we could get Jake to open the gate and we could drive out slowly so that the infected can keep up with us and follow, then, once clear, Jake closes the gate and if any are left inside, they can be dealt with by the others waiting for them."

Steve bit his lip. "You don't think that's a bit of a risk, Gary?"

"Everything is a risk these days. We're taking a big risk ourselves venturing out there and crossing miles and miles of potentially hostile ground. For us to get out of here, it's a risk that the people inside will have to take. Everyone has to earn their keep around here, Steve, and that means taking risks now and then."

Kevin nodded from between them. "Yup, I think he's right, Steve. Everyone has to pitch in these days. It can't be just us shaking our meaty, juicy arses at those puss brains while everyone else sits back."

Steve nodded. He didn't like the idea of leaving a gap that could be exploited but he knew that the plan and philosophy made sense.

"Okay then, get Jake on the radio."

Ten minutes later, four others from the mansion arrived in the gate area but kept themselves out of sight from the infected on the other side. Jake was among them, carrying a length of metal piping. There was nothing camp about him now; which Steve was sure he deliberately put on for the sake of entertainment to the others. He was all business and looking serious and focused.

Two men named John and Carl had also volunteered to help.

Steve's heart skipped a beat when he saw Helen with them. He knew better than to say anything. Though, no doubt Helen would appreciate his attempt at chivalry if he insisted that she go back and stay out of harm's way. He also knew that she would tell him where he could piss off to. Instead, he nodded to her and she gave him a short smile in return.

"Okay, Jake," Gary spoke into the radio, "you know the plan. Keep outta sight and once we're clear and the gates are shut again, only then do you come out of the trees, and only if some of those things manage to get inside."

"I understand, Gary. Be careful out there yourself."

The gate gave off a low electric whirr and began to slowly move, sliding open from the locking mechanism and toward the opposite wall. Immediately, the dead began to push through the gap and stagger toward the vehicle. They slapped and banged at the doors and glass and surrounded the vehicle as it unhurriedly moved toward the opening that led out from the park.

Steve sat behind the wheel, fighting the urge to slam his foot down and speed away from the ghastly visions he could see all around him. He did his best to keep his eyes focused straight ahead and not to look at the mottled pale green faces that pressed up against the window at the side of him, the bony hands that clutched at the glass in an attempt to pull it away and reach inside. Their smell began to permeate the air vents of the Range Rover, and all three of them gagged at the stench of rotting flesh.

"Fuck me, that's hideous." Kevin had the neck of his t-shirt pulled up to cover his nose. To him, the dead smelled like a cross between the chicken he had once left out on the kitchen counter at home while he was away for a weekend, and dog shit. He gagged. "You think they're all gonna be smelling this bad?"

"Probably worse when we get into a built-up area, especially if we run into large groups of them," Gary answered over his shoulder as he too covered his mouth and nose.

Steve couldn't afford to loosen his grip on the wheel and he had to grin and bear the smell that assaulted his nostrils. He could feel his stomach churn and his gag reflex beginning to twitch with each intake of breath, and he opted to breathe through his mouth instead.

He caught a glimpse of the face of one of the nearest bodies to the driver's side. "Jesus!" he exclaimed.

It had once been a woman, but was now unrecognisable as it slammed its bloated, festering arms and rake-like fingers against the doors of the vehicle. Her long, dark, greasy hair was missing in large chunks in places and the rest was matted to her scalp.

Her pale skin was peeling from around her cheeks and jaw, and underneath Steve saw what looked to be fresh, healthy pink flesh. For a moment he doubted that they were actually dead and that maybe the scientists had gotten it wrong. But just one look at the eyes told him they hadn't. They were a dull grey as a misty film had covered the already rotting eyeball, with a darker circle in the centre where the iris and pupil remained under the film. The eyes stared at him blankly and the swollen, dark tongue flopped from the ravenous mouth as it stretched wide in an attempt to bite through the glass. The teeth were gnashing together and biting clear through a large portion of her tongue. Her eyes seemed to register that she had gotten what she wanted and the creature pulled away, chewing vigorously before realising its mistake and letting the rotten cold meat drop from her mouth before approaching the vehicle again.

The sound emitting from the walking cadavers never ceased, but at such close range, the men in the vehicle were able to distinguish individual voices, tones, and pitches. Even in death, it was easy to differentiate male from female. The moan and whine of their lament held their masculine and feminine touches, though unrecognisable as speech.

Black clouds of bloated flies swarmed in the air around them. They constantly buzzed and added to the sound of the dead; the air seemed electrified, like the sound produced by large transformers attached to the power grid.

They pushed through the gate and slowly headed down the approach road. The dead continued to stumble after them and when Gary was sure they had all followed, he keyed the radio, "Okay, close the gate, we're clear and I think they've all come with us."

"Closing it now, Gary," Sophie called from the control desk in the mansion.

Steve watched in the rear view mirror as the gate began to slide back into place behind them. Once it slammed shut, he sped away.

"Any of them get in, Jake?" Gary asked.

The radio crackled and hissed then Jake's voice could be heard. "No Gary, they all followed you. It worked perfectly."

"Good good, get back up to the house. We'll push up to the junction and try and give you a call on the radio to see what the range is like on this."

"Will do, Gary, good luck," Jake replied.

The range was good. They were still able to talk with the people at the Safari Park from as far as a kilometre away as Steve negotiated his way through wrecked and stalled traffic and the wandering corpses that littered the roads.

There seemed to be dozens of them shuffling along the lanes and roads and they all seemed to be headed in the direction of the Park.

"I think that we could be in for some trouble back at the park eventually," Gary was thinking aloud.

Steve glanced across from the driver's seat. "You think that's where they're all heading?"

"Could be, there were more than just a few out there this morning. Maybe they have a sixth sense? Or maybe they just see others like them and automatically follow? But either way, I think that if we're not careful, we could find ourselves stuck and surrounded."

Kevin asked, "Where else could we go anyway? Maybe we should just sit it out there regardless of how many there are outside?"

"I've thought that myself, but we don't know how long we could be there for. I mean, how long will it take for them to rot away? It's better to at least have an escape plan. As well as that though, if there ends up being thousands of them surrounding our walls, disease could become an issue. I'm no doctor but rotting flesh and the millions of insects feeding off the dead make for a bad combination health-wise."

Steve was concentrating on the road ahead as he swerved around a cluster of static cars. "It's something that we will have to consider when we get back; either a get out strategy or a way of keeping them away, maybe both. For now, let's just get on with the job at hand."

They were travelling, as per the plan, along the same route that Steve had taken to get there. But it now looked completely different from what it had just a few days earlier. It seemed that people had given up on waiting for instructions from the government and police officials and had begun trying to make their own way to safety.

Kevin looked disgusted as he peered out the window nearest to him at the scale of the destruction and horror of the reanimated.

"You not been out recently I take it, Kev?" Steve asked glancing at him in the mirror.

"Not recently. Well not at all really. I came to the park at the beginning when we believed it was all just riots and flu. I was inside the safety of the walls when it was announced what was actually happening, had no desire to venture out since to be honest, Steve."

"Why come now?"

"I couldn't let you go out with just this old fossil," he nudged the back of Gary's seat, "you'd never make it back having to carry him too."

Gary looked over his shoulder. "Hey, Kevin my boy, there's still plenty of life in this old man yet. I was running marathons and a black belt in Judo when I was your age and I played rugby every Sunday up until a few years back. Unlike you, sitting in your bedroom playing computer games with the door barricaded shut and eating nothing but pizza, like a Japanese teenager."

Despite the situation outside of the vehicle, Steve burst into laughter and Kevin's only response was, "Fuck off."

They made sure that the main roads that led into the town were given a wide berth. They travelled along a bypass road that would bring them out on the far side of the main built-up area and not far from where they were headed.

Steve tried to call Claire that morning and had no reply. The automated voice told him that the number was out of service. He decided to send a text instead, informing her that they were on their way and to be ready to move. Now his phone beeped and vibrated in his pocket.

He didn't want to take his eyes off the road or his hands from the steering wheel. "Gary, can you reach into my pocket and check my phone, it could be Claire."

Gary did as he was asked and when he read the message notice he said, "It says 'Saggy Arse'." He looked to Steve questioningly.

"Yup, that's Claire. What does it say?"

"It says that she's ready and that there aren't many infected knocking about in the street and she asks how long."

"Tell her fifteen minutes if all goes to plan."

Gary began typing the reply, using the thumbs from both hands. "I hate this predictive text thing. It never spells what I want it to. I'll probably end up sending the recipe to Christmas cake or something."

Ten minutes later they turned off from the junction that led up to the housing estate that Claire lived on. It was an upper working class area with large double drives and long front gardens that were overlooked by large bay windows.

The place didn't look much different from all the other chaotic residential areas of the country with burnt houses, trashed cars, bodies, and other detritus lying in the street.

As they turned a corner, a van bolted toward them. The driver's eyes bulged from their sockets when he saw the Range Rover and he fought with the wheel and swerved just in time to avoid colliding with them before the van screamed past and out of sight. Close behind, a small crowd of five or so infected sprinted after it, but when they saw Steve and his companions, they diverted their attention to the four by four and charged at it.

They pounded at the hood and doors, their faces pressed up against the glass, smearing it with all manner of filth as Steve pushed the car forward and trampled one below the wheels. The soft crunch of the bone as the heavy treads churned up the body below them could be heard from inside and Kevin winced in the back seat.

They surged forward and away from the pursuing infected and soon lost them in the twists and turns of the streets on the estate.

Close to where Claire lived, they saw the body of a person who had been burnt to a crisp and beyond recognition, still sitting on a scooter that had its kick stand down. The sight was completely bizarre and even with all that was going on, it seemed out of place.

"Jesus," Gary commented, "I wonder what happened to him?"

They slowly passed the gruesome sight and Steve could see the charred and blackened features. He could even see the teeth as the lips had been shrivelled away leaving the body sitting upright and with a permanent grinning expression on its face.

They turned onto the road where Claire lived. There were two infected in view and they decided that they would go ahead with the plan and deal with them if they approached. He forced the car to a stop outside the house and considered using the horn for a moment to get Claire's attention, but then decided against it.

"If there are only two of them in sight, then we'll just have to knock. I don't fancy attracting the whole estate down upon us."

Gary gripped the handle to the door. "You get the ex with the saggy arse and me and ginger balls back there will keep the area clear."

"Fuck off silver fox," Kevin retorted.

"Hey, my grey hair shows maturity and wisdom, your bright red locks show that you're just cursed." He glanced back and smiled at him then opened the door and stepped into the road. "C'mon lad, let's do our bit."

Kevin and Gary stood in the road wielding iron bars, ready to swing them down onto the heads of anyone who approached.

Steve climbed out and headed toward the door. The van that Roy used for work was backed up close to the front door with a gap of less than a foot for them to squeeze through. The door was already open and he saw Claire's face in the gloom as she spoke.

"You'll have to move the van, it's open and it should move forward once the handbrake is off, we'll push from here."

Steve nodded and did as instructed. Soon Claire and Roy were trotting down the driveway, carrying the three bags they had packed, and heading straight for the Range Rover. Claire stopped as she came level with Steve. She looked at him with tears in her eyes and a smile on her face. "Thank God you made it. I was worried." She kissed him on the cheek and threw her arms around his neck, sobbing. "You kept our little girl safe, and I could never repay you for that."

"You can start just by getting into the car." He looked down at her and smiled.

As Steve approached the driver's side, he saw two bodies in the street close to where Kevin and Gary stood. Both had virtually no heads left and pools of congealed blood seeped out from the broken skulls. Gary looked over at him and shrugged. Steve nodded and began to climb behind the wheel.

"C'mon, Kev, that's us."

Both of them piled into the car and quickly nodded to their new passengers by way of introduction, "I'm Gary, this is Kevin."

"Pleased to meet you, I'm Claire, and this is Roy," she replied and Roy nodded with wide frightened eyes. Steve glanced at him through the mirror as he put the vehicle into gear. He looked scared out of his wits.

The Range Rover turned in the street to face back the way they had come. Steve struggled with the heavy vehicle, and soon they headed back for the junction toward the bypass road.

Steve could see that Gary had something on his mind. "What is it?" he asked, finally acknowledging the glances that Gary was giving him to gain his attention.

Gary looked over his shoulder sheepishly to check if anyone would be able to hear what he was about to say. Claire was speaking to Kevin about where they were headed.

In a hushed tone, almost a whisper, Gary asked, "Why do you call her 'Saggy Arse'? It looks pretty decent to me." He nodded to the side as he said it, indicating toward Claire.

Steve checked his mirror again to make sure she hadn't heard. "Dunno really," he muttered back trying to keep the same low tone. "It's an ex thing I suppose."

"It's okay, Gary," Claire's voice spoke over their shoulders. "I have him listed as 'Dick Head' in my phone."

Gary threw his head back and let out a snort. Steve shrugged his shoulders in resignation. "Told you, it's an ex thing."

The rescue had gone well. Too well.

They were on the bypass and making good progress. Steve knew not to let his guard down but he was almost feeling relieved, then he saw it. Up ahead was a dark throng of people, infected people. They were stretched across the width of the road and Steve couldn't see a way through. They were shoulder to shoulder and heading straight at them.

"Shit!" he slammed on the brakes. "Where the fuck did they come from?"

"Dunno, and I don't think they'll tell us if we ask them. Get us out of here, Steve." Gary's voice trembled. He had never seen so many of them. He was always the one that dealt with them at the gate to the park and around the walls, but he had never seen them in such numbers. Now, his eyes were fixed on them as the crowd staggered toward the car. Their numbers were terrifying and he imagined that there must be thousands of them.

It was hard to distinguish individuals within the mass. They were still over a hundred metres away, but steadily gaining ground as Steve considered his options. Their bodies were just a dark wall of browns and blacks. The grime and filth clung to their clothes, their flesh rotting and becoming discoloured as they festered and remained exposed to the elements.

The sound of their moans and wails became louder as they closed the gap that separated them from the warm living flesh that they sought. It was a haunting chorus of pain and anguish and the drone of the millions of insects that surrounded them provided the rhythm and, now and then, a higher pitched shriek as a dead voice broke into a solo over the rising din of the horde.

Steve turned as quickly as the vehicle would allow him and headed in the opposite direction, deeper into the urban area.

"Where do you think that lot came from?" he asked.

Gary looked shaken. "Dunno, maybe we attracted them as we passed through earlier and they just headed toward the road and followed it?" He wiped the sweat from his brow. "Where we going?"

"I dunno. I just want to put some distance between us and them," Steve replied, watching the infected behind them in his rear view mirror.

Claire placed a hand on his shoulder. "If we keep going this way, we'll end up in the city centre. There's probably millions in that area."

"I know, Claire. I don't intend on going into the city. But we can't go back the way we came, so I'm gonna try and find another way."

Steve was getting annoyed. He cursed under his breath because he knew what the town would be like. The road system was badly designed and to get from one side of the town to the other, you had to travel through the centre. There was no ring road that would allow them to circumnavigate the crowded centre.

"There is a way around, but it'll take a lot longer and we could hit more trouble," he said.

Gary glanced across at him. "We will deal with that if and when we have to, Steve. Anything is better than driving across a city of a million dead people that want nothing better than to eat you."

"I'm inclined to agree with the old dude on that one, Steve," Kevin said from the back.

They picked their way through streets and avenues full of the infected that charged at them whenever they passed, and headed through the suburbs. The car was starting to look beat-up and the numerous dents, scratches, and stains would be hard to explain to his brother.

They had left the majority of the built-up area behind them and began to approach the retail parks and industrial areas before they would hit the country roads again. Steve turned a bend that was overhung by trees and bushes that poked out from the fences of the factories and warehouses they surrounded. A loud crunch and bang from underneath the front wheels sent them tumbling in their seats as the vehicle dropped at the front. It settled on a forty five degree angle and everyone found themselves pressed up against the windows of the right hand side.

"What was that?" Gary was pushing himself back up in his seat and checking out of his window before he tried to open the door.

Steve was trying to get the car into reverse. "I don't know, Gary. If I knew what it was, then I would've seen it before I hit it wouldn't I, and we wouldn't be in this position." He growled as he fought with the clutch and accelerator.

Outside, Gary saw the problem. It was a pipe or conduit of some sort that had burst and caused the road above it to collapse and create a trench in the tarmac close to the curb. Just one look at it told Gary that there was no way of getting their vehicle free and even if they did, the steering arms were probably damaged.

"I think it's the end of the road for the Range Rover, Steve."

Steve eased off on the pedals and climbed out to see for himself. Kevin, Claire and Roy followed suit, glancing all around them, checking for any approaching infected in the area.

Kevin looked at the front axle that seemed to be buried in the asphalt. "Fuck, looks like we're walking then. Which way we heading? We can't stay here."

"We will have to keep going in the direction we were going and hope that we can find another vehicle. There's a drive through McDonalds up there so maybe there's still parked and undamaged cars outside." Steve rose to his feet from surveying the damage and looked at Claire and Roy. "Grab your bags and let's get going then."

They began walking in the direction they had been travelling, leaving the Range Rover that was the pride and joy of his brother, Marcus, far behind.

"I think your brother is gonna kill you, Steve," Claire was trying to make light of the situation.

"No doubt, but I'll happily take a kicking from him rather than getting eaten." He was in no mood for chatting and he walked on ahead, his hammer in one hand and the small axe in the other. Gary walked beside him and Kevin brought up the rear while Claire and Roy carried their bags in the middle.

"We should've stayed at the house, Claire," Roy commented when he saw that no one would hear him.

She rolled her eyes and huffed as she adjusted the strap of the bag over her shoulder. "Don't start, Roy. You know we couldn't have stayed there forever, and there was no way I was gonna stay separated from Sarah even if there was a slight chance of me getting to her."

"I know," Roy's voice quivered and he was back to being on the edge of a breakdown, "but this has all gone wrong. We have no car and we're walking about in the open with those things running around. We should turn back and wait in the car."

Claire stopped and turned on him. "You fucking serious?" she hissed. "And then what, we sit and wait while Steve and the others find a car and come back for us?"

He looked down and mumbled something as he continued to walk.

"You need to grow a pair, Roy," she said to him as she stomped on ahead.

A while later they approached a large junction that had a number of exits leading into and away from different parts of the city. The one directly across from where they stood would bring them onto the country lanes that would eventually filter them back toward the Safari Park.

They stopped in the shadows of the trees that grew by the fence line of the road as it approached the junction, and watched the large open area to their front. The sun was still high and there were virtually no clouds in the sky. Birds twittered and trees swayed in the soft, cool breeze of the perfect summer's day. It was almost enjoyable to be out, but there were things missing. The beep of horns, the rumble of engines and the voices of people and music from car stereos as they passed through the junction were completely absent and left the atmosphere feeling surreal.

It unsettled Steve and seemed to affect Roy even more; he was close to panic. They had been in the open for almost an hour and even though they had seen no sign of the infected, Roy felt all the more apprehensive. With every minute that passed by without any appearance from them, the anxiety built up in his mind. He expected them at any minute, and the longer it went without them showing, the more the fear rose up inside him.

He fidgeted and glanced all around him continuously as though he expected to see groups of reanimated corpses sneaking up on them. "Why are we standing here? We should keep going."

"We can't," Kevin replied in a hushed voice as he eyed the far side of the junction staring at a car showroom, "there's a fucking million of them over there."

He slowly raised his arm and pointed toward the tops of the numerous heads that he could see above the grass verge, wandering just fifty metres away in the open area in front of the showroom.

Gary was caressing his beard as he eyed the scene. "We can't go back the way we came in case they followed us out of the suburbs, and the second we walk into the open, the infected over there will see us." He turned to Steve who also stood watching from the shadows of the trees that overhung the railings. "What do you think?"

Steve glanced along the length of the fence and back toward the junction. "The drive through is just on the other side and to the right. If we made a break for it and keep low, maybe they won't notice us, and we could maybe find a car there that still runs."

Gary wasn't convinced, "There's too many 'maybe's' in that, Steve."

"I'm open to suggestions if you have any better ideas." He looked at each of the group in turn and no one replied. They knew he was right and they had to go forward whether they liked it or not now.

They sprinted along the fence line and headed straight for the low single-storey building of the drive through. Their feet pounded against the tarmac and Steve cringed at the thought of their heavy steps attracting the attention of the infected.

A figure darted out from the edge of the fence line and collided with Roy as they bolted out into the open to cross the road. Cold fingers clutched at his face and they tumbled to the ground in a heap. Roy let out a loud shriek as the creature's teeth clamped down on his shoulder; the sharp incisors puncturing the soft skin and tearing away at the cloth of his shirt and muscle underneath.

The two of them writhed and struggled as Roy tried to push the body away from him. Steve turned when he heard the scream and Kevin ran at the pair, aiming a kick at the face of the attacker with all his strength. It connected under the jawline. Its head snapped back with a loud crack and its jaw dislocated, causing the piece of bloody flesh to fly from its mouth. Blood splattered across its face. Kevin swung his iron bar from the right and it smashed against the back of its skull with a wet thwack, forcing it to fall forward again onto the still screaming Roy beneath.

The body lay motionless and Kevin and Gary grabbed Roy and hauled him to his feet and dragged him toward the road.

Steve had continued to run toward the drive through, grabbing Claire by the forearm as the others took care of the problem. He glanced over his shoulder to see Gary, Kevin and Roy making their way across the road. Beyond them, he saw the mass of corpses from the showroom climbing the grass verge and crossing the open road. The sprinters were out in front and approaching fast.

"Fucking run you three, run!" he hollered.

Roy was a dead weight, and Kevin and Gary had to use all their strength to keep him on his feet and moving. "I've been bit," he sobbed, gripping his shoulder as he was forced along. "Shit, I'm gonna die aren't I?"

"Keep moving, Roy, we're nearly there." Kevin pushed hard at his back, forcing Roy's legs to run as Gary pulled.

They reached the other side and saw Steve and Claire rounding the corner. Kevin looked back and saw five infected charging toward them at full pace. He turned back to the front and pushed harder.

"If you don't run for yourself, I'll fucking leave you here, Roy."

Steve stopped for a moment to glance around, hoping to find a place to head for. On the far side of the restaurant was a garage forecourt and a red family style saloon still sat idle at one of the pumps.

"There," he panted and pointed with his axe as he dragged Claire towards it.

He hoped that the keys were still inside. As he got closer, a man walked out from the shop attached to the fuel station, carrying a bundle of food and other goods in his arms. He saw Steve and the others heading for his car and dropped his load.

"No you fucking don't. It took me ages to find a car that works," he shouted as he sprinted for his car and stopped in front of the driver's door holding a rifle in his hands menacingly, showing the invaders that he was willing to fight for what was his.

Steve didn't slow in his stride. "Help us, there's a load of them things chasing us, we need a ride outta here," he shouted to the man as he approached.

The man looked past Steve and saw the other three as they turned the corner and followed. He reached across to his right and pulled the rear door open and waved them toward the opening, "Get in then, they're right behind you."

"No, they're with us, they're okay, but the infected aren't far behind them," Claire said, indicating Gary Kevin and Roy, as she climbed in to the car.

"Run, Gary, get in here," Steve called as he piled into the back seat, pushing Claire to the far side to make room for the others.

Gary and Kevin were exhausted. They had had to push and drag Roy the whole way and they were slowing. They saw the car and the open door and Steve and Claire disappear inside and they pushed their legs and drained their final reserves of strength to gain the last few feet of ground. They could hear the feet of the approaching infected behind them as they pounded across the concrete and the moans as they reached out in anticipation of the living feast ahead of them.

The man with the car was now behind the wheel and gunning the engine, screaming for them to get in. Kevin pushed at Roy's back and forced him forward, and then his feet slipped from under him and he crashed to the ground.

Gary felt the sudden drag as Roy slowed without Kevin to push him forward and, after a moment, turned to see his friend sprawled on the floor ten metres behind him. He hesitated, and then dragged Roy past him hoping that the momentum of his sudden jerk would propel the dead weight of the useless Roy forward the rest of the way to the vehicle.

Steve clambered back out of the vehicle, shoved Roy into the back seat and turned to see Gary moving toward the collapsed form of Kevin as he struggled to his feet. "Gary, move," he screamed at him. There was now a pack of seven infected racing toward Kevin who was almost back on his feet.

Gary was still moving toward them when they closed the gap and tackled Kevin to the ground.

"Kevin!" he cried.

He heard the crunch as Kevin and the infected crumbled to the ground in a ball of arms and legs. He charged at them, swinging his iron bar and smashing it into the face of one of the creatures that ran at him after it had broken away from the group. It hit the ground with a splat and remained motionless.

Steve grabbed him from behind and pulled him back; there were many more approaching fast and they needed to run. He saw Kevin struggling from beneath the pile of clutching and biting corpses that swarmed him, and he moved toward them with his axe raised, ready to help his friend.

Kevin was screaming as he struggled, and Steve saw a bloody tear appear on the side of his neck and across his throat as a set of teeth ripped away the flesh, tendons and veins. Kevin squealed and a cascade of bright red arterial blood sprayed onto the tarmac below his face, forming a large pool within seconds. His windpipe had been torn open, and he was now face-down, drowning in his own blood. His ruined tracheal reflexes squelched as his body continued to try and take in air.

Gary struggled against Steve and tried to break free, but Steve held his grip and pulled him toward the waiting vehicle and bundled him into the rear seat. Steve forced himself into the passenger seat and the driver released the clutch and sped away in a screech of smoking tyres, heading straight for the exit.

Gary was shouting and screaming, trying to reach out from the open window to help Kevin, who now lay motionless on the ground as hundreds of infected clambered over him and tore him to pieces.

Claire was gripping him around the neck with both arms in a strangle hold and, eventually, he stopped struggling as he went limp and lost consciousness in her grip.

The car bounced over the exit ramp and the driver slammed it to the right, ploughing through the few infected that remained on the road and toward the opposite side of the junction.

"Sorry about you friend, Steve," the driver said.

Steve looked at him in surprise and confusion. "How do you know my name?"

The man behind the wheel turned and looked at him, a slight smile creasing the edges of his lips. The piercing blue eyes, thin wavy light brown hair, and that smile; a smile that Steve had seen a thousand times as if to say in complete innocence, 'It wasn't me,' and Steve's eyes widened in recognition.

"Lee, Lee Gorman?" The man turned his attention back to the road.

"Yep, that's me. I recognised you when I saw you up close, but I didn't think it was the best time to reintroduce myself. But really, I am sorry about your friend, Steve."

"Me too, but I'm more sorry for Gary." Steve indicated with his thumb to the unconscious form still in Claire's arms. "They were close."

Lee nodded, "Poor guy. What were you all doing back there?"

"Trying to get back to the Safari Park, we had an accident and had to abandon our car and we were hoping to find one at the drive through."

"Well, you did find one. Why are you going to the Safari Park?"

"That's where we've been living. We came here to rescue my daughter's Mum and bring her back. Obviously, things didn't work out as planned. Lucky we bumped into you though. Thanks, Lee."

"Don't mention it, Steve. Mind if I come with you?"

Steve looked across at him in. He had already taken it as read that he would be coming along, but then he realised that he hadn't even considered that Lee could have others dependent on him.

"Of course not, you're more than welcome. You not got a family here now?"

"Nah," Lee kept his eyes to the front. "My Mum died a few years back and my sister is living down South somewhere. Not got a missus at the moment, and I was only at the garage mainly through boredom. I didn't need the food but I just thought I would grab it while I was there."

"Boredom," Steve raised an eyebrow.

"Yeah," Lee patted the rifle by his leg, "I was just taking a few pot shots for a laugh."

Steve looked down at the weapon and realised it was just an air rifle. "With that?" he exclaimed. "It's nothing more than a toy."

"Best I could get hold of though." Lee couldn't understand the problem that his old friend had with his statement as he shook his head and looked away.

Lee Gorman had been Steve's childhood friend and, despite his instability, he had always been loyal and unflinching when it came to standing up for his friends and family. Steve knew that having him on board would be both beneficial and interesting in the same breath.

He looked back to Claire who sat silent in the rear seat, still holding the unconscious Gary in her arms. Tears poured from her eyes and cascaded down her cheeks. She hadn't known Kevin, but she had seen that he was a good man all the same. He didn't need to come with Steve and help him save her, but he had nevertheless, and he had paid with his life trying to save Roy.

Roy.

Steve glowered when he looked at him, his jaw muscles flexing and his teeth grinding. He sat huddled in the corner of the seat by the window, whimpering and holding the wound on his shoulder. Steve wanted to say something, to stop the car and leave him at the side of the road, but he knew that it would make no difference. Roy was going to die anyway. And Kevin had died trying to help a 'dead man walking'.

21

His heavy feet scuffed against the surface of the road as he trundled into the outskirts of the city centre. Something familiar registered in his deteriorated mind and caused him to stop in his tracks and gaze around at his surroundings.

His instincts had guided him along for miles and miles, shuffling in the same direction, as though he had somewhere he needed to be. Nothing spoke to him inside or told him where or what he was headed for, he just kept walking. It was something deep down that surged him forward and to place one foot in front of the other.

He had trailed along streets, through residential areas and along open country roads. Nothing much along the way had enticed him to look up or even raise his head a little. For the majority of his journey he had stared at the unending and unchanging black tarmac below his feet as he shambled along.

It was only when his ears registered the sound of the leaves rustling in the trees, and the birds twittering away in the country lanes, that he became distracted from his line of travel.

The sun blazed in the sky and the billowy white clouds scurried across the expansive blue heavens as he gazed up. His eyes could distinguish the change in the brightness of the light as he stared straight into the large, glowing white ball of the sun, but he didn't squint, he had no desire to protect his eyes. He had no desire at all.

A light breeze caused the long grass in the fields to sway and he could feel, in a numb and deteriorated sense, the slight touch of the wind against the bare flesh of his fingers. He looked down to his hand as though expecting to see the source reaching up to him from the ground.

He had stood for hours below a tree, and looked out over the rooftops of the city in the distance. Something resembling appreciation took in the view ahead of him and a diluted sense of content seemed to wash over him.

Something about the rolling fields and the crisscrossing walls and fences of the rural areas that led up to the dark blue silhouettes of the high buildings in the distance made him want to sit down, and he shambled across to a wooden bench by a gravel path that crunched below his feet as he crossed it, causing him to stop and look down at his feet in wonderment.

He sat and watched and listened. The only sounds he could hear were the birds and the wind, and the insects that swarmed him.

He looked down at his position on the bench and placed his hands either side of him, and slowly leaned back as a trace thought spoke to him and told him that that was what he should do.

Below his feet, stalks of green, topped with budding yellow petals, sprouted and he stared at them for a while, studying them, before he reached down and plucked one from the soil. He raised it close to his face and eyed it as he twisted it around in his fingers, before dropping it and reaching for another.

Nothing was encouraging him to move, and he felt no desire to. In fact, he didn't feel anything; he just sat there and stared out in to the far distance. Only when a bird landed close by did his attention shift. The flurry of its wings as it came in to land just a couple of metres away from his seat, caused his eyes to snap in that direction. It walked, bobbing its head and pecking at the ground.

A feeling, deep and undeniable, thrust its way through his body to the forefront of everything. It urged him to grasp the bird, to consume it no matter what. He didn't understand the feeling and nothing inside him tried to. It was so forceful and all consuming that his sole focus was now on the living warm flesh that moved about at his feet.

His hands pushed him up from the bench and a long faltering moan escaped from his throat as he lunged toward it. He tripped and stumbled as he closed in on the agile creature on the ground and just a step away, the bird took to the sky in a flutter of feathers and a squawk.

His cold, shrivelled hands vainly clutched at the air in its wake as it soared into the sky. He was left flailing his arms, not realising that even though his eyes could still see the creature, it was too far away for him to touch. His teeth gnashed together once, hands dropped to his side, and his attention was brought back to his staggering legs that began to shuffle back toward the road.

As he continued his mindless journey, he could see the other figures that shuffled and lurched close by as he stood in the open street of the shopping area, but he paid them no attention. It was the buildings themselves that he watched. The large glass fronts of the shops and stores seemed to ignite a deep forgotten memory in him and he glanced around in confusion as he searched for the source of the new thought pattern.

He was standing at the end of the main high street, lined with row after row of department stores and fast food restaurants. He swayed in the breeze and focused in on the nearest of the other shambling figures that moved about close by, aimlessly.

It slowly staggered across his path and lumbered toward the window of the nearest shop front. Its clothes were soiled and ragged, with speckles of dried blood all over and a large patch of the same blood around the shoulder of the once white blouse that was now a dull, mottled grey.

It had been a woman; maybe he had even known her, but there was no sign of recognition or familiarity now. Something was happening inside his badly functioning mind and it forced him to reach out to the body of the wandering corpse as it staggered by.

His cold hand grasped at the loose cloth of her shirt, causing it to tear across the front, exposing a shrivelled and bare breast that was a light greenish blue in places with weeping sores filled with puss and squirming larva.

The fingers closed around the upper arm and pushed through the top layers of the already paper thin and deteriorating flesh. She stopped in her tracks and turned to face him. She remained slightly hunched forward and her tangled hair hung toward the ground and ruffled in the breeze. The skin of her face was a pale blue with black tinges around the ears, nose and lips as they began to shrivel and rot away. A large festering wound down the side of her neck squirmed with hundreds of maggots as they wriggled and burrowed their way deep into her putrid flesh.

For a brief moment, their gazes met. Her eyes were much the same as his; flat and clouded with no signs of life or even a spark of thought behind the misted lenses. After the brief encounter, he released his grip and the woman shuffled sideways for a few steps before turning and walking away again.

He looked down at the hand that had grasped her. Coagulated blood and a greasy layer of her skin had remained on his palm as he released his grip from her. He looked at it and then raised his other hand to see if there was the same to be seen there. There wasn't and he instinctively wiped the soiled hand along the length of the front of his jacket.

He shuffled toward the large window front of the nearest shop and caught a glimpse of movement beyond. He moved closer and reached for the moving figures and his hand suddenly stopped with a clunk. He pulled it back and tried again. It stopped again in the exact same place. He pressed both hands against the invisible barrier and brought his face closer, until eventually his nose and lips made contact with the glass.

It was cool and solid against his skin, and the change in the sensation caused him to remain that way for a moment before he pulled back. Then he saw the movement again and began walking the length of the window as he followed it. It was close, just beyond the barrier, but when he reached the end of the glass wall, the figure disappeared. Instead, he found himself staring at the reddish brown of a brick wall.

He stepped back and peered up the side of the building toward the roof top, then began to shuffle back the way he had come. He saw the figure again, moving with him in the same direction. He reached out with his grasping fingers and then he stopped. The vision on the other side of the glass was doing the exact same thing. It was reaching out for him and he stepped further back.

Staring at his fingers and then back at the window, a moment of clarity flashed in his mind. Somehow, he knew that he was seeing himself. He glanced around and then back to the reflection.

He stood with his shoulders slumped and his hands dangling at the side. He was wearing a dark bomber jacket and a dirty, grime-smeared pair of blue jeans. The front of his jeans had a dark expanding patch emanating from the centre of his groin area where his bowels and bladder had released their loads with nothing to keep the muscles contracted. He looked down and touched the area and a film of clear liquid transferred to his fingertips.

His skin was pale, his black hair was flat against his scalp and his features were saggy and lifeless. There was no indication of where his lips merged around his mouth. Normally they were a clear deep pink colour, flushed with blood and slightly inflated, giving them the appearance of fullness. Now, they were flat and colourless.

His legs swelled beneath the clothing around them, the blood having settled in his extremities while he had been upright. The fabric of his jeans was taught around his bloated lower limbs leaving his legs with the appearance of being waterlogged.

He turned away from his faint reflection and trundled along the high street. He heard the moans of the others around him and saw the tightly packed crowds that pressed themselves against shop windows and doors in an attempt to gain entry for whatever reason.

There were thousands of them in the streets, black clouds of flies swarming them and emitting a constant hum as they all buzzed together. Some of the dead were starting to swell, their internal gases expanding in their rotting stomachs and their skin stretching and forming ugly blisters as the outer layers began to putrefy. Now and then, a distended stomach would burst causing a loud trumpet of sound as fluids and gases escaped through the many orifices, including the rectum and mouth.

The ground was gluey with excreted bodily fluids and internal organs as some of the bodies, bloated from unreleased gasses, had exploded. Their innards had spilled out at their feet and become tangled around their ankles, and were then dragged and tripped over by the others in the street.

Some had lost the soft tissue of their faces already and some of them were blind as their eyes had been eaten away by the fat, bloated, squirming maggots that infested them. Lips and noses had receded and rotted away, creating grotesquely grinning expressions showing yellowed teeth that gnashed together over black, bloated tongues.

Most of them walked slowly along in no particular direction until something blocked their way and they would turn and follow the path of least resistance. With modern cities being designed specifically to keep the consumers in the high streets and stores, it was even easier to contain the mindless dead within the tightly packed walkways.

Nothing about the drab figures around him roused his attention and he continued shuffling along the street, now and then stumbling into others as they crossed his path. He scraped along walls and bounced from glass fronts, his eyes staring blankly at the floor and emitting the odd moan or groan.

As he came level with a particular shop front, he paused. He looked up and around at the faces that passed by, there was no life or spark in them to hold his curiosity, but something had. Something had caused him to stop and look up.

A glimmer of a memory, a familiarity hit home and for a fleeting moment as the electrical impulses fired and misfired in his partially working brain, he knew the place and a faint vision of figures, very much unlike the ones his damaged eyes could see now, passed in front of his mind's eye and were gone just as quickly.

He moaned loudly and remorsefully and reached out, trying to claw back the vision and the healthy flesh that he had just, for a brief moment, witnessed. He stopped and turned around, studying the large glass front of a shop spanning wide in front of him. In the window, he saw the shapes of people in glamorous clothing and in different poses, smiling and looking every inch, the healthy human being.

Pressed against the glass, his face left a smear along the clear window as he travelled along it, slapping his open-palmed hands against it and trying to reach the people beyond. He slumped against the door and the weight of his body forced it open slightly. He looked down at the gap and pushed a little harder, expanding the gap and forcing his way through into the shop.

Pictures of beautiful people covered the walls, and he looked from one to the next, scrutinizing each one with his pale, dead eyes. He scanned around the room and his eyes fell upon a picture of a close-up of a man, smiling broadly at him. He was a healthy-looking figure with dark, wavy hair, sparkling teeth, and chocolate brown eyes.

He became confused, his brow furrowed and he moved closer. He stared unblinkingly at the large face. To the right of the picture, he caught a glimpse of movement; he saw the reflection of himself in a large full length mirror. He looked from one image to the other, continuously comparing the moving image of himself in the mirror and the smiling picture on the wall and then, the comprehension hit and his brow rose in surprised recognition as he let out a questioning murmur.

The large, smiling image was him. Andy Moorcroft was in his own shop where he had run his modeling business. The reception desk, the trendy leather sofas in the lounge area, the heaps of portfolios and the camera equipment that lay about were all his. He glanced from one item to the next, shuffling on his unstable feet as faint and distant distorted memories flashed before him, causing him to shuffle in circles as he tried to reach out for the visions.

He approached the mirror and brought his hand up to touch the cold skin of his face and the hair on his head. Locks fell away in his fingers and he groaned as he tried to place them back into his scalp. He looked up, moaning sorrowfully at the image that had once been him, and a feeling of what could only be interpreted as sorrow passed over him. It dawned on him that he would never be that man again.

Still staring at the picture, he staggered back until he hit a low, stylish leather couch. His knees buckled when they made contact with the hard surface, causing him to sit down. On the seat next to him was a camera. Its black surface with its long lens and silver buttons and switches were vaguely familiar to him and he turned it in his hands. He studied it from different angles, before he finally and clumsily lifted the view finder to his eye. He glanced around the shop, pausing as the pictures came into sight.

Slowly, he lowered the camera again and it fell from his grasp and clattered and smashed against the floor. His eyes stared at his pale, bloodless, and wrinkled hands and then back up at the picture of him hanging from the wall as he let out a muffled, despondent moan that sounded more like a quiet sigh.

He slumped down into the soft cushions and sat staring for hours as the walking dead of the city shambled by in the street beyond the window.

22

"Jake, can you hear me?" Steve pulled the radio away from his mouth and tilted it toward his ear. There was no reply.

Lee slowly rolled the vehicle toward the junction that led onto the main approach to the Safari Park. Steve signalled with his hand to slow even further as he waited for a reply from Jake. He didn't want to draw any closer until he knew how the situation looked outside the entrance to the park.

They had been gone for nearly ten hours and they were keen to get back to safety, but Steve didn't want to rush in and he insisted on making sure that the coast was clear, and if it wasn't then he wanted to know what they faced.

He keyed the radio again. "Jake," there was urgency in his voice. "Can you hear me? We're on our way back."

A moment of silence, then a crackle of static as the radio squawked. "Yes, Steve, I can hear you. Where are you?"

"We're at the top of the main road leading to the gate. How does it look, are there any infected around?"

"Yeah, more than this morning actually," Jake replied. "What do you want to do?"

Steve bit his lip and hummed, "We'll have to try and draw them away mate, then make a break for the gate. Same drill as this morning, only in reverse. Have a few people ready to deal with any that get in and open the gate when I give you the word."

"Will do, Steve. I'll let you know when we're in position."

Steve turned and looked at Lee and then to the rest of the group. Gary sat with his hands in his lap and stared at the floor while Roy continued to gaze into space out the window, nursing his shoulder and whimpering and mumbling to himself.

Only Claire looked like she was alert and ready to deal with whatever trouble lay ahead.

Five minutes later, Jake called to say that they were ready.

"Okay, Lee, take us down to the gate. As soon as they start to follow, back up slowly and draw them away. Once we're about a hundred metres from the entrance, put your foot down and we'll get in without any of them following us, hopefully." Steve didn't look wholly convinced when he said it and he looked at Lee with a dubious expression.

Lee nodded. His eyes doubtful and tinged with fear, but as Steve knew he would, he did as he was asked and began to edge his way toward the dark entranceway, overhung by large trees and cast in shadow.

The dead at the gate saw them as they approached and turned their attention in the direction of the rumbling vehicle as it came to a halt just twenty metres away from them. The grey, emaciated, and slowly rotting faces of men, women and children gazed at the car and the people within. Their arms outstretched and their moans were audible over the sound of the engine before they were even fifteen metres away.

They staggered and shuffled at different paces and Steve had to place a hand on Lee's shoulder to steady him and stop him from reversing too early. They had to let the whole crowd gather and be sure that they had their complete attention, leaving none behind to push through the gate once it was opened.

They lurched toward them, their injuries and abominable appearances becoming apparent in the light of the day as they left the shade of the trees. They limped and hobbled, staggered and shuffled. Some were smeared in dried blood and others had limbs hanging loose, held on by threads of sinew or missing altogether. Clouds of buzzing flies circled them, unnoticed by the dead. Their skin was blackened in places, and puss-filled blisters bubbled from underneath as their bodies broke down from the inside out.

They crowded the car and pressed their faces against the windows. The people inside kept their eyes focused anywhere else other than into the haunting, dead eyes all around them.

There was a loud crack from the rear left hand window behind Steve, and Claire let out a startled yelp. Steve spun in his seat and saw that the glass had been splintered and was ready to crash inward. He caught a glimpse of a pair of hands brandishing a piece of broken masonry.

"Shit! The window is gonna go, back up, back up, Lee!" Steve shouted in terror.

Claire was leaning across the back seat and pushing up against Gary, who remained silent and inactive, to try and put as much distance between her and the window as possible. Another blow hit the glass, shattering it and showering Claire with small pellets of safety glass as a set of ashen hands were thrust inside. They clutched at the air in an attempt to grasp her and pull her through the gaping window and into the pack of waiting corpses on the other side.

Lee increased speed and the grasping arms clanged against the side of the door frame before disappearing back through the window as the car pulled away from the advancing dead mob.

They were far enough away from the park entrance.

"Okay, Jake, open the gate," Steve shouted into the radio.

Lee slammed the car back into first gear, and the bumper soon came into contact dead legs as they bounced over the front of the car and to the side, leaving bloody smears as their heads hit forcefully.

Bodies were slammed to the side as Lee ploughed through them and towards the gateway. The gate was only a few metres away when it began to close again, missing the side of the car by inches as it raced through and slamming shut just seconds after they passed on to the other side. Jake had timed it perfectly.

The dead were too slow, and by the time they reached the gate, the car was out of sight. They were left behind, hopelessly clawing at the air as they thrust their filthy, skeletal hands through the bars.

Back at the mansion, a crowd of people thronged toward the car to meet them as they pulled up. Helen and Jennifer were there, as well as Karen, Gary's wife.

Claire searched frantically with her eyes, looking for Sarah, and was out of the car before it had even come to a complete halt, calling for her. She wanted nothing in the world more than to see the beaming smile of her little girl and hold her tightly and tell her how much she loved her.

She wasn't there.

Steve climbed out. "Where's Sarah, Jen?"

Helen approached him, looking grave. "Steve, she's sick. It came on her after you left this morning and she's steadily gotten worse." She looked down, not wanting to meet his gaze, "I think it's the flu, Steve."

His knees became weak and he stifled a whimper as he felt fear rise in his chest. The colour drained from his face and he stepped closer to Helen, gripping her by the shoulders and pulling her close.

"Where is she?" he demanded.

"She," Helen struggled with her words, "she's upstairs in her bed. Sophie is with her."

Steve pushed past her and through the doors to the mansion, closely followed by Claire. He sprinted up the stairs, bounding two steps at a time, and burst into the room where Sarah lay, silent and pale with sweat soaking her hair and clothing.

Sophie looked up, startled as Steve entered. "She's been asleep for a few hours, Steve. I tried to give her some soup but all she could manage was a glass of water." She looked at the still form on the bed and back to Steve. "I'll leave you two alone with her, but I'll be outside if you need me."

Steve just nodded in acknowledgement without taking his eyes from his daughter as Sophie walked past him. Claire tried to appear appreciative with a brief smile, "Thank you," she said and the door closed behind her as the young girl left the room.

Sarah looked peaceful and didn't show any signs of discomfort, and both Steve and Claire began hoping, in optimism that is typical of a parent as they suppress their worst fears when faced with such a thing, that it was just one of the many illnesses that can easily be picked up and not necessarily the deadly strain of flu.

They sat in silence and watched her sleep. Her face was pale and clammy, and dark rings had formed around her eyes, making them appear sunken. Neither of them had anything to say to each other and neither had a desire to speak. They just sat and stared at the limp figure of their daughter, wrapped in the sheets, and willed her to be okay.

A short while later there was a knock at the door. It was Jake, and Steve reluctantly left the room, leaving Claire and Sophie to watch over Sarah.

"Steve, I know you're worried and you want to be there for your daughter, but there's nothing you can do and she is in good hands with her Mum and Sophie, and Helen will do all she can. You know she will." Jake was almost pleading with him. "But we need you downstairs. Gary is catatonic, he's not spoken a word or moved from the couch since we carried him in, and that other bloke, well, he's been bitten on the shoulder."

Steve nodded gravely in agreement with his previous statement, and went on to answer his second. "Yeah, his name is Roy, and it's 'cause of that fucking oxygen thief that Kev is dead." He said it with unreserved venom in his voice and stared into the distance as he spoke, remembering the geyser of blood and the squeals as Kevin had his throat ripped out.

Jake looked down at the floor and nodded. "I'd assumed that Kev hadn't made it when I noticed he wasn't in the car. I take it that Gary saw it happen too? I know they were close. Who is the other guy, the one who was driving?"

"Yeah, he saw the whole thing, and so did I." He looked Jake square in the eye. Tears were forming and he felt his heart pang at the memory. "The driver is Lee; an old friend of mine actually." He took a step toward the stairs and turned, "Thanks for your help today, Jake. C'mon, we better go and see to this mess then."

They walked into the lobby of the mansion, a gaggle of people stood and watched as they entered, glancing from Steve and then to Roy, who was lying on one of the large sofas, still not speaking. Gary sat at the table, the chess board in front of him, and Karen sat waiting for him at his side, her hand across his broad back and gently rubbing him between the shoulder blades.

Stephanie approached Steve with her weasel-like husband hot on her heels. She already had her ample chest puffed out and her sternest looking face, which she always used to intimidate others.

"That man has been bitten," she said in a booming, almost masculine and unmistakably authoritarian voice as she pointed to Roy. "He can't stay here. He will turn into one of them and..."

Steve held up a hand and spoke over her, "Listen to me you bag of shit," he leaned toward her, speaking through gritted teeth. "You did fuck all to help us today. You didn't step a foot outside this building, so until you have earned your place here, you need to walk on egg shells, or *you* won't be staying here either."

Her eyes bulged and her jaw fell open as her tongue lolled about inside her mouth like a swollen slug, trying to form words. "You, you can't speak to me like that, I'm the senior staff member here." She was trying to claw back the ground she had lost by using her position at the park as leverage.

Steve stepped toward her, his eyes flaring with rage. Their faces were just inches apart and he growled as he spoke. "You are nothing here, Stephanie, nothing but an overly vocal bully. The world has changed and you had better hurry up and realise that. You have no authority in this place and you're not the most popular either. So, be careful or you could find yourself as a living buffet for those puss brains out there."

He turned to Jason, who stood in silence, cowering in the large shadow cast by his wife. "And you, you fucking rat, you get in my way or cause any problems for me and mine, and I'll feed half of you to the lions and the other half to your bloated wife after she has turned. Okay?"

Without waiting for a reply, Steve stepped away and walked toward the rest of the group leaving Stephanie and Jason stunned. Jake was in shock and it took a moment for him to recover before trotting after him and falling into step beside him as he headed for the centre of the room.

"Jesus, Steve, did you mean all that?"

Steve stopped and turned to face him. "She needs to be knocked down a few pegs, Jake. Given half the chance, that fat butter mountain would run this place like Auschwitz. There is trouble coming from her, mark my words. And the moment I see her as a threat to me, Sarah, or anyone else in the group, I'll do what I have to in order to protect them. I meant what I said to her. The world has changed, Jake, and we all have to earn our place in it and I'll dispose of anyone I see as a threat to me and mine."

Jake smiled. "Hey, I agree one hundred percent with you, Steve. I only asked because I wondered how you would lift the fat bitch over the gate and I was gonna offer to help."

Steve had to hide his grin from the others. Despite the predicament he was in with his daughter sick, Roy being infected, and Gary in a state of shock and grief that he may never pull out of, Jake had made him smile, and he was grateful.

Helen was tending to the wound on Roy's shoulder. He sat in silence, chewing at his knuckle. She looked up at Steve and Jake as they approached and nodded as she finished off the last bandage.

Lee joined Jake and Steve. "I'm Lee, hope you don't mind me joining the gang?" he said as he shook hands with Jake.

"Of course not," Jake said in a hushed tone. "There's plenty of room and the more help we have, the better."

Helen came over. "I can see the infection already setting in. The wound is turning black around the edges as the skin is dying. His arm is swollen and red because his body is trying to fight it. I've never seen anyone survive though, and I don't expect to. The only thing I'm not sure of, is how long it will take and what we should do with him in the meantime."

"We'll put him in a spare room and keep a guard around the clock on him," Steve muttered. He wasn't particularly interested in Roy. He was more concerned for Gary. "What about him?" He indicated his friend to Helen with a nod of his head.

"I can't tell," she sighed. "I'm not a psychiatric nurse and don't know where to start. I can treat him for shock and stuff, but his state of mind is completely outta my hands. Best I can suggest is that he should have those closest to him around him for support and comfort while he comes to terms with it in his own time."

Steve met Helen's eyes, "Thanks, Helen."

"Steve," she paused, thinking of the right words. "I'll do all I can for Sarah. I promise you. I'll spend every minute of every day with her if need be to nurse her through this."

Steve nodded his appreciation and watched her as she left, heading for the stairs that led to Sarah's room.

"Fucking hell, she'd get it," Lee announced from behind.

Steve had to smile as he shook his head. Some things never change. His appearance had, but Lee was still mentally the young teenager, and he was reminded of all the crazy things that Lee had done during their childhood.

Lee had always said the most inappropriate things at the most inappropriate times, and could never understand or comprehend what all the fuss was about when the offended people reacted the way they did. To him, his actions and comments were always perfectly acceptable.

Steve saw that side of him as a positive. Even though he had found himself in many a scrape and sticky situation due to Lee and his inability to think before he spoke or acted, he always knew exactly where he stood with him and Lee didn't and *couldn't*, pull his punches.

Never shy of taking the fight to the enemy, Lee could never be accused of lacking balls, even when the odds were stacked highly against him. Steve knew that he could count on Lee to stand by his side and watch his back, regardless of the hopelessness of any situation.

Though slightly mentally unstable and completely unpredictable, Steve could rely on Lee as an ally.

He left Lee in the capable hands of Jake to give him a tour and introduction to the grounds and the people there, while he went to see what he could do for Gary.

He sat down beside his friend and watched him for a short while before speaking. "Gary, I'm not gonna waffle shit to you, what happened back there has hurt you, and hurt you badly. I know that and I know Kevin was a good guy. He proved that just by volunteering to come when he didn't have to and you had known him longer than I had, so the loss is hitting you hard.

"All I can say, Gary, is he wouldn't want you to unravel over him now. By all means mate, grieve for him, but there's a lot of people here who need you too. You and your wife are the two that have kept all these people together, and they still need you. I need you. You're one of the strong ones here and there's a lot to get done before we can afford to lose you in grief. Use the grief, as Kevin would want, and turn it against those walking bags of shit out there and wield it as a weapon for the people in here."

Gary continued to stare, unblinking at the chess board in front of him.

Steve looked up to Karen, looking for a sign in her eyes that he may be getting through; she nodded, encouraging him to continue.

"We need to look at options of getting out of here if it comes to it, Gary, just like you said. You know this place better than anyone. So when you're ready, I could use your thoughts on the matter. Also, any ideas you have on how to keep them things away from the main gate. There's no rush mate, and we will deal with it when you're ready. I'm sorry about Kevin, I truly am. He was a better man than the wanker he gave his life trying to save.

"If you just need a friend to talk to, I'm always happy to share a bottle of whisky and bang the world to rights with you. Just hang in there buddy. I'm sorry for Kevin, and I'm sorry for you, Gary. Anything, anything at all, just let me know." He gave him a squeeze on the forearm and stood up from the table.

"Thanks, Steve," Karen had tears in her eyes. "He thinks you're a good man and he needs a good friend like you."

Steve nodded. "I'll be here for him whenever he needs me, Karen. I wouldn't have survived today without his help. I owe him. I'm gonna go and see how Sarah is now, but I'll be back soon."

He left the table and made his way to his daughter's room. It was dark and cool in the room and he could see faint figures, dimly lit by lamps that had been turned low. Helen and Claire sat vigil at the side of her bed.

"How is she, has she awoken at all?" he asked Claire as he sat down beside her.

Claire was fighting back the tears. "Briefly, she didn't recognise me." Her voice broke as she said it.

Steve placed his arm around her shoulders as she sobbed against him. He had to keep himself strong for them both. "It's okay, Claire. She's in good hands. Helen will take care of her. You should try and get some sleep. Sarah is a strong girl, you know how tough she is."

She was crying uncontrollably now, "I just can't bear the thought of losing her, Steve. She doesn't deserve this. She's just a little girl, our little angel." Her words were distorted as she tried to control herself but the tears forced their way through.

He led her away and into one of the spare rooms, lying her on the bed and tucking her in as she continued to sob. He stroked her brow and promised her that Sarah would be fine. He didn't know what else to say. He stayed at her side until she fell asleep and then went back to sit with his daughter.

Helen stayed by Sarah's bedside, refusing to leave and even taking her meals in the same room. She remained there throughout the second day and into the night, watching for any change in her condition.

Steve hardly slept in the forty eight hours since he had returned from rescuing Claire.

His thoughts troubled him and they were full of 'what if's' and worst case scenarios. He neglected everything else around him and devoted his whole time between his daughter's bedside and his own room, refusing to bother with anything else. He felt lost and spent hours sitting on the edge of his bed, staring out the window into the dark trees as the heavy windswept rain lashed against the glass and the old wooden frames. Tears rolled down his face as he contemplated the possibility that Sarah may not pull through.

Jennifer had come to see him at one point during the second day. "I didn't mention it yesterday, because you had enough to deal with, but I got a phone call from Marcus."

He turned to her, waiting for the rest of the news. "And?" he asked.

"He's in Turkey. He didn't say much. He said they're all okay but I know Marcus, I could tell they had a rough time of it."

"Yeah," Steve nodded as he sat at the edge of the bed clasping his hands together between his knees. "He did mention to me that there was a chance that the border could be closed and heavily defended."

"Well, he didn't say much, except that they were okay and heading for the crossing at Istanbul. He also asked about the radio we have here. I wrote it down." She pulled a piece of paper from her pocket on which she had scribbled a series of words. "He said they have something called Codan. Some kind of radio I think, and he wants to know if anyone here knows about high frequency radios and all that."

"I think Jake is the technical guru here, so we can see what he knows tomorrow. Did he say where he is exactly?"

She shook her head. "No. Knowing him, he probably couldn't pronounce it anyway." She chuckled.

It was five in the morning when he woke, still dressed and sprawled on his bed. He rushed out of the room and in to see Sarah. He asked Helen if there was any change. Sarah had been sick for almost three days and running a high fever. She had been delirious most of the time and during her brief moments of consciousness, she recognised no one.

"Her fever broke during the night, Steve." Helen was smiling as she said it, a glint of tears in her eyes. "She still has a temperature, but that's to be expected. She woke a couple of hours ago and asked for water, so at least she's coherent." She looked at him as she pushed the hair back from her clammy forehead. "You were right, Steve, she really is a tough one and she's fighting it like a Spartan."

Steve crouched by the bed and looked at the pale, sleeping face of his little girl. "Hey tiger," he whispered, "you'd better pull through this, or you'll miss out on the big treat. I've already organised it with Sophie and Gary that all the kids, and anyone else who wants to come along, will be doing a full tour of the park, with picnic baskets, while they check on all the animals and you'll even get to pet some of them.

"But you've got to pull through for me, darling. Please Sarah, I can't..." He pushed his face into the bed sheets and sobbed as he gripped her hand.

"Dad," her voice was weak and croaky. "Dad, why are you crying?"

He looked up, wiping the tears from his eyes. "Hey buddy," his voice faltered, "how you feeling?"

"My throat is sore and my legs ache. When are we going to see the animals?"

Steve let out a low snort, a smile stretching across his face. "When you're better, you have to get completely better first. Don't worry. I won't let them go without you buddy. As soon as you get yourself right, we will go and see the animals."

She managed a weak smile. "All of them?"

"Yep, all of them."

"Including the lions and tigers?" she asked.

"Of course, but I don't think you will be able to feed them. They're more likely to want to bite your arse off."

Another smile from Sarah. "They wouldn't, because you would be with me and you're bum is a lot fatter than anyone's."

Steve was stroking her hair and giggling along with her. Even in her weakened state, she managed to ply him with all the banter he needed. "Righty dokey then buddeo, you get yourself back to sleep and save your strength. When you next wake up, promise me you'll try and eat something?"

She nodded slightly and rolled her head to the side and drifted back to sleep. He leaned over and kissed her on the cheek. "I love you the entire world, Sarah."

He made his way to the kitchen and poured himself a cup of coffee. Karen was making breakfast and hummed cheerily as she worked.

"How's the wee one this morning?" she asked looking over her shoulder at Steve.

He shrugged between gulps of the hot liquid. "She actually spoke and managed to joke. Her fever broke in the night, so I suppose it's a good sign. But it's too early to say. How's Gary?"

"Oh, he's a tough one, Steve. He's hurting, but he will bounce back. I've seen him like this in the past. He needs you though. You're what will give him a purpose. You're pretty much the leader of the group here and these people are already looking on you in that way. You're a doer and that's what they need. And you don't take nonsense, especially the way you dealt with that Stephanie."

Steve looked up as he drained the last of his cup. "Oh, you heard that then?"

She grinned at him. "Listen to me sunshine, I have ears like a shit house rat and there's very little that gets past me. As well as that, I'm very good at reading people and I've noticed the whole Helen and Steve thing that's developing too."

"Eh? There's nothing going on there, Karen," he stated, feeling slightly embarrassed and like a kid being scrutinised by his Mother.

"Not yet there isn't." She poured him more coffee and winked at him.

Claire entered the room. Her hair was unkempt and her eyes were red and puffy. "Morning, Steve. Listen, thanks for the other day. I should've thanked you sooner, but I wanted to get you alone."

"No worries," he shrugged.

"I'm serious." She touched his hand and stared at him. "Thanks."

He shifted in his seat, feeling a little uncomfortable and changed the subject. "Did you look in on Sarah?"

She sighed. "Yeah, she was still sleeping. Helen told me that she is starting to seem better. The fever has gone and she said that you and her spoke too."

"She recognised me this morning and even managed a smile. I think she'll be okay, Claire."

She tried to feed from his optimism. "I hope so, Steve," she sighed as she ruffled her hair into some sort of presentable shape.

He looked down at his cup, biting his lip and then back to Claire. "There's something else we need to discuss, Claire."

"I know. Roy," she replied without looking up from the table.

"Yeah, Roy. Jake has kept an eye on him but we are gonna have to do something about him soon. From what I know, there's no cure, and every bite is one hundred percent fatal and he will come back, Claire."

She nodded as she stared down at the table top. "I know, Steve. He may be a coward and self-centered, but I wouldn't wish this on him."

"I don't, Claire. I wouldn't wish this on anyone."

She looked up, flicking her hair from her face. "What do we do then?"

Roy had been made as comfortable as possible and dosed with pain killers and sedatives. Jake and Lee had handled him into one of the spare rooms and took turns sitting watch over him.

His fever had strengthened and he had become delirious and incoherent. He continuously shouted out at no one in particular, and his words could rarely be understood. His arm had swollen to almost twice its natural size and his veins were visible underneath the skin as the infection coursed through his blood stream and around his body.

"He's gonna die soon, you know that, and we need to be ready for it. We need to restrain him. I dunno about you, but I think it would be better to put him out of his misery before the infection gets any worse."

Her brow creased. "He's not a fucking horse, Steve."

"I know. I know that, Claire. But it's too dangerous to let him turn. You've seen what happens and you've seen what they can do. For fuck sake, Claire, remember what they did to Kevin the other day?" He was pleading with her but it came across more as him lecturing and trying to lay the law down at her.

"Yes, Steve, I remember what they did. I had a front row seat remember? But we can't just start killing people when they get bitten. Or sick. Would you kill Sarah, could you kill her if you knew she would turn?" She looked at him questioningly and accusingly.

Steve raised his voice and spat his words. "Don't even fucking say it, Claire, that's different."

"Not when you look at it the way that you are. In a 'not taking any chances' sort of way."

He realised her point and backed down with a sigh as he slumped into his chair. "Sarah wasn't bitten, Roy was, and it's not a dead cert that anyone catching the flu will turn, but Roy will. I just don't want to take any risks, Claire."

"Like you said," she leaned forward and took his cup and raised it to her mouth, "we can keep him separated, and restrained if need be. And when he turns, it should be me that kills him. I owe him that much."

Her last statement shocked Steve. He had always known she was strong and fiery, but still, it shocked him. He just nodded.

Later in the morning, Lee approached Steve. He looked troubled and he pulled Steve to one side in the lobby of the mansion to speak quietly. Discretion wasn't exactly Lee's forte and instead of a private conversation, it was more of a loud one, just removed from the rest of the people, who could actually still hear every word.

"Steve, that Jake, is he a bender?"

Steve laughed. "You mean gay? Yeah he is. Why?"

"Fucking hell, I've been spending loads of time with him lately and people may think I'm a sausage bandit too." He was rubbing his head, clearly uncomfortable and afraid that his masculinity, as well as his sexuality, may be in question.

Steve knew that unless dealt with in a more diplomatic manner, Lee was likely to climb on a chair and begin announcing that he wasn't gay to the whole house. It would be meant in a purely 'clearing the air' sort of way to Lee, but Steve knew it wouldn't be taken like that by others. It would offend some, because he wasn't likely to use the politically friendly terms, and others would think him mad.

He placed a hand on his friend's shoulder. "Lee, no one here thinks you're gay. It's as plain as the nose on your face that you're straight because since you got here, you've been walking about like a dog with five dicks, drooling over Sophie and Helen."

"You don't think he fancies me do you?" he asked with a worried tone in his voice.

Steve was shaking his head and grinning broadly. "Don't flatter yourself mate. Just because he's gay, doesn't mean he wants a piece of you."

"Yeah, Lee," a voice came from behind, "I don't want to bum every bloke I see you know." Jake walked past with a mug of steaming coffee, speaking casually between sips. He paused and smiled at Lee. "What's up, did I seem too butch? I can go and put my hot pants on and mince about for you if you want?"

Lee looked at Steve then at Jake, his eyes wide. "Look, I didn't mean to offend you or anything, I just didn't know."

"Hey mate," Jake was smiling, "it's cool. I'm happy with being a 'bender' as you call it, and you've nothing to worry about Lee. You're far too ugly for me, even if it is the end of the world."

Lee grinned, relieved that he wasn't an object of desire for a gay man, and also that it was still okay for him to be friends with someone he had clearly already begun to bond with.

Steve waved Jake over. "Anyway, if you have time Jake, I want to talk to you about the radio."

"What about it?" he asked as he lowered the cup from his lips.

"Well uh, will I be able to talk to my brother on it?"

"Depends what he is using. Has he said anything about their equipment?"

"Something called Codan? Does that mean anything to you? I'll be truthful, I don't know the first thing about that kind of stuff." Steve was hopeful that Jake did.

Jake nodded slowly. "Yeah, the Australians developed it for the outback originally. It's HF," he looked from Steve to Lee and saw they were no wiser and rolled his eyes. "High Frequency. Depending on the frequency and the antenna types and lengths and times of day, you can talk to someone on the other side of the planet. If it has been supplied by the military though, it could be encrypted and we would be unable to pick it up, at least with the equipment we have here."

Steve and Lee swapped glances then both looked at Jake.

Steve said, "You've just given me a big bowl of Greek salad there Jake, but you obviously know what you're talking about. Have a play about with the radio and I'll try and get more info from Marcus on what he's carrying."

"I'll have a look at it this afternoon. What are you two gonna be doing?"

"We need to start working on an escape plan for this place and the possibility of blocking off the road to stop those things from wandering up to the front gate. We need to be better organized and start having people doing set jobs around here. Obviously, you're the Bill Gates and Steven Hawking of the group rolled into one, so you're the tech guy."

Jake raised his eyebrows. "Lucky me eh?"

Sarah began to slowly recover and with each hour, she looked and seemed to feel better, but Helen was adamant that she should remain in bed and under constant supervision. Steve was happy to comply.

As Sarah fought the virus off, Roy deteriorated rapidly. Four days after being bitten and he was close to death.

Lee, Jake, Steve and Gary helped to carry him down and out through the back on a makeshift stretcher, out of sight from the rest of the people of the house. Sophie had been detailed to take the children out the front and to entertain them to prevent them from seeing the almost lifeless Roy as he was brought through the house.

He was placed onto a mattress that had been set aside for him, in an annex that was used as a large storeroom for the mansion. He was completely incoherent and didn't seem to notice his new surroundings. His hands and feet had been bound to stop him from lashing out or being able to move in case he turned suddenly.

Helen took his vital signs, feeling for his pulse and listening to his breathing. "I don't think he will hang on much longer," she said gravely, shaking her head as she stood.

He was ghastly pale and gaunt. His features had withered as though he were already dead. His sunken eyes were rolled into the back of his head and he struggled to breathe. His entire body was soaked with sweat and as he was unable to take in more fluids to replace what he was losing, his body began to dehydrate and shrink to nothing.

Claire approached, pushing her way to the front of the gaggle that had formed around the mattress. "Leave us. I'll deal with it from here. I'll wait with him. I owe him that much."

Steve looked down and saw that she was carrying a pick axe. "Claire, are you sure?"

She nodded. "Just leave please." She looked around at their faces, pleading, with tears in her eyes.

They left the room and went back into the main part of the house.

Steve went to see Sarah. She was still weak, but the colour had started to return to her cheeks. Jennifer sat beside her as she slept.

"She is gonna be okay, Steve," she said to him as he took up position on the other side of her.

"Looks that way don't it? Jesus, I was so worried."

"Is Claire with Roy?" Jennifer asked. She lowered her voice as she spoke, more from respect than to keep it a secret.

"Yeah," he nodded, staring down at the blankets on the bed. "She insisted and wanted us all to leave."

She blew out a long, loud breath. "God, that can't be an easy thing to do. Understatement I know."

"Yeah, she's a strong woman and has always been independent when it comes to making difficult choices."

Sensing that Steve wasn't comfortable to go on speaking about what needed to be done for Roy and the decision that Claire had made, Jennifer changed the subject.

"I don't think Marcus is gonna be too impressed about his baby," she said.

Steve looked at her and then realised what she had meant. "Oh, you mean the Range Rover? Yeah, I think I'm gonna have to come up with a good story on that one aren't I?"

"Nah," she smiled as she shrugged. "It was used to save us all and besides, he can have his pick of cars when he gets here."

It had been hours since Claire entered the room and stayed with Roy. Steve and Helen had remained in the lobby, the door leading into the storeroom just in view down a small corridor that led away to the back of the house.

They watched the door, waiting for Claire to emerge.

It had been almost twelve hours when the door finally opened. Claire appeared, she staggered, clutching the door frame and then she slowly and unsteadily made her way toward the sitting area.

Steve watched as she approached, casting nervous glances at Helen, who returned the same expression. Claire came closer and stopped. She raised her head and looked at them both in turn before closing her eyes tightly.

Finally, she nodded. "It's done."

She slumped into one of the large antique leather armchairs and reached for the crystal canter in the centre of the low table in front of her. She flipped off the top and poured herself a generous helping of brandy into a glass tumbler. She raised the glass to her lips and threw her head back, swallowing the contents of the glass in one gulp before pouring another.

Steve and Helen sat in silence and let her get on with it. They refrained from asking the usual stupid questions such as *'Are you okay?'*

Those very same questions, though meant well, always annoyed him.

Of course she isn't okay, she just slammed a pick axe through her boyfriend's head, Steve thought to himself.

Later, Steve helped Jake and Lee to move the body when Claire had gone to clean up and sleep off the six large glasses of brandy.

She had done a clean job of dealing with Roy. There had been no unnecessary suffering. It had been quick and Roy would've felt nothing. Steve wondered whether the dead felt pain at all.

She hadn't panicked and missed or hit with a glancing blow. There had been one swing and it had punched clean through the centre of his head, the point of the pick sticking into the wooden floor boards underneath with very little blood or splatter.

Steve didn't know whether or not Claire had waited for him to reanimate or if she had taken care of him as soon as he had died. He didn't need to know; it was done and nothing more needed to be said.

They wrapped him in sheets and carried his body into the garden, to a grave they had already prepared earlier in the day, and gently placed him in it. They left it open in case Claire wanted to see him one last time and say anything over him before the hole was filled in.

Steve thought it was only right that he should be buried with a degree of respect given the chance. He would want that for himself and he would see to it that others had the same treatment if it came to it.

He couldn't help but think of Kevin. He hadn't been buried, or taken care of when he died.

23

He felt powerful and strong.

It was a whole new experience to him. All his life he had fantasised about being the dominant male among his peers, but he could never live up to it. Instead, he spent his lonely evenings acting out his daydreams in front of a mirror; arguing with himself and being assertive and standing up to the people he had always been trodden down by as he imagined them standing before him.

Now, he was probably the only remaining survivor of his colleagues. He was sure that they would all be dead by now. If they hadn't died on the night of the riot that had swallowed most of his workmates up, then surely they must have died since. They would've been too busy trying to look after family and friends and with people to look out for; it increased the chances of getting killed.

Tony had neither. It was just him and he had the world at his feet now. There was no one to tell him what was right or wrong anymore. He didn't have to pretend to be like everybody else. He could indulge himself and be who he really was without hiding behind the uniform and using his position of power to elevate him above the poor excuse of a man he really was.

He was now the almighty and powerful and he thrived on the feeling.

For weeks he had moved about the city and outlying towns, helping himself to whatever he wanted and doing as he pleased. He had free reign and he had shrugged off the shackles of ethics and what society had deemed as moral conduct.

He broke into houses and businesses and took what he pleased. He always secretly hoped to find survivors. People who were weak and easily manipulated that he could then mold to adore and revere him.

More often than not, the houses would be empty and abandoned. He had developed the habit of sifting through family photographs, looking for pretty women or young girls, then he would head upstairs and find their room and begin sifting through their drawers and laundry baskets, masturbating as he wore their underwear over his face. He would become completely lost in himself and without realising it, he would be howling as he reached his climax.

Tony had pushed the boundaries one day, even for his own warped mind. He broke into a house and found the owner to still be inside, dead of course. At first he had considered making a sharp exit, but decided against it.

"Hello gorgeous," he slurred as he eyed the walking corpse that had once been a pretty female.

Even in death, it was obvious that she had been extremely attractive in life. Now though, her skin had a yellow hue and looked clammy. Her eyes were lifeless and misted, and her swollen tongue flopped from her lips as she snarled and lunged toward him. He punched and kicked the body to the ground and proceeded to subdue and tie her up.

"Time for a bit of fun for you and me darling and, of course, I'll still respect you in the morning."

He stripped her and wore her soiled underwear over his face as he spent the entire evening drinking and masturbating over her decaying body as she squirmed and writhed beneath him. He imagined her struggles to be that of orgasmic ecstasy from his prowess and skill in the bedroom.

What very few morals he had had before the rising of the dead, they were long since gone now. There was nothing and no one to tell him what was socially acceptable anymore. Before the world crumbled, there had been the police uniform and other people and television to steer him right. Now, all that was gone and the restraints of civilisation were broken and he had no intention of ever allowing himself to be shackled by them again.

He drank a lot. There wasn't a day that went by when he wouldn't be driving around with a bottle of vodka or whisky in his lap, continually swigging from it until he was blind drunk. One time, he had pulled over to sleep it off and hours later he awoke to find himself surrounded by the faces of the dead, packed tightly together and banging against the windows and rocking the car as he slumbered.

Sometimes, when he became bored, he would taunt the dead and lure them into areas of his choosing where he would trap them and take his frustrations out on them. His weak past still haunted him from time to time and he would need to replenish his depleting dominance by doing something brave and daring.

In reality, there was nothing brave or daring about his actions. He always made sure that he was well protected and all possibilities were covered. He left nothing to chance and avoided any situation that even remotely held a risk of him being hurt.

One of his favourite pastimes was to dress in full bike leathers with helmet and gloves and trap two, sometimes three of the infected in a large room, normally a warehouse on the outskirts of town and then, fight them as though he were a gladiator in the arena, raising his arms in triumph to his imaginary audience as he pulled off a particular feat or a killer blow that he thought worthy of applause.

He collected an assortment of weapons, from steel bars and tools like large spanners and wrenches, to a cheap copy Samurai sword that he had found in a shop window. One of his favourite weapons was his homemade mace. It had originally been a small baseball type bat, and he hammered long nails in to it, creating a ring of spikes around the head of it that he would smash into the bodies and faces of his opponents.

He would play with them at first, crippling them as they charged him and smashing their legs to a pulp with blow after blow with one of his weapons. Normally, the coup de grace would be given after he had paraded around the arena, waving his arms and standing with hands on hips as he rested a foot on the vanquished that lay squirming on the floor. He would draw his sword and slice through the neck, severing the head and then proceeding to walk through his make-believe Arch of Triumph.

Depending on how he was feeling, sometimes he would even catch specific kinds of infected. If he was particularly brave on a given day, he would try and trap a couple of runners, or even people with the aggressive strain of the flu, though the latter were few and far between since the dead had risen.

He drove aimlessly, heading to nowhere in particular. He had made a point of avoiding the larger of the built-up areas and kept to the backroads when he could. Now he drove his shiny new people-carrier through the countryside with the window down, playing his favourite music, his favourite items in the back, locked in a large black box that he patted and spoke to in a soothing tone now and then.

He really felt alive. Everybody dying had given him a new vitality. He had a purpose, and that purpose was to enjoy life while everyone else had theirs snatched away from them. But there was a problem; he had killed Elaine without a second thought and he had enjoyed the feeling afterward. She had provided him with a distraction when they were cornered by the dead and she had, in the process as he listened to her die, aroused him.

He had become damn right horny over the whole thing.

Now though, the killing of people who were already dead had lost its lustre and he was becoming tired of it. There was no excitement in it anymore.

They didn't feel pain, or at least not on the level that he desired, and they didn't scream or beg for their lives before he dealt them the finishing blow. Instead, they just kept coming at him, even without their legs or arms, or blind as he had gouged out their eyes. They never backed down or cowered from him; something that would have fed his sense of power and complete control.

He needed more. He needed living people to give him his sense of Godliness.

He looked into the mirror as he drove, adopting his strongest and most intimidating face. "I am the Emperor. This is my world now," he said in a deep growling voice at his reflection.

"You're just the Emperor of the dead and that's nothing," his reflection argued back. "They don't fear you and they don't respect you. Worst of all, they don't worship you. You're nothing, nothing but a fucking loser."

"Fuck you!" he screamed. "Fuck you, cunt, cunt, fucking cunt!" He was ragging the steering wheel, his veins distended in his neck as he roared at his own image in the mirror.

He pulled to the side of the road and sat staring at the path ahead for a while. He was sweating and his heart pounded against his chest wall. "I'm not weak. I'm strong." He lowered his head and rested it against the wheel. "I'm strong. I'll show them."

He glanced back up through the window. It was a clear sunny day and the heat shimmered slightly from the black surface of the road. The birds were singing and the insects buzzed by as they went about their business.

Tony smiled. All was right with the world. It was how it should be; just him and his possessions, with no one else to interfere with him doing as he pleased.

He put the car in to gear and drove on, the argument with himself forgotten, and singing along again to the sounds of Led Zeppelin.

24

People took it upon themselves over the weeks to perform certain tasks and duties, and within a short period things were running as smooth as could be expected with something that resembled a normal routine. As normal as could be expected given the circumstances.

Steve, Lee and Gary had taken on the responsibility of ensuring and maintaining the security of the park. With regular patrols and checks of the walls and gates, they identified weak points and possible blind spots that would need to be reinforced eventually. But, with such a large perimeter and such a small amount of manpower, they decided that the best course of action was to conduct a daily physical check of them and to also have a dedicated guard to stand watch around the house twenty four hours a day.

Everybody who was considered as being able bodied enough and with good eye sight took a turn in the shift that was posted on the roof of the house. The guard on duty was given specific points and directions to check regularly with the binoculars, as they stood watch. The elevated position of the house provided good all around visibility for a considerable distance, giving the people of the group ample warning of anything approaching, and time to react.

Gary had even assembled the entire group together at one point and given them a full presentation on the do's and don'ts when it came to ensuring the safety of everyone involved. The walls, including all gates and access points, were declared out of bounds to all, unless they were escorted by either Steve, Gary or Lee.

There was a sort of curfew introduced without people being made to feel too restricted. No one, and it was emphasised that it was for their own safety, was to travel anywhere within the grounds alone during darkness, and without first letting other people know where they were going. To avoid panic of the thought of infected being on the loose in the park, Gary explained that it was mainly due to the fact that people could fall and hurt themselves or become lost in the extensive grounds of the park without anyone knowing they were missing until the morning.

The night guard wasn't exactly a hard job to do. It wasn't the army and no one was expected to sit and stare out into the blackness of the night for hours, or endlessly pace to and fro on the roof. The average stint was rarely longer than two to three hours and it was agreed that whoever stood watch during the night was excused any chores for the next day. Most people on duty took a book or magazine to read and it was the norm to make sure that there was always a flask of hot coffee and sandwiches stacked inside the guard position; which consisted of a couple of fold away chairs and a gazebo to keep the rain off.

On the second night that the watch had been introduced, Lee had checked up on the guard position and found Jason fast asleep and snoring in his sleeping bag, the radio and binoculars nowhere to be seen.

Steve was awakened by the crashing and banging and the screams of pain from the rooftop. Lee ploughed into Jason with his fists and feet as the scrawny man lay zipped up to the neck in his sleeping bag and unable to protect himself as he was kicked around the roof, while Lee bawled and shouted at him for putting their lives at risk with his incompetence. It was decided after the incident that anyone found asleep on duty would be banished beyond the walls. Just the thought of such a punishment terrified most people into staying awake.

Of course, there were people that argued against such decisions and voiced their concerns and fears of the situation becoming a totalitarian regime. Gary, in his calm schoolteacher manner, explained to everyone that it was a matter of safety for the group and pointed out that should the worst happen, if the guard was asleep, they could all be overrun and killed by the infected. With visions of the dead tearing up the path etched firmly in their minds, the people at the house saw reason, all except Stephanie.

"Why do we have to obey the rules that you decide? Who voted that you should be calling the shots? The way I see it, you three," she glanced from Gary to Steve and to Lee in turn as she spoke, "have pretty much taken over the place and now dictate what we can and can't do. I mean, look what that thug," she pointed to Lee who had his usual 'butter wouldn't melt' look on his face, "did to my husband." She was doing her best to pitch an audience and rile people.

Steve, remembering the last confrontation he had with the vile woman stepped forward, his arms folded across his chest. He breathed in deeply before he looked her dead in the eye and spoke.

"Stephanie, I really don't care what you do." He emphasised the word 'you' and rocked slightly on the heels of his feet as he said it. "You do very little around here anyway and the little that you do, is under duress. As for the thug, well, your husband placed everyone of us here in danger by sleeping on duty and if it takes a kicking for him to realise that and to stop it from happening again, then so be it. Next time, I won't pull Lee off him like I did.

"Honestly, Stephanie, you're not a prisoner here." He looked at every face in the room. "None of you are, and you can leave anytime you want. We will even help you. But if you are to stay here, then you help with the running of this place and you obey the rules, especially when it comes to the security of all.

"Nothing is being asked of any of you beyond your physical capabilities, and everyone can even choose what it is they want to help out with. We," he glanced behind him, indicating Gary and Lee with a nod to each, "could use more help with security, but if no one else wants to go to the walls, to see the dead at the gates, then that's fine. No one will force you. But we all do our bit."

Stephanie sat glowering at him. She huffed, "I just don't think someone like you should be in charge."

"I'm not in charge, Stephanie." He said it with slight arrogance to annoy her. "No one is. Should we make you the boss? And what do you mean 'someone like you'? Am I not enough of an egotistical self-absorbed bully like you? Is that what leadership is? Stephanie, don't sit there making your statements and trying to upset people, try working with us for once, or fuck off!"

They discussed the options for escape should the worst case scenario happen and the main entrance be breached. They decided on the wooded path at the far end of the park to the rear. In that direction there was nothing but private farmland and footpaths through nature reserves for miles. Steve had argued that they were less likely to run into any infected in that area because of its isolation and inaccessibility.

A secluded track led down to a gate that was used by the previous security staff for access to and from the rear guard box and private access point for park vehicles. It was approximately three kilometres from the house and it would mean having to move there either by vehicle or on foot. Four cars were left to one side of the car park with the keys in the ignition at all times. They were the escape vehicles and they were checked and their engines turned over every day to ensure that they were reliable and ready to move at short notice.

Gary had insisted that the house be strengthened in case they find themselves trapped and surrounded and unable to escape to the cars. The windows within arm's reach on the ground floor were boarded both inside and out, and the doors had boards and planks of wood placed close by for a quick and dirty defence. They would be crudely hammered into place to secure the entrances should the worst happen, and could be reinforced later once the house was locked down.

Karen declared that she would take on the majority of the cooking duties, and most people were happy to let her. Karen loved being in the kitchen and she seemed to get a real kick out of people's reactions to the small miracles she was able to perform with the limited ingredients available to her. Regularly she would take adults and kids alike out around the woods of the park to hunt for mushrooms and natural herbs and plants that could be added to the food.

She was a magician in the kitchen and with few pleasures left in the new world, meal times were always looked forward to with glee and excitement and anticipation at what delights could be laid out for dinner.

"That wife of yours could make a gourmet meal from a scabby dog, Gary," Helen had remarked one evening after another of Karen's glorious meals.

Gary laughed. "Well, it looks like the secret is out my dear, cause it's scabby dog stir fry for dinner tomorrow."

Sarah had recovered within a week of falling ill and was soon back to full strength. As promised, Sophie and Gary took all the children and a few of the adults on a tour of the park as they checked on the animals and ensured they were healthy. Sophie was concerned about one of the Rhinos and the kids had even been able to approach and pet the animal as Sophie carried out her checks.

That night all that could be heard throughout the house were children talking and chatting excitedly about the animals in the park and which were their favourite.

The children developed a sense of duty also and even though it was fun to them, they took on the responsibility of helping with the animals and learning all they could about caring for them. The parents and adults also found it a great distraction for the children, to take their minds away from the horrors of the new world.

Even Lee took an interest and began spending time helping out, particularly with the monkeys, helping to feed them and clean out their paddocks. It surprised Steve; he had always thought that Lee was more likely to want to throw stones at them and taunt them. He shrugged off the thought and put it down to Lee having matured since his wild and unpredictable childhood.

The only person in the group who had even a remote idea of what he was doing when it came to the technical workings of the park was Jake, and he had managed to get the radio up and running. It took a lot of fiddling about and fine tuning with antenna types and lengths before he felt confident enough that it was ready to use.

The power grid had shut down and they filled and primed the generators in the basement for use. It was agreed that it would be the job of one person to regularly check around the house, turning off lights and appliances that were not necessary and to enforce the conservation of fuel. They had a supply of fuel expected to last for some time, but it was agreed that it wouldn't last forever and the more regulated they were with it, the better for the long run.

Stephanie had immediately volunteered for the job.

"Anyone but her," Karen had remarked.

Gary mused, "Let's give her a go at it. The moment she starts carrying a whip though, we set Lee on her."

Phone communications had pretty much died off. Over the weeks it had become more and more difficult to get through or even get the usual calm recorded female voice saying that the signal was gone or that there was a network error. Now, all that happened was the phone would just beep then go dead. Text messages had become a thing of the past also as the networks began to crash. It surprised many at how reliant they had become on mobile communications and as the internet developed problems as servers crashed, more pressure was placed on Jake to get the radio up and running.

"Okay, Steve, I think we're good to go."

Steve looked apprehensive. "You think it'll work then?"

"We'll soon find out I suppose. Marcus said he will be calling at ten tonight, his time. So that should be within the next half hour," he said looking up at the clock. "Best we can do is leave it tuned in and ready."

Steve looked over the radio, taking in the knobs and dials. "I wouldn't know where to start Jake."

"It's not easy, even for me, and I've been working with communications equipment for years. Marcus is working on the High Frequency decametre band with the Codan. That means he's between three to thirty megahertz. What it does is it fires its signal up into the ionosphere where it reflects off charged particles in the atmosphere. It bounces around up there and is picked up by our transceiver which is tuned in to the same frequency.

"Marcus is gonna be on the forty one metre band which is seven thousand two hundred to seven thousand four hundred and fifty kilohertz. It's the best one to be on at this time of night and less likely for us to have difficulty with.

"If we both have our sets right, at his end and ours, then we should be able to speak to one another."

Jake turned to look at Steve and saw a vacant and dreamy look wash over his face.

"You've completely fucking lost me there, Jake. It's all too complicated and nerdy for me. I think you need to get out more to be honest."

The first night of the radio being set up, they had made contact with Marcus and his team. A dozen people had crowded into the small room at the rear of the house where Jake had the camera monitors and radio set up. They waited eagerly to see if it would work.

At first, there had been nothing but the hiss of static as Jake had turned the dials very slightly in order to fine tune the antenna as he watched the monitor read out that indicated the strength of the signal.

Then, very faintly, they heard a voice.

"Hello, Steve can you hear me?" The voice was distorted with the distance and the fluctuations in the signal strength, but it was unmistakable.

Instantly Jennifer squealed, clasping her hands to her mouth as she recognised the voice of her husband. The rest of the room erupted with a cheer as the survivors felt they had achieved a small victory as they managed to cling onto an element of civilisation that was still in their hands.

From then on, they were able to speak with Marcus every night and receive updates on where he was and their condition as he made his trek across the Middle East, headed for the southern tip of Europe.

The first thing that would happen was, Marcus would give Steve the exact position and location of where they were and where they planned to be the next night, and whenever possible, he would tell them the route. Steve and Jake could then plot it on the maps they had on the walls of the radio room. Afterward, Jennifer and the two boys were always given time alone in the room so they could have a private conversation.

People began to feel better about the situation as they settled into their new lives. As to be expected, there were a few hiccups. Some people still had difficulty adapting and coming to terms with what was happening and their losses. There were people in the house that had lost their entire family, some in front of their very eyes.

A few still remained withdrawn and glided around the house on auto-pilot, not completely unlike the dead roaming the streets outside. They would sit and stare at nothing, rarely interacting with anyone else and consumed in their own thoughts and emotions.

One such person was a woman named Lisa. She had seen her two young sons and husband torn to pieces in front of her, and in the brief moments that she did stumble onto the same plane as everyone else, she would say very little other than she should have died with them.

An elderly couple had decided that life wasn't worth living anymore since losing their daughter and grandchildren. Seeing no good left in the new world, they had taken their own lives. They both swallowed all the sleeping pills they had between them one night and went to bed with the intention of never waking up. They hadn't realised or considered the consequences of their actions and during the early hours, they had revived and crashed into the bedroom of another couple.

Screams of terror had echoed through the house and only through the quick reactions of Gary and Jennifer, were the two newly revived dead subdued. They rushed the room with clubs and bars; everyone had adopted the habit of keeping some form of weapon by their bed, and beat them to the floor and then restrained them by ripping the sheets and blankets from the bed and throwing them over the couple, pinning their flailing bodies down. The couple were disposed of with as much dignity as could be provided and buried alongside Roy in the garden.

As always, everybody gathered every evening to watch the news reports and learn anything they could on the situation. There was always the hope that somehow, the situation would stabilise or be completely reversed.

One night, they learned that it was to get worse first.

Steve recognised the reporter from the days before the virus. Then, he had always been smooth shaven, wearing a neatly pressed and finely cut suit with impeccable hair and skin as he smiled at the camera and flashed his whitened teeth. Even when he was announcing bad news, many people had swallowed it easier because it was being read to them by someone who looked like they belonged on the front of a Men's Health magazine and they were dazzled by his persona.

Now, he sat in front of the camera wearing a faded blue t-shirt that looked stretched around the neck as though he had slept in it. His eyes were bloodshot and swollen and dark rims had developed around the lids. His unshaven cheeks looked sunken, his hair was unkempt and greasy, and his reporting was bare bones. There was no glitz and no bullshit with bulletins and fancy visuals. His voice was strained and he smoked as he read from the papers laid out in front of him.

"Jesus," Gary commented, "the world really has gone to pot when reporters are sat puffing away on TV."

The man went straight into his report. "Ladies and Gentlemen, reports from existing government and army officials have informed us that all remaining military and police units still operating on the mainland, are to be evacuated immediately into the so called 'safe zones' of the Channel Islands and the Outer Hebrides, where they will consolidate and regroup.

"A massive relief effort is currently underway to retrieve as much equipment and manpower of the depleted security forces as possible and I am informed that once they have undergone a period of refitting and planning, there will be a renewed effort to claim back the mainland from the infected. However, we have not yet been told of when this is likely to take place or given any indication of how they plan to do it.

"In the meantime, people are encouraged to seek whatever shelter they can. Remain indoors and await the outcome of the renewed attempt from the security forces."

He glanced back down at his papers and shuffled to the next announcement as he cleared his throat.

"All major cities have been declared as overrun and no one is advised to try and enter them for whatever reason. There has been no news to come out of London, Liverpool, Birmingham, Nottingham and Manchester for the past few days and it is believed that they are now completely devoid of the living. Newcastle, Leeds Glasgow, Edinburgh and Cardiff are also believed to be dead, but no official confirmation has yet been received.

"It is advised for those that are able, to head away from the built-up areas and seek shelter in the country. However, small villages and towns still untouched by the virus and the infected have reported that they have been inundated with refugees as they flee the cities and Red Cross and local hospitals are overwhelmed with the influx of the sick and dying.

"We recommend that if you're in a secure and safe location and have adequate stocks of supplies, that you stay there and do not attempt to head further into the rural areas. It is speculated that many people could still be surviving in some of the urban areas just by keeping out of sight and avoiding all contact with the infected. We have been asked to inform any surviving people in the cities not make any unnecessary movement or noise and keep any light to a minimum.

"There is no further news on the plague itself or what is being done about the spread of it. Many have begun to suspect that scientists and governments have given up trying to find a cause or even a cure and are now looking at using tactical nuclear weapons to try and bring down the numbers of the dead before they attempt to retake the mainland. An interview with the Defence Secretary some weeks ago aroused suspicions when he stated that,

'We haven't looked into using our larger weapon capability as yet, but maybe we should.'

"The statement sparked outrage from other remaining government officials and spokespeople alike. The Defence

Secretary hasn't been seen since and it is suspected that he could be the victim of an infected attack.

"Other countries around the world have released statements that their cities are now uninhabitable and consumed entirely by the thousands of reanimated bodies that now infest them. The United States have announced that their National Guard Units have been mostly overwhelmed and with the bulk of the regular army and air force still en-route from the various conflicts in the Middle East, it is believed that they won't arrive in time to repel the infection and its spread.

"France, Spain, Belgium and Germany have all declared that their countries are overrun as well as the rest of Europe, with all military units fighting a retreating battle to the coasts in all directions, in the hopes of joining forces with the remaining British military units in the 'safe zones' of the Channel Islands, Gibraltar and Malta."

He shuffled through papers again, then looked up, an apologetic look on his face and a reluctance to look directly into the camera.

"We have also received word that we will be going off the air as of tonight and we will be evacuated to a new facility where all the news stations and information will be consolidated and will come under direct control of the government."

He shook his head and glanced off camera. "There will be no more broadcasts from this station after tonight as we will be shutting down immediately after this."

The room around them was silent. No one had moved during the news broadcast and now everyone stood and stared as the television went blank.

Lee broke the silence. "Does that mean that they won't be giving us the weather report now then?"

Though it was a stupid remark and completely out of place, it broke the ice and dragged a few people from their trance.

"Looks like they won't be telling us anything anymore, Lee," Gary answered, still staring at the dark TV. "And you can bet your last penny that when they do finally start broadcasting under the government's gaze, we will only get bits of the bigger picture and rarely the truth." He paused and looked around him at the people gathered in the lobby. "We really are on our own here now."

The next morning, Steve, Gary and Lee walked to the main gate and began their checks. They stood back in the shade of the trees and out of sight from the gateway. The mass of bodies pushing against the entrance had more than doubled in the last week and Steve guessed there to be possibly fifty of them clawing and wrenching at the iron bars of the main gate.

Their emaciated and lifeless faces pushed and squeezed into the gaps between the bars. Claw-like hands reached into the empty space beyond and into the park grasping at thin air. A steady low hum radiated from the dead as they moaned and gurgled constantly, and the buzz from the clouds of insects that continually circled them added to the noise, creating an unremitting murmur.

Steve eyed the throng of bodies in front of them. "Shit, we could find ourselves in real trouble here fellas if we don't find a way of keeping them back from the gate, even the road if possible."

Gary was at his side. "There's more of them every day."

They moved back into the trees and headed to the far end of the park where the wall ran close to the road that accessed the area. They stopped in front of it and looked up and along its length. It was eight feet high and made from solid sandstone. All along the perimeter wall, large fir trees grew at regular intervals on both sides of the stone, their long branches hanging over the wall's edge and sheltering the inside from view. The wall had stood for a couple of hundred years, from the time before the land within had become a Safari Park and when it was the land of a rich Lord who had encompassed his estate with the tall barrier.

Lee scaled the wall and peered over the edge for a moment before climbing back down. He wiped his hands together to clear them of the small pieces of grit that crumbled away from the stone and the moss that had grown at the top.

"Well, you want the good news or the bad news?" he asked.

Steve shrugged, "You may as well give us both Lee."

He nodded. "Okay, well I don't think the walls will be a problem. It's about two feet lower on the other side, so unless they learn how to use a ladder, they have ten feet to climb. Don't think even I could manage that easily, never mind them things."

Gary spoke, "Well, that's the good news. What's the bad?"

Lee looked up from dusting the knees of his jeans. "Um, there's fucking loads more on their way."

Gary and Steve swapped glances and then looked at the wall. Steve began scrambling up it to get a look for himself. The road was just a few metres from the wall, separated from it by a narrow grass verge. The road spanned twenty metres to the other side where it then crossed onto the path of another, more modern brick wall running parallel to it along the access road. The junction was to his left and at the tip of the road. It was the main entry point for the access road to the Safari Park and it was wide open to anyone that walked along it.

Shambling bodies approached. A few were just metres away from him as he watched them travel from the direction of the crossroads and onto the access road. They didn't see him as he peered over the wall in the shade of the large trees and he counted at least twenty of them while he watched through the branches, spread out and all headed in the same direction, toward the gate.

Some shuffled and staggered on unsteady legs, others walked slowly but with more coordination. A few seemed to struggle to stay upright at all. With each step, their bodies lurched and their dangling arms swayed with them, giving Steve the impression that their hips were mounted on some kind of seesaw. Most of them still looked relatively fresh, apart from their colour and gait. But others couldn't be mistaken for anything other than what they were. Green, sagging, rotted skin hung from their bodies, grotesque wounds betrayed their deaths. Some were missing limbs or trailed fetid intestines along the ground in their wake as they lumbered forward.

He dropped back down to Gary and Lee with a deeply concerned look on his face. "I think we're gonna have to take a more serious look at blocking off this road boys."

Back at the mansion, people gathered around to discuss and give ideas. After hours of consideration and deliberating their alternatives, Gary came up with the best suggestion.

"Well," he began, "as far as I can tell, the dead at the gate are all coming from the junction up here." He pointed his finger to the diagram that had been drawn on a piece of paper and everyone murmured their agreement.

"If we can find a way of blocking off the road, then I think they will stop coming. I'm not talking about building a wall or anything particularly heavy or formidable. I'm thinking more along the lines of breaking up their line of travel and what they see in front of them."

A few confused faces looked up from the group and glanced to each other before asking what was meant by 'breaking up their line of travel'.

"Think about it. These things don't seem to be too bright to me and from what I've seen they will walk forever in a straight line unless something makes them veer off in a different direction. Like the road for instance; it's unending really because one road leads into another across the whole country.

"They tend to be bordered with footpaths or guard rails that act as guides and they all look the same if you're staring straight down. So the dead are channelled really and will carry on walking in a straight line, until something attracts their attention or the road stops. If we could just find a way of obscuring the road ahead of them at the junction, hopefully they will just turn left or right and continue following the black tarmac away from the area."

Helen raised her eyebrows and looked at Gary. "Okay then, I see what you're saying, but how do we obscure the road?"

Gary shrugged, "Dunno, the idea has only just occurred to me, I haven't thought that far ahead to be honest."

"Trees," Jake had been quiet through most of the discussion but he had picked up on Gary's concept immediately and came up with a solution, "we cut down some of the tall trees on the other side of the wall close to the road and lay them across the carriageway as close to the junction as possible. That should be barrier enough for them, and with their branches, the access road should be obscured enough for it to work."

It was agreed they would use the trees to block the road and now they needed to come up with a plan of action.

There would be three groups. One group would fell the trees while another stood as their protection, and the third group would keep the infected occupied down by the gate to stop them from approaching the people on the outside as they chopped the trees down.

"I've never chopped a tree down before," Lee announced to the group. "Not that I'm a tree hugger or work for Greenpeace or anything, just never found reason to."

Steve turned around from the planning board that they had erected showing the positions and job labels of who would be doing what.

"Yeah, me neither. There's a knack to it isn't there, to get it to fall where you want it to?"

"I'll take care of the trees," John, a burly man, stepped forward from the back of the room. "I think I could get them to fall right, you just keep them rotting shits back while I do it."

John had been a great help over the past few weeks with his handyman skills and his knowledge of a wide range of practical subjects. He proclaimed himself to be a 'jack of all trades, but master of none' and he was able to put his hands to almost anything, from mechanics and electrics to carpentry and building.

Gary turned to him. "Have you cut down trees before John?"

He nodded. "Once, yeah. I stormed into my neighbour's garden with an axe and chopped his tree down. He was pissing me off with it because it blocked the sun from reaching my garden and he wouldn't trim it."

Gary looked at Steve questioningly, then back to John. "And did it fall how you intended?"

"Not exactly, no. I wanted it to smash into his greenhouse, but it fell the other way and landed on his conservatory instead. All I'll do now is go for the opposite approach and hopefully, they'll land exactly where you want them."

Gary still didn't look convinced and seemed troubled by John's experience.

John sighed. "Look, you may not be too impressed with my axmen experience and my reasons for it, but none of you have chopped a tree down and I have, so really, that makes me the expert of the group."

Gary, still looking troubled, glanced around the room, but without an alternative it was decided that John would be their resident lumberjack.

Every tool that could be used was gathered together. A number of axes and saws were dished out to the tree felling team and the protection lot were armed and clothed as best they could be for the job. They wore multi layers of thick clothing and gloves; mainly denim and leather, despite the warmth of the day. Soon everyone was headed to their positions along with two sets of ladders to scale the wall.

Jake, Stephanie and Jennifer were the gate team. They were armed with a radio and headed off through the wooded road that would bring them out at the main entrance. They were to approach the gate at a safe distance and keep the attention of the mass of bodies focused on them.

John, Gary and Jason set out to cut the trees.

"Okay, Jason, time to earn your keep," Gary told him.

Jason looked anything but eager to be part of the job, but he knew he had no choice.

Steve, Helen, Lee, Sophie and Carl would be the protection group for the tree cutters. Carl had volunteered against his wife's wishes and had ignored her protests all the way out the building as she followed him down the path, pleading with him not to go.

"I have to darling. I can't just let them go on their own can I? And if I can help, then I should. You know we all have to help out around here."

Down at the wall, Steve keyed the radio. "Okay Jake, we're up at the far end on the other side from the junction. How we looking?"

"Uh, well they're all pretty riled up down here, and I think we have their complete attention, Steve."

"Good, keep it that way." Steve clipped the radio back onto his belt and turned to his group. "Okay, the moment of truth."

He took the first set of ladders from Carl and placed them at the wall. He climbed them and looked out into the road and then at the junction. There were bodies in the area but they were spread out and he judged that, if they were quiet and could remain unseen until the last second before everyone sprung into action, then they could very well get away with it.

He signalled for Carl to pass up the second ladder, and straining under the weight of them, he hefted them up and over the stone wall, careful not to allow them to bang against it. He eased them down to the ground and pushed and gently pulled them, ensuring they were secure and unlikely to topple or slip.

He looked back down to the others and gave the thumbs up. "Okay, first group up. Once Sophie is over," he pointed to Gary and his team, "you three get over behind us."

Everybody nodded.

Steve swallowed hard, feeling a shiver run down his spine and his gut churn, and then he climbed down onto the opposite side, closely followed by Lee, Carl, Helen and then Sophie. They paused in the shade of the trees as they drew their weapons and readied themselves to step out into the open.

To their front and slightly left was the turn of the junction and directly across was the opposite pathway and high brick wall. Steve looked up into the trees and estimated that three good sized ones should do the trick.

His heart was racing and he could feel his legs and arms shaking as nervous beads of sweat coursed down his forehead and the back of his neck. He flexed his hands around the handle of his hand axe and looked around at the faces of the others. They all had the same apprehensive look about them, but at the same time, steadfast and determined.

Gary, John and Jason began to descend the ladder behind them. Steve watched as each stepped onto the grass verge beneath the trees. He looked at Gary and nodded; the nod was returned and Steve and his group moved forward into the open.

The nearest body was fifty metres away and moving toward the access road. It saw them as they broke cover and immediately let out a moan and quickened its step as it raised its arms. They had all agreed to allow the infected to come to them, to stand their ground and meet them as they approached to within striking distance.

Gary and Carl began chopping at the first tree in turns at the base as Jason stood ready with the saw. Once Gary and Carl had cut most of the way through, they would jump to the next tree and Jason would come in and finish off the first one.

Gary and Carl struck the trunk alternately, the axes cutting away at the bark and then into the softer pulp in the middle. They sweated and grunted as they swung their axes and tried their best to block out the moans of approaching infected, laying their trust in the other team members to protect them.

The first of the shambling bodies approached Helen. She stepped back as it reached for her and slammed the claw end of the hammer that she wielded into the side of its head, felling it in one blow. She had to step on the side of its neck to wrench the hammer free and she raised it again, dealing it a second blow to be sure.

Two more approached from the rear, their attention being drawn from the crowd at the gate further along by the commotion of the cutting at the trees. Lee was the closest and he laid into them both, swinging his length of rebar at them and beating their heads to a pulp, leaving their rotting brains and smashed skulls smeared across the road.

As he turned, puffing and panting with exertion he noticed a car headed in their direction from the opposite side of the junction. He paused and pointed as he shouted, "Someone's coming, Steve."

Steve was hacking away at a motionless body on the ground beneath him with his axe when he heard the shout from Lee. He turned to look at his friend and followed his gaze. A silver people-carrier was racing toward them. He looked up and saw the tree swaying as it began to weaken.

"Shit!" he shouted. "The tree is gonna fall any second." He waved to the people-carrier to speed it along toward them in the hope of making it through the junction before it was blocked by the first tree. "Come on, move it!" he shouted.

The first tree was almost ready to fall and Steve saw the signal from Gary and told his team to pull back a few steps to avoid being crushed as it fell. Jason jumped in with the saw, and to Steve's surprise, he attacked the tree with vigour. He wasn't sure if it was fear that drove the man, or whether he had turned a moral corner, but he was impressed with the way he went at it.

The car screamed across the junction as a loud creaking emitted from the tree and it began to lurch. The driver kept his foot to the floor and continued in the direction of the gate.

"There's a car on its way, Jake. Don't let it in though; we need to be sure none of the infected will get through first." Steve called over the radio.

Jason jumped back and looked up for an indication of the direction the tree would fall, and from what he could tell it would land straight across the road, forming the first layer of the barrier. It tumbled perfectly, with a loud screech followed by a crash as it smacked against the ground. It hit the opposite pavement, spanning the whole width of the road.

Steve glanced back toward the gate and saw that the car was now backing away from the entrance and reversing up the road in the opposite direction, leading the crowd of infected away from them.

When it was fifty metres away from the gateway, Steve heard Jake's panicking voice over the radio. "Steve, Steve, Stephanie has opened the gate!"

He watched in horror as the car shot forward and disappeared as it drove into the shade of the trees that obscured the gate area. The infected turned and followed, chasing it up the entrance path toward the park. He could only hope that the gate was closed in time before they breached it.

Carl and Sophie had begun working together to deal with the dead that had approached from the rear after the first tree had fallen. The noise and commotion caused by the tree felling team had attracted their attention away from the throng of infected at the gateway.

They swung both their clubs and bars at the cadavers and screamed obscenities at them as they did so. They ploughed through them and managed to keep the area clear as Gary and John hacked away at the trees.

"C'mon, Sophie girl, c'mon!" Carl screamed across at her as he charged, swinging into the advancing dead.

Sophie was calling the dead every name and curse under the sun and screaming with each swing, sounding like a female tennis player. She let out loud sighs and grunts with each swing as she hefted her golf club.

Helen and Lee were on the opposite side of Gary and John, plugging the gap that still left a small entrance onto the access road from the junction. Gary, John and Jason also shouted encouragement to one another as they cut their way through the second tree.

The second two trees quickly followed the first. They crashed on top of each other and became an interlocking tangle of thick green branches and tree trunks, six feet high with the greenery stretching higher still.

More bodies were approaching from behind and Steve, happy with the barrier, gave the word for them to get back inside the walls. He was the last to leave the ground and he raced up the ladder. He made sure he didn't forget to raise it behind him before jumping down on the other side. All of them stood, panting and sweating. Jason was physically sick, leaning against Gary and blowing sighs of relief.

Steve straightened up and raised the radio to his mouth. "Jake, the barrier is good from what I can tell and we're all okay. Please tell me the gate is closed?"

"Yes, Steve, it's closed, but three of them did manage to get in. Jen and I had to deal with them. That useless bitch, Stephanie, ran back to the house."

Steve clenched his jaw muscles and growled. "We'll deal with her when we get back, where is the car that came in?"

"It's here with me. A guy named Tony, a policeman, was driving it."

Lee rolled his eyes at Steve. "That's all we need, a fucking copper."

He nodded to Lee in agreement. "Okay, Jake, we'll meet back at the house."

He turned to Jason who looked back at him and then down at the ground, ashamed for his wife. "That bitch of a wife of yours has done it now mate. She opened the gate and then ran off."

"I'll fucking kill her," Lee growled from behind him.

Steve stormed up the path with the rest closely following. He could feel his anger bubbling over and his blood pressure rocketing. He still hadn't decided what he was going to do about Stephanie; he just wanted to get his hands on her for now.

She stood in the lobby area, speaking loudly with two others and Steve heard her mention something about her being told to return to the house. She turned and saw Steve and his party storm into the foyer. Her face turned white and her lips quivered.

"Ah, Steve, I was just telling them about how it all went. I came back to make sure that everything was okay and to let them know about the new arrival."

Lee, without a word of warning, launched himself from over Steve's shoulder and planted a punch straight into the centre of her plump face. It landed with a wet thud and the bone cracking under the impact echoed around the room as she was knocked backward and onto the floor. Bright red blood spurted from her smashed nose and Lee moved in and stepped over her, cocking his arm for a follow up.

Steve grabbed him and pulled him back. "Don't Lee, that's enough."

He stepped in front of him and crouched by the sobbing Stephanie who sat, spread legged on the floor with a stream of blood dripping over her fingers as she was unable to stop the flow.

"Tilt your head back; it'll clot and stop bleeding that way." He spoke calmly and he leaned in closer as she angled her face to the ceiling. "Now then, listen to me Stephanie, I warned you not to cross me.

"You put the entire group at risk with your little stunt down at the gate. You heard me tell Jake on the radio not to open it, but you went ahead and did it. Not only that, you ran away, leaving Jennifer and Jake to deal with the infected that got in." He shook his head and looked down at the ground with a sigh.

Stephanie followed him with wide and scared eyes as she kept her head back, with her hand still pressed to her nose. The lack of emotion in his voice and his calm approach made her feel uneasy, more so than if he had been ranting and screaming at her.

"Now luckily, they were able to deal with them without being hurt. Imagine what would happen now if they had been hurt? For a start I wouldn't have stopped Lee. But now I'm having a dilemma, what do I do about you? You clearly don't want to play along and be part of the team, and anyone that isn't a part of the team, I consider as a part of the opposition. So, that means I now have to look at you as a serious threat, Stephanie." His voice was still calm and monotone. There was no anger or excitement in his words, they were just cold and composed, and it terrified Stephanie.

Her eyes widened still and she began to cower away, pushing her legs out in front of her and forcing herself backwards. Steve hobbled on his heels, still crouching, after her.

He leaned in closer, his eyes now glowering with rage, and hissed, "You're a piece of shit. Do you know that?" He checked over his shoulder to make sure he couldn't be heard. "I'm going to feed you to the dead, Stephanie." Her eyes bulged and she whimpered at his words.

He left it at that, leaving her unsure and wondering what would come next as he stood and walked across the room to the rest of the group and the new arrival.

"I'm Steve and I hear your name is Tony?" He held out his hand and Tony accepted it.

"Yeah, my name's Tony. Sorry about the hassle down at the gate." He nodded to the fat form, still seated on the floor with her head held back.

Steve shrugged, "It wasn't your fault. She made her own choice."

Tony was led away by Gary to undergo the usual check over for bites and any injuries suspected of being caused by the infected. He went without question and as Steve stood and watched him leave, the rest of the group dispersed, except Lee. He approached him and spoke into his ear.

"I don't like him, Steve," he whispered.

Steve screwed up his face and turned to him. "Eh? You've only just met the bloke, Lee."

"There's something about him. And I'm sure he was the same cop that did me for being half a point over the limit five years ago. I got an eighteen month drink driving ban, and it really fucked me up, especially work wise. And you try being a grown man having to go shopping at the supermarket with your Mum every week. The staff at Tesco must've thought I was a right Mummy's boy."

Steve snickered. "Look, we'll just keep an eye on him for now. He could turn out to be an okay bloke, just give him a chance. It's that fat bitch there," he nodded at Stephanie who was now seated at the table and crying into her hands, "that we need to look out for."

Lee grunted, "If it were up to me Steve, I'd feed her to them fuckers down there." He gestured toward the gate with a sideways cock of the head.

Steve nodded and hummed. "Yeah, that's what I said to her. If it was just me, I would do it mate."

A week went by. Tony was integrated into the group pretty easily. Everyone seemed to get along with him and actually liked having him around. He was pleasant and helpful, especially when it came to entertaining the children.

Only Lee kept his distance, and as suggested, he also kept an eye on him from afar.

The first day he arrived, he had seemed quite protective over his people-carrier; something that Lee couldn't understand considering he wasn't likely to use it again. He had climbed in and taken it for a drive around the park to 'find his bearings' as he put it, and he refused all offers of people to sit in the car with him and show him around. Instead, he insisted that he always preferred to explore new places alone and without distractions and that way, he could get a feel for the place. Most people just shrugged it off, understanding his point of view, but Lee saw something sinister about it.

He watched him from the window of the house as he drove away in the direction of the Information Centre and restaurants. There was still something wrong, and it was really starting to annoy Lee what it was.

An hour later and Tony returned his attitude to other people approaching his car had completely changed. He no longer hovered around anyone who went near it, and he even donated it to the house, adding the keys to the pile as a group vehicle.

No, Lee really didn't like the guy.

25

"What do we do now then?" Ian asked as he bit off another piece of Slim Jim that he pulled from the ration pack.

They were looking out onto a flat, open, green plain that stretched as far as the eye could see. It finished in a stark line where the clear blue sky took over and stretched high above them. The heat waves shimmered from the ground and the birds in the sky squawked and dived into the long grass of the open steppe.

Marcus shrugged as he eyed the ground ahead of them. "We crack on, I suppose."

They were now in Serbia, north of Belgrade, and stood watching the dust trail of the car as it faded into the distance along the dirt track. Yan and Sini had departed in an old Soviet-made white hatchback they had found at a farm, and now headed for their home town. Marcus and the remainder of the team were forced to say a regrettable farewell to them and watched as they disappeared over the horizon.

For weeks they had hidden, sneaked, and scavenged their way across the Middle East and into Europe. Turkey had been hard. The army had tried to lock the country down, throwing up checkpoints at every major junction. Marcus and his men were forced into a battle of wits and cunning. Using the maps they had recovered after the border attack, they were able to bypass the main troop concentrations and major checkpoints. They hid during the daytime and made a run for the crossing at Istanbul over the Sea of Marmara in the dark hours, scavenging and raiding as they went.

As much as possible, they left no trace behind them. They didn't want to attract the attention of the Turkish army down on them by leaving a trail of bodies in their wake for anyone to follow. The infected were everywhere, but it wasn't difficult to avoid them due to their route selection. The dead that they come across tended to be individual stragglers and small groups from villages close by.

It was decided that all contact with the living should be avoided if possible. They were headed for the coast and with very few options on how to get across, the last thing they needed was someone giving the security forces up ahead advanced warning of their approach.

They gave wide berths to the large towns and cities and kept themselves to the interior of the country and the less densely populated areas as much as possible. Sticking to mountain tracks and river roads, they crept from one village to the next, stopping each time to scout the ground in front of them and moving on once they were confident they could continue undetected, siphoning fuel from broken down or unguarded vehicles as they went.

At the end of each night they had to find a lie up position that provided them with cover from view while they rested during the day time. They found themselves in caves, woods, barns and dried up riverbeds. The process had been repeated over and over every day until they had reached to within five kilometres of the coast and sat watching the Northern Faith Bridge that spanned the Istanbul Straits.

Marcus had expected it to be much like the border with Iraq; heavily defended and an unavoidable battle to get across. But it seemed that during their weeks in the wilderness, Turkey also had a hard time of the plague and now the bridge lay open before them.

Marcus and the rest went firm on the high ground to the East that overlooked the Northern edges of the city on the East side of the straights and where the start of the bridge was situated. The main highway that linked onto the road that fed across the stretch of water came up from the South and joined onto the bridge road directly ahead of them in a tangle of ramps, slipways and flyovers that formed a spaghetti junction.

From where they stood, they could see the faint plumes of blue and black smoke from the obvious fighting that had taken place there within the past few days. Hundreds of cars and other vehicles sat bumper to bumper, crammed into the area of the junction. The road that led up to the bridge was much the same. Stu, using binoculars, pointed out destroyed tanks and other armoured vehicles as well as aircraft amongst the wreckage.

"What do you think happened?" Stu asked as he pointed to more of the carnage.

Sini took the binoculars from Stu's hand and peered through them, scanning the area for himself. "Looks to me like they didn't get along and ended up turning on each other. There must've been a battle for the bridge. Maybe one lot wanted to keep everyone in Turkey and the other lot, like us, wanted to make a run for Europe and the open? Either way, it looks like our job is gonna be a little easier than we thought."

"Don't be too sure." Marcus pointed further along the road toward the bridge and then shifted his finger to the destroyed and smouldering buildings at the outer edges of the suburbs to the North, close to the highway. At both points, thousands of black figures could be seen, staggering around the buildings and out into the road, making their way from one vehicle to the next as they headed for the bridge.

"Looks like there must've been thousands killed, and now they're all up and at 'em." Stu blew a low whistle under his breath as he took in the number of reanimated dead before them. More and more were piling into the road, headed for the bridge.

Marcus made a face. "Why they all headed for the bridge?"

Ian shrugged, "Maybe that's where they were headed before they were killed and it's a left over memory or instinct, or something?"

"Shit," Jim hissed through his teeth as he lowered his own binoculars. "That bridge is gonna be packed tighter than a whore's cunt in a gang bang if we wait too long, then we'll never get through." He was shaking his head as he said it.

Stu glanced from the corner of his eye at him. "Lovely choice of words there, Jim."

"Hey, that's about as best I can describe it. I dropped outta school when I was in eighth grade, what you expect?"

"Ah right, because when I was thirteen, my vocabulary consisted of words like 'cunt' too. I mean, they hadn't taught us anything else like History and Maths at school by then, just the basic profanities at that point. We moved on to insulting hand gestures in the next term." Stu grinned, taunting him.

"Fuck you, College boy," Jim replied and held up the middle finger.

Before the crowds could build up anymore, Marcus decided on racing for the other side, opting to plough through the mass of bodies that had already accumulated, rather than wait for the bridge to become completely impassable with them. It was early morning and the sun was on the rise, but they couldn't afford to wait and their path to be blocked. They had to act there and then.

There was no resistance from anyone living, and it was clear that anyone that was capable had fled the area completely, leaving it for the dead. They bobbed and weaved their way through the tangles of smashed and destroyed vehicles and the piles of broken bodies that littered the roads, hammering their way across from the junction and toward the bridge. At first, they had been slowed by the roaring crowd of infected as they all turned and assaulted the convoy. But, once again, they manned the machineguns in the turrets to cut them a path through the infected and crushed them below their heavy armoured wheels as they fell.

It took them less than five minutes to cross the bridge that spanned nearly a kilometre across the straits, from the moment they hit the junction leading to the bridge, to their wheels hitting European tarmac.

Once across, they had kept on going, putting as much distance as possible between them and Istanbul. They pushed along the highway, crossing over onto the opposite carriageway, to avoid the piles of stalled and wrecked traffic crammed together at the toll booths for the bridge. The road on that side was completely deserted. It seemed that everyone wanted out from the Middle East, but no one wanted in.

They continued along the road for another ten kilometres before they hit a junction and turned North, following the lesser roads that led them through the central part of the Istanbul Peninsula and toward the border with Bulgaria.

They raced across the country, sticking to the back roads and remote areas as they had done in the East. They managed to get to within sixty kilometres of the Bulgarian border, but it was getting dark and the team members were about ready to drop. They had been on the move for almost forty eight hours and the lack of sleep and rest was starting to take its toll.

They found an abandoned farm complex to the East of the large city of Kirklareli and after clearing out the stray bodies that meandered around the buildings, they hid the vehicles in the barn and bedded down for the night, deciding to push on through the daylight hours.

Except for when they passed close to cities and large towns, the dead were sparse on the roads and the team encountered mainly long columns of refugees headed West until they closed in on the border. The closer they got, the more they began to see Army units that seemed to be retreating away from the coastal areas. Long stretches of tanks and vehicles carrying men and supplies lined the roads, creeping along in a never ending snake as they made a strategic withdrawal.

Marcus surmised that they were headed to join forces with other units from other countries, such as Bulgaria and Macedonia, in an attempt to create a new defensive line further inland. It looked as though the Middle East had been written off completely and left to die.

The soldiers stared at them as they passed by. Some just gazed, the horror of their experiences etched across their faces as they looked through and beyond the men of the team. Others looked quizzically and began speaking excitedly to each other and gesturing toward the SUVs as they zipped by.

Ian, still riding in the front vehicle as the lead scout, spoke over the radio. "Marcus, we're getting a lot of eyeball action from these troops." He sounded nervous.

Marcus replied, "Roger that Ian, but we're committed now and if we turn back, we'll lose ground and also give them reason to take more of an interest in who we are."

Stu broke in on the conversation over the speakers. "We should bluff it like we did in Tikrit that time with the Americans. Whack on the sirens and flashers and maybe they'll think we're carrying someone important from the government, or a General who needs to get to the front."

Marcus nodded to himself as he remembered the ruse. "Roger that, Stu. Ian like he said, let's go noisy and we'll brass it out."

"Roger," Ian replied. Marcus, travelling in the second vehicle, began to hear the loud wailing horn of the sirens up ahead of them. He flicked the switch in front of him and looked across at Sini and winked, as their audio warning systems began to blare their own rising and falling high pitched tone.

They stormed along at breakneck speed, horns blasting and the red and blue strobe lights attached to their bumpers flashing alternately, looking to all intents and purposes, very much like a group of people with important and immediate business further up ahead. They just had to hope and pray that nobody would actually have the audacity to wave them down; they would have no choice then but to start the shooting and Marcus knew it would be a one-sided battle with the amount of men, armour and air support in the area. He counted on their guts and the confusion of the moment to carry them through. After all who else, other than an important official of some sort, would be driving around with sirens and lights in an armed escort with men waving guns?

Once they got to the border, to their amazement, they were waved through and sent on their way without having to even slow down. They kept their speed up, turned due North at the first possible chance to break away from the military units that were massing in the area, and headed inland toward the central hilly peaks and mountains that ran across the width of the country, and then followed it East toward Serbia.

It took them three days to cross Bulgaria. Each night, after pushing hard on the road, avoiding groups of infected or just smashing through them, scrounging and bartering for fuel, they bedded down wherever they could and tuned in the Codan to speak with Steve and to see what other information they could pick up from other transmissions.

Mostly, the situation worldwide seemed grave. Between the team, they could speak a number of various languages and it was when Sini and Yan recognised their native tongue over the radio signals, they learned that the situation in Serbia and most of the Balkans had already pretty much crumbled into chaos. Most of the military forces were destroyed, deserted or had broken away to become independent rogue armies. The more that Yan and Sini interpreted to the rest of the men, the more they realised that crossing that part of the continent wasn't going to be easy and they were more than likely headed directly into trouble.

Hussein approached Marcus and Ian as they stood discussing routes on the maps. "Yan has told me about the problems we may face in Serbia. Are we still going ahead?"

Marcus nodded, "Yes, we are. We have to cross that area anyway, either that or take the long way around and pass through Romania. We could have just as much trouble there too. Sini and Yan are our friends, and we have to help them as far as we can."

"Yes, I understand that. It is strange, a month ago, I never saw you as real people. I saw you as animals, worse than pigs. But you are no different than us."

"Except we don't wear dresses on our days off," Ian mumbled from the corner of his mouth as he looked in the opposite direction, away from Hussein.

Hussein smiled, "Well, Mr Ian, it keeps the air circulating and stops us from getting, how you say it, sweaty balls?"

Ian almost choked on his cigarette and spluttered a laugh. Still coughing, and thumping his chest with one hand, he leaned over and patted Hussein on the back in complement for his quick retort.

Hussein nodded his appreciation at the now red-faced Ian and turned back to Marcus. "Anyway, I find it a very honourable thing that you are doing. I am pleased to be part of it, and I speak for Zaid and Ahmed too. They think that you are great men and great soldiers too."

"Thanks, Hussein," Marcus replied with a smile. "I quite fancy you too."

Ian creased up into more laughter, snot and drool exploding from his already strained nasal passages. Hussein looked perplexed for a moment and then, realised that they had cracked yet another joke at his expense. He laughed along, not fully understanding the joke but able to construe that it wasn't meant in a malicious way.

"I'm still getting used to your humour, Mr Marcus," he smiled.

"Yeah, wait till we start the fart jokes. You'll be completely lost."

They crossed the border close to a Serbian town called Pirot and pushed through the low farm lands to the south, heading for central Serbia.

With Yan and Sini acting as the convoy commanders, they were able to talk their way past many army units that took an interest in them. Mainly, it was a case of one of them climbing into a turret and shouting insults at the soldiers or patriotic slogans and the soldiers would holler a reply. Mostly, the banter was enough for the troops on the ground to wave the vehicles by, showing disinterest and more than likely, they had had their fill of looting and raping their way through the dozens of burned and massacred villages that the team had already passed by.

Piles of bodies lay in the baking sun, attracting swarms of flies and birds as they rotted and bloated in the heat at the roadside. Their destroyed villages, now just smouldering and collapsed ruins behind them, having been picked clean by the marauding troops as they swept the land.

On more than one occasion, Marcus saw tears streaming down Sini's face as they passed through the massacred towns and saw the heaps of his dead country folk sprawled at the roadsides. Men, women and children, soldiers and civilians alike were targeted by the alcohol-fuelled anarchy that the rogue army units brought down on them.

At first, they had stopped at the sites of the carnage to check for survivors and see what help they could offer. They soon realised that they need not bother. No living people were ever found. A few dead had managed to reanimate and stagger about in the ruins, but the majority of the people had been executed with head shots.

The team stood around a large depression in the ground on the outskirts of a large village. It was full of bodies. Heads and limbs poked up from the pile with the bodies being twisted and clumped together, having been tossed into the pit after their execution.

Flies had found them and thousands of little black dots swarmed and buzzed through the air above the pit. The massacre couldn't have happened more than twenty four hours earlier judging by the look of the dead, but the pungent, sickly-sweet smell of rot was already rising into the air as they festered in the blistering sun.

Ian and Marcus stood to one side, looking down on a line of dead men that looked as though they had been executed separately from the rest. Marcus guessed that they were the town leaders and had possibly been killed last, after being forced to witness the murder of the all the men, women and children.

"Why do you think they left them separated?" Ian asked as he looked down along the line of dead.

Marcus grunted, "Fuck knows. Maybe they just couldn't be arsed picking them up and tossing them into the pit after they had humped and dumped the others?"

"Bodies never look like they do in movies." It was a rhetorical statement from Ian. They had all seen hundreds of bodies and created many themselves, but now and then there were always a few that caught the attention. Not that there was anything in particular about them, just sometimes, it played on the mind and made them think of their own mortality.

Many times, Marcus had looked on the still and lifeless body of a person and thought to himself, *Just hours ago, that was a person; a living, breathing, thinking and feeling person. Now, they're dead and will never live again. Their desires, memories and ambitions, lost with them.*

In the movies, dead people always look pretty normal, even attractive to a degree. Gunshot wounds; always represented by just a neat hole in the front of the head and a trickle of blood running down the face, eyes staring into space.

In reality, the entry point would often be caved inward, the bone being smashed and fragmented by the impact of the solid slug and the vacuum in the wake of the bullet causing the bone to implode as it pushed its way through. The exit wound was normally just a jagged hole like a collapsed 3D jigsaw puzzle where the bone had been blown outward, leaving the skull to crumple in on itself while the remnants of thick blood and brains oozed from the hole.

The face would lose its normal shape with the integrity of the skull being destroyed, making the features unrecognisable sometimes. With the lack of blood pressure, the nose loses its plumpness as well as the lips and the cheeks, and the eyes look sunken, giving the impression of the dead having lost weight.

Eyes never close or remain completely open together, especially with a traumatic death. At least one eye is always half open, with the other either wide or closed. The eye itself would become flat without the blood pressure to keep it rounded and the white of the eye turns dull while the pupil expands and takes up nearly all the iris, resembling fish eyes. The mouth would always end up gaping open, leaving a gormless expression on the face.

The dead never died in a dignified position either. If someone is shot, they're not dying naturally and they are not going to fall into a natural position. Most of the time, they would land in a twisted or sprawled, spread eagle position, the clothing always seeming to ride up from the waist or a shoe would come off. To Marcus, he was always given the impression that their clothes didn't fit them anymore after death.

"Nope," Ian sighed, "there's no such thing as a good looking corpse."

Sini and Yan came from the town of Temerin in the North and as they came close, they said their goodbyes and went to find their family and friends. Marcus, Stu, Ian, Jim, Hussein, Zaid and Ahmed stood and watched as the vehicle disappeared from sight.

With heavy hearts, they turned and climbed back into their SUVs. They had given their two Serbian friends as much ammunition and food as they could spare to help them on their way, and the loss, both in manpower and friendship was felt immediately within the team.

Marcus told them of their intended route and that they were welcome to follow them if they changed their minds.

Hussein took over as the driver of Marcus' vehicle and Zaid climbed behind the wheel for Stu. They travelled in silence for a while, all of them lost in thought. The strain was starting to show on all their weather-beaten, bearded faces. They had been hard on the road for over a month and they were now running on their reserves. They needed to find somewhere to rest for a day, maybe even two.

They could've gone with Sini and Yan, but Marcus felt that it could attract too much attention to them if they approached any major built-up areas, and the two Serbs had insisted on going alone and that Marcus and the rest of the team were to push on and make it to their own homelands as quickly as possible.

That evening, they found a place to rest. A wood line, a few hundred metres back and overlooking the road running in front of them, providing the team with good cover from view and advanced warning of anyone approaching.

They rested for the whole of the next day and into the evening before deciding that it was time to move again. They pushed on and headed for the North, hoping to make it across into Hungary the next day.

Close to the border, Ian's vehicle had a blow out. The tyre exploded like a grenade and they came to a stop. Jim and Ian began fixing it while everyone else saw to their own vehicles, replenishing what fuel they had used and checking over their own tyres to avoid any more stops.

They were in the middle of nowhere, close to Lake Zobnatica in the North of Serbia and no more than fifty kilometres from the border. Thick forests flanked them on both sides with trees that were so tall they left just a thin slither of blue sky above the road, casting the ground into perpetual twilight.

As they huffed and sweated, heaving off the damaged tyre and discarding it as they replaced it with one of the spares, an agonising scream rang out from their rear. Marcus turned to see Zaid approaching from around the back of his vehicle, clutching his neck with blood oozing between his fingers and running down his arm. He staggered and swayed, using his spare arm to guide him along the vehicle as he tried to remain upright against it.

He struggled forward, gurgling something through his damaged throat. Marcus drew his pistol as a figure lurched out from behind Zaid. Fresh blood smeared across its pallid face and neck, its pale features shimmering in the gloom as it began to lumber after the wounded man, its arms outstretched in an attempt to grasp its prey and to stop it from escaping.

Marcus closed the gap, pulling Zaid behind him and pushing him toward the rest of the team and into Hussein's arms. He raised his pistol and pointed it between the infected's eyes. It had been a man once and he stopped still just a few feet in front of Marcus, his faded dull eyes staring down the barrel of the gun pointed straight into his face. He seemed to straighten up, almost with a touch of pride or dignity, then he looked beyond the pistol and focused on Marcus, his mouth gaped and a loud lingering whine erupted from within as strings of blood dripped from his teeth and lips.

Marcus squeezed the trigger, the pistol bucking in his hand, a loud crack that echoed through the trees as the round left the barrel. The left eye of the dead man in front of him disappeared into the back of his head, ripping the skin and tissue of the cheek with it, and he collapsed to the ground as his knees gave way.

Everybody checked their immediate area, ensuring there were no more infected creeping up on them. Marcus and Stu approached Hussein, who sat with Zaid across his lap. He looked dead, but Marcus saw the rise and fall of his chest.

"How bad is it?" he asked.

Hussein looked up at him, his eyes wet with tears. "I don't know, but we know what will happen to him."

Stu crouched and began checking over Zaid's unconscious body, and after a minute, he spoke. "It's not that serious actually. Well," he paused and thought, looking back down at Zaid, "under normal circumstances it wouldn't be. He won't die from blood loss, but he will turn eventually. We know that." He turned as he said his last statement and stared questioningly at Marcus.

Hussein looked down and pulled his friend close as he sobbed over him.

Stu asked, "Do you want us to take care of him?" The question was intended for Marcus, but he looked at Hussein as he said it.

"No," Marcus shook his head from behind him, "we give him a chance."

They dressed the wound and treated Zaid for shock and blood loss, then loaded him into the second SUV, where Marcus could keep an eye on him as Hussein drove. They moved on.

Soon after, they cleared the forest. The sun blinded them as they came into the open. "Stop," They heard Ian say from the lead vehicle. "Shit, Marcus, I think you need to come up and see this."

He motioned for Hussein to push forward and to come alongside Ian to see what the problem was. Before them was a wide expanse of open ground that stretched far into the horizon and into the distance on either side of the road. Hussein stopped the vehicle suddenly, slamming on the brakes and causing it to lurch forward as he stared, open mouthed, through the windshield at the sight before them. Marcus didn't notice the jerk as the vehicle stopped sharply as he too was gaping out the window; the radio slipped from his hand and clattered to the foot well of his seat.

On either side of the road, tall wooden posts lined the route and nailed to each post, a body, flailing and struggling against its bonds as they saw the team approach from the trees. The poles stretched far into the distance, and as far as Marcus could tell, there were bodies attached to all of them. He regained his composure and glanced into the fields to the left and right. There too, more bodies, impaled on tall wooden stakes, hanging by the neck or crucified. With every possible method, bodies were erected onto posts in endless lines across the open ground. Everywhere they looked, they saw the scarecrow figures, pinned to the wood above the ground and unable to break away from their bondage, left to rot in an eternal torture.

Everyone began to dismount from their vehicles. No one had advised that they take a closer look, but the spectacle was too overpowering and Marcus and his men couldn't help but be horrified by what they saw. It was almost hypnotic.

"There must be thousands of them, Marcus," Ian said as he noticed his friend standing at his side, staring up at the figures stuck to the long posts above them, gawking from one body to the next.

The body directly above them looked down, twisting and straining against the post, grasping at the air that separated it from the living human flesh below. It grunted and wailed continuously, causing the other bodies close by to join in the tortured chorus of the dead. Soon, the entire field on either side of the road was a deafening mantra of wailing voices, all reacting to the sounds of the other moans close by to them.

Marcus didn't reply to Ian, he couldn't, he just nodded and continued nodding for sometime without realising it. Some of the bodies had placards attached to them, written in Serbian and unintelligible to anyone in the team, but from what they could guess, the placards probably read supposed crimes that had resulted in the cruel and final punishment.

Without a doubt some, if not most, had been alive before they were put into the field as part of a gruesome display of man's inhumanity to man. Marcus suspected that many would have survived for a lengthy period of time, particularly the ones who had been crucified, before they succumbed and died before reanimating.

He looked up at the nearest body. He couldn't tell if it had been male or female. Its skin was black, with large fluid-filled blisters all over it from baking in the hot sun. Its ribcage was ripped open, a cavern where its innards had once been and its dull white bone tips poking through the rotted flesh. The skin of its face was stretched tight over the skull, and the eyes were all but gone, but it knew they were there as it snarled and moaned at the men below, flailing its arms in an attempt to reach them.

Some of the bodies were little more than torsos, nailed to the poles or stakes that had been driven into them from the rectum and up through the neck. Some bodies were completely decomposed with nothing left except for bones, held together with dried out sinews. In some places, just heads on pikes were visible, the jaws still flexing but making no sound from the lack of vocal cords.

Flocks of birds and insects swooped and dived continually above the spectacle, as they spotted another particularly tasty morsel on one of the dead. The smell was overpowering. There was very little breeze and the stench of the thousands of rotting and putrefying bodies lingered in the air like a thick haze, permeating into everything.

They were mesmerised by the sight, and didn't hear the approaching vehicles. In their shock at what they saw, they made the mistake of leaving their weapons in the SUVs, leaving just side arms at their immediate disposal.

Four trucks emerged from the tree line and headed toward them.

Stu was the first to react. "Stand to," he screamed, snapping the attention of the rest of the men back to reality. They all spun and saw the trucks and turned to run for their vehicles.

Before they could move, a stream of tracer rounds zipped in front of them, cracking loudly as they split the air and creating a demarcation line that told Marcus and his men not to move any further. They all stopped in their tracks and glanced nervously to each other. Whoever it was that was approaching them, they had them zeroed and any attempt to move, they would be cut down before they could take more than two steps.

The trucks pulled up in a screech of brakes and men began spilling out from the back of them, shouting commands and orders to one another and gesturing with their rifles. They were dressed in mixed uniforms of different nationalities, including civilian clothing. Nearly all of them wore a bandanna of some sort. Not a good sign as far as Marcus was concerned. Nearly everything he had seen or read of atrocities in the Balkans had been committed by men wearing bandannas. It was a rebel thing.

A man, who appeared to be their commander, approached and began shoving people in different directions and shouting. They began to climb in and out of the vehicles as their new prisoners stood and watched, helpless to do anything. Their weapons were removed from their belts and collected in a pile in front of the rebel commander. He picked up Marcus' pistol and hefted it in his hand, then looked approvingly at Marcus with a smile.

"Thank you," he said.

Two men appeared from the SUV, Zaid between them as they helped him from the vehicle. The rebel commander approached them and ripped the dressing away from the injured man's neck, causing Zaid to wince with pain. The rebel commander studied the wound for a short moment then nodded. He stepped back and without a moment's hesitation, he raised the pistol and fired a shot into Zaid's face. His head snapped back, then forward as he fell to his knees and onto his face, causing a cloud of dust to rise around him as he landed.

Hussein and Ahmed stared and watched in silence, then lowered their heads in silent prayer for their friend.

The commander shouted a few words and then Marcus and the rest were blindfolded and bundled into the back of the trucks and driven away.

It was the unknown that they feared. They had been caught off-guard and now lay at the mercy of their captors without any control over their own fate. Marcus felt scared, but more than that, he was angry, angry with himself.

26

Jennifer paced the lobby, wringing her hands together as she nervously and continually looked to the main door, waiting for Steve to return from the perimeter checks.

She heard the sound of voices as the door opened and Steve stepped inside, speaking loudly with Gary.

"We can't just leave them there. We need to do something about them," he was saying over his shoulder to his friend as they entered.

"I agree, Steve," Gary replied, "but what do you reckon we should do?"

Steve stopped and turned. He hunched his shoulders and cocked his head. "Well, I was thinking we should..." he was interrupted by Jennifer's anxious voice.

"Steve, have you heard anything?"

He turned at the sound of her voice. "Sorry, Jen, I've no news for you." He looked at her apologetically.

She looked down, her eyes blurry from the tears and her voice croaky with emotion. "It's been two days, Steve." She continued to look at the floor as she spoke. "I know it's not always possible to get in touch every night, but it's never been this long, never longer than a day."

Gary tapped him on the shoulder and said in a low voice, "I'll crack on, Steve, and leave you to it. We can discuss things later." He nodded to Jennifer, acknowledging her need to speak to Steve more urgently than he did.

"Okay, Gary, I'll catch you in a bit then," Steve said glancing back at him.

Steve turned back to Jennifer and placed his hands on both her shoulders and stooped his head so that they had eye contact. "Jen, listen, I'm sure he's okay. It's probably just the area where they are, or they're having radio trouble or something. You know Marcus, he gets into all sorts of scrapes, but he always comes out on top, and I'm sure that he will be in touch soon. You'll do yourself and the kids no good worrying about it."

She sniffed back the tears and wiped her eyes as she looked up. She breathed deeply to compose herself and even managed a faint smile as she nodded in agreement with him. "Yeah, you're right. I just need to stop flapping."

Steve nodded. "As soon as I hear anything, you'll be the first to know, Jen. Jake is virtually living in the radio room, keeping a round the clock radio watch. If any transmissions come across, he will let us know. Now, go and get some sleep. You look wiped out, Jen. The kids are out with Sophie and Helen, seeing to the animals, so enjoy the peace before they all come back pretending to be lions and monkeys."

A hoarse and nervous laugh escaped Jennifer's throat and she turned and walked away toward the stairs. She stopped with her foot on the first step and turned to Steve, who stood watching her. She smiled.

"Even if I'm asleep, Steve, if he gets in touch, wake me."

"Will do, Jen," he replied and watched as she turned and climbed the stairs.

Steve was worried too, but he had kept his inner concern from Jennifer. Increasingly over the weeks, he had become more of a leader for the group, and he saw it as his duty to hold his composure. The way he looked at it, if he were to lose his head, then how could any of the others rely on him, or keep theirs?

He rushed to Jake's room and threw his head around the doorway. "Anything?" he asked hopefully.

Jake looked up from the laptop he was working on and removed the earphones. With a regretful look in his eyes, he gave a solemn shake of the head. "Sorry, Steve, nothing."

Steve slouched and rested his head against the door frame as he sighed. "Let me know though, Jake, will you?"

"Of course, Steve."

Later that night, a meeting was held. At the far end of the lobby, a group including Steve, Gary and Lee sat talking quietly. They discussed the food and fuel situation, as well as that of their other provisions. After being given the rough estimates of their supplies, Steve was satisfied with the conclusion. They had enough food, water, and fuel to last for a while yet, and it wasn't a pressing matter at that moment.

Also, the animals and their current condition were brought up by Sophie. "Most of the animals seem fine, the monkeys and the primates seem a little more lively than usual, but it's the lions and the tigers I'm concerned about."

"What do you mean, what's up with them?" Gary asked.

"They're agitated," Sophie replied, "constantly roaring and pacing the fence, and fighting amongst each other. Some of the kids were even scared by it earlier when we did the rounds."

Gary nodded, as though he had expected this and had an answer ready. "Ah, it'll be the dead. They can smell the rotting bodies. Don't forget, cats have a very strong sense of smell, just like dogs. The scent of the decaying bodies all around will be driving the lions and tigers nuts. Especially with the lot at the gate so close."

As he made his last statement, he switched his eyes across to Steve.

Steve took that as his cue and moved on to the problem that he and Gary had spoken about earlier in the day as they conducted their security checks.

"The infected at the gate," Steve inhaled as he looked about the group, "what do we do about them?" He paused and no one spoke. They just watched him blankly, assuming the question to be rhetorical.

He continued, "Okay well, we can't just leave them there to rot and wander about for a number of reasons. Firstly, they're a health hazard. The weather is getting hotter and animals are feeding off them, as well as the insects and then they're flying around here. I'm not clued up on the whole health stuff, but I'm sure that having a bunch of dead people on your doorstep isn't wise." He nodded across to Gary. "We were down there this morning, and we could smell them from hundreds of yards away, before we could even see the gate.

"Secondly, they're making too much noise and movement. The way I see it, the longer they're down there, the higher the chance that other infected will be attracted to the area. The sound of their moaning and rattling of the gate carries well beyond the junction at the top, bearing in mind that there's no other noise to drown it out.

"On top of that, they're constantly moving about. I'm not sure how good their vision really is, but it seems to be good enough to distinguish the living from the dead, so I'm sure that with fifty to a hundred of them bouncing about at the gate, any that stumble close enough to the barrier at the top of the road will see them as well as hear them."

Helen sat forward. "Yeah, but I thought the trees and their branches would block the view?"

Gary spoke, "Not completely. Remember, it was only supposed to obscure their view, not block it completely. With the wind blowing the branches out of the way, or even the infected hearing the commotion, they can always see past the barrier if they try. The way we see it though, if there's no noise or movement on the other side, then they'll not investigate."

"Will the barrier not hold them back?" Claire asked. She sat by Jennifer. The two of them had become close over the weeks, helping each other as they struggled through the loss of Roy, and the possibility of Marcus not returning.

"Again," Gary answered as he took a sip from a glass of whiskey, "it's not strong enough to stop them from getting in if they want to. And, there's the gap."

Everyone in the group looked up at Gary. "The gap, we didn't leave a gap, did we?" Helen asked.

Gary nodded as he swilled his drink. "Yeah, we did, between the base of the trees that we felled and the wall. It's only about a metre wide on the grass verge, but that's big enough for them to get through. If there's nothing attracting their attention though, then they won't notice the gap, or have reason to wander through it. We can handle the odd stray now and then."

Carl nodded. "Yeah, there's always gonna be the odd one that turns up. But we can handle that."

"So, how do we deal with the unhealthy noisy gaggle at the gate then?" Helen asked.

Steve glanced at Gary then, answered, "We burn 'em."

A murmur sounded from the group as some people hummed in agreement and others gasped at the thought.

Karen was the first to speak. "Can we do that, I mean, just set fire to a load of people?" She looked to her husband for his stance on the matter.

Gary returned a shrug.

"We've killed them before, what's wrong with killing them again? The only difference is the method," Steve said to the group as a whole.

"Yes," Karen replied, a look of disgust on her face, "but isn't that a bit inhumane, setting fire to them?"

Gary leaned forward, rolling his glass between his hands as he spoke. "Karen, there's no other way to deal with them. We can't risk trying to kill them individually. There's too many. We need a way of dealing with them en masse and from a safe distance with no risk to ourselves. Steve and I discussed it earlier, and fire is the only option we came up with."

Steve backed him up with his own argument. "Gary is right, Karen. Besides, from what I've seen, they don't seem to feel pain like we do."

"Yes, but it still seems a little barbaric and extreme to me. They're still human."

Steve shook his head. "They ceased to be human the moment they died, Karen. What they are now is some new and unholy creature. I only see them as dangerous rotting lumps of meat."

"Yeah, that walk about," Lee said from his left. He was staring straight ahead at the table, a dreamy look on his face as he spoke.

Steve nodded, "Yeah, that too."

"And attack you."

Steve hummed his agreement.

"And eat you."

"And that," Steve concurred again.

"And turn you into them."

Steve turned and looked to his friend, "Yeah, Lee, we get the point."

"And they stink."

Steve nodded, trying to move on.

Lee was still staring at the table top as he spoke, "And they moan,"

"For fuck sake, Lee," Steve slapped the table with his palm and rolled his eyes, "we get the picture."

It was agreed, contrary to Karen's disdain, that the infected in the area of the gate would be burned. They knew that there was a chance of the smoke and flames attracting the attention of more infected from the area, but they agreed that it would be a case of dealing with them individually as they came in.

Steve and Lee collected the fuel and poured it into plastic bottles that could be squeezed, affording them range so that they could spray the infected from the wall without being too close. They made a bunch of Molotov cocktails from glass bottles that were intended to be thrown to the rear of the group, ensuring that the fire spread throughout the swarm at the gate and not just the ones at the front.

Later, from the house, everyone watched in the direction of the park entrance as they saw the thick black plumes of smoke rise into the sky. Soon, the acrid smell of burning flesh twitched at their noses, forcing them back inside and away from the horrible stench. Some were physically sick and people walked around the house for the afternoon, holding scented tissues to their mouths and noses. Others made a point of getting out of the house for a while and joining in with the animal checks with Sophie and the children.

The next day, a party was handpicked to go to the gate again with shovels and digging tools, to remove the burnt and charred corpses that littered the area. Only those of a strong constitution were asked to volunteer and they made their way there, led by Steve.

"Do we have face masks and gloves and stuff?" Carl asked. "Not that I'm squeamish or anything, I just don't like the idea of breathing in that shit."

"Yeah," Sophie answered. "I've already thought of that. I've got us aprons and boots too."

Steve hadn't thought of that and he smiled at Sophie, grateful for her forethought. "What about disinfectants and stuff, do we have any of that too?"

Sophie turned on him. "You serious? Of course we do. This is a frigging zoo, Steve. You ever smelled lion piss when they're in heat?"

They moved off to the gate and stepped out, careful where they placed their feet among the blackened and vile smelling remains mangled and mixed into the ground. Charred black skeletons were everywhere, surrounded by a thick, fly-infested, putrid soup.

Steve remembered setting fire to the crowd with Lee. The infected had sizzled as the fire had taken hold. Their skin and muscle tissue bubbling and dripping away from their bones, their eyes had popped from the heat. Many had swelled up as their already gas-filled stomachs had distended further as their innards had boiled inside them, eventually bursting and spilling their stomach-churning, fetid contents onto the ground as the fire continued to consume them.

What had bothered Steve though, was the lack of acknowledgement from the dead of their ultimate demise from the flames. They had made no move to back away from the flames, and continued to scramble at the wall and gate beneath Steve and Lee as they watched from above. Their moans were not of pain, but the usual low wail, with the odd excited screech or holler from within the mass. None had retreated.

Steve and the burial party moved away from the gate and stopped further along the grass verge and began digging graves along the roadside. It didn't take long; there wasn't much left to bury. They stripped from their aprons and gloves and tossed them into the holes too, glad to be rid of the filth-stained garments.

Tony stood mumbling to himself as he filled in one of the holes. Steve and Sophie watched him, a disturbed silence between them as they witnessed his ramblings.

"See, you're dead," Tony spat into the grave. "I won. You can't get me. You will never get me. I'm the king, the emperor."

He was shaking his head and snorting to himself. A shiver ran down Steve's spine as he watched.

Afterward, bleach and any other industrial style cleaning fluids that Sophie thought would do the trick were poured all over the area in front of the gate to disinfect the vicinity.

They returned to the house, feeling better and more secure, knowing that there was no longer a pack of flesh-eating ghouls clambering at the park entrance. Everybody drank that night to wash away the dirt and filth of the day's task from their minds.

The next day, Sophie did her rounds. It was early morning and she drove the zebra-painted Land Rover along the track to the side of the Monkey Paddock. A flurry of movement to her left caught her eye. At first she struggled to see what had caught her attention, then she focused on something by the trees.

Her eyes grew wide. She slammed on the brakes and jumped out, moving closer to the fence. In the shade of the trees, she saw the figure of a man. He turned and looked at her, then sprinted into the woods after the monkeys.

Steve sat in the lobby talking with Jake when Sophie burst through the door, distraught and looking angry.

"Steve, can I have a word?"

Steve looked up from his seat. "Of course, what's wrong?"

She looked slightly awkward and unsure of how to put her words. "Uh, it's about Lee."

He raised his eyebrows and glanced at Jake before returning to Sophie. "Go on,"

"Well, I wasn't sure I had seen what I thought I had at first, but as I was driving the Jeep along the track past the Monkey Paddock I, uh, saw something."

"You saw what?" Steve was getting anxious and wanted her to spit it out.

She steeled herself then, spoke in a hushed voice. "I saw Lee, in the enclosure with them."

Steve rolled his eyes. "For fuck sake, what's he doing in with the monkeys? I wouldn't worry about it, Sophie. I'm sure he means them no harm and I'll have a word with him about it later."

Sophie wasn't finished and she hovered, still wanting to say something but unsure how. Steve saw that there was more to come. "What?"

"He," she paused, "he was naked Steve."

She had seen him from the corner of her eye as she passed by. A blur at first, but she had stopped and looked again and saw him clearly. He was running and jumping about with the animals, completely nude and when he saw the vehicle on the road, he took off into the trees.

At the dinner table that night, the story broke.

"So, Lee," Steve said during a hushed moment around the table, "what's this about you and the monkeys being at one with nature?"

Lee stopped, hunched over his plate and his fork midway to his mouth. He looked up across and at the faces that now gazed at him from around the table.

After a moment's pause, he shrugged. "Ah you know, I was just having a laugh."

"Sorry, Lee," Steve replied. "I don't know. When I want to have a laugh, I'll watch a funny movie or play a joke on someone. It's never crossed my mind to get naked and run around with monkeys."

He shrugged again and carried on shovelling his food into his mouth. "Each to their own, I guess."

Jake had to ask: "But why naked Lee?"

Everyone wanted to know the answer and the silence around the table as they waited for his reply, was deafening.

Lee dropped his fork onto his plate with a clatter and wiped the corners of his mouth with the back of his hand as he straightened up in his seat.

"Look, I just like the monkeys is all. It's not that I'm trying to shag them or anything. We just get along." He looked around, hoping that his explanation struck a chord; it didn't. He sniffed, "As for the naked part, I came here in the clothes I stood in. I didn't have any spares. I've no problems with wearing someone else's trousers and t-shirts, but I'm not wearing another man's underpants, I don't care how well they've been cleaned."

Jake mused, "So, what you're saying is, if you had some clean underpants, you would be running around with the monkeys in your duds instead of having your bare arse on show?"

Lee was trying to dislodge a piece of food from his teeth with his tongue. He nodded, "Yeah."

"Oh, that's okay then. And there's me thinking it was just weird, when all along, given the choice you'd be running around with a bunch of primates in your underpants instead. I mean, Diane Fossey and David Attenborough must have had it all wrong. Never mind studying them for years. Living among them and being accepted by the group but all the time, keeping their clothes on. All they had to do was get in the buff and there you go, it's the 'missing link'. Glad we cleared that up, Lee." Jake nodded to the man and raised his glass, a broad grin spread across his face.

The rest of the table erupted into fits of laughter.

Sophie, seeing that it was just the eccentric way that Lee was, and not something sinister, even joined in with the laughter and soon found her cheeks and jaw muscles aching.

All the time, Lee sat with a straight face, wondering what all the fuss was about.

27

The next time Marcus saw daylight, he was in a room that appeared to be a sort of storage room, with tiled floors and flat whitewashed walls and high small windows. On a second look, it seemed more like a cell. He was tied to a chair and three men stood in front of him, silent and staring at him with angry looks.

Without a single word, they laid into him. The first hit felt like a train had smashed into his face. A blinding flash and his vision blurred as his head spun and he lost all sense of direction. They didn't let up, punching and slapping him over and over until he lost consciousness.

He was sharply awakened again from the cold stinging water that they threw over him. He was still tied to the chair, but now he lay horizontal on the cold floor where he had toppled over from the force of the blows.

His face was swollen and he could taste blood in his mouth. His lips were split and he could feel the sting as the air hit the open sores. His head throbbed from the countless lumps and gashes he had sustained and his right eye was almost completely shut from swelling.

Again, they laid into him and within seconds, Marcus' vision faded.

He must have been unconscious for hours, because when he awoke again, he was in darkness. At first he thought he was back under a blindfold, but as his eyes adjusted, he was able to see the faint beams of light from under a door to his left. He lay face down on a cold hard floor and as he raised his head, he felt the sharp stinging pain as sores were forced open again as he pulled away the clotted blood that had formed around the cuts, sticking him to the floor.

He was no longer bound to the chair and his hands were free. He reached his fingers to his face and immediately pulled them back as the pain from his nose, jaw and cheek bones shot through him. He cringed, waiting for the agony to subside. He quickly ran his hands over his body, checking for broken bones, and to his relief, he couldn't feel any and he slowly stood up on shaking legs. The last thing he needed was broken limbs or ribs; they would slow him down if he was able to escape.

Reaching out into the darkness, he began to feel his way around the room, moving from wall to wall, developing a mental image of his immediate surroundings in his mind.

Once he was satisfied with his bearings, he whispered into the darkness, "Anyone else in here?"

There was no answer and he began to feel around the floor, hoping to find another body in the cell with him. There wasn't.

After carefully and quietly checking the door and testing its strength, he sat himself in the corner, dejected and scared of the unknown. He didn't know what was going to happen to him. He didn't know if any of the others were still alive and the thought of being impaled terrified him, even more than being killed by the infected.

Then the screaming began.

It was Jim. Long howls of pain lingered and reverberated from further inside the building, along a corridor to the left Marcus suspected, from the way the sound echoed toward the door of his cell. Even though he knew that Jim was in pain and being tortured, it gave Marcus a connection to his friends. At least one was alive and he wasn't alone.

The idea of being the only one was a lonely and demoralising thought and, as selfish as it seemed, it did his spirit just that little bit of good to know that others were in the same shitty boat with him.

For two days, as far as Marcus could tell, they were held and tortured again and again. He was able to distinguish the different screams of his friends. He recognised Ian's deep throaty cry, Stu's ear-splitting screech, and Hussein's bone-chilling, high-pitched shriek.

He was becoming weaker and weaker with every beating and still, no one had even spoken to him. He had no idea why they were being held or what they intended to do with them. He would have felt better if he had actually been interrogated. At least that way he would have an idea of the rules of the game.

He was dragged from his cell with his hands bound behind his back. With a guard under each arm, they didn't give him the chance to get to his feet and he was hauled along the corridor, his feet and toes scraping along the rough floor and causing more pain to his already stretched senses.

He was thrown onto his face, landing in a muddy puddle in a courtyard. He coughed and spluttered as he turned his head to save himself from drowning in the dirty water. He looked up, and to his right, he could see the rest of his friends, in a line on their knees and bound in the same way he was. Stu stared at him, his eyes wide with anticipation and fear. With the way that they were lined up, Marcus was sure that the time had come for their execution. He just hoped it would be from a bullet in the head.

A hand grasped him by his hair from behind and pulled him upright and onto his knees. He glanced back along the line of his team members. They were all in a bad way. Jim looked the worst. His head was black and blue and he swayed continually, about to collapse. A guard stood behind him, a hand on his shoulder to stop him from falling over.

Around them, in a circle, Marcus saw his captors. They stood as though they were waiting for something and watching Marcus and his men as they knelt in the mud. Marcus counted six of them, with maybe another two behind him.

From across the yard, a door flew open with a bang and another two guards appeared, dragging a man with his hands and feet tied. He was babbling and struggling frantically as they hauled him into the open. They approached the centre of the courtyard and threw him to the ground, hitting the loose stones with a sickening thud, creating a large gash along the side of his head that instantly began to pour blood down his face and neck.

A tall man walked into the clearing. His short blonde hair and rugged features identified him as the same man who had shot Zaid. He walked with an air of confidence and supreme command, his shoulders pushed back and his head raised. Marcus could picture him in an SS uniform.

He stopped and looked down at the bloodied man, squirming on the ground. He coughed and spat a wad of phlegm onto the wretched figure below him, and motioned to his men.

One nodded and approached with two others. From the back of a flat bed truck, another two pulled a long pole and began to move toward the man on the ground. Two of the men grabbed the bound man and hauled him to his feet. On seeing the stake, he began to struggle all the more, crying, pleading and shaking his head toward the men who held him. He was mumbling something that Marcus couldn't understand, but it was obvious he was begging for his life.

The tall blonde-haired commander stepped in front of Marcus and his men, a smile spread across his face as he spoke.

"My name is Colonel Vladimir. I prefer Vlad though, Vlad the Impaler. That is funny, no?

"I am the big boss around here. I choose who lives and who dies. This man," he pointed behind him, still smiling, "he was my personal bodyguard, but his loyalty was in question. Now you shall see."

He turned back to his men and nodded.

Marcus felt his heart sink. *Shit, now we have our very own Dracula,* he thought.

The struggling man had the ties around his ankles cut and a man on either side began to splay his legs. He jerked and screamed as two others brought the stake into position, the sharpened end pointing into his groin. Four men held him in position, jostling and fighting to keep him under control.

The men carrying the pole took aim, and thrust hard, driving the tip into the man's flesh. They had aimed at the groin, but with him kicking and thrashing, they missed and the spike pierced into the area below his abdomen, just above his groin and genitals.

An ear-splitting screech rung out around the yard as the soldiers pushed the stake further into him. Blood gushed from the wound and began to flow along the length of the wooden stake. They pushed it further and the man began to convulse and gurgle as the tip of the spike was forced up and into his ribcage. His head shot back as they drove the stake deeper, blood bubbling up from his throat and splashing over his face as he continued to scream.

By now, the man was gasping and spluttering, his head shaking and twisting as he weakened and died. The tip of the spike pierced through his shoulder, forcing the skin apart and stretching it as it accommodated for the circumference of the stake. With a final shove, the stake was forced another half metre and the men restraining their victim helped to bring the body and the pole upright leaving the dead man completely impaled.

Vlad clapped. "Ah, this is good, no?" He turned to Marcus, proud of the work his men had achieved.

Marcus could hear whimpers from his right, they were the sounds of despair and he couldn't tell which of his men the noise came from, but he felt like doing the same.

Later, they came for him again. The door was kicked open and two men dragged him to his feet and back into the whitewashed room. This time, he was thrown to the floor in front of a wooden chair. They didn't tie him to it as usual and when he looked up, he saw the rebel commander, *Dracula*, seated in front of him behind a fold away metal table. The light from the high windows behind silhouetted him, casting his face in darkness.

"Sit down," his voice boomed, and Marcus struggled to the chair and sat.

"What is your name?"

"Marcus," he was staring at the floor, not wanting to make eye contact and provoke another beating.

"You are Muslim, yes?"

Marcus suddenly looked up, confused. "No," he replied as the consequences of such an accusation from a Serb flashed into his mind, "I'm Roman Catholic, a Christian."

Vlad looked down at his folded hands on the steel table. "Then why did you have Arabs with you? I think that you are Albanian and here to rape and murder your way through our country."

The irony hit Marcus. He was tempted to retort with the fact that they weren't the ones who were nailing people to spikes or impaling them, but decided in the interest of self preservation, not to mention it.

"We are just trying to get home to our families. We came from Iraq. Hussein and his friends helped us."

"So," Vlad lowered his voice, a hint of finality in his tone as though he had got to the bottom of something, "you are the commander of a group of Islamic Extremists from Iraq seeing the current world situation as your chance to attack us? That's not good, Marcus."

Marcus began to reply when he heard vehicles pull up outside the window. The sound of voices hollering to one another, then the screams and yelps of a woman followed by laughter and cheers, rang around the room.

Dracula was about to speak, when the thunder of automatic fire erupted from outside. He rose to his feet and looked to the door. Men were screaming and shouting from inside the building, their footsteps thundering down the corridors and stairs as the sound of the gun battle outside grew in intensity.

Marcus remained seated, his head lowered, and he watched from the corner of his eye as Vlad began to move toward the door hesitantly. As he came level, Marcus sprung from his chair, his hands aiming for the throat of his captor. Vlad turned, too late, shock in his eyes, as Marcus closed in on him, his fingers closing around his windpipe and bringing his knee up into his groin. Vlad groaned and folded, dropping his weight onto Marcus's shoulder, their faces close.

Marcus continued to pound his knees into the man's groin and abdomen as he gripped tighter at his throat, blocking off any attempt at a scream for help. They were now against the wall and Vlad had nowhere to back up and no chance to recover as Marcus never let up with his assault.

He opened his mouth wide and bit down on Vlad's nose, tearing at the man's face and coming away with a large chunk of flesh between his teeth. He dropped it and brought his head forward again, his teeth clamping shut again, this time tearing away at the lips and soft tissue around the mouth as Vlad flailed his arms, pounding at Marcus' back and head with his fists, trying to break his grip.

Bloodied and drowning in his own blood, Vlad spluttered into Marcus' face as he weakened and tried in vain to escape his grasp. Marcus tightened his grip and felt his strength surge with his own instinct for survival.

He pulled his head back and began to launch his forehead, over and over again, into the face of his enemy, smashing it to a pulp with each blow, feeling the bones crunch and shatter beneath his assault.

He released his grip on the throat and grasped his hands on either side of Vlad's head as the rebel commander began to slump down the wall. Marcus dug his thumbs into his eyes and pushed down with all his weight, feeling the soft jelly inside the eyeball pop and burst over his thumbs.

Vlad was screaming, a faint spluttering squeal that didn't reach far. He didn't have the strength to carry his voice and his scream became lower and lower until it was nothing more than just a whimper as Marcus continued to headbutt his face into oblivion.

Marcus brought his head down again and gripped his throat between his teeth. He clamped them shut, feeling his incisors meet on the other side of the windpipe as they punctured through the skin. He pulled his head back as hard as he could. He felt the skin tear and pop as the warm blood gushed into his mouth and over his face.

He released his grip and stepped back, looking down at the jerky movements as *Dracula* died below him. He finally lay still and Marcus reached down and grabbed the pistol from the belt of the dead man.

The battle outside still raged and men screamed as they were hit. Holes appeared in the walls as rounds punched through the brick and into the room, sending splinters of stone and plaster flying around him. He opened the door and peered down the corridor.

A man crouched at the end, holding an AK47 and taking cover around the corner. Now and then he reached around and let off a long burst at his attackers outside.

Marcus quickly made his way along the narrow walkway and came up behind the man, placing his pistol to the back of his head. The man didn't even realise Marcus was behind him, and probably didn't even realise he was dead when the bang of the pistol blasted out from behind him. Marcus had shot him through the base of the skull, and he dropped like water into a heap on the floor, sending his rifle clattering on the tiles.

He reached down and picked up the weapon and ammunition and began to make his way back along the corridor, hollering for the rest of his men. He could hear Ian further along, shouting his name from within a room. He kicked the door open and found him laying on the floor, his hands and feet tied together.

He could hear more familiar voices from other rooms close by, and after releasing Ian, they went and collected the rest of their men.

Jim was in a bad way. He was virtually unconscious with only fleeting moments of clarity. Marcus feared that he had a skull fracture as they helped him along the corridor and to the light of the open door at the far end around a corner.

Shots still rang out, but they had now become intermittent and Marcus began to hesitate again as they approached the corner. Thoughts raced through his head. *It could be another rebel group, or it could even be the same rebel group, just making a few changes to their leadership.*

It had gone quiet outside now, and Marcus and Stu decided to try and creep around from another angle, leaving Ian, with the rifle, to defend the doorway.

They walked in a crouch along the hallway and to what they thought was the back of the building, exiting through an old rickety wooden door. They hugged the outside of the building and followed it around to the right, hoping to remain out of sight and able to come up on the flank of whomever was outside.

They rounded the corner. Marcus held the pistol out in front of him, trying to focus with his good eye. It was hard to see anything, let alone aim. He paused before peering around the corner into the courtyard of the house. Their vehicles were there, though one of them looked worse for wear, full of holes and with steam spouting from beneath the bonnet. Men lay sprawled all around in the open, weapons and ammunition mixed in with the pools of blood as the bodies continued to leak.

To his front, twenty metres across the courtyard, stood a man staring at him, an M4 rifle clutched at the ready in his hands. He didn't move and he didn't raise the weapon. Marcus also paused and strained to focus on him.

Then he heard a voice from his left.

"What do you intend to do with that little thing in your hand then, Marcus? Throw it at us?"

Marcus spun, the pistol at the ready, but he saw nothing.

"Don't shoot, don't shoot. Marcus, it's us, Sini and Yan." The man across the yard was quickly walking toward him, waving his right arm and his rifle pointed to the ground with his other.

Marcus became dizzy, his head spun and his knees weakened. He leaned against the wall of the house and collapsed into a sitting position. "Fucking hell," was all he could manage.

Stu sat down beside him, wincing with pain and giggling at the same time. It was the laughter of relief and the pair sat there watching Yan as he approached from behind a wall.

Yan and Sini had followed Marcus after reaching their home town and seeing that everyone had either run or died there. They reached the field of the impaled dead and noticed the tracks formed from the SUVs in the dirt and the unknown trucks that accompanied them. They followed, and come across the farm complex the night before. They watched the comings and goings through the night and listened to the torture and decided that they would attempt a rescue the next day.

Sini had found only his girlfriend in the ruins of their town. She had been hiding in the loft of her home and they soon realised that they would find no one else, and decided to try and join back up with Marcus.

Sandra was used as a decoy. Sini and Yan knew that the prospect of a woman to beat and rape would put the rebels off-guard and bring the majority of them into the open, easy prey to be gunned down, and they sprung their ambush. Yan had moved to the right flank and while Sini drew their fire, he was able to pick the rest off from his position.

The team was reunited, and they immediately began to collect weapons and ammunition from the dead rebels. Sini walked into the interrogation room and looked down at Vlad's body and whistled.

"You really didn't like this man, did you Marcus?"

Marcus shrugged. "The fucker was gonna impale us." He looked down at the body with disdain and spat. "We better round them all up before they all come back."

Sini turned to him. "Don't worry about them; me and Yan will take care of that, you see to the others. I think Jim is in serious need of Stu's med skills, Marcus."

Marcus nodded and left the room.

Stu had already carried Jim into another room and lay him down on a cot, stripping him and assessing his wounds. He looked up at Marcus as he entered; a grave look on his face.

"He isn't doing too well, Marcus. I don't think his skull is fractured, but he definitely has a serious concussion, at least two broken ribs, a fractured jaw and sunken cheek bone. His eyes are so swollen I can't get a proper look to see what damage has been done."

Everyone was in a bad way. Marcus moved through the house with Ian, hobbling and wincing with pain, checking each room and ensuring that there was no one left alive from the rebel group. Specifically, they looked for any evidence of other rebel forces in the area, maps showing their dispositions and radios with call signs and frequencies. They couldn't find either in any of the buildings they searched.

Marcus felt relieved.

"This means they were on their own, Ian. They aren't part of any higher organisation and no one probably knew they were here or even existed."

Ian screwed his face up. "Yeah, so, what you getting at?"

Marcus smiled. "It means we have free bed and board for as long as we need it while we recover. There isn't likely to be anyone coming here, especially other rebel forces. We're out of the way and not likely to be stumbled across."

The realisation hit Ian and a grin spread across his bloodied and battered face. "So does that mean I can have a shit in a real toilet then instead of the bushes, or my trousers 'cause you won't let us pull over?"

It was decided, they would stay and recuperate. Jim needed a lot of attention, attention he wouldn't receive if they were back on the road and pushing hard across Europe. With the state he was in, he was no use to the team and his condition would probably worsen if they were travelling.

"This is Sandra," Sini presented his pretty brunette girlfriend to Marcus. "She is coming with us."

Marcus raised an eyebrow. "With us?" he asked.

"Well, I have no reason to stay here, so we may as well come with you."

Marcus nodded his approval, and smiled at Sandra. He turned back to Sini. "What about Yan?"

"You know him; he always does whatever I do. He was like that when we served in the army together. He doesn't have any close family anyway, why do you think he rarely went on leave? He was saving most of his money to move to the States and become a porn star or something like that, knowing him."

They recovered their vehicles. Ian's SUV was beyond repair. It had taken too many rounds in to the engine. Even the armour was damaged in places and it had taken on the appearance of a colander. They began stripping it out to use what parts they could salvage, to refit the other vehicles.

Marcus got to work on the Codan.

"Steve, this is Marcus, you there?" He waited for a reply. It took a long time to get the Codan to work properly again but eventually he was able to hear the faint reply from the other end.

"Marcus, thank Christ. We've been worried about you bro."

Marcus smiled and began to explain the situation. He refrained from going into too much detail and ambiguously referred to the incident as 'trouble with the locals'. He gave them their location and intentions, explaining that they would be going firm and staying at that location for up to two weeks then pushing on, headed across Hungary, Austria, Southern Germany and into France. It sounded a lot easier than it would be, and Marcus knew that there were a lot of miles to cover and possibly more trouble, similar to what they had already encountered.

After the brief conversation with Steve, he had his usual ten minutes with Jennifer and the boys. They all sounded strained, but relieved to hear from him. Marcus could tell that Jennifer had been at her wits' end, wondering what had happened to him.

That night, Marcus took his first bath in over a month. He dipped his foot into the hot steaming water and felt the tingling heat race up his leg. He placed both hands on the side of the bath and slowly lowered himself. The water gave him a shock as it reached his backside and as he sat his breath was momentarily taken away from him as the water swished up to his chest.

Every sore and niggling ache and pain screamed at him in protest from the hot water. His body ached from the weeks of travelling and scurrying about in the wilderness. Now, he had the cuts and bruises from the countless beatings he had sustained over the last few days to add to the moment of agony before the pain settled in the hot water.

As he splashed his face, he almost howled. His lips screamed at him and threatened to explode while his cheeks and eyes throbbed as they swelled up again with the heat. His beard was matted thick with dried blood and snot and his hair was a greasy mess of tangled, overgrown locks. It took forever to get himself washed. But once he was clean, all the pain and suffering seemed worth it.

Now it was time to shave, and get some kind of haircut.

He walked into the room where Stu was tending to Jim on the bed. The cool air felt good on his freshly bare face. For weeks he had forgotten how it felt to have a smooth chin and the sensation of a breeze on his skin.

Stu looked up from Jim as Marcus entered. He did a double-take, and his eyes showed surprise at the sight of him.

"My God, Marcus, you look like a new man."

"I feel like one," he replied, "but it was fucking agony getting this way. I never knew that shaving with a blunt razor could be so painful. You should try it, you look like a tramp. How's our patient doing?"

Stu turned to look at Jim. "Early days yet mate, but we should have a more solid answer after tonight hopefully."

Marcus nodded, rubbing his smooth chin, understanding that the first twenty four hours would be critical to Jim's recovery. "Go get yourself sorted, Stu. I'll keep an eye on him for a while."

Stu left to get cleaned up.

Marcus moved over to the cot where Jim lay. His breathing was shallow and his body was still.

"Jim buddy, you've got a lot more sightseeing of Europe to do yet, so get yourself well. You hear?"

For twelve days they stayed at the farm. They collected weapons, ammunition, repaired their vehicles and filled up on what supplies, fuel, and equipment they thought they could use. By the end of their stay, they looked like a ragtag bunch of mercenaries in a mixture of clothes and vehicles.

They discarded their M4 rifles and opted to use the more robust, larger calibre AK47s that they took from the dead rebels. They were low on ammunition for their old rifles anyway but there was an abundance of rounds and magazines for the AKs. They also took one of the smaller rebel trucks, fitting it out as best they could with a machinegun and communications equipment, but it would be used mainly to hump and dump the majority of the ammunition and supplies.

Jim was in much better condition; still not back to his old self, but far away from death's door. He still had trouble moving about as his ribs slowly healed and his face still bore the marks of a broken nose and jaw. He was placed in the back of the truck and Sandra was tasked with watching over him while Stu and Ahmed rode up front in the cab.

Marcus, Sini and Hussein were back in their old SUV, only this time, Hussein would stay behind the wheel, freeing up Sini to man the guns when needed while Ian and Yan took over Stu's old SUV at the front of the convoy.

They moved out, headed for the border with Hungary. They had to pass through the field of impaled dead again and Marcus felt a shudder run through his entire body as he avoided looking directly at the elevated corpses that stared and moaned back at them as they passed.

28

A cool breeze was blowing in from the open ground in front of the house. The dark sky was completely devoid of any cloud cover and the tiny twinkling lights of millions of stars were stretched across the heavens, like a scattering of diamonds over a black silk sheet.

Lee had always loved summer nights. They had been his favourite since he was a young boy, and now he sat on the roof of the house, leaning back in his chair and savouring the moment. Without the ambient noise and light of the days gone by, the night seemed all the more complete. Nothing stirred. There was no glare from street lights and no steady murmur of the hundreds of cars as they travelled the roads in the distance.

The gentle wind rustled the leaves in the trees around the house, and the occasional hoot of an owl or squeak of a mouse could be heard in the underbrush. But it wasn't the noises of the nocturnal animals that suddenly caught his attention and made him sit upright. It was the unnatural and unmistakable sound of a door closing. Whoever was responsible for the sound was doing their best to go unheard. But Lee distinctly heard the click and the almost inaudible thud of the wood as the door met the frame.

The noise came from his right, toward the back of the house. Lee rose from his chair and made his way over to the edge of the roof, taking gentle steps, careful not to alert whoever was below to his presence by crunching too heavily on the gravel that coated the flat areas of the roof.

He reached the edge and peered over and into the gloom. At first he saw nothing, but a moment later his eyes adjusted to the change and he was able to make out the foot of the trees, the dark line that marked the edge between the long grass at the side of the road and the tarmac, and the figure walking away from the house.

It looked like a man. The gait was unmistakably masculine. He couldn't tell who it was. All he saw was the silhouette as they walked along the road and hugged the grass verge, remaining obscured in the dark shade of the trees.

The figure stopped, Lee could see a very faint cloud of misted breath escape from his mouth as he slowly turned, looking in all directions. It was then that Lee realised who he was watching.

Tony.

His movements were unmistakable and Lee couldn't understand why he hadn't recognised Tony the moment he saw him. For weeks, he had watched him like a hawk and scrutinised his every move. Even though no one had found any reason to distrust the man, Lee always had a gut feeling about him and it niggled at him constantly.

Now he was watching him again, in the middle of the night, skulking away from the house and into the darkness. To Lee, just by that very act, there was reason enough not to trust or like the man.

Lee rushed back through the door that led onto the roof from the inside of the house and pounded his way down the three flights of stairs to the ground floor. He paused at the rear door and sneaked a look through the window, careful to make sure that Tony hadn't seen him or suspected he had been noticed.

Lee couldn't see him anymore, and he slowly turned the handle and crept out into the gloom and after Tony.

Following the path that he suspected he would have taken, Lee trod carefully. Avoiding the crunch of stones and the snap of twigs beneath his heavy feet, he crept along, blinking into the darkness for any sight of his quarry.

He continued blindly, hoping to pick up a sign or sight of Tony. He was about to give up when, from somewhere up ahead, he heard the faint deep grumble of someone clearing his throat. Lee quickened his pace, hoping to close the gap to a distance where he could see him with his naked eye without having to rely solely on his hearing.

A minute later he could see the hunched shape of Tony, fifty metres ahead of him. He was walking, hands in his pockets, and Lee could now hear another sound in the air. Tony was humming a tune. He couldn't tell what tune he was humming, but Lee got the impression that he didn't have a care in the world and was just out for a nighttime stroll.

For a moment, Lee doubted his own judgement. *Maybe he was just out for a walk? Maybe Tony enjoyed the summer nights just as much as he did?* Lee shook himself. No. His gut feelings about the sinister side of Tony were still there. He was going somewhere specific and Lee wanted to see where.

Tony headed for the restaurant and gift shop area of the park. He left the gloom of the trees and made his way to the Information Centre, still humming away to himself.

Lee stopped in the darkness of the woods and watched as Tony crossed the open area and began to fumble at the side door that led into the Information Centre. He paused as he pushed the door open, glancing about and checking for anyone in the area before disappearing inside.

Stepping out from the trees, Lee quickly crossed the open area and into the shade of the building. He followed around its exterior wall, hoping to see some sign or hear a noise that would pinpoint Tony's location for him.

Toward the back of the building, he heard the sounds of footsteps inside through the thin corrugated iron and plasterboard lined walls. It sounded like Tony was in the manager's office.

"Ah, hello again." His voice was muffled through the wall, but Lee could make out what he was saying without any undue effort.

"I hope you've been good while I've been away. Have you? You know I don't like you misbehaving. We must always keep order."

Lee screwed up his face in confusion. *Who could he possibly be talking to? Is he using a phone or talking to himself? Does he have a pet?* Lee wondered.

"Yes, if we don't have order, we have anarchy. And that will not do, will it? You do understand, don't you?"

There was a pause as he continued in a calm friendly voice. "That is why I keep you here, to teach you the ways of the new world. You are pure, you have been taught by me, the right and wrongs of the new era. If I were to mix you in with all the whores and scum up at the house, you would be polluted and no better than the filthy, impure creatures that roam the streets. Believe me, it won't be long before those festering inbred swine at the house are staggering about as they rot on their feet too."

Lee couldn't see what was going on, but he was hearing plenty and what he heard turned his stomach and boiled his blood. He moved around to the other side of the building and paused below a window that he suspected would look into the room where Tony was. He slowly raised his head to the bottom of the ledge and paused again, listening for Tony's voice and ensuring that his movements hadn't been detected.

His eyes cleared the ledge, and in the glow of candlelight, he saw Tony pacing the room, a long cane clutched in his hands as he spoke. He seemed to be ranting, but in a hushed voice. Lee turned his head, straining his eyes to see what Tony was ranting at.

He focused and saw something in the gloom.

His eyes bulged, a cry knotted in his throat and his stomach tightened, as if someone had reached into his abdomen and twisted his guts in their clenched fist. His anguish turned to rage, he gritted his teeth and staggered back from the window, shaking his head. He steeled himself, and then stormed toward the door.

Steve's eyes shot open. At first, he wasn't sure what it was that had awoken him until the blur of sleep subsided a few seconds later. He could hear shouting, crashing, and banging. And screaming.

He sat bolt upright and reached for his trousers at the side of the bed and quickly pulled them on, hopping to the door as he buttoned them. Without bothering to pull on his t-shirt, he bolted out into the corridor, where the commotion became louder. He stopped and looked to his right, checking that the noise wasn't coming from any of the other bedrooms.

It was coming from downstairs, in the lobby.

He bounded down the steps, taking two at a time until he skidded to a halt in the open area in front of the main door.

Before him were two men. One was on the floor and the other stood above him, his arm pulled back, about to land another punch.

Steve watched as Lee's fist shot forward and pounded into Tony's head with a sickening thud. A scream echoed through the house and Lee cocked his arm, ready to strike again.

"Lee, stop!" Steve was holding his hands out to his friend, pleading with him.

Lee looked up with wildly shining eyes and a ferocious snarl. He was panting with the effort of the obvious beating he had inflicted on the man at his feet. He lowered his arm to his side, and stepped back, slightly, but not too far to give the floored figure the chance to wriggle away.

Steve slowly approached, still looking into the eyes of the madman that had possessed the body of his friend, Lee. He was confused and concerned and wondered what could have happened to make Lee turn into a maniac. He knew there would've been something, but for the life of him, he couldn't imagine what.

The man on the floor groaned and rolled onto his back. His face was a mess. He was covered in blood and thick strings of it dangled from his mouth. He spluttered and turned his head and spat. Steve heard the tinkling sound as three white teeth skittered across the tiled floor, leaving dots of bloody spittle in their wake.

Jake, Gary, and John had heard the commotion and came down the stairs behind him. Further up, Helen and Claire stood at the top of the stairs, straining to see what was happening.

Gary looked back at them and held out a hand, telling them to stay where they were.

Steve recognised the limp form, now curled tightly into a ball and whimpering. He looked back up at Lee, his eyes wide and questioning.

"What happened, Lee?"

Lee's chest was heaving, and Steve saw that it wasn't from the exertion. He had tears in his eyes and he struggled to speak as he sobbed. He gestured at Tony. His hand was swollen from the beating he had dished out.

In a voice that was on the verge of breaking as he fought to control himself, he spoke, "Ask that bastard there. Send someone down to the Information Office to see for themselves." Lee looked up from Tony, his head shaking at something he was struggling to comprehend. His tears had broken through their floodgates and they now streamed down his cheeks in glistening rivulets. "Kids, Steve, they're just little kids."

He let out a howl and began to throw kick after kick into Tony's ribs as he writhed and screamed under the blows.

Jake and John moved to the door and ran out into the night to the Information Centre.

Lee continued to rain down kicks and stomps onto the quivering and pulverised mush that was Tony. Gary approached him from behind and grabbed him by both arms, speaking soothingly into his ear as he pulled him away to allow Steve in to see to Tony.

"It's okay, Lee, it is okay. He isn't going anywhere. You can leave him for now. Come over here and sit down. Your hand looks hurt, let me have a look." Gary took his hand in his own and began examining it, trying to distract Lee from launching any further assaults.

Steve knelt over the now still and unconscious Tony. His face was unrecognisable and Steve wondered how Lee hadn't managed to kill him, though from the look of it, it had been his intention.

Helen came into the lobby, her hair sticking up and a scruffy old baggy t-shirt just barely covering her perfectly formed thighs and buttocks. Steve couldn't help but steal a second glance, even with the carnage and emotion around him.

They moved Tony to the couch and gently placed him down under the lights so that Helen could examine him better. Steve left her to it and moved over to the table where Lee sat, sobbing into his folded arms with Gary and Carl sitting either side of him.

More people had come down the stairs and Steve noticed that the room was now pretty full. He saw them staring and heard the odd mutter here and there, including Stephanie's whispered voice.

"He's finally done it. That psycho has actually gone and killed someone."

Steve turned in her direction and gave her a hard stare that shut her up immediately and forced her to shrink back into the crowd.

"Lee. Hey mate, what the fuck is going on?" He was leaning over his shoulder and speaking into his ear, pleading with him as he rubbed him on the back.

Lee raised his head and tried to speak, but his words were gibberish.

"It's okay, calm down and tell me what happened."

Lee sat up, sniffing up his tears and breathing deeply as he wiped his eyes. He looked to Steve, his eyes pleading. "They're just kids, Steve," he said again, "chained up in an office, just a couple of little kids."

Steve sat back and looked at Gary, who returned with a shrug. "That's all he told me, Steve."

The lobby door crashed open and Jake entered, followed closely by John. They looked flustered and out of breath and headed straight for Steve and the others, pulling them to one side when they got there.

Jake looked severely shaken, even terrified and spoke in a hushed voice. "Lee was right. This sick fucker had a couple of kids changed up in the Information Centre. It looks like he's had them there a while too."

Steve glanced over his shoulder at Helen and then back to Jake. "Where are they now?"

John looked down and Jake followed suit. "They're dead, Steve," John replied.

Steve felt sick. The room began to spin and he had to steady himself against one of the chairs behind him.

"A little girl and boy, Steve, I think they had been alive for a while. There were food wrappers and water bottles lying about, but it looks like he killed them a week or so ago. Steve," John's voice was grim but urgent. Steve looked up into the burly man's staring eyes, "they were naked, Steve. I think he, I think that bastard, he..." John couldn't finish the sentence and looked away, shaking his head, but Steve knew what he was trying to say.

Lee was sedated with what pills and potions the people of the house could come up with, as well as a good helping of whiskey and brandy, then placed into his bed. Carl stood watch outside his door while he slept.

Tony was carried into a back room, his hands and feet bound to a table that he was laid upon. Helen, upon hearing the story, refused to treat him any further and no one in the house could blame her.

The two reanimated corpses of the young children, Amy and Robert, were removed from the Information Centre and John was burdened the responsibility of taking care of them. He argued with his inner-self and justified it with the fact that he was putting them at rest and bringing them peace. It was still no easier for him to do, and Steve saw how deeply it had affected him when he returned and opened a bottle of whiskey. He sat in silence, acknowledging the existence of no one, and didn't move until the bottle was empty.

Steve now found himself at odds. What was he to do? All the time he fought to keep his rage under control and stop himself from bursting into the room to beat Tony to death. Images of the boy and girl, snarling and clutching at him, fighting against their restraints as he entered the room, flashed into his mind.

He guessed that the girl would have been about ten and the boy, maybe eight, probably brother and sister. He couldn't imagine what horrors and tortures they had been forced to endure. He held his head in his hands, clutching at his hair and sobbing.

He also remembered how well Tony had interacted with the other people of the house, especially the children, including Sarah.

All the time, there had never been a single, obvious warning sign. No alarm bells or inclinations of his ulterior motives. He felt sick to his stomach, ashamed of the fact he had failed to protect and keep the people he felt responsible for from harm.

Instead, he had let the bastard in and welcomed him with open arms.

Only Lee had been right.

Gary called a meeting in the lobby. Only Steve, Helen, Jake, and John were asked to attend, but many more turned up, feeling that they had the right to be there, some being parents themselves.

Gary held his face in his hands as he sat at the head of the table. He looked up and glanced about at the people who stood in silence, watching him.

He let out a long sigh and sat back, resting his hands on the tabletop. "Well, what do we do?" He tried to meet the gaze of the assembled people, but each one turned away or looked down as he made eye contact.

"We string the fucker up," Carl said without hesitation. He sat at the far end, staring at his hands.

Steve sighed and leaned back in his chair as he looked up to the ceiling. "I dunno what is right and I don't care, but I agree with Carl."

Murmurs rippled through the crowded room as people gave their own hushed opinions amongst themselves.

Helen nodded, "Me too."

"Is that it, as simple as that?" Gary asked, glancing from Steve to Helen.

Steve glared at him, "What do you suggest then, Gary, counselling?"

Gary held up his hands in defence. "Whoa, Steve, you're getting me all wrong here. I'm not disagreeing with you. What I'm asking is: do we decide it as easily as that?"

"What other action should we take?" Steve changed his tone. In a cold and calculated voice he said, "Okay, let's look at it logically then. There are no police, no prisons, no psychiatric hospitals, no judges anymore, and no other treatment as far as I'm concerned. He is a threat to everyone here. Even Lee told us that he heard Tony speaking of plans to kill us. We can't turn him loose, he could come back, or other survivors could fall victim to him." He looked down into his lap and then back up, staring straight ahead at the far wall. "I hate to say it, but I quote Joseph Stalin here: if you have a problem, get rid of the man. Then you have no problem."

A woman named Julie spoke up from behind. "Are you really gonna just, kill him? How can you?"

Jake turned on her and growled. "Hey, we've been killing much better than him for weeks now. They may be dead but they're better people than Tony as far as I'm concerned."

"But still, we can't just kill him. What about the law, what about justice? The man needs help, not execution."

A few more mumbles could be heard within the group.

Helen spoke, "I was a pediatric nurse before all this, and I've seen what those monsters do. I've seen kids beaten to within an inch of their lives and heard the excuses that they had fallen down or walked into something. I've seen the blood smears between the legs of little girls and boys and the withdrawn faces and whimpers of children as they suffered in silence with no one to fight their corner.

"I've even reported my suspicions and findings to the hospital administrators, to the police, only to be met with excuses about how the law can't do anything for this or that reason. I was even suspended for three weeks after taking the law into my own hands and refusing to allow a girl's father to take her home because I suspected he was abusing her." She turned to Carl and nodded. "I agree with him, we string the bastard up."

Julie erupted with emotion in her voice. "For the love of God, can you listen to yourselves? You sound no better than him. We are not barbarians who summarily execute people. Capital punishment was abolished in this country a long time ago."

Slamming his hands down on the table with a loud echoing bang, Steve suddenly rose to his feet and turned to face the crowd, singling out the source of the voice of reason from the woman, Julie, who had spoken up.

He spat and hissed his words, "Listen to you. Are you fucking serious? I've already told you there is no law, no police or prisons. What shall we do? Try and make him right?

"He held those two children for Christ knows how long, right under our noses. He raped them, beat them, tortured them for weeks, and eventually, killed them.

"Were you one of those bleeding hearts in the past, who always insisted that monsters, like him can be cured and placed back into society? To be allowed the protection of the police while he stalked the schools again, surfed the net, and spent his time picking his targets?

"Tell that to the parents that lost their children to fiends like him, who then found out that the powers-that-be knew about him all along. The law has protected him and failed us for long enough, and this time, right here tonight, that bastard in there," he growled and pointed his finger in the direction of the room where Tony was being held, "gets the treatment that all of those animals should have gotten from the start.

"No counselling, no chemical castration, no prison sentence followed by a new identity and government hand-outs to see him through afterward. No, he dies, simple as that. And I dare any fucking one of you to try and stop me."

He stomped around the table and toward the back room. Anyone in his path quickly stepped aside and made way for him.

Jake, John, and Carl followed, and after a moment, so did Gary. They burst into the room and dragged Tony's limp body to his feet. He was barely conscious and struggled to walk as they marched him out into the lobby. The crowd hushed and stared at the beaten man before them, then parted, showing that most of the people in the house agreed with the verdict. That was the final confirmation for Steve. *How could everyone in the room be wrong in their judgement?*

They pushed Tony to the door and outside, bundling him into the back of one of the cars. Jake took the wheel and drove straight for the far side of the park, toward the corner where they had felled the trees to build the barricade.

Tony had come to and began to realise what was about to happen. He sat crying and begging for forgiveness, pleading with them to let him go and that they would never see him again.

Carl slapped him hard across the face. "Shut up, cunt. You die tonight, and believe me, you will suffer."

They reached the corner and gagged Tony to stop him from screaming and attracting any attention before they wanted him to.

John and Steve grabbed the ladders Gary had attached to the roof of the car and placed them at the wall while Jake and Carl climbed and waited on the other side after securing the second ladder.

Gary remained by the car. It wasn't that he was reluctant. He knew that the others were far more agile than he was and once they were ready, they would need to be fast at getting back over. He watched as Steve and John hoisted Tony over the wall and down the other side.

Tony was carried and dragged beyond the barricade and placed in the centre of the road at the junction. His muffled cries and pleas were already attracting some attention and they could hear the slow shambling footsteps approaching in the darkness. Carl rested a foot on Tony to keep him in place while John kneeled against his back.

The four of them peered into the murky night. No one had any uncertainty at all in their minds about what they were about to do and the ethics of it.

"Can you see any?" Jake hissed.

"There," Steve said from his left, pointing down the road at two figures that staggered toward them in the gloom. They lurched and dragged themselves closer, moaning and gurgling as they approached.

"Okay, remove the gag," John said.

"Wait," Carl whispered and stepped over the immobilised Tony.

He reached into his pocket and as he removed his hand, Steve saw a faint flash of silver. Carl moved in close and began to tear at Tony's trousers. A second later and Tony was writhing and screaming from behind the gag as Carl worked on him. He stepped back and in the gloom of the night, Steve could see the almost black blood that covered Carl's hands and the lump of fleshy meat he held in his palm.

"Eat this, you fucking cunt," he snarled as he reached down and ripped the cloth from Tony's face and stuffed the severed penis into his screaming mouth.

The dead were closing in. More of them had appeared from the darkness. Tony began to beg and plead, whimpering and crying as he squirmed on the ground, clutching at the men's legs with his tied hands as they moved away from him.

"Please, please don't let them get me," he cried.

Steve looked down at him in disgust. He felt nothing. No remorse, no empathy, or sympathy. Most of all, he felt no doubt.

The four men began to shout and holler into the night, hoping to attract more infected. After a moment, satisfied that they must've caught the attention of the whole area, they turned and ran through the gap of the barricade and to the wall, scampering up and over to safety as the first screams began to ring out behind them. Long, bone-chilling shrieks, filled with pain and suffering reverberated in the night and the haunting moans of the dead could be heard even inside the car as they drove away.

That night, Steve sat on the edge of his bed. At odds with himself and asking questions he couldn't answer. There was a knock at the door, and without waiting for a reply, Helen entered. He looked up and in the twilight of the room, he could see her beautiful outline and the distinctly attractive features of her face.

She sat on the bed beside him and placed a hand across his back, rubbing him gently between his shoulder blades.

"Steve, you okay?" Her voice was soft and soothing.

Steve shrugged and looked down at his hands as he picked at his nails. "Do you think we did the right thing? I mean, my heart says we did, but my head isn't sure now."

"Steve, what you said was right. It's a new world now, and there is enough danger as it is. You were also right about what you said regarding the treatment of such monsters. They shouldn't be allowed to live, Steve, even before all of this started." She shook her head as she spoke.

He turned and looked at her. She made him feel calm and sure of himself, even content. When he looked into her eyes, he had no doubt that they had done the right thing.

She leaned in close, a slight smile on her face and she stared at him, unblinkingly. "I think we both need this."

And without another word, she kissed him, long and hard.

29

A brown sticky puddle had accumulated around his feet and it spread out across the floor and under the couch. Flies buzzed around it and some became caught in the gooey mess and struggled to climb free.

His bodily fluids had drained to the lower extremities and finally burst through the flesh as the skin had putrefied and became thinner, until it finally gave way and the fluid seeped out over his shoes and onto the tiled floor of the shop.

It wasn't just the floor that was soiled. The couch was covered in all manner of filth. More of the stomach's contents had become dislodged as the organs rotted and dissolved and passed through the rectum and oozed out around his body.

His skin had dried substantially, withdrawing and losing much of its moisture as it clung to his rotting muscles and bones. It now took on the appearance of soft leather with a deep green and blue hue.

His eyes had sunken back into his skull casting deep dark shadows in their sockets and making the brow seem more protruded. His lips had shrivelled to hard, crusted, and curled lines above his teeth that were constantly visible now, while the skin of his face had tightened and made his cheek bones seem more prominent.

For weeks, Andy Moorcroft had sat in the same place, occasionally looking up and staring blankly at his surroundings. Always, his gaze would fall upon the large smiling picture that hung on the wall. Every time, he reacted the same way. At first, confusion as a faint memory stirred, then an emotion that could only be described as sorrow. Something inside his rotting mind told him, *that image had once been you.*

The healthy smile, the glittering shining eyes, and that soft plump flawless flesh, was something he craved.

He desired it more than anything, to do what with it, he didn't know, but he did know that he couldn't have it. Somehow he knew the image in front of him wasn't real.

The others were constantly there, outside in the street, staggering about and tripping over and into things, forever groaning and wailing. Andy never reacted to any of it. He just remained seated, staring directly ahead of him, watching the slowly increasing ooze spread across the floor beneath him.

He would have stayed there forever, but something stirred in the distance.

There was a noise; a strange noise that he was unused to. It was a deep rumbling and it became more audible in his ears as it came closer. He could hear a blaring horn too and hoots and hollers of voices followed by a screech and the crash of glass shattering.

The voices were different from the others like him, and it caught his attention and snapped something to life inside him. His instincts made him want to go to the noise, to be part of it, to consume it.

Andy's head raised, his eyes widening and moving from side to side and his mouth opening and closing, gnashing his teeth together. He turned in the direction of the door and saw figures, grey and dull, waterlogged and wretched, all staggering in the same direction, moaning and reaching out with their clasping hands ahead of them.

For the first time in a month, he forced his body up and away from the couch. His feet slipped with a squeak in the sticky mess on the floor and he barely kept his balance. He saw more of the lifeless figures staggering past the large window in front of him and he felt the urge to join them. He reached out and a rasped moan came from his parched throat as he moved to the door.

He didn't try to walk through the glass this time, something reminded him that he just needed to force his way through the door and he would be out in the open and able to move toward the noise that had now become even louder as the rumble echoed between the tall buildings around him.

In the street he paused and looked up, expecting to see the source of the sound above him, around the roof tops. He looked back at the other figures and followed their line of travel with his gaze. There was something further up the street. A large crowd was gathering and the noise was more distinct now. The voices were more animated, more vibrant.

He turned and staggered along with the others.

Other shambling bodies came from all directions. They poured into the main street from side roads, alleyways and shop fronts. To Andy's left he saw the smashed window front of a large designer clothing shop. The rotting grey figure of a woman stumbled and fought past the mannequins, batting them out of her way as she headed for the open street. As she stepped through the shattered window, she lost her balance and crashed to the ground. A large piece of jagged glass was dislodged from above and it fell like a guillotine, severing her legs. She glanced behind her at the space where her lower limbs had been for a moment and then back to the source of the noise and began to drag herself along the bare concrete with her hands.

Andy's joints creaked with stiffness and it was difficult for him to keep walking in a straight line. One knee seemed more lubricated than the other and that leg was able to take longer strides. He began to veer off to one side, colliding with others that were headed in the same direction. He stopped and turned to face the sound again and resumed his slow march forward. Again and again he had to stop before he walked into one of the building fronts on the opposite side of the street, and readjusted his position to aim him in the right direction.

As he closed in on the mass of bodies in front of him, he saw something that stopped his eyes in their tracks and he became completely entranced by it. Above the heads and outstretched arms of the others in front of him, he could see the flat top of something. He recognised it as something that could move and he used to sit in.

It was a van. On top of the van was a figure, but it wasn't like the others in front of him. This figure moved differently. It was fast, agile and most of all, it had bright, healthy, pink flesh. His mouth opened and his black rotten tongue flopped from the open cavern and lolled to the side of his chin. He began to gurgle and groan as he reached up with his hands and quickened his pace toward it.

He reached the first of the others that blocked his way but he was still too far from the thing he desired so much. His whole body and instincts were set on reaching his goal. With a snarl, he looked down at the backs of the bodies in front of him and began to grab and tear at them, pulling them out of his way as he pushed into the writhing throng.

With each yank and tug, he was closer to the side of the van and eventually his hand slapped the cold hard side of the vehicle. He pounded at it, moaning and growling as he stared up, catching the occasional glimpse of the fast moving figure on top. The crowd around him was wailing and screaming and the noise buzzed in his ears.

He could hear the noise the fast moving figure made. It was nothing like the noises Andy made, and they excited him and made him beat the side of the van all the harder as the figure dashed to and fro.

Andy could hear more voices coming from his left, possibly from inside the building that the van seemed to be pushed up against. They all sounded lively compared to the lifeless drones of the figures around him that he had listened to for so long. Now he was hearing something that made him feel something and he wanted it.

More of the fast moving, healthy figures jumped onto the roof of the van as they came out of the building. They headed to the front and climbed down into the cab, high up and out of reach. The crowd erupted with excited wails and shrieks as the spectacle of four energetic and living people darted before them.

The van began to rock with the combined weight of the mass and the voices of the living changed. They seemed different now, higher pitched and urgent, but the sounds caused the crowd to pulsate and push at the van even harder.

Andy heard a sudden roar as the van tried to move. The wheels were spinning and churning up the bodies behind it as it tried to pull away. It couldn't move. There were too many bodies all around it and it wasn't long until the door at the front flew open and a figure darted out and into the mass. A large portion of the crowd swayed in that direction, leaving Andy in an open area, staring directly at the door when another living person jumped out and ran straight into him.

He closed his arms around the person and they both toppled to the ground. Andy was underneath and he could feel the form on top of him trying to pull away. Andy pulled harder, he didn't want to lose what he had wanted so much and he brought his head up, close to the soft underside of the face. He began to bite at the air between him and the fleshy neck but the person was pulling against him and trying to flee.

More of the lurching, moaning crowd closed in around them and the weight began to push down on them both. For a moment another feeling – fear – raced through Andy. They wanted to take his prize away from him.

He opened his mouth wide and clamped down hard on the figure's neck as it squirmed on top of him. A high-pitched sound emitted from its throat, ringing in his ears and causing Andy to tighten his grip as he pulled his head away, ripping at the flesh he clamped in his mouth.

A gush of warm fluid flowed over his face. It ran into his eyes, over his skin, into his nostrils. It ran into his mouth. His dry throat felt the sensation of the life-giving fluid. A moment of serenity gripped him. The screams of the struggling figure above him faded into a distant sound as he clung on and began chewing, savouring the sensation of the warm and tender flesh in his mouth as the body above him writhed and shuddered in his arms.

He swallowed as more blood poured over him. By now the body above had stopped struggling, but it was being tugged and jostled as more wanted to experience the same thing that Andy had. He felt it being wrenched away from him and he gripped onto it and pulled his head close again, taking a large bite from the shoulder. The blood didn't flow as much now; it seeped and oozed onto him and into his mouth as he chewed.

His lips smacked as he ate. His tongue slurped and he made gratified groans and murmurs as he swallowed and closed in for another bite.

In his euphoria, his grip loosened and the body was dragged off and away from him.

He moaned and reached out, scrambling to his knees and crawling after it. To his left there were more screams and cries similar to what he had heard from the body that landed on top of him. There were more people, but he couldn't see them. What he could see was the body he had bit into just ahead of him, being dragged and torn apart, leaving a long smear of intestines and blood along the ground that others fell upon and fought over as they consumed the remains.

Andy climbed to his feet and charged ahead, knocking figures away from him. He reached the body and dropped down with all his weight onto the limbless torso on the ground, and began chewing at the face and neck, digging his fingers into the eye sockets and clawing at the cheeks until there were gouges of flesh missing.

He ate and chewed his way through the tendons, veins and bone. Eventually, he scurried off to one side with just the head in his hands. He propped himself against a wall and sat eating mouthfuls of soft succulent flesh until there was nothing but the skull left. He was smeared in fresh blood, his face and neck red with it, his hands covered in tiny slivers of flesh and tendon.

When there was no more to be had, he discarded the jawless pink skull, the brain still intact inside.

After awhile, the others moved away when they realised there was nothing left. Dried blood stained the entire surface around the stalled van. Body parts picked clean, lay scattered all around - a skull here, half a ribcage there.

A child, its skin pale and waxy, dressed in what had once been a pretty summer dress, passed him as he sat, leaning against the wall still. It was carrying the lower half of a leg, stripped of all flesh and the tibia and fibula and foot bones were held together by nothing more than sinews.

Flies swarmed the area, the steady hum and the occasional moan from the others was all that could be heard. There was nothing to make Andy want to move, but he stood and looked around, eyeing the others like him.

The little girl stopped in front of him and looked up into his eyes. For a fleeting moment, Andy felt sorrow. As he watched her walk away, he somehow knew that she wasn't supposed to be the way she was. The thought forced him to turn and study his reflection in the nearest shop window again.

Something inside him had changed. He looked at the child in the dress, then at the remains from the feast around him. Then he raised his hands to his face and studied the shrivelled and damaged skin. He caught sight of himself in the reflection of a shop window again and the memory of the picture in his shop flashed before him.

He glanced around one more time, a low whimper and a huff escaping his freshly lubricated vocal cords, then he shuffled away toward the outer edge of town.

30

Marcus sat in his seat in his SUV, staring out of the windscreen over the grassy hills and rolling countryside of Northern France in front of him. It looked like a patchwork quilt of different shades of greens and browns, broken by dry stone walls and high privet hedges. Here and there, he could see the outline of the cottages and farm buildings that dotted the land. It was beautiful, Marcus thought. The sun was beginning to set and it cast its golden rays over the scene, creating the impression that he was looking at an old sepia photograph from many years ago.

He reached onto the dashboard and grabbed the handset to the Codan. "Steve, Marcus, you there, bro?"

He waited then he heard the voice of his brother coming through the speaker. "Yeah, Marcus, how's it going? Are you close to the coast yet?"

"Not far," Marcus replied. "We've gone static for the night, to the East of Calais and West of Cassel, about twenty miles from the coast." He paused and thought, realising that Steve was probably looking at the Ordinance Survey maps that are measured in the metric system. "That's about thirty kilometres, give or take. Not sure what we will do once we get there, but I think we'll have to ditch the vehicles and try and find a boat. It's only about twenty miles or so across the Channel to Dover, so it shouldn't be a problem. If all else fails, we'll swim if we have to."

Steve laughed at the other end. "Yeah, Marcus, I don't doubt that you're mad enough to try it."

"After all we've been through, Steve, we couldn't give up now. Home is so close, I can taste it. Speaking of which, how's the food? Is that Karen lady still working miracles in the kitchen? It feels like we've been living off rations and tinned food for a lifetime."

"Yeah, the food is good, bro. We can organize a banquet for when you return. There's still plenty of food at the moment, but I think we are gonna have to look at going out for more eventually. We have time yet to plan stuff like that and look at the options. In the meantime, make sure you get here in one piece."

Marcus looked to Sini, a grim expression on his face, and then keyed the handset again. "Yeah well, are you in the radio room alone, Steve?"

"No, Jake is here with me. Jennifer will be here in a minute or so."

Marcus felt a sense of urgency and sat forward in his seat, keen to say what he needed to before Jennifer was able to hear. "Okay, listen, Steve, if she turns up at all while I'm speaking, cut me off."

There was a pause, then a confused sounding reply, "Uh, okay, Marcus. What's up? Is everything okay there?"

"Not sure, bro." Marcus sighed. "We've been seeing a lot of bad signs lately and I think we're in an area controlled by some rogue militia. We tried to backtrack, but it seems we're pretty much surrounded. I dunno if they know we're here or if they're even interested in us, but it could get rough. I just thought you should know mate."

"Yeah, cheers bro. It's best to be in the picture, even if it's a shitty one." Steve sounded quietly worried. Then his voice was back to normal as he put on a facade for Marcus' wife, "Ah, here's Jen."

"Hey there, doll face." Marcus said as he smiled. "How are you and the boys today? This time tomorrow, I'll be speaking to you from within the same country."

Her voice was soft over the speaker, "I can't wait to see you, Marcus. I miss you so much. Every day the boys are hounding me, asking me how much longer it will be before you're here. They need their Dad. All they have here is a bunch of retards to look up to."

A round of 'hey' could be heard from her end as she was reprimanded by Steve and Jake.

It was good for Marcus to hear them all laughing.

After speaking to Jennifer for a while, he climbed from his vehicle and sat down next to Stu. Marcus didn't like having to tell his brother of possible danger ahead of them, but he needed to know, just in case things went wrong as they moved closer to the coast. At least that way, Steve would have an idea of what might have happened.

"How is the missus then, buddy?" Stu asked as he handed him a steaming, half full cup of coffee.

Marcus shrugged and smiled at his friend. "Ah you know, the usual."

Stu could see Marcus was troubled and that his mind was elsewhere.

"You really think we're in for trouble? I mean, we haven't seen anyone. Granted, there's been plenty of signs, but maybe they've moved on." He was doing his best to sound optimistic.

Marcus bit his lip as he sat, leaning against a tree and staring at the ground. "I don't think they've moved on, Stu. Looks to me like whoever is in this area, they're very territorial, well armed, and well organised.

"Think about it, we've seen very few infected in this area. Someone has cleared them out. Did you notice anything about the bodies we've seen, the ones hanging from trees and street lights? Some of them were soldiers. French, German, even British troops had been through here, and they weren't travelling together." He glanced up and swatted at a fly that buzzed around his face. "They were in different stages of decomposition, meaning they were caught at different times. So, whoever is here is here to stay and they see this area as their turf."

Stu nodded. He realised that Marcus was right and when he thought back, he could see that it was obvious.

"Well, it won't be the first lot of trouble we've run into. It's just a case of fighting through, we're well armed too and we have a good crew here."

Marcus shook his head. "I don't think it'll be as simple as that, mate. They have armour. Those tanks that we passed, the ones burnt out and full of holes? They were Leopard 2's, Stu, German tanks. I remember from my days in the Anti-Tank platoon, we were always told that, '*the only thing that can destroy a Leopard 2 is, another Leopard 2.*'"

Stu nodded again, remembering being told the same thing. "Yeah, I heard that too. Well, whatever they have, they're effective. They'll cut through our SUVs like tin cans then."

"That's my worry. We will have to look at the maps and see what routes we can find. We'll travel the roads least likely to be defended. Hopefully, they're a mobile unit, constantly on the hunt and might not be around in this neck of the woods tomorrow.

"But if they're as organised as I suspect, they will have observation posts and communications everywhere to dominate the ground. And mobile units acting as rapid reaction forces, placed in positions where they can deploy to any given grid in their area of responsibility."

They moved back to where the rest of the team sat huddled around as they ate.

As was the custom, no one made a hot drink that was intended for just themselves, it was always passed round so that everyone had a drink from the 'communal brew'.

Ian passed his cup across to Sini who took it in his hands as he looked up and asked, "What is it?"

"It's tea, NATO standard," Ian replied.

Sini's brow creased as he stared at the hot steaming drink before looking up again. "Serbia was never a part of NATO."

Ian rolled his eyes and grumbled, "You thick communist bastard. It means, tea, with milk and two fucking sugars."

Sini smiled at Ian. "Ah right, you mean a homosexual drink. Why don't you drink real coffee?"

"Because the first and only time I drank that Serbian stuff was when I was in Kosovo. It caused my teeth to grow a fur coat and I didn't sleep for a month. On top of that, it was fucking disgusting."

They were in high spirits. Morale was good and it was mainly due to the fact that the final leg was in sight. They were all fully aware of the possible danger and they had seen the scenes of battle and torture, but their confidence was soaring. Not because they dismissed the threat as something trivial, but because they knew what they would be fighting for; to get home.

Marcus looked over his men as he stood beside Stu, watching them laugh and insult each other.

Sini and Yan, as always, sat close to each other. They had been pretty much inseparable since their days in the Serb army together and now Sandra, the husky, raven-haired, Eastern European beauty, made up the trio. She didn't speak much English, but she could read people and anticipate what needed to be done most of the time. She had taken good care of Jim during his recovery, and as a result, a friendship had developed between them.

Ian, the human bulldog, as usual took every chance to make fun of people. Especially Jim, who was seated to his right.

Jim still wasn't completely healed from his torture by the rebels in Serbia, but he was making a steady recovery. Marcus could see him wince now and then when he moved his upper body suddenly, causing the healing ribs to shoot a bolt of pain through him, reminding him of the damage they had sustained. He dismissed the broken bones of his face as "all adding character to my Hollywood-style looks". Hussein and Ahmed had continued to grow with the group. They were always quick to smile and tried their best to join in with the jokes. Though sometimes, it did take a lot of explaining of the punchlines and by then, the moment was gone. When Zaid was executed, Marcus feared that they would become withdrawn but the opposite happened. Having been through the same torture and anguish as the team, they grew closer.

It took the team nineteen days to reach the coastal area of Northern France after leaving Serbia. They had crossed into Hungary and on to Austria the next day. The journey hadn't been too difficult, and with the isolation and seclusion of much of the Austrian and Southern German countryside, it was easy for them to avoid the larger cities.

Most of the small, picturesque towns and villages such as Salzburg, Augsburg, and Ulm were, to a degree, secure and still intact.

Army units had abandoned their posts within the large urban areas like Stuttgart and Munich and fled, taking their equipment and tanks with them to the mountainous regions of the Austrian Alps and the heavily forested areas of Bavaria, in Southern Germany, and set up defensive rings around villages and towns.

Marcus noted to himself at the time, *Typical of the Germans, they always get themselves organised. The rest of the world falls apart, and they do the logical thing and turn back to their roots.*

A few times, Marcus and his team were stopped by German patrols who wanted to take a closer look at them. At first, Marcus had considered opening fire on the men of the checkpoints, but decided against it when he saw that they were lightly armed and of no serious threat.

In conversations of broken English and German, they were able to retrieve snippets of information and advice on their journey and routes. The German soldiers and villagers always insisted that Marcus and his men should stay and rest, but they always politely declined, explaining that they needed to push on for the coast.

The team was warned of places to avoid, and always left with the well wishes of the soldiers and civilians, who understood how far they had travelled and what they had been through. Where possible, the German soldiers would radio ahead to other units, informing them that they were to offer what assistance they could to the group of 'ragtag mercenaries' headed West.

They passed close to Stuttgart before they crossed the border into France. The once vibrant city was nothing more than a smouldering ruin and from a distance, through the binoculars and on elevated ground, the team watched the swarms of dead that moved around the outskirts and along the main roads leading in and out. Even from afar they could hear the noise the dead made. It was a continuous murmur, like an electric buzz, as hundreds of thousands of black distant figures massed together, staggering within the city and singing their haunting chorus as one.

The sound sent chills down Marcus' spine, and he knew in his own mind that there was not a living soul left in the city.

From far off to the North, two tiny black dots appeared over the horizon. Soon, Marcus and his men could hear the distant roar of jet engines as the fighters drew closer to the city. They watched as the two planes dropped their ordinance over the buildings and saw the fountains of smoke and debris as they exploded. A moment later, they heard the report of the detonations as the sound travelled the distance to the team while they looked on. They circled and closed in for another pass. They began to fire their rockets and incendiary bombs into the crowds that stood and stared at the spectacle above them before being obliterated in the blasts.

The fire began to spread and grip the city, sending dark plumes high into the sky as the orange flames licked at the buildings. The two fighter jets veered off and with a roar of thrusters, turned back North and flew from view.

Now, the team faced possible trouble ahead as they thrust for the coast.

They had begun to see signs of battle and ambush along their route as they travelled through Northern France, and Marcus ordered a turn around, hoping to pick up another route to the South. As they backtracked, they saw clouds of dust in the distance and heard the rumble of heavy vehicles headed toward them from the East and further to the South.

They were trapped.

Marcus decided that they needed to quicken their pace and continue to push West. They passed through small villages and saw the bodies of the infected lying in the open, sprawled over vehicles, crushed under crumbled buildings. The houses were peppered with bullet holes and Marcus judged that some of the weapons used were of a high calibre, maybe 20mm and 40mm.

Bodies were strung up, hanging from road signs and street lamps, swaying in the wind, having been executed by whomever it was that was roaming the area. In some places, rows of heads lined the road, placed on spikes and left to rot as warnings.

The team had no choice but to push on, trying to keep the distance between themselves and the suspected militia that was following.

The next morning, as they readied themselves to move out after spending the night in a wood, they heard the unmistakable loud rumbling of approaching tank tracks. The noise seemed to come from all around and they struggled to pinpoint the direction of the possible threat.

Stu jumped down into position beside Marcus, hefting an RPG.

"Sounds like there's a few of them. Not seeing any on the road yet though," he said as he prepared the launcher for firing.

Marcus whispered into his radio, "Everyone, hold your fire. Hopefully they'll just pass us by." He glanced back at Jim and Ian, who covered the rear, facing into the wooded area with Ahmed. Yan and Sini were positioned on their left flank, covering the road leading up to their position, with Sandra tucked in close behind them.

Marcus nodded to them and they nodded back.

Soon, they began to hear voices along with the grinding and rattling of the tanks. The tanks came to a halt and a voice, speaking English and with a strong French accent, rang out around them.

"Hello, you come out now. If you come, we will not hurt you."

Stu glanced at him, eyes wide. Looking back to Ian and Jim, Marcus signalled, pointing both his fingers to his eyes and then shrugging his shoulders. Ian shook his head; he couldn't see any of them at the rear, but they all knew that they were surrounded.

Stu squinted, peering out to the road. "I can't see fuck all, Marcus. What do you think?"

Marcus bit his lip and looked down at his weapon in his hands. "I think we're fucked, Stu." He looked at his friend and a wry smile spread across his face. "I'm not walking out to be executed like a dickhead."

Stu looked about him, glancing at the rest of the men. "Me neither."

Marcus keyed his radio again. "Lads, I don't think we'll get to the vehicles in time if we just run for it. We will have to go at them and try and create confusion, then pull back and see if we can bug out in the trucks. Jim, see if you can get eyes on with the nearest tank. If we can hit that, it could make them panic and give us a chance."

"Will do, Marcus," Jim replied and he began to edge his way forward, further into the wood line.

A minute later, Marcus heard Jim's voice through his earpiece. "I've got eyes on. There's one about fifty metres to our half right, just outside the trees. I can see dismounted infantry ahead, moving through the wood toward us."

"Roger that." He turned to Stu and nodded.

Stu raised himself into a crouch and nodded in return, knowing what he needed to do. "Right, don't go anywhere, I'll be back in a jiffy".

Marcus spoke again over the net. "Okay, Stu is gonna push forward with a launcher. Once he hits the tank, throw whatever smoke grenades you have. Then empty a magazine into the direction of the approaching troops. Once you hear the horn of my vehicle, fall back and mount up. Sini and Ian, get straight behind the guns in the turrets and begin hammering the bastards as we bug out. We're gonna head straight for the road and toward the West."

Marcus could feel the tension in the air. That moment between making the decision to fight, and the actual initiation was always the worst. Sweat leaked down into his eyes and he felt the hollow of his stomach and the knot that was steadily growing within.

His body was taught and ready to pounce, but the 'fight or flight' instincts were making his legs tremble and shivers run the length of his spine. His mouth was dry and it was hard to swallow as he sat, waiting for the moment to come.

He watched Stu stalk forward with the RPG cradled in his right arm. He stopped and dropped to a kneeling position and turned back to look at Marcus. He held up a thumb then pointed it to the ground and then pointed in the direction to his half right. Stu had visual on the tank.

"Standby, standby,"

Everyone tightened their grips on their weapons. All safety catches were off and Sini and Ian held smoke grenades at the ready.

A blast to the front and a whoosh, followed by another loud bang, initiated the start of the fight. Immediately, a crescendo of fire erupted from every weapon within the team. A cloud of smoke hung in the air around where Stu had been kneeling. Marcus watched as he bounded through the mist and back toward him. At the same time, the smoke grenades were thrown. As soon as the RPG struck the tank, they poured a massive weight of fire into the approaching troops. The cracks of the rounds hitting the trees and the screams of men as they were hit echoed through the woods. The rapid automatic fire was constant and never let up, denying the enemy the chance to recover from the shock and ferocity of the wall of fire that was unleashed on them.

Marcus darted back and climbed behind the wheel of his vehicle and began to pound on the horn. "Move, move!" he screamed for the men to pull back.

One by one, they emerged from the fog of battle and piled into their vehicles. The engines roared to life and the machineguns in the turrets began to blaze away into the wood line. No enemy were visible yet, but as far as Marcus was concerned, that was a good thing because it meant they were too busy taking cover and not advancing or returning fire.

The drivers slammed their feet to the floor as the gunners continued to pour their deadly fire into the trees, and the vehicles bounced along the track and toward the road. Marcus turned left and glimpsed something on the road to his right. It was another tank.

"Tank! We've got a tank to our rear!" he heard Sini screaming from above him.

The other vehicles crashed onto the main road from the track and followed Marcus. The flatbed truck was in the middle and Ian and Stu with Ahmed brought up the rear in their SUV, an easy target for the tank whose turret had turned and was aimed at the convoy. Marcus increased the speed, the guns in the turrets still firing at a rapid rate in the hope of keeping the enemy suppressed and busy, taking cover.

Marcus' ears popped and his vision blurred momentarily as a fountain of dirt erupted close to his right. The tank had missed just by a couple of metres. The blast wave rocked the vehicle and threw

Marcus about in his driver's seat. Hussein sat beside him, holding his hands to his ears and opening and closing his mouth as his face screwed into a canvas of pain and disorientation.

The doors buckled, the windows cracked, and spider webs formed across them from the shockwave of the blast. Marcus struggled with the heavy vehicle, trying hard to keep them on the road as the chassis twisted and groaned beneath them.

Sini collapsed into the vehicle from the turret. "Shit. That was close. Get us out of here, Marcus. I can't see a fucking thing!" he screamed as he scrambled back to the gun and continued to fire.

Before the tank was able to reload, the convoy had turned a bend and was out of sight as they ploughed along the narrow road ahead of them, trying to put as much distance between them and the follow-up that would inevitably come.

The gunners changed their ammunition for fresh belts and checked their arcs, making sure they weren't in the sights of other enemy units about to ambush them. Sini could see over the hedges that lined the roads and he continually swivelled his gun turret to cover their front, while Ian covered the rear.

They thundered for the coast, never slowing. They had seen no other enemy units and they hoped they had put enough distance from their attackers. With the speed they were travelling, Marcus judged that they would have a bit of breathing space between them and the tanks due to their reduced speed. He hoped that the infantry wasn't stupid enough to follow up without their armoured support.

They were close to the sea. They could smell it.

A fireball erupted from the rear. A deafening bang and shockwave followed it that rocked the entire convoy. Machinegun fire rattled from the right. Tracer rounds zipped over and around them and more rounds thumped into the sides of their vehicles creating a deafening crescendo of noise on the inside as the rounds cracked and pinged into the armour.

The flatbed began to slow and swerve to the side. It lost control and collided with a low wall on its left and the front wheels landed in a ditch. The windows were shattered and the body of the truck was full of holes and tears as the rounds had pumped through and out the other side.

Sini was firing continuously into the positions he could see to the right. He screamed as he worked the gun; the belt feeding through from his left and the empty cases flying out from the ejection opening to the right while the used link piled at his feet, creating a little mountain of black steel.

Marcus spun in his seat, trying to see what had happened behind. He saw the crashed and perforated truck behind and glimpsed the rear SUV. It was static and on fire.

He slammed on the brakes. "Sini, vehicles two and three are down. Have you got eyes on with them?" he screamed up into the turret.

Sini was still firing and hollering, the vibrations of the gun shaking him as he leaned into it to stabilize his aim and unable to hear a word that Marcus had shouted at him. Marcus quickly decided that it was best to leave Sini behind the gun, and he grabbed Hussein and bailed out. They headed to the rear to see if there were any survivors. He still hadn't seen any of the enemy, but he placed his faith in Sini to suppress them while he extracted who he could from the other vehicles.

The air was alive with screams and the cracks of the rounds as they slammed into the vehicles or passed over their heads. In front of him, as he moved toward the flatbed, a stream of red tracer rounds shot across his path, snapping at the air like a hundred whips. Hussein ducked behind him, then raised himself and fired a burst through the bushes and into the general direction of where the enemy fire had come from.

Smoke and shrapnel were thick in the air as the enemy fire continued to disintegrate the vehicles. Clods of mud and debris flew up as the sustained fire slammed into the embankments at the sides of the road. It was hard to see or hear and Marcus wasn't sure if there was anyone left alive from the rear two vehicles.

Then, through the smoke and fire, he saw movement. It was Stu and he was dragging someone. Jim was close behind him and Yan and Sandra staggered out from behind the flatbed.

Jim was firing into the bushes and screaming for the people in front to speed up. Marcus began to do the same and Hussein followed suit, screaming for them to hurry.

As Stu approached, Marcus saw that he was dragging Ian. He was still conscious but clutching at a bloody wound to his abdomen. He was groaning with the pain and unable to walk unaided.

"Where's Ahmed?" Hussein shouted over the noise as they passed.

Jim shook his head gravely. "He didn't make it. We need to move." He pushed Hussein ahead of him and the survivors continued toward the lead vchicle, firing into the bushes and beyond, crouching and ducking as enemy fire came close.

Marcus motioned for Sini to dismount the gun and follow. With the amount of rounds the vehicles were taking, he knew that they were on foot from there on. The enemy fire eased off and Marcus wasn't sure whether they had been killed by Sini, or they were moving for a new position.

At a junction up ahead, he got his answer. An embankment spread out across their front with open fields beyond. Marcus headed for the far side of the road toward the cover of the embankment, hoping to steal a moment to consider their next move.

More rounds zipped toward them, cracking as they passed. Marcus sprinted forward and ducked into cover on the opposite side of the road and pressed himself close in against the earth mound of the embankment. He couldn't tell where the fire was coming from. It seemed to be all around and the air was alive with the white hot steel hornets as they thrashed around them. He could hear the steady barking of machineguns to his far right and he suspected they were to his front as well.

Marcus dropped to his knees and turned, just in time, to see Yan sprinting across the open junction toward the cover that Marcus ducked behind.

His body jerked and bent at the waist and his eyes grew wide. His hand reached up to the side of his chest as he continued forward without reducing speed. His face screwed into a mixture of determination and agony. Then, Marcus saw a spray of blood as a round smashed through Yan's neck. He stumbled to his left as the force of the bullet pushed him off course. A moment later, the side of his head imploded and an eruption of blood and brain shot from the other side as another round thumped into him. His legs buckled and his body slumped to the ground with a crash, then his body lay still.

Sini was close behind him, sprinting with the machinegun in his arms and the long belt of linked ammunition dangling around his legs. He glanced down at the body as he passed, unable to recognise it in the fleeting moment. He crashed into the embankment and began to set the gun up so that he could fire through the sparse bushes along the top of the dirt embankment. He looked about as he did so, then he realised the body behind him was his friend, Yan.

For a moment, he looked at Marcus bewildered and questioningly. His face turned cold but his eyes burned wild as they filled with tears. He swallowed hard and nodded to Marcus, understanding that he had no time to mourn and they still needed to get out of the ambush.

Jim and Sini took up the firing and began pounding away with their guns at where they thought the enemy was. Marcus glanced over the embankment and saw what he suspected was a machinegun position to their front. He could see heads moving and the flash from the muzzle of the gun. He glanced to his right and saw more tracer rounds coming from the high ground.

Marcus looked at Stu; he was squatted over Ian, who lay at his feet, still clutching at his wound while Sandra tried to stop the bleeding. Stu motioned for her to pick up Yan's weapon and Ian began to draw himself into a squatting position, using his weapon to steady himself.

Stu looked up to Marcus and screamed from further down the line of the embankment, "We need to move, Marcus, we need to go forward. They've got us pinned down and we're fucked if we stay here."

Marcus understood what he was saying. They were caught in an ambush. He knew that in an affective and well prepared ambush there is no way out, except to charge and take the fight to the enemy. It was a case of turning and facing the enemy and drawing from every ounce of aggression and determination and fighting through.

They were trapped in an 'L' shaped ambush. Meaning that they were caught in a crossfire, and no matter whether they went, forward, back, left or right, they were in the killing area.

"Sini, give us fire support." He turned to Jim, panting and breathless. "You ready, Jim?"

Jim nodded and grunted as he steeled himself for the assault.

Sini increased the rate of fire and screamed that they were to move.

Marcus began screaming out his commands to the group. "Fight through, fight through."

Marcus and Jim bounded forward from the embankment, screaming and roaring as they ran. He could see Stu, Ian, and Sandra also moving to his left. The team was rushing forward in an extended line together, toward the enemy positions to their front. Tracer rounds were flying both ways, from Sini and the gun and their own weapons as they fired on the move. The enemy position was also sending fire toward them. It cracked over their heads and pounded into the dirt at their feet, sending up fountains of mud all around them as they sprinted across the field. Red beams flowed in both directions, like mini flares being fired horizontally or lasers in a light show.

Marcus couldn't hear anything other than his own hard breathing and the screaming inside his head as he willed himself forward into the fray. He was roaring with fear and the resignation of his impending death gripped him, and he felt anger. They had come so close and now he was about to die, just a few kilometres away from the narrow strip of sea that separated him from his homeland.

Everyone was charging, screaming and firing as they moved and sprinted toward the enemy; their sheer aggression carrying them forward.

Marcus could feel the weapon vibrating in his hands as he squeezed the trigger. From the corner of his eye, he saw Ian doing the same thing; the pain of his wound forgotten as he charged for his life at the enemy positions ahead of them, screaming and roaring as he took the fight to the enemy. His body folded as rounds impacted into his abdomen and legs, and at the speed he was running, Ian tumbled forward into the ground.

They couldn't stop, they had to fight through.

Jim and Marcus continued forward, never slowing their pace. Sini fired from behind, the rapid fire of his machinegun sounding like a large piece of cloth being ripped.

Men began to spring up from numerous positions ahead of them and they turned and ran. Some stood their ground, only to be cut down by the wall of fire that the team had unleashed in their desperation as they charged.

A heavy thundering began to blast away from further to their front and spouts of dirt and smoke flew up all around them, flinging shrapnel in all directions as a heavy calibre weapon zeroed in on them. The cracks and the impacts of the rounds as they smacked into the ground all around left them deafened and disoriented but the momentum of their assault carried the team forward regardless.

Marcus was panting. He was close now, just a few more metres from the position.

A flash to their right, and Marcus felt himself thrown to the left and toward Jim. It felt like he had been hit with a massive fist.

His vision blurred and his ears rang. Something burned in his side and the wind was knocked out of him as he sailed through the air then crashed to the ground.

Everything went dark.

31

Gary chopped at the frozen meat. He stood in the cellar of the house with a cleaver in his hand and pounded away at the solid chunks of flesh he had spread out on the table. To save more power and ease the strain on fuel, all the stores of food for the animals had been moved to the basement of the mansion. Every chest freezer they could get their hands on had been carried across and placed into the spacious room below the house.

To save space and to use as few freezers as possible to stop the drain on fuel, Gary and Sophie had suggested that they turn all the frozen meat into bite-sized chunks so that they could be packed tighter into the storage freezers.

There was a lot to get through and he needed to work fast before the meat thawed and spoiled. He stood panting and sweating in the gloomy room. He raised his hand and mopped his brow with the back of his sleeve before raising the hatchet for another chop.

A voice from behind startled him. "You should take it easy, Gary. You're gonna have a heart attack."

Gary spun, the cleaver still held aloft. His face was red with the exertion and the veins stood out on his forehead. "Ah, Steve. You should be careful creeping up on people. I could've got carried away and cut your head off with this." He waved the cleaver menacingly then lowered it and smiled.

"You need a hand?"

Gary shook his head. "Thanks, but I'm okay. I'm treating it as a workout. Since this whole end of the world thing started, I've lost about twenty five pounds and I'm feeling much fitter and more energetic than I have in years." He patted his stomach with pride.

"Yeah, you're looking good, Gary. Maybe we could make a gym?" Steve smiled, but it was forced. He looked down and kicked at the dust on the floor of the basement.

Gary noticed his friend's uneasiness. "Something on your mind, Steve?"

He looked up and sighed as he stepped closer and leaned against the edge of the bench, thrusting his hands into his pockets. "Marcus, he's not been in touch since the day before yesterday. Last time we spoke, he said something about possible trouble ahead. They're in France, not far from the coast, and he said that they'd been seeing some bad signs. I know him well enough to tell when he's being vague, and if he has concerns, then it's for a good reason."

Gary hummed and looked down at the cleaver in his hands. He placed it onto the table and then stepped closer to Steve. "Look, it's pointless worrying about it. I know it's easier said than done, but there's nothing you can do about it at the moment. Does Jen know?"

Steve shook his head. "That's the other part, he asked me to keep it from her. He doesn't want her worrying. But it must be something worth worrying about in that case."

"I dunno what I can say to help you take your mind off it, Steve, or stop you from worrying. Other than; so far, that brother of yours has proved to be pretty resilient and an expert at getting himself outta tight spots. I'm actually looking forward to meeting him." Gary patted him on the shoulder. "Let me finish this lot, then we can go walk about and do our checks with 'Crazy Lee'. Karen is doing something special for grub tonight too." He smiled and squeezed harder at his friend's shoulder. "Don't worry, Steve."

Later, the group sat around the table. Platter after platter of food was brought from the kitchen. There was beef, turkey, and even duck. Between the large plates of meat, there was a huge selection of side dishes and vegetables. Bottles of wine and whiskey were placed at regular intervals around the table and Jake and Lee had already polished off the better part of a bottle between them.

The children had their own table off to the side with balloons and hats laid out for them. The sounds of their laughs and shouts of excitement echoed around the house.

Lee's mouth watered as he gazed at the feast. He turned to Carl who sat beside him. "What's the occasion?"

Carl shrugged, "Haven't a clue, it's definitely not Christmas."

"It's Gary's birthday," Karen announced as she appeared from the kitchen with a large bowl of gravy in her hands. "I just thought it would be nice to celebrate it."

"Ah, how old are you Gary?" Claire asked from the other side of the banquet.

"Let's just say, I'm as old as my gums, and a little older than my teeth," he replied with a grin.

Jake looked up from a bowl of soup. "Bollocks old timer, you haven't got any teeth of your own left."

"Yeah," Lee added, "next year, we're making you a coffin as a present."

Gary wagged his finger at him. "No, there's plenty of years left in me. Don't write me off just yet. In fact, Steve and I are thinking of building a gym here, aren't we?"

Steve nodded, trying his best to seem jovial. "Yeah, and next year, we're holding our own Mr Universe. It shouldn't be too hard to win it by then."

Sophie appeared from the kitchen. "Check this out everyone, Karen's own homemade sausage."

"Mmm sausage," Jake murmured.

Lee saw an opportunity and lowered his glass of wine as he swallowed. "Yeah, we all know how much you love the sausage, don't we?"

Jake shrugged. "It's my favourite. You should try it. I bet you would love it too."

"No thanks. I'm strictly off the sausage in that sense."

"Ah, come on," Jake was taking advantage of Lee's homophobic side, "I wish I had a pound for every straight man I've shagged."

Shocked laughter rang out around the table and Lee squirmed in his seat.

Since Tony's execution, a number of the people at the mansion had left. Julie, who had spoke out against it, decided that it was too barbaric for her to live with and decided to leave with her husband and son. Also, no one had seen or heard anything of Stephanie or Jason since the following day.

"Where do you think they are?" John asked as they were brought up in the conversation.

Helen answered, "I don't really care to be honest. That Stephanie was a real nasty piece of work."

"You think they're still alive?"

Steve shrugged, "Dunno." He looked across at Lee.

Lee lowered his glass, and poked his finger into his own chest as he spoke. "Hey, don't look at me. You lot are the ones who feed the people you don't like to the infected. I just broke her nose and gave that skinny little shit husband of hers a hiding."

The party raged into the night and Steve, having drunk very little, saw an opportunity to slip away and take over in the radio room. As he sat twisting dials and adjusting frequencies, Helen walked in.

She sat his side on a stool and rubbed his thigh. They had become an item over the weeks and now she sat watching him, a look of concern on her face.

"You're worried aren't you? You think something bad has happened?"

Steve continued to play about with the radio, avoiding her gaze. "Yeah, I just have a feeling, Helen."

They stayed in the radio room the entire night, monitoring the airwaves and hoping beyond hope that they would hear something.

When Steve awoke, it was early in the morning and the sun had not yet risen. He had fallen asleep at the desk with his head in his folded arms. Helen had also drifted off beside him, her head resting against his shoulder.

He raised himself and Helen stirred and rubbed her eyes. "What time is it?" she asked in a croaky voice.

Steve glanced at his watch. "Just gone four. I'm gonna go and see about getting us some coffee."

He stood up and stretched, feeling his stiff joints loosen, and the bones in his spine crack. He walked toward the door then stopped. He turned and cocked his head, his brow furrowed. He took a step closer toward Helen, who sat watching him, squinting with sleep.

"Did you hear that?" he asked as he moved closer.

Helen looked confused, "Hear what?"

"There, I heard something." He rushed to the radio and increased the volume and adjusted the signal strength. A hiss of static and a faint crackle could be heard in the background. He continued to twist and turn the knobs, ever so slightly.

He paused, holding his breath to cut down the sound in his own head and enable him to focus his hearing. Very faintly, almost inaudible, he heard a voice.

"Steve, can you hear me? Steve?" It was Marcus.

END

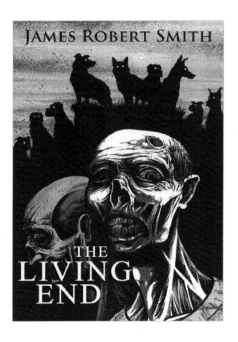

THE LIVING END
James Robert Smith

One Hundred and Fifty Million Zombies.

Sixty Million Dogs.

All of them hungry for warm human flesh.

The dead have risen, killing anyone they find. The living know what's caused it-a vicious contagion. But too late to stop it. For now, what remains of society are busy shutting down nuclear reactors and securing chemical plants to prevent runaway reactions in both. There's little time for anything else.
Failed comic book artist Rick Nuttman and his family have joined thousands of other desperate people in trying to find a haven from the madness. Perhaps refuge can be found in the village of Sparta or maybe there is salvation in The City of Ruth, a community raised from the ashes of Carolina.

ZOMBIE PULP

Tim Curran

Dead men tell tales.
From the corpse factories of World War I
where graveyard rats sharpen their teeth on human bones to the
wind-blown cemeteries of the prairie where resurrection comes
at an unspeakable price...from the compound of a twisted
messianic cult leader and his army of zombies to a post-
apocalyptic wasteland where all that stands between the living
and the evil dead is sacrifice in the form of a lottery.

Dead men do tell tales. And these are their stories.
Zombie Pulp is a collection of 9 short stories and 2 never before
published novellas from the twisted undead mind of Tim
Curran..

The Official Zombie Handbook: Sean T Page

Since pre-history, the living dead have been among us, with documented outbreaks from ancient Babylon and Rome right up to the present day. But what if we were to suffer a zombie apocalypse in the UK today? Through meticulous research and field work, The Official Zombie Handbook (UK) is the only guide you need to make it through a major zombie outbreak in the UK, including: -Full analysis of the latest scientific information available on the zombie virus, the living dead creatures it creates and most importantly, how to take them down - UK style. Everything you need to implement a complete 90 Day Zombie Survival Plan for you and your family including home fortification, foraging for supplies and even surviving a ghoul siege. Detailed case studies and guidelines on how to battle the living dead, which weapons to use, where to hide out and how to survive in a country dominated by millions of bloodthirsty zombies. Packed with invaluable information, the genesis of this handbook was the realisation that our country is sleep walking towards a catastrophe - that is the day when an outbreak of zombies will reach critical mass and turn our green and pleasant land into a grey and shambling wasteland. Remember, don't become a cheap meat snack for the zombies!

Available at www.severedpress.com, Amazon and most online bookstores

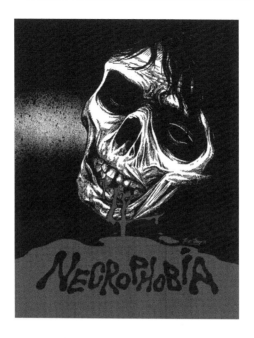

NECROPHOBIA
Jack Hamlyn

An ordinary summer's day.
The grass is green, the flowers are blooming. All is right with the world. Then the dead start rising. From cemetery and mortuary, funeral home and morgue, they flood into the streets until every town and city is infested with walking corpses, blank-eyed eating machines that exist to take down the living.

The world is a graveyard.

And when you have a family to protect, it's more than survival.

It's war!

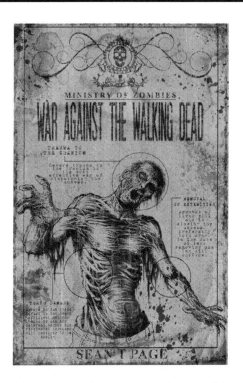

More than 63% of people now believe that there will be a global zombie apocalypse before 2050...

Employing real science and pioneering field work, War against the Walking Dead provides a complete blueprint for taking back your country from the rotting clutches of the dead after a zombie apocalypse.

* A glimpse inside the mind of the zombie using a team of top psychics - what do the walking dead think about? What lessons can we learn to help us defeat this pervading menace?

* Detailed guidelines on how to galvanise a band of scared survivors into a fighting force capable of defeating the zombies and dealing with emerging groups such as end of the world cults, raiders and even cannibals!

* Features insights from real zombie fighting organisations across the world, from America to the Philippines, Australia to China - the experts offer advice in every aspect of fighting the walking dead.

Packed with crucial zombie war information and advice, from how to build a city of the living in a land of the dead to tactics on how to use a survivor army to liberate your country from the zombies - War against the Walking Dead may be humanity's last chance.

Remember, dying is not an option!

RESURRECTION

By Tim Curran
www.corpseking.com

The rain is falling and the dead are rising. It began at an ultra-secret government laboratory. Experiments in limb regeneration-an unspeakable union of Medieval alchemy and cutting edge genetics result in the very germ of horror itself: a gene trigger that will reanimate dead tissue...any dead tissue. Now it's loose. It's gone viral. It's in the rain. And the rain has not stopped falling for weeks. As the country floods and corpses float in the streets, as cities are submerged, the evil dead are rising. And they are hungry.

"I REALLY love this book...Curran is a wonderful storyteller who really should be unleashed upon the general horror reading public sooner rather than later." – *DREAD CENTRAL*

www.severedpress.com

Dead Bait

"If you don't already suffer from bathophobia and/or ichthyophobia, you probably will after reading this amazingly wonderful horrific collection of short stories about what lurks beneath the waters of the world" – *DREAD CENTRAL*

A husband hell-bent on revenge hunts a Wereshark...A Russian mail order bride with a fishy secret...Crabs with a collective consciousness...A vampire who transforms into a Candiru...Zombie piranha...Bait that will have you crawling out of your skin and more. Drawing on horror, humor with a helping of dark fantasy and a touch of deviance, these 19 contemporary stories pay homage to the monsters that lurk in the murky waters of our imaginations. *If you thought it was safe to go back in the water...Think Again!*

"Severed Press has the cojones to publish THE most outrageous, nasty and downright wonderfully disgusting horror that I've seen in quite a while." – *DREAD CENTRAL*

ZOMBIE ZOOLOGY
Unnatural History:

Severed Press has assembled a truly original anthology of never before published stories of living dead beasts. Inside you will find tales of prehistoric creatures rising from the Bog, a survivalist taking on a troop of rotting baboons, a NASA experiment going Ape, A hunter going a Moose too far and many more undead creatures from Hell. The crawling, buzzing, flying abominations of mother nature have risen and they are hungry.

"Clever and engaging a reanimated rarity"
FANGORIA

"I loved this very unique anthology and highly recommend it"
Monster Librarian

BIOHAZARD

Tim Curran

The day after tomorrow: Nuclear fallout. Mutations. Deadly pandemics. Corpse wagons. Body pits. Empty cities. The human race trembling on the edge of extinction. Only the desperate survive. One of them is Rick Nash. But there is a price for survival: communion with a ravenous evil born from the furnace of radioactive waste. It demands sacrifice. Only it can keep Nash one step ahead of the nightmare that stalks him-a sentient, seething plague-entity that stalks its chosen prey: the last of the human race. To accept it is a living death. To defy it, a hell beyond imagining

"kick back and enjoy some the most violent and genuinely scary apocalyptic horror written by one of the finest dark fiction authors plying his trade today" HORRORWORLD

www.severedpress.com

Printed in Great Britain
by Amazon.co.uk, Ltd.,
Marston Gate.